Praise for *This Fatal Kiss*

★ "A delightfully queer polyamorous romance teeming with splashes of ethereal magic."
—***Publishers Weekly***, Starred Review

"Lovingly detailed Slavic folklore forms the basis of this gripping fantasy, with particular focus on the water and forest spirits. The mystery of Gisela's death provides a strong and unsettling undercurrent, helping to up the ante and ground the romantic hijinks. The subversion of a typical love triangle will also delight readers. Engaging and immersive—a delight from start to finish."
—***Kirkus Reviews***

"A found family of other rusałka with diverse sexualities and gender identities, their irascible (but hot) immortal water goblin 'grandfather,' and the small town setting with its witchy cottagecore aesthetic make this an appealing destination for fans of Jasinska's *The Dark Tide* as well as readers in search of a cozy, flirty, folklore-inflected good time."
—***The Bulletin of the Center for Children's Books***

"Told from three alternating perspectives and influenced by Slavic folklore, this polyamorous romantasy successfully juggles themes of identity, family, and queerness, all while building a crisp, clear, beautiful world where readers will want to linger with these characters."
—***Booklist***

"The rich Slavic fantasy world unfurls throughout, weaving folklore with fairy-tale, as it reimagines elements of 'The Little Mermaid.' . . . The multiple points of view build suspense as each character learns that in this world of magical spirits, not everyone is as they seem."
—***School Library Journal***

THIS FATAL KISS

Alicia Jasinska

This Fatal Kiss

Spirits and Saints

1

PEACHTREE
Teen

Peachtree Teen
An imprint of Peachtree Publishing Company Inc.

Printed in September 2025 at RR Donnelley in China.
Edited by Jonah Heller
Book design by Lily Steele
PeachtreeBooks.com
First Hardcover Edition, 2024
First Paperback Edition, 2025
ISBN: 978-1-68263-736-4 | 3 5 7 9 10 8 6 4 (hardcover)
ISBN: 978-1-68263-856-9 | 1 3 5 7 9 10 8 6 4 2 (paperback)

Library of Congress Cataloging-in-Publication Data

Names: Jasinska, Alicia, author.
Title: This fatal kiss / Alicia Jasinska.
Description: Atlanta, Georgia : Peachtree Teen, 2024. | Audience: Ages 14 and Up. | Audience: Grades 10–12. | Summary: Cursed to haunt the river where she drowned, Gisela, a water nymph longing for humanity, strikes a deal with Kazik, a spirit-hunter losing his magic, to help her gain a mortal's kiss, but complications arise when both fall for Aleksey, an enigmatic young man with ties to Gisela's past.
Identifiers: LCCN 2024022710 | ISBN 9781682637364 (hardcover) | ISBN 9781682637371 (ebook)
Subjects: CYAC: Fantasy. | Kissing—Fiction. | Water spirits—Fiction. | LGBTQ+ people—Fiction. | LCGFT: Fantasy fiction. | Novels.
Classification: LCC PZ7.1.J393 Th 2024 | DDC [Fic]—dc23
LC record available at https://lccn.loc.gov/2024022710

EU Authorized Representative: HackettFlynn Ltd, 36 Cloch Choirneal, Balrothery, Co. Dublin, K32 C942, Ireland.
EU@walkerpublishinggroup.com

A NOTE TO THE READER

IN SLAVIC FOLKLORE, a rusałka is a female water spirit or nymph. Stories vary, but most describe these creatures as the restless spirits of young maidens who died violent and tragic deaths in or by a lake, river, or body of water. Sometimes malicious and sometimes playful, they are famous for bewitching mortals with their beauty and dragging them into the depths.

As such, while lighthearted for the most part, this story does contain brief depictions of fantasy violence and death, drowning and near drowning, abusive relationships, a history of sexual assault, physical assault, struggles with sexual identity, and suicidal ideation.

Readers who may be sensitive to these elements please take note.

Pronunciation Guide

Characters

Aleksey – ah-LEHK-see

Babcia – bahp-CHAH

Gisela – gee-ZEH-lah

Kazik – KAH-zheek

Leszek – LEH-shehk

Wojciech – VOY-chyeh

Places

Leśna Woda – LESH-nah VOHD-ah

Spirits

bannik / banniki (bathhouse spirit) – BAHN-neek / BAHN-neek-kee

bies / biesy (forest demon) – BEE-es / BEE-esey

czart / czarty (devil) – CHART / CHART-ey

domowik / domowiki (house spirit) – doh-MOH-veek / doh-MOH-vee-kee

latawiec / latawce (air demon) – lah-TAH-vyets / lah-TAHV-tse

leszy (forest spirit) – LEH-shee

ognik / ogniki (fire spirits) – OG-neek / OG-nee-kee

rusałka/ rusałki (water nymph) – roo-SOW-ka / roo-SOW-kee

skrzat / skrzaty (gnome) – SKSHAT / SKSHA-tey

utopiec / utopce (drowner) – oo-TOH-pyets / oo-TOHP-tse

wiła / wiły (nymph) – VEE-wah / VEE-wee

wodnik / wodniki (water goblin) – VOHD-neek / VOHD-nee-kee

1

THE DROWNED MAIDEN

GISELA

"YOU'RE SNEAKING OFF RATHER early today," Wojciech called out. "It's not even dusk yet."

Gisela's steps faltered. A wash of rainbow light poured through the Crystal Palace's domed ceiling, rippling over the floor to shine a watery spotlight on the elegant figure making his way down a monumental flight of steps toward her.

For a brief disorientating second, Gisela thought she might be staring into a mirror. Wojciech's green-black hair and hooded wine-red eyes could have been a reflection of her own. Only, his skin was darker, a warm clay brown next to her ghostly blue-green complexion. His lips were carmine, where hers were tinged violet. She usually preferred it when the water goblin took human form—his true form was honestly quite terrifying. But this new guise was just creepy.

"You're looking awfully youthful, Grandfather. You're not feeling self-conscious about your age again, are you? You can be honest with me. You're only *at least* a thousand years old."

Wojciech, who currently didn't appear to be a day over

twenty, pinned her with a flat, unimpressed look. A soft chime-like tinkling, the noise a spoon made when it tapped against a teacup, filled the air like a warning.

Gisela glanced over her shoulder at the giant pillar in the center of the palace atrium. The glittering monstrosity shot to the ceiling and was so wide around its base that even a half dozen water nymphs couldn't have touched hands if they'd stretched their arms around it. A honeycomb of shelves cut into its surface, and on those shelves rested thousands and thousands of seemingly innocuous teacups upturned upon their saucers.

"May I remind you, child," Wojciech said, his voice low and melodic, "that growing old is an accomplishment. I've outlived civilizations, survived more than you could imagine."

The ethereal tinkling increased in volume, the drowned souls he'd trapped inside each teacup pushing against the walls of their tiny porcelain prisons. Only the Sea Tsar himself was said to have a grander collection of human souls.

Wojciech reached the ground floor of the atrium. "If you're going out, take Tamara with you. *Don't* make me ask you twice."

"What? Why?" Gisela whined.

A second figure appeared at the top of the stairs: a girl with soft chestnut-brown curls and anxious red eyes; her skin had the same ghostly pallor as Gisela's.

The new girl.

Gisela's gaze darted back to Wojciech, her eyebrows pinching together in a silent plea.

Wojciech's smile was sharklike, full of unreasonably sharp teeth. Even in this handsome human form, he maintained a few monstrous traits. "This is Tamara's first time celebrating Green Week with us. Show her where the humans leave their offerings. Get to know each other. I think the two of you might have a lot in common."

Gisela doubted it. Saints, she didn't want to be stuck playing nursemaid for somebody who was new to all this. Perhaps she shouldn't have joked about Wojciech needing dentures—or maybe this was punishment for accidentally smashing one of his precious teacups and setting a soul free?

Or it was another one of his games. You never could tell.

Tamara came down the stairs and paused, shifting her weight from foot to foot, twisting her fingers in the ghost-white fabric of her flowy dress. She rubbed her hands up and down her bare arms as though she were anxious or cold. The air was always cooler down here in the depths of the river, in Wojciech's realm, and strangely wet, as though you were constantly walking through a mist.

As a mortal child, Gisela's favorite bedtime tales had been about the wodniki—the water goblins, the old river gods, the keepers of the drowned—who lived in grand underwater palaces carved from crystal and gold. Not that she'd ever admit as much to Wojciech.

You'll know the water goblin by his dripping clothes, by the sodden squelching of his boots, and by the wet footprints he leaves behind, her Great-Aunt Zela had told her. *If you ever visit the old country, darling, when you cross a river, you must carry breadcrumbs in your pocket and say a prayer so as to avoid meeting with him. He can drown you on dry land so long as he has even a spoonful of water.*

Gisela's skirt billowed about her knees, free from the bonds of gravity that governed the living world. It hadn't been so very long ago that she'd been the new girl here, waking in a strange and unfamiliar place, in this palace built upon the riverbed. When Wojciech told her that her mortal life was over, that she'd never turn seventeen nor grow old nor see any of the people she loved ever again, she'd almost despaired.

She'd wanted so badly to go home.

She still wanted to go home, was determined to, which was why she didn't have time for *this*.

"Can't one of the drowners do it?" she asked, already knowing the answer. "Or Yulia. Can't Yulia show her around? She's good at that. I'm busy. I have things to do." She shot Tamara an apologetic glance.

"Yulia's already on the surface," Wojciech said. "She snuck off earlier, muttering something about honey cake."

Gisela cursed. Every spring during Green Week, the local townsfolk honored the rusałki—water nymphs, like her and Yulia and Tamara. They left shiny baubles and trinkets by the riverbanks, strung gifts from the branches of the trees in the forest: garlands of bright flowers, hair ribbons dyed eye-catching colors, and necklaces of glossy beads. They'd even leave offerings of food: eggs and sweet grain puddings, honey cakes and handfuls of sugary berries. They were bribes, prizes left out to placate hungry ghosts. People hoped that if they appeased the water nymphs, they wouldn't bewitch and harm their loved ones.

Competition for such offerings was fierce. There were only so many treats to go around, and no matter how many years you spent haunting the deep, how accustomed you grew to the water goblin's feasts of catfish and eel, you never quite forgot the taste of human food, of home.

If Yulia ate all the honey cake, Gisela was going to make sure she drowned in the river.

Again.

"Oh, and Gisela?" Wojciech drew a handkerchief from a pocket of his emerald-green suit and began polishing a teacup he'd selected from one of the pillar's little nooks. "Make sure you tell Tamara what will happen to her if she strays too far from my river. I want to avoid trouble this week. Keep an eye out for our resident exorcist. He's been overzealous in his duties lately. So overzealous, I can't help but wonder if *somebody* has been provoking him."

"Whoever could that be?" Gisela said, trying for innocence and not quite succeeding.

The teacups on the shelves rattled ominously. The sudden sharp glint in Wojciech's eyes was a reminder of just who she was dealing with.

Maybe it was better to go along with what he wanted for now.

"Fine, fine. I'll take her with me. But are you sure you don't want her to stay behind and help you with the polishing? I mean, should you really be doing all the housework at your age?"

Wojciech's lip twitched.

Gisela quickly grabbed Tamara by the wrist. "We'll see you later, then! Don't break a hip!"

2
THE LAND OF THE LIVING

GISELA

A SINKING SUN HALOED the scene as Gisela and Tamara emerged from the river, rising from the water below a deserted stone footbridge as if it were a portal to another world. Gisela helped Tamara clamber onto the bridge beside her. Lazy clouds floated overhead, tossed by a balmy breeze.

Gisela fished a compact out of the pockets of her white slip dress and started dabbing powder and rouge on her cheeks to disguise the deathly pallor of her skin. Lipstick would hide the purple of her lips. She couldn't do much about the unnatural color of her eyes, but soon it would be dark enough that most people wouldn't notice unless they looked closely.

Tamara watched curiously, wringing water from her dress. "What did the water goblin mean when he said to tell me what will happen if I stray too far from the river?"

"Have you ever seen a frog that's been trapped indoors for days?" Gisela had. She'd found a dead frog in the library at her school once. Its body had shriveled into a sad little dried-out husk. "It's like that. You'll dry out and die."

There wasn't any point in sugarcoating it. Tamara would discover the truth for herself soon enough—the same way Gisela had when she'd tried to leave, determined to find a way home to her family. She'd barely made it past the old forest shrine at the edge of town before the dryness hit her throat and her lips began to crack, her parched skin demanding she turn back.

They couldn't leave this place even if they tried.

Gisela finished painting her lips a sweet strawberry red. "We can't stray far from where we died. And it's important to stay hydrated. Leave your hair wet," she instructed, when Tamara started to twist water out of the strands. "Don't worry. People will just think you've come from visiting one of the bathhouses." She offered the other girl her powder and lipstick. "Are you from around here? Or did you just—" Gisela slid a finger across her throat.

Tamara shook her head. "I was told I could find work as a maid here. I wanted to get out of the city. It was supposed to be a fresh start. But I—I fell in love with somebody I shouldn't have. He made me a lot of promises, and like a fool, I believed him. He wasn't a good person, and he has an awful temper. . . ."

Gisela grimaced at the unpleasant implication.

In any case, it made sense Tamara had thought she'd find work here as a maid. Leśna Woda was a famous and fashionable tourist destination. Tens of thousands of visitors came and went throughout the year. The dreamy scenery and miraculous powers of the town's blessed waters, its magical hot springs, had drawn people here for centuries: commoners and the cream of society, as well as the cultural elite—poets and artists and emperors and queens. It was one of the oldest spa towns on the mainland.

Gisela herself was not a local. Her father had taken their family on a trip abroad. He was always doing business in faraway places. Most of the time, he left Gisela and her little brother behind, but this time, this one time, he actually listened when she'd begged to accompany him. She promised they wouldn't interrupt his work nor wander off nor cause any kind of trouble, though Gisela suspected he gave in simply because she had a vague understanding of the language spoken here. She'd picked it up from Great-Aunt Zela. Her father had been keen to use her as a translator.

"I'm not from around here either. I'm from Caldella."

"The witches' island?" Tamara said, wide-eyed.

Gisela smirked. "Relax. I'm not a witch, I promise. I've been here for almost a whole year now. I know the place like the back of my hand." It occurred to her that it would be easier to simply abandon Tamara here—she must already know her way around. Gisela could simply tell her where to find the offerings the humans left out. But if Wojciech found out . . .

Gisela didn't want to deal with that.

She led Tamara across the footbridge. The streets of the town rose around them. Gisela's mood lifted. As always, the charming old-world architecture made her feel like she'd traveled back in time or stepped into the pages of a story. Leśna Woda looked like a place where a fairy tale began.

The meandering cobblestoned lanes were shaded by leafy trees, while the grand bathhouses were ringed by lush parks and gardens filled with ornamental ponds and burbling fountains. A gust of wind blew, showering blush-pink petals across their path. Because it was Green Week, everything was adorned with greenery. A profusion of wildflowers and fragrant herbs decorated every shop front, every window, every doorway leading into a hundred-year-old guesthouse. The honeyed scent of roses laced the air with sweetness. It was as though the whole town were in bloom.

"You know Villa Lilia, right?" Gisela pointed at a distant rooftop. There were five main springs running through the town, and each bathhouse drew from a different one. Drinking or bathing in Villa Lilia's waters would enhance your beauty and leave your skin shimmering like stardust.

"Most of the bathhouses are heavily warded so spirits can't enter, but Villa Lilia's owner doesn't mind if one or two of us sneak in so long as we don't snack on any humans. Oh, and those spires, the church over there—avoid it."

"Because of the exorcist?" Tamara asked. "Is he really dangerous?"

"He's more of a pest than anything. Don't worry. He's probably off working toward sainthood somewhere." Gisela pulled Tamara to her side, leaving space for an elderly dark-skinned man with a walking stick to shuffle past.

The streets were growing increasingly busy as they ventured closer to the heart of town; tourists and locals alike were meandering toward the night market in the main square: Girls in airy sundresses with ribbons braided through their hair and lace trim on their socks. Boys dressed in crisp button-down shirts and suspenders. Happy couples with their heads bent close together.

The air was full of chatter in a multitude of languages. The mainland was a continent made up of countless countries and little kingdoms, so many that they all blurred together in Gisela's head. Her gaze lingered on a family stopped outside a souvenir shop. The parents were busy picking through racks of whimsical watercolor picture postcards, while the children, a little boy and girl, whispered and giggled and pointed at something on display.

Memories hit her like a wave, threatening to sweep her under. Her heart squeezed.

"It's not the worst place in the world to haunt," she said after a pause.

Tamara gave a considering look. "Do you mean that? Yulia told me you're trying to cheat death, become human again so you can go home. Is that true?"

Yulia.

Of course, *Yulia* had said something. She couldn't keep her stupid mouth shut. She'd been acting all weird and standoffish ever since Wojciech had admitted there was a way for a water nymph to regain her humanity. Yulia hated the idea. She didn't seem to care about the home she'd left behind, whereas Gisela desperately wanted to get back to hers. After all, she'd have to be a true monster, wouldn't she, to not want to return to her family?

She wished she knew why Yulia was so willing to let go of the people who'd raised her, but another part of her was too afraid to ask.

"Is there really a way to become human again?" Tamara asked.

Gisela chewed her bottom lip. Was this why Wojciech had insisted they visit the surface together? Was this what he'd meant when he'd said they had something in common? The other water nymphs didn't seem to feel the pull toward the mortal world that Gisela did.

"It's simple." Or at least it had sounded simple when Wojciech shared the secret. It had turned out to be much harder in practice. "All you have to do is get a human to kiss you."

"Kiss you?" Tamara echoed in confusion.

Gisela nodded. Rusałki were maidens who had met untimely and violent ends. They were cursed to haunt the waterways in which they'd drowned, bound to live as restless spirits, unless one of two things happened.

The first was if their death was avenged. If they revenged themselves on those who had wronged them and resolved the lingering grudge that had caused them to become a spirit in the first place, they could move on to the afterlife—which was what Yulia had suggested Gisela do if she hated being a water nymph so much. Which she didn't. The whole being-an-undead-spirit thing was *so* not the point. The point was Gisela was angry. She wanted her life back. She wanted what had been stolen from her.

Which was ironic, really, because when she had been alive, Gisela hadn't been all that attached to *being* alive. She was prone to bouts of melancholy and was regularly overwhelmed by dark and negative thoughts. How many times had she joked about how dead she felt inside? How many times had she daydreamed about never waking up again?

How many times had she thought, *Wouldn't it be easier if I just weren't here?*

Some days, she felt like the biggest, most pathetic cliché

because it was only once she'd lost her life that she'd realized how much she cherished it. Even now, the hungry animal desire to *live* still shocked her.

So, option two.

"We're bound here by our grief, by our anger and regrets," she told Tamara. "It's what made us rusałki. If you want to regain your humanity, you have to find a way to tether yourself to the mortal world with another equally as powerful, transformative, and all-consuming feeling—like love. You need to forge an emotional connection with a human who'll act as your anchor."

And then, once she'd accomplished that, once she'd dragged herself out of this strange liminal state between life and true death, then Gisela would see to resolving her grudges. She would unravel the mystery of her death. She wanted vengeance *and* her humanity back, and she didn't care if Yulia thought she was greedy for desiring both.

They paused to catch their breath, standing at the edge of a paved square surrounded by quaint tea- and coffee houses, art supply stores, and cute little kiosks selling handmade crafts and curiously shaped porcelain spa cups with built-in straws.

Gisela's eyes were immediately drawn to a boy fooling around with his friends over by the central stone fountain. Above the splashing water rose the curvaceous statue of a mermaid. The boy himself was short and reedy, with a head of adorable honey-brown curls. One of his friends elbowed him, shoving him off-balance as he cast a furtive glance her way. Gisela feigned shyness, watching him through the damp black curtain of her waist-length hair.

He wasn't her usual type. His friend was more to her taste—tall and effortlessly cool, with a grin that bordered on a smirk. The kind of boy everyone admired.

But the reedy boy was the one shooting glances at her, and she couldn't afford to be picky. She was getting desperate. It wasn't important if she liked or wanted him anyway. She didn't need to find someone perfect for her. What was important was that *they* wanted her badly enough to kiss her.

Because she couldn't just ask for a kiss. That was the catch. It had to be freely given. The other person had to initiate it. But every time she got close, when she started to lean in for that perfect meeting of lips . . . that was when trouble struck. She was rudely interrupted, or the person she was with suddenly realized what she was. Their expression would morph from lust to confusion to outright horror, and they'd flee from her in fear.

Even so, she wasn't giving up.

Gisela linked elbows with Tamara. Maybe it was actually a good thing Wojciech had foisted the new girl on her. She had yet to collect any Green Week treats, but Tamara might help her get something even better. "Do you want to help me?"

"Help you?"

"To become human." Gisela checked her reflection in a shop window. "Okay, here's the plan. We're going to stroll past the fountain, and you're going to pretend to trip and push me into the arms of that shy curly-haired boy."

"What? Why?"

"So he has an excuse to catch me and start a conversation, obviously." Gisela reapplied her lipstick and was just about to start tugging Tamara across the plaza when something flashed at the corner of her vision.

Sunlight catching on the lenses of an all-too-familiar pair of wire-rimmed glasses.

Shit.

Gisela let out a hiss. Tamara cocked her head in question.

God damn him. Why was he always, always interfering?

"Change of plan," Gisela said, pulling Tamara in the opposite direction, away from the boys at the fountain. "Run! *Now!*"

3

HIDE-AND-SEEK

GISELA

A THUNDER OF FURIOUS footsteps chased them down the nearest side street. "Oh, Kazik," Gisela called over her shoulder, "always interrupting at the best part. It's like you don't want me to have any fun!"

The only reply was a curse and a shout as a crowd of pedestrians jumped out of the exorcist's path.

Gisela ducked around the next corner, dragging a breathless Tamara after her. They deftly avoided a man pushing a baby stroller, very nearly running into an old woman carrying a wicker basket full of wild strawberries.

"Why are we running?" Tamara gasped. "Who is that?"

"Quick, hide in here." Gisela pushed Tamara toward the open doors of a bakery famous for its delectable blueberry yeast buns.

"What about you?"

"If I don't come back, head for the riverbank. The other girls will be there. If there's trouble, just use your hair comb. You have one, don't you?"

Tamara looked bewildered.

Saints. Was Wojciech expecting Gisela to do literally everything? She fumbled in the pockets of her dress before fishing out an ornate bone-white hair comb. Its handle was embedded with dark river pearls, and its teeth were fine and sharp as needles. Every water nymph carried one like it, a hair comb crafted from coral, amber, or bone.

Gisela pressed hers into Tamara's hand. "You can borrow mine. I'll take you to get yours later. There's a whole chest of them in the palace. You can use it as a weapon or to conjure and control water. Just hold it tight and focus. The magic will do the rest."

Beneath her fingers, Tamara's grip was loose and uncertain. But Gisela didn't have time to spare on more instructions. She gave Tamara another shove, and then Gisela was off, leaving the mouthwatering scent of fresh-baked bread behind. She knew Kazik would follow her. It wasn't the first time they'd played chase. He was always ruining her plans, constantly interfering, popping up like some reverse matchmaker determined to sabotage her love life.

Sure enough, when she dared to look back, she caught a glimpse of messy dark brown hair rounding the turn, practically on her heels. But, as Gisela had told Tamara, she knew the spa town like the back of her hand. She was familiar with every crack in the pavement, every sudden bend and hidden alley, every garden, every shortcut.

"Am I that irresistible?" she called, her bare feet slapping the footpath. "Don't you have better things to do than stalk me?"

"I warned you! How many times do I have to send you back to your river, demon?" Kazik's dark eyes were flinty behind his glasses, flashing with an anger hot enough to burn.

"But I like it here!" Gisela grinned and put on a burst of speed, the exorcist's threats fading as she put distance between them. Her speed and agility as a water nymph was far beyond a human's. She was almost flying.

In a single bound, Gisela hurdled over a manicured hedge in the gardens circling Villa Lilia. Skidding sideways, barely out of breath, navigating past a silvery pond and a sun-warmed bench, she squeezed down a narrow pathway between two buildings, heading for the busy lane on the other side. She crossed it. Another square opened before her, and she slid with calculated ease into a crush of pedestrians exploring a market of stalls, weaving in and out of the bustle, blending in.

Vanishing.

Vendors haggled in loud voices. Chalk signs displayed the price of herbal butters and scented candles, homemade liqueurs and strings of fresh bagels. Gisela snatched a headscarf embroidered with roses from one of the displays, wrapped it over her damp hair, and threaded into a line of tourists lining up to buy waffle cones of cheap ice cream from a stall shaded by a red cloth awning. She held her breath when Kazik staggered into the market mere seconds later.

His hands gripped his knees as he bent almost in two, wheezing and trying to catch his breath. The saintly medallion he wore on a chain around his neck and the silver cross dangling from one of the piercings climbing the curve of his left ear caught the light when he lifted his head, scanning the crowd with a fierce scowl on his sun-browned face.

Kazik was always scowling or frowning or glowering at something or somebody, and yet, for all his brooding looks, Leśna Woda's resident exorcist was surprisingly pretty. His features were delicate. His angry brows as fine as brushstrokes. His intense brown eyes were fanned with the longest, darkest lashes Gisela had ever seen.

She hid a smile as he stalked out of view, searching for her in vain. While it was true that Kazik was actively trying to exorcise her, she couldn't help finding his little efforts amusing.

The line she was in moved, taking her forward. The couple behind her chattered loudly, debating which flavors of ice cream to order: saffron and lemon cream or raspberry and pistachio. Gisela's stomach grumbled, reminding her that she hadn't eaten in hours. She'd been saving room for all the Green Week treats.

Standing on tiptoe, she tried to see how far she was from the head of the line.

The boy in front of her was unfairly tall, but he chose that moment to bend down and fix his shoelace. There was something about the set of his broad shoulders, hunched over like that, something about the sweat-darkened curl of blond hair at the nape of his neck . . .

An inexplicable chill swept over Gisela's skin. All the giddy relief at her escape evaporated. Something stirred in the recesses of her mind as she stepped back instinctively, but whatever it was slipped away before she could make sense of it as she knocked into the couple behind her.

They let out twin growls of annoyance. "Hey! Watch it!"

"Sorry, I—" Gisela stumbled away from the line. What *was* that? Before she could pull herself back together, a hand seized her elbow, and a fistful of wormwood was flung in her face.

She shrieked, throwing her arms up to shield herself, her eyes burning and watering. She coughed violently. Wormwood was poisonous to water nymphs.

A loop of shining amber prayer beads roped around her forearm.

"Wait—" She gasped, trying desperately to yank free.

The prayer beads flared with bright light, glowing hot, cinching tighter, cutting into her skin.

"Ow, ow, ow! Wait, let go. You're hurting me! Oh, come on, Kazik. You really want to do this in front of everybody? Here? You're going to look like a crazy person!"

4
THE WITCH'S GRANDSON
KAZIK

THE PRESSURE BEHIND KAZIK'S brow bone was rapidly building into a migraine. Rusałki were always a nuisance in the warmer months, especially during Green Week, and this year he had to deal with them all by himself. He just needed a minute—one goddamn minute—of peace.

He gritted his teeth against a swell of nausea. His vision was blurring, which was not at all helpful when he had a literal demon in his living room.

Leśna Woda's number one public menace.

"Kah-*zeek*! I'm bo-*oored*," Gisela whined, dragging out each word. "How long are you going to keep me here? Let me out!"

Kazik spared a brief glance at the corner of the room, where the water nymph was imprisoned within a circle drawn with blessed chalk. It formed an invisible barrier that she couldn't cross. His heart swelled with satisfaction at the sight. Finally, *finally*, he had her trapped.

Gisela pouted up at him from where she sat puddled on the floor. She looked oddly pathetic, her wrists bound with rosary beads and her knees hugged to her chest, but there was no danger of him feeling sorry for her. Gisela was as hauntingly beautiful as any of the water goblin's bloodthirsty granddaughters with her long black hair and tiny heart-shaped face. Human in appearance, until you registered the deathly green-blue pallor of her skin and the unnatural bloodred glint of her eyes.

You couldn't let yourself forget those pretty faces hid wicked hearts.

The boy she'd been eyeing in the market probably didn't even realize what a lucky escape he'd made. But then, Kazik's childhood classmates weren't exactly known for their intelligence.

Gisela huffed. "I didn't realize you were so desperate for my company that you'd actually kidnap me."

"Yes, I realized I couldn't possibly live without you," Kazik replied with a deadpan expression.

Gisela grinned. "So the other spirits don't get this kind of treatment? I'm special? Did you ruin my little meet-cute at the fountain because you were jealous? You know you're looking very handsome today. Are those new glasses?"

Kazik didn't rise to the bait; engaging with her antics was only asking for trouble. He knew her tricks. The flirting didn't fool him. Gisela flirted with everything that breathed. She'd say literally anything. Sometimes he couldn't even process the ridiculous things that spilled from her lips. She had no shame whatsoever.

Turning his attention to the wicker basket on the living room table, he sorted through bunches of mint, milk thistle, skullcap, and chamomile. This had all been so much easier when his grandmother had been alive. Babcia had kept the terrors that preyed on Leśna Woda's inhabitants in check. She was revered by the townsfolk; everyone knew they could turn to her in the case of a fever, sore back, or strange happening. She'd been called a faith healer, an herbalist, a witch—though she'd hated that last one.

They weren't witches.

It was a dangerous thing to be called a witch in these parts. The only powers they had, Babcia had made Kazik repeat time and time again, were a gift from God to be used in the service of others. There was nothing sinful about that. They could undo charms cast by *real* witches and scare off sickness, give water healing qualities just by praying over it. They read the future in pools of cooling candle wax, spoke with the saints and the dead, and exorcised wicked spirits.

Kazik had come to live with his grandparents after his father had left. His mother was unable to care for him by herself. She'd also been a talented healer once, but that was before she'd misused her powers and lost them for good. She sent money she earned working a secretarial job in the city but rarely visited. To her, this was a place full of painful memories.

It didn't stop him from resenting her. And now his grandparents had passed away—his grandfather from a fever that had resisted even Kazik's best efforts at healing and his grandmother after a lethal encounter with a forest demon. He was left to carry on their traditions, to deal with the unholy creatures drawn to the town and its sacred springs.

A palpable loneliness clung to the house now.

"My wrists hurt," Gisela whined, jolting Kazik from his thoughts. He watched her stand and pace the diameter of the chalk circle like a wild beast trapped behind bars. White flames flared when she pushed her bound hands against the invisible barrier surrounding her. She shrieked and let out a curse.

Kazik rolled his eyes and mentally ran through the list of things he needed to get done. He had bigger concerns than one exasperating water nymph. Half a dozen or so patrons visited the house every day except for Sundays. Locals mostly, and folk from neighboring villages. Some people traveled great distances seeking his family's services. But only those who could be trusted were invited into the tidy little room at the front of the house decorated with its gold and gleaming pictures of the saints.

Kazik still had to prepare some linden bark and make a cloth charm for Mr. Novak to bury beside running water to cure his toothache. He frowned, trying to ignore the incessant tapping of Gisela's feet, the rustling of her dress while she moved and complained and generally made as much of a nuisance of herself as she could. Eventually, she even started to sing, each insidiously soft note designed to cloud his mind and entice him to step a little closer to her—it was the same song the water nymphs used to draw mortals into their river.

With saintlike self-control, Kazik kept his expression determinedly blank. He'd be damned if he gave her the satisfaction of bewitching him so easily. When she sent a hopeful glance his way, he scrambled to look busy, trying so hard *not* to pay attention to her that he banged his knee against a table leg.

Gisela winced with exaggerated sympathy. "Ouch" was her helpful commentary. "That's definitely going to bruise."

Kazik took a deep breath through his nose.

"Come on, Kazik. Let me out. I'll be good. I promise."

"I don't believe that for a second."

"You know, it's almost as if you don't like me."

"I don't."

Gisela gasped, feigning shock. Her eyes welled with fake tears. "You wound me."

"I might if you keep annoying me."

"You know, it's kind of sexy when you're mean. Have I told you I love it when you get all forceful with me?"

Kazik felt his ears get hot.

Gisela leered. "Okay, okay, I'm just teasing. I'll stop if you let me go."

"So you can run off and attack more innocent people? I warned you the last time what would happen if you kept causing trouble."

"I've never attacked anybody!"

"Oh, so Jacek Adler tried to drown himself in the river?"

For a split second, Gisela almost looked guilty. "That was an accident. We were having a tickle fight, and he tripped and *fell* into the water. How was I supposed to know he couldn't swim? I was annoyed too! Do you have any idea how much time I wasted trying to get his attention? And then he went and almost died. Why am I so unlucky, Kazik?"

"And Sara?" Kazik named the tourist girl he'd found wandering dazed and shivering along the grassy riverbank at dawn the other week. Dressed only in her nightgown, she'd spoken of beautiful ghostly girls, of cold clammy hands pulling her away to dance with the dead in endless circles.

"What, I can't ask a girl to dance now?"

Kazik tried to will away his growing migraine. "What about Dmitri?"

"I invited him for an evening stroll, and it was hot, so I suggested we go skinny-dipping in the river. I don't know why he started acting all weird." Gisela pouted. "I didn't think he'd be such a prude. I think he might've started to suspect what I am. I only grabbed him to try and stop him from leaving. I wasn't trying to drag him into the water. Did he tell you I was? Because that's a lie!"

Kazik shoved his glasses into his hair and pressed the heels of his hands into his eyes. At least Dmitri had some inkling of self-preservation. So many people Kazik's age didn't believe creatures like Gisela existed, even as they took part in the Green Week festivities. They didn't heed the old tales of how it wasn't safe to bathe in the river before Saint John's Eve.

"I'm just trying to make somebody like me!" Gisela said.

Kazik scoffed disbelievingly.

"Did you know, Kazik, that if a mortal kisses a water nymph, she can regain her humanity?"

"I didn't know you still believed in fairy tales. But if you're so tired of living as you are, I'll do you a favor and perform an exorcism. You can go to the next world, where you belong."

Kazik raised his hand threateningly, meaning to scare her, reaching for the spark of divine power at his core, for the magic he'd been blessed with—though some days it felt more like a curse than a blessing. He relished the feeling when his palm warmed, a bright current of power humming through his veins as he called on heaven to grant him strength.

Those saints who protect me, hear me now. . . .

Across the room, Gisela's eyes widened in alarm. It was so satisfying finally having her at his mercy. Leśna Woda would be so much more peaceful with this nuisance gone.

Grant me your . . .

Abruptly, the magic recoiled, writhing in his hold like an eel before it slipped from his grasp.

What—

Kazik froze in place, his arm still raised in the air. He turned his head, staring at his palm. What the hell? He glanced at Gisela, but she looked as confused as he felt. She lifted an eyebrow.

Heat seared up Kazik's neck. Of all the spirits to screw up in front of. He didn't even understand how he'd screwed up. His magic never failed to respond to his will. So why?

The old grandfather clock in the corner let out an exceptionally loud *clang*. His eyes flew to the time. Saints. He had no time to figure this out. He was supposed to meet Zuzanna at the bus station. His cousin had sent word she was coming to stay for a few days. She had time off before her summer exams.

He brooded for a moment, debating. Was it safe to leave Gisela here alone? She was sealed within the bounds of the chalk circle, and he'd scattered cuttings of wormwood over the floor as an added protective measure. Her wrists were bound with his amber rosary, a family heirloom. How much trouble could she get into? He'd be gone for half an hour at most. He'd walk fast. Zuzanna could help him deal with all this when they returned.

Kazik tugged on an earring then patted down his pockets for his house keys before he spied them on a shelf near the clock.

He grabbed them.

"What are you doing?" Gisela said. "Where are you going?"

"Out."

"Out? But you can't leave me here. There's no water. You know I can't survive for long on dry land!"

"Can't you? How sad. I'll pray for your soul."

Gisela shot him a look that was equal parts livid and desperate. "I'll start screaming," she threatened. "Someone will hear me."

"You think so? Out here on the very edge of town? Stay here and reflect on your sins." Kazik turned on his heel.

"Wait! Come back! You can't just— Kazik!" Gisela's voice cut off as the front door clicked shut.

Peace at last.

A cool breeze ruffled Kazik's hair. It was quiet outside, save for the faint sound of a dog barking somewhere in the distance and the persistent singing of the crickets. As he'd just reminded Gisela, his grandparents' cottage sat in loneliness on the very outskirts of town, on the edge of a dark and endless forest.

Dusk was falling, the long day finally giving way to night. Walking fast, casting the occasional glance over his shoulder and keeping his ears pricked, Kazik strode down the road. You never knew who might appear nor what you'd run into here. The next sound to break the quiet might be a twig snapping beneath the heel of a god or a monster.

Water nymphs weren't the only creatures causing trouble. There were the male drowners and the water goblin, with his propensity for snatching up humans and trapping their souls in teacups. There were the noon wraiths that stalked the fields at midday and the deadly night demons that crept like cats into houses after sundown. Leśna Woda was haunted by all manner of devils and hungry ghosts, by wicked forest spirits that liked to slip inside mortal bodies and wear them like new coats.

Every one of those abominations would rejoice if they knew Kazik was having trouble with his power. The way his magic had seized up just now. . . . His head pounded. Maybe that was the cause. He just needed to rest.

A soft, spine-tingling chittering sounded from the bushes.

Kazik stilled, tensing, searching for eyeshine and teeth gleam amid the foliage, scanning up and down the rough dirt path. He saw nothing out of the ordinary, only innocent wooden houses with gabled roofs and window boxes bursting with flowers. A neighbor's cat side-eyed him, its long black tail flicking slowly back and forth.

He continued walking, a little bit faster now. His fist clenched around the vial of holy water he always carried in his pocket. If any unholy terror thought they could take him without a fight, they were in for a world of disappointment.

5

THE TASTE OF KINDNESS

GISELA

SOME DAYS, GISELA THOUGHT Kazik wasn't as terrible as everybody said. Sure, he took his role as Leśna Woda's self-imposed protector far too seriously, but that was why it was so much fun to push his buttons. She couldn't resist playing with that overly righteous fire, testing to see how far she could take things before he snapped and tried to douse her with holy water.

But clearly, she'd thought wrong.

He *was* just as terrible as the other spirits claimed. And cruel. Completely and utterly heartless. For the shadow of a second there, she'd really believed he was about to exorcise her. She wondered what had made him change his mind. Maybe he thought letting her dry out was easier.

What was his problem anyway? It wasn't as though she was indescribably evil. She was just a dead girl trying to get her life back. He didn't have to be so mean.

She spun in a circle, examining her surroundings, trying to determine how the hell she was going to get out of this. Kazik's house wasn't a place she'd ever imagined visiting. She wasn't sure what she'd expected: Bloodstains on the floorboards? Devils chained to the walls, imprisoned in iron cages?

Technically, Gisela supposed *she* was the devil in this case.

Was there anything in here she could use to free herself?

Grim-faced saints frowned at her from the walls, their holy pictures gleaming gold. Dried herbs and paper ornaments hung from the ceiling on strings. Vials of holy water and blessed salt filled rows of crowded shelves. A small wooden table covered with a white tablecloth occupied one corner—a private altar. Upon it rested candles and a Bible with gilded edges and pages so papery thin, it looked like an ancient grimoire with which a witch would cast their spells. The scent of beeswax, incense, and burnt flax that she'd come to associate with Kazik infused the air and made her nose itch. The whole house smelled like a chapel or a church.

And it was tiny, by Gisela's standards. The living room bled into a plain little kitchen with a woodstove and cast-iron pots hanging from the wall. Two doors branched off from the open space: one leading into a bedroom, the other into a shadowy corridor. She could just make out a rickety wooden staircase leading up to a second floor.

Kazik lived alone, so there was probably no one upstairs whom she could beg for help. Screaming, as he'd pointed out, would've been a waste of breath.

A severe old grandfather clock was *tick-tick-ti*cking away in the corner. Gisela watched its hands count down the hour. The light seeping through the lacy window curtains was fast losing its golden luster.

Night was approaching.

It seemed Kazik really did intend to leave her here to shrivel up and die.

Cautiously, Gisela approached the edge of the chalk circle. The air in front of her nose shimmered like the skin of a soap bubble, with a rainbow iridescence. She raised her bound hands, tentatively reaching out.

It was like when she'd pushed two magnets together at school. The air itself pushed back. An invisible barrier. The white lines of chalk flashed brightly. Sparks flared, and she snatched her hands back with a curse.

She didn't know if it was panic making her imagination run wild, but her skin suddenly felt dangerously parched. She hadn't been lying when she'd told Kazik she couldn't survive for long on land—she should probably have mentioned that to Tamara too. It wasn't just that they couldn't venture far from the river; they had to constantly return to it or find another way to rehydrate.

Gisela hoped Tamara had the sense to have found the other water nymphs by now. With any luck she'd tell them about Kazik chasing Gisela, and they'd come looking for her. She didn't know if they'd dare look here though.

She tugged at her hair, trying to think. Earlier, the silky black strands had been a cold heavy weight against her back. Now they felt almost dry.

Shit.

She wished she hadn't been so quick to give Tamara her hair comb. She could've used it now to wet her hair or, if she'd been really petty, to conjure waves and enough water to flood the entire house. Kazik deserved it, and doing so would've drastically improved her mood. If only Wojciech hadn't insisted she play nursemaid. She was trying hard not to think about the scolding she'd get from the water goblin when she finally got out of this mess—if she got out of it before she turned into a husk and withered to dust.

If she did wither to dust, would Wojciech get off his ancient ass and flood the town to avenge her? He was going to be so incredibly pissed.

Gisela shook the intrusive thoughts away. "Focus," she mumbled. Her mind had a habit of getting stuck in circles, imagining worst-case scenarios. Anyway, conjuring water from thin air wasn't the only useful skill she'd gained since becoming a spirit. She smiled grimly at the chunky prayer beads looping around her wrists. The bonds were tight, the glossy beads still warm against her bare skin.

Forcing herself to still, Gisela shut her eyes and concentrated. Magic responded to your will, Wojciech had taught her. It was all about intent.

After twenty-two great deep breaths, the voice in her mind finally fell quiet. A shiver ran through her. Her skin tingled, and a silvery-white light engulfed her body. With a bubble-like *pop*, Gisela vanished. The white slip dress she'd worn crumpled to a silent heap upon the floor. Kazik's rosary landed atop of it with a crash. A second later, a small green frog poked its head out from beneath the fabric, hopping to free itself.

That was better. She wouldn't dry out as quickly like this. And maybe, if she couldn't *step* through the barrier in human form . . .

Gisela leapt—only to smack against an invisible wall. Her little green body slid, as if down a pane of glass, before falling with a sad wet squelch back to the floor.

God damn it.

Dazed, bruised, and mentally vowing dark revenge against Kazik—he was going to suffer when she was free, she'd make sure of it—she took a full minute to register the distant rapping of knuckles against wood. Someone was knocking on the front door.

A voice called faintly: "Hello?" The door handle rattled. "Is anyone home? Oh." The exclamation was followed by the groan of the front door's hinges creaking open. There was a pause, then the sound of tentative footsteps. "Hello?" A tall, broad-shouldered, and densely built silhouette darkened the entrance into the living room.

A chill ran down Gisela's back—the same inexplicable sense of foreboding that had frozen her body back in the marketplace. A boy roughly her age stepped into the room, into the last of the day's light.

She didn't recognize him.

At least she didn't think she did. His short honey-hued hair was swept back from his pale face. It was a fairly ordinary face, narrow, with a long thin nose and impishly pointed chin. His eyes . . .

His *eyes*.

Gisela's breath caught. His left eye was as blue as a summer sky, while his right eye was as green as spring leaves.

He was studying her in turn, his brows raised, looking as surprised to see her as she was to see him.

Gisela stayed deathly still, animal instinct screaming at her to shrink herself to be as small and inconspicuous as possible. Should she try shifting back into human form? No. He'd definitely freak out, and she'd be stark naked, which was always so damn awkward.

A touch of amusement lifted the corners of his mouth. "Now how did you end up trapped in here, little frog?" The deep timbre of his voice startled her. It sounded almost familiar.

Had she tried flirting with him before? But surely, she'd remember those eyes.

He moved closer, his gaze darting from the silver-green wormwood cuttings scattered across the floor to her crumpled dress and the fallen rosary beads, until only the curved line of the chalk circle separated them.

Gisela let out an encouraging croak. *Yes! Good human.*

If he could just smear the chalk with the toe of his shoe, then she might be freed from Kazik's magic circle.

She hopped backward, trying to draw him in closer. The boy shot her another faintly amused glance. There was something endearingly unkempt about him. A bright green leaf was stuck in his hair, and his left shoelace was coming undone.

He crouched before her, squatting on the balls of his feet, and scrubbed curiously at the chalk line, breaking it. He lifted a powder-caked fingertip to his face.

There was no great flash nor crackle of magic. No thunder nor lightning. No sign a spell had even been broken. But Gisela swore she felt something ripple through the room. The air lightened as the invisible barrier dissipated.

Ha! Now she'd show Kazik. She readied herself for another leap. She was going to make him regret ever having—

A hand, shockingly warm and large, closed around her small body. Gisela squirmed and writhed in panic, survival instincts kicking in at full force. The hand squeezed tighter.

"Hey, hey! Wait, it's all right. I'm not trying to hurt you." The boy laughed and made soothing noises as he caged her between his giant palms. "You can't stay here. Let's get you back outside, where you belong, okay?"

Gisela's stomach lurched at the sudden upward motion as she was buoyed into the air. Why on earth had she thought it a good idea to change form?

They left the living room and then the house itself. Outside, the air was lighter, free of the choking scent of incense. The boy carried her down the front steps and around to the garden at the back of the cottage, deftly avoiding three curious hens and two terrifying geese who came to peck at his ankles. They passed the outhouse, a small tumbledown barn, and a vegetable patch overflowing with young cabbages and cucumbers. A whitewashed fence marked out the garden's boundary, half the posts collapsing from age.

The boy stepped through a gap, following a path worn into the dirt that headed away from the house and into the surrounding forest. The dense canopy drenched them in deep green shadow. A loud caw echoed through the branches as a bird took to the sky in a flurry of dark wings.

Dread filled Gisela anew.

But eventually, and ever so gently, with a care that made a

strange warmth blossom inside her chest, the boy deposited her beside a mossy log, among a patch of vibrant purple wildflowers.

"There. Off you go. I'd stay away from town for a few days if I were you. Don't let Kazik catch you again." He gave her a conspiratorial grin, an impish dimple appearing in his cheek.

Butterflies fluttered in the pit of Gisela's stomach.

"You should find some water. You don't want to dry out." The boy straightened, raising his arms above his head in a stretch.

Gisela let out a soft croak, the tiniest thank-you.

Her savior cast her one final bemused glance, then started back the way he'd come. Gisela listened until his footsteps faded, until his broad back vanished amid the shadows of the trees.

6

SONGS SUNG TO THE MOON

GISELA

NIGHT HAD SETTLED OVER the spa town by the time Gisela returned to the river. Starlight clothed her fellow water nymphs in ghostly silver. The girls, all six of them, were lazing barefoot on the grassy bank, weaving flower crowns of marigolds and honey-scented frog orchids while Zamira, the smallest of their number, she'd only been thirteen when she was murdered, sang a love song to the moon. Each melancholy note unspooled from her blue-tinged lips, weaving a haunting melody through the dark.

Gisela waved but didn't join them. She was a *little* offended that they hadn't been panicking over her absence. And anyway, her goal right now was to rehydrate.

She let out a relieved sigh as she dipped her toes into the cool water. Almost immediately she felt soothed, refreshed, and less like she was about to dry up and wither away to nothing. The river ran narrow here and at a leisurely pace; the currents were slow-moving, the water thick with reeds and water lilies. She waded in farther, enjoying the smooth slide of the river pebbles beneath her feet, lifting the hem of her skirt as the dark water rose above her knees. She'd shifted back into human form and swiped a billowy white nightgown hanging from a clothesline in somebody's garden. Two tiny silvery fish swam a loop around her ankles.

"Gisela!" A series of splashes followed the sound of her name. Tamara burst into view. She threw her arms around Gisela's neck in a crushing hug, sending her stumbling back a step. "I was so worried! I thought you'd been captured."

"Well, I kind of was." Gisela patted Tamara awkwardly on the back, trying to disentangle herself from the embrace. "But I can handle Kazik. Really, it's all—" She took another step back, and the pebbles beneath her feet shifted, giving way to slippery mud and silt. Gisela lost her footing, her balance, and she toppled backward.

Cold black water closed over her head, and panic took her. The reasonable part of her knew that, as a water nymph, she could swim like a fish and being afraid was ludicrous. But the old nightmarish terror of drowning overwhelmed her.

She floundered and flailed. Screamed. Water rushed into her mouth and nose, soaked her nightgown, weighing her down. She was trapped and tangled in the fabric.

Rough hands grasped her under the arms and hauled her upright. Gisela broke the surface with a gasp. Cool air hit her drenched skin. Her hair was plastered to her face. Over the noise of her own coughing and spluttering, she could hear Tamara apologizing and someone telling her not to worry.

Yulia.

Because of course it was *Yulia*. The older girl fished her out of the river and dragged her up onto the grassy bank. Gisela collapsed in a sodden trembling heap.

"Breathe," Yulia ordered in her annoyingly commanding way. She was their unofficial leader. The one they all went to when they needed someone strong to lean on, when they needed help or advice or something heavy lifted off a shelf. Yulia was one of those reliable older sibling types. Of all of them, she had lived in the water goblin's realm the longest.

Kneeling beside Gisela, she cut a dashing figure. Her sandy hair was cropped boyishly short, and she wore tight high-waisted breeches with a floaty white blouse that laced closed at the collar. She'd rolled the sleeves up to her elbows, revealing her lean forearms. Yulia had confessed once that she didn't know if she really belonged here among the rusałki. Some days she felt like she might be one of the utopce, a drowner—what humans called a male water spirit.

Wojciech would likely have let her join the drowners in their wing of the Crystal Palace if that was what she'd wanted. After all, according to the others, he'd merely shrugged and handed Miray a water nymph's comb when she'd shyly informed him that she wasn't a drowner as he'd first assumed. Unlike humans, spirits like Wojciech seemed to view the concept of gender as something of minor importance.

Gisela didn't feel strongly either way about her own gender. It was easier, really, to let everyone think of her as a girl rather than exhaust herself explaining that she didn't always feel like one.

She envied Yulia's willowy figure though, her flat chest and slim hips, and the fact that she could pass easily as a boy or girl according to how she was feeling. Maybe in another life, Gisela could be reborn as a tall buff guy or something. Now *that* would be awesome.

"You back with us yet?" Yulia asked briskly. She started to reach out, then drew her arm back just as quickly, as if she'd been about to take hold of Gisela's hand or give her a comforting punch to the shoulder and then thought better of it.

Swiping at a riverweed stuck to her cheek, Gisela nodded. "I'm fine," she lied, the words coming out harsher than she intended. She was annoyed to find her eyes stinging. She hadn't let herself cry in ages. She really wished Yulia would stop watching her be so pathetic.

Gisela fixed her gaze on the river, on the reflection of the sickle moon drowning on its dark surface, the stars mirrored in the inky depths. She dug her nails deep into her palms, hating that she had to resort to self-harm to calm herself. Her nails bit into flesh, but the magic within her healed the cuts almost immediately, barely giving her a second to savor the pain.

A fragrant breeze stirred the air. It took another minute for Gisela to reorient herself, to convince her body that she was safe, that she was all right. The other girls came to sit around her, circling like a family of hungry ghosts. There was cheery Miray; solemn-faced Clara; little Zamira with her tumble of dark ringlets; blonde and bookish Nina-Marie; and of course, Tamara and Yulia. Their skin varied in shade from pale ivory to deep bronze, though they all shared the deathly pallor of the drowned. They ranged in age from thirteen to twenty—not counting the years they'd spent as spirits trapped between earth and heaven.

Tamara shyly handed Gisela back her hair comb. Nina-Marie set down a wicker basket crammed with delectable Green Week offerings: boiled eggs and bloodred apples and small jars of syrupy dandelion honey. There was raspberry cloud cake topped with dreamy meringue and sugar cookies with flowers baked in, even a dish of sweet grain and poppy seed pudding, the kind mixed with nuts and dried fruit that people placed on their altars at home for the ghosts of their ancestors.

"It helps to eat something sweet after you've had a scare," Nina-Marie said wisely.

"Clara, you cow," Zamira complained. "You ate all the oatcakes!"

"And?" Clara said. "If you'd wanted some, you should have said something earlier."

Miray nudged Gisela with her elbow. "The new girl said Kazik got you. We thought you were dead. Or you know, like, more dead."

"And none of you thought to come to my aid or, I don't know, send out a search party?" Scowling, Gisela reached for a spoon and helped herself to a mouthful of pudding. It melted on her tongue, nutty and rich and sticky sweet, conjuring memories of the days when Great-Aunt Zela would cook the dish for her and her little brother. It had been one of their childhood favorites. "He did get me. He imprisoned me inside his house."

"How did you get away?" Yulia demanded at once.

"Saints!" Miray shuddered dramatically. "He is *the* worst."

"This is why I hate humans," Nina-Marie said.

"You used to be one," Clara replied in singsong.

Nina-Marie pushed her glasses up. "Please don't remind me."

"Don't worry," Zamira said. "One day it'll have been so long since you were alive that nothing left in you will remember being human."

Gisela shivered.

"You're lucky to have escaped." Clara struggled to wrench the lid off the jar of dandelion honey. "They say Kazik has immense spiritual powers. He's exorcised countless demons and wicked spirits. The strzygi call him a holy terror."

"He blames spirits like us for his grandmother's death," Yulia said, taking the jar from Clara and opening it for her. She gave the contents a curious sniff. "He wasn't this bad when she was alive. Even the drowners have been whining about 'that vile exorcist' lately."

"I wouldn't say he's vile." Miray tapped a finger to her chin. "He's kind of pretty for a monster slayer. Especially when he's all fired up and sweaty and angry."

Nina-Marie rolled her eyes. But privately, Gisela agreed. It was one of the reasons she liked to tease Kazik. She didn't say so out loud though, especially not in front of Yulia.

"How did you escape?" Zamira asked again.

"Well . . ." Gisela paused for dramatic effect. She quickly swallowed another spoonful of grain pudding and sat up straight, making sure she had everyone's attention. Clara and Zamira hugged their knees as she spun the tale, embellishing slightly to make the story more exciting, leaving out the moment when Kazik had frozen up. Nina-Marie let out a hiss when she told them how he'd thrown wormwood at her and threatened to leave her to dry out, while Tamara stared in admiration and

Miray squealed and clapped when Gisela described the mysterious stranger who had freed her from the magic circle and carried her out of the house. Throughout it all, Yulia wore a vaguely judgmental look on her face.

"We should stay away from town for a while," she decided, when Gisela finally paused for breath.

"What?" Clara protested. "But it's Green Week."

"Exactly. Kazik will be watching for us." Yulia cast a meaningful look at Gisela. "You keep antagonizing him. You're taking things too far."

Gisela bit down on her spoon. Once upon a time, Yulia had been her staunchest defender. It was Yulia who explained to her the ways of the spirit world. Yulia who dragged her along when she was hesitant to join the others. They bonded over the fact that they both liked pretty girls and makeup and clothes. Yulia even stood up for her when Gisela hadn't shared the story of how she'd ended up like this. The others seemed to revel in the telling of their own gruesome ends. There was a morbid kind of competition to see who'd had the most tragic death. Gisela actually would've liked to join in, but the truth was she didn't remember how she'd died.

She remembered the journey here, the queasiness in her stomach as the ship crossed the sea, the teeth-jarring rock of the train carriage as it rattled through fields and valleys, and the final jolting bus ride. She remembered arriving in Leśna Woda and the first few days of their stay and then . . . nothing.

It was like a pair of claws had gouged a great hole in her memories. It had worried her at first. But once she'd listened to the other girls' tales of murder, rape, and suicide, she'd come to think of it as a blessing. Part of her was relieved her mind was blocking out what had happened to her.

"You're so obsessed with rejoining the mortal world," Yulia continued, "that you're causing trouble for everybody."

Gisela kept her chin up even as guilt and hurt bubbled in her stomach. She was desperate to get her life back, but she didn't *want* to cause trouble. Not if she could help it. Especially not for these girls who had so readily accepted her as one of their own, who had never done anything but welcome her into their strange undead family.

"Oh, come on," Miray said, coming to her rescue. She was the second oldest and the only one who dared argue with Yulia. "Give her a break. Most of us have tried it once. Don't you remember Zamira dragging us along to look at that artist who'd set up his easel by Villa Hyacinth's boathouse? She was obsessed with him."

"Oh my God, shut up!" Zamira threw an apple at Miray, who dodged it effortlessly.

Clara snatched the apple out of the air with inhuman reflexes. "Hey, don't waste the offerings!"

"You're only worked up this time because it's Gisela." Miray finished with a meaningful look at Yulia.

Yulia looked like she, too, would like to throw something at Miray.

"It's sweet that you're worried about me," Gisela added.

"I'm not worried about you," Yulia said immediately. "Kiss and flirt with whoever you like. *I* don't care. I just think you're being an idiot. The living will always choose to be with the living. That's how it works. No human is ever going to choose to be with a dead girl."

Gisela flinched.

"Mortals and spirits aren't meant to be together," Yulia said. "You're defying the natural order of the world."

"A true love story for the ages," Miray chimed in with a wink. "So, this boy who rescued you, tell me again what he looked like. I want all the details."

"He was . . ." Gisela blinked, thrown by the abrupt change of subject but grateful for the chance to let her thoughts drift back to the moment she'd first seen him. She still couldn't put a finger on it, but there was something about him. Something almost familiar. Those spellbinding eyes—one a perfect summer blue, the other the startling green of spring leaves—gleamed in her memory so clearly, he could have been sitting directly across from her. "He has the most delicious voice and these amazing eyes and hair the color of honeyed wheat."

Miray nodded eagerly.

More importantly though, the thing that really stuck in Gisela's mind was the fact that he'd been kind. How carefully he'd cradled her in his hands as he carried her into the forest, taking her to a place where she'd be safe. How many people would have bothered to do that for a frog? It was such a small thing, but it was those small things that mattered most.

"The moment I saw him, I felt like we had a connection. He's really tall and built, so at first he seems intimidating, but he's really gentle and softhearted toward animals."

She liked that.

Yulia snorted. "You'd fall in love with anyone who did you a kindness. A little attention and you're ready to throw yourself at them."

"So," Clara interrupted loudly, "what are we doing tomorrow?"

Her attempt to change the subject was even less subtle than Miray's, but Gisela gave her points for trying. Zamira did better, tugging on Yulia's arm and distracting her by asking if she could cut up the raspberry cloud cake.

"We could show Tamara the shipwreck," Nina-Marie suggested, lying down and resting her head in Clara's lap. "Or we could feed the swans or dive under the rowboats the tourists take out on the river and steal their oars. Drag our nails along the underside of the hulls until they start to scream."

"Oh yes," Clara said, deeply sarcastic. She fed Nina-Marie a sugar cookie. "That will definitely not piss off the exorcist."

Miray roped a noodle-thin arm around Gisela's shoulders. There was a wicked gleam in her ruby-red eyes; unlike the others, she enjoyed throwing fuel on the fire. If there was one thing the flame-haired water nymph loved, it was drama. "So, are you going to try and see him again? The boy who rescued you."

"Well, I mean . . ." Gisela said, twirling a strand of damp hair around her finger, pointedly ignoring the fact that Yulia was listening in. "I owe him a thank-you at the very least, don't you think?"

7
LOST SOULS
KAZIK

"I DON'T THINK YOU'RE going to find her."

Kazik scowled, listening with only half an ear as he continued to scan the street. Beside him, Zuzanna sighed and raised a hand to shield her eyes from the glare. While they'd both inherited their grandmother's gifts, Kazik and his cousin were a study in contrasts. Kazik was short and thin with dark eyes, darker hair, and skin that tanned after only a few seconds in the sun, while Zuzanna was tall and curvy, flaxen-haired and moon pale. Her eyes were angelic blue, and she liked to dress like a wicked saint in velvet and lace, her neck draped with shiny rosaries so that the snicking of holy beads always heralded her appearance.

She was the coolest person Kazik knew. He missed her fiercely when she wasn't there and was annoyed out of his mind by her when she was. They were more like siblings than cousins. Zuzanna was one of the only people who could still make him feel like a child.

"It's not like you to get so worked up over a mere water nymph," she said as they made their way down Leśna Woda's busiest street, striding past the expensive shops where the tourists spent their riches. "I've never seen someone get to you like this."

Kazik glanced across the road to the spot where he'd once caught Gisela peering through the windows of a fancy bookshop. "You don't know what she's capable of." He'd spent half the night cursing himself after he'd returned home to discover she'd somehow escaped the chalk circle.

Really, what had he expected? There was no way an insatiable, troublemaking spirit like Gisela was just going to sit back and let herself be captured. She was a flirtatious force of chaos. You couldn't leave her alone for a second. How could a single girl be so positively infuriating? He wasn't going to show her any mercy this time. He would perform a proper exorcism and get rid of her for good.

His eyes flicked from shop front to shop front, scouring the bustle and the sidewalk for any glimpse of long black hair, for any trace of dewy footprints.

"She thinks," he scoffed, "that if she seduces a mortal, she'll somehow become human again."

"Oh?" Zuzanna tilted her head to one side. "Like in the story?"

"What story?"

"The one Dziadek used to tell us. 'Rusałka and the Monk.' The one where a water nymph—" Zuzanna clamped a hand around Kazik's wrist, stopping him midstride.

His head whipped toward her in surprise, and then he saw what she had seen: Father Paweł stepping out from behind a glass-encased phone booth. The bony old priest startled when he made eye contact, his face flushing such a mottled purple red that Kazik half expected him to start frothing at the mouth.

"Good to know he's still thirsting after our blood," Zuzanna commented once he'd passed.

Kazik snorted. There was no love lost between their family and the local priest. Father Paweł considered their rituals and dealings with spirits paramount to witchcraft. The tension when he and Babcia had crossed paths had been enough to strike a match. He'd even banned her and Kazik from taking candles and holy water from the church. Which was incredibly frustrating because altar candles were the best kind for magic. Ordinary candles didn't cut it. They had to have been blessed.

Fortunately, most members of the parish were also their loyal patrons, including the elderly woman who cleaned the church and whose husband's life Babcia had saved when he was possessed by a forest demon. Mrs. Mróz was more than happy to supply Kazik with stolen candle stubs and even a few snipped threads from Father Paweł's priestly vestments to use for his charms. In this part of the country, there was a whole racket in the trade of holy goods. If Mrs. Mróz ever got tired of helping, there were plenty of others who would take up the task. Almost everybody they passed acknowledged the two of them in some way—with a covert glance, a wary nod, or an openly nervous stare. Everybody, excluding the tourists, knew everybody in town, and everybody knew Kazik and Zuzanna were Babcia's grandchildren. Every resident here had sought their grandmother's services at least once in their life, even if it was only as a child when *their* grandmother had brought them to the house to help with their night terrors or to have their fortune read.

Everybody knew healers like their grandmother passed their secret knowledge down to the youngest members of their family.

"I've missed this," Zuzanna said. "Don't get me wrong. I love the city and studying at the university. But I mean, how many people can say their profession is 'town witch'?"

"We're not witches, Zuza. We're healers."

"I think there were witches in our family once. Who do you think taught Babcia all the things that she taught us? *Her* grandmother could've been a witch. Where do you think all the witches in these parts disappeared to?"

The jingle of a shop bell was her only answer.

"They fled to safer countries," she continued, "*or* they went into hiding, disguising their spells as spell prayers. Adding the names of angels to their charms. Appealing to the saints instead of spirits."

Kazik pressed his lips together. He knew some of the old rites and rituals passed down to him had their roots in pagan practices. It wasn't as though he hadn't noticed the similarities between their charms and the curses witches worked. It was only his devout nature that stopped him from letting his mind wander into that dangerous territory. A part of him worried that Heaven might sense his faith wavering and punish him for it.

"Is that what they're teaching you at that fancy university of yours? Babcia would be horrified."

Zuzanna cackled. "Everybody in the dorms calls me a witch. They keep asking me to cast love spells for them. They even offer to pay me. Good money too. And I mean, what *is* the point of having God-given magical powers if you don't use them to turn a profit? Joking," she added, catching the look on Kazik's face. "I'm not an idiot. I'm not like, well, you know."

The *your mother* went unsaid.

There were rules that governed their magic. Unreasonable rules, Kazik sometimes thought. Like the one that decreed you had to help anybody in need, no matter how much of a monster they might be. Or the one that said you could never receive payment, only thanks and small trinkets of gratitude: a basket of hen's eggs, a crate of sour cherries, a curd cheese, an apple soufflé. Votive offerings made to the church in your stead, were, of course, acceptable. Cash slotted into the donation box and candles lit before the icons. But if so much as a coin was left on Babcia's kitchen table, it was forcibly refused.

No healer should ever use their abilities for personal gain, lest they lose their gifts forever.

Like his mother had.

It was all just another reason why Kazik knew they weren't witches. True witches could use their magic however they pleased. They weren't beholden to a higher power. Magic was so much a part of a witch that if they ran out of it, they would fade to nothing. Kazik was merely a devout vessel, a conduit for the saints.

He spared a moment to side-eye his cousin. *He* followed the rules like they were sacred commandments, even when they felt wrong, but Zuzanna had a dangerous habit of treating them as though they were merely guidelines.

"It's not even about the money, really," she said, twirling one of the rosaries hanging from her neck. "I just think some of the people who've asked truly need my help. And I don't like turning my back on anyone in trouble."

"If you wanted to help people, you could've come and lived here."

Zuzanna hummed. "You know *you* don't have to stay here, right? If you don't want to."

"Someone has to take Babcia's place." And it wasn't as if Kazik had any grand ambitions beyond living up to his grandmother's expectations. He didn't have any other talents. He wasn't clever nor particularly studious. Not like Zuzanna. Not when it came to things like math and history and geography and all that stuff. He'd dropped out of school as soon as he was legally allowed to, three years ago, when he'd turned fifteen.

It didn't matter if at times he felt it too, that desperate urge to climb on a bus or a train, to slip away and never return. To leave it all behind. The responsibility. The danger. He could abandon it all.

But those were treacherous thoughts. There were too many people relying on him. Who else was going to chase away the demons and evil spirits and protect Leśna Woda's sacred springs?

He'd promised Babcia. His grandmother had never once doubted that he would follow in her footsteps. Despite the circumstances of her death, she'd passed peacefully, knowing he'd take care of things.

Even so, he couldn't help feeling like he wasn't ready. He didn't know if he could do this alone. Without her wisdom and guidance. He felt like one of his old teachers had just called on him in front of the whole class to answer a question that he couldn't solve.

He needed to do better. He needed to be stronger. He had

to show the spirits that he was someone to be reckoned with. He had to strike before they struck him or anyone else he cared about.

Kazik unbuttoned his collar. It wasn't even noon, and the day was already heating up. He squinted into the shadowed space between two buildings.

Still no sign of Gisela.

It was like searching for the fern flower—impossible. Where the hell had she gotten to? She'd left no clues behind at the house, only her empty dress. And Kazik really didn't want to think what that implied about what she had or hadn't been wearing when she'd escaped.

But he knew her well enough to know she'd be back to her usual routine of evil. She was out there somewhere, probably already stalking another would-be victim.

Or worse, she was out there telling all the other spirits how he'd seized up when he'd threatened to exorcise her yesterday. Of all the times for his magic to fail, it had to have happened in front of Gisela. The last thing he needed was her spreading rumors that *he* was losing his gift.

"You know you've been at this for hours," Zuzanna pointed out, as they turned the corner into a more secluded lane. "I don't think—" She maneuvered around a dark-haired figure carrying a bouquet of sunflowers larger than their head.

Kazik pivoted sharply, but it was only Adele, one of the shop girls from the post office. She gave him a shy nod.

They slowed again at the end of the lane, where a rapt audience had crowded to watch Mr. Czerny sweep out his shop with a twig broom made of birch branches. He was making a show of it, informing his gullible tourist spectators that they could purchase hair ribbons from his shop to leave out as offerings for the water nymphs.

"Careful," Zuzanna warned, "the wind will change, and your face will get stuck like that."

"People need to stop encouraging them."

"We've always left gifts for the rusałki. It's tradition."

"That's doesn't mean we have to keep doing it. The bribes don't actually work."

Realistically, Kazik knew he'd never convince anyone to stop. The spa town's whole economy was based on tourism; most residents ran souvenir shops or offered rooms for hire or worked as domestic help at the bathhouses. And the Green Week traditions were a big tourist draw. Families planned their trips just so they could take part in the festivities. He'd have as much success as Father Paweł had trying to stop Babcia from dabbling in folk magic—which was to say zero.

In his grandmother's words: *I heal, and there is nothing Father can do about it.*

Plus, a lot of people here were of double faith. In Leśna Woda the borders between the old beliefs and the dominant religion were fluid. Some people even believed that the water nymphs' dewy footprints and dripping-wet hair brought blessed moisture to the plants and flowers each spring. They thought the girls were only playful and not the malicious creatures Kazik knew they were.

"Sometimes," Zuzanna said, "I feel sorry for them."

Kazik threw his cousin an incredulous look.

Zuzanna raised an eyebrow. "What? They're sad things, really. Lost souls who weren't able to travel to the afterlife. The spirits of maidens who died before their time. Girls cursed to haunt the bodies of water where they suffered violent ends. You don't think that's sad?"

Kazik didn't answer. Of course, he knew how a water nymph was born. He knew the origins of all the unholy terrors that haunted the mortal world. Violence, tragedy, and human cruelty birthed monsters. Spirits like Gisela didn't materialize from thin air.

But it wasn't his business, even if it did make him wonder . . .

He'd never given much thought to how Gisela had become a water nymph. How *had* she died? What had happened to her, to make her what she was now?

Did he really want to know? It was easier to believe she was just another wicked spirit with devious intentions than to think of her as a victim herself.

Despite the heat, Kazik couldn't repress a shiver. He tugged on an earring, ignoring the uncomfortable twisting in his stomach. He didn't want to hear their sob stories and justifications for causing chaos. There was no justification. Everybody had it hard. That was no excuse for lashing out.

"They should move on to the next world instead of causing trouble in this one. Babcia always said they were pests."

"Babcia used to call *us* pests," Zuzanna said. "'Pest' was practically an endearment coming from her."

Kazik bit back a smile. Saints, he missed his cranky grandmother.

"They'll take the decorations down eventually. Are you going to perform the ritual to protect the cows on Sunday?"

Kazik nodded and tried not to think about the looks he was going to get from some of his childhood classmates. A furrow reappeared between his brows.

"Don't worry," Zuzanna reassured him. "I'll be there to make sure you don't screw it up."

"Your faith in me is *so* appreciated."

"Will any of your friends be there?"

Again, Kazik didn't answer. Zuzanna was always nagging at him to socialize. He'd endured enough of her lectures that he could recite them from memory.

I really think more human interaction could be good for you!

You can't keep shutting everybody out.

I know it's hard to interact with people because of what we can do, but you can't forget how to live in the ordinary world. You need to let people love you. You need people who'll keep you grounded.

She seemed to believe he was doomed to a life as a miserable recluse.

"What about that boy you had a crush on?" she pressed. "The popular one? Arek? Aleksey?"

"I don't know who you're talking about."

For a second, they were separated, both forced to weave through a crush of bodies taking up the entire sidewalk: Foreigners and city folk taking strolls between spa treatments. Tourists who babbled on about escaping the hustle and bustle and reconnecting with nature, until some unearthly terror crept out of the trees and tried to eat them.

Slipping down a shaded pathway running between a coffee-house and a famous chocolatier, Kazik looked back for his cousin . . . and felt the hairs rise at the nape of his neck.

He spun just in time to catch a glimpse of golden eyes, a skittering of limbs. Hot power surged through his chest and down his arm. Light flashed beneath his palm as he caught the cat-sized czart with one hand.

The little devil let out a wretched howl and twisted free, clutching at its face with unsettlingly human hands. Panting in pain, its skin smoking, it fled into the shadows.

Before Kazik could decide whether to chase after it and burn it to ashes, footsteps sounded and Zuzanna reappeared. "You all right there?" she asked.

"Never better." Kazik adjusted his glasses. The power in his veins was cooling, withdrawing with unnerving speed. He frowned at his palm and briefly considered asking Zuzanna if her magic had ever fluctuated like this before he dismissed the idea. She'd only fuss over him even more than she already did.

He stalked back down the path between the shops. Stepping out onto the main thoroughfare, they came to another fork in the road. Wrought iron signs pointed the way to the nearest bathhouse, Villa Hyacinth, and to another of Leśna Woda's popular landmarks, the old stone Wishing Bridge, where you could toss a coin into the river and request a miracle.

Legend said these miracles were performed by the local wodnik, the water goblin, who was either evil or helpful, depending on the tale. During the war, he was said to have kept the river stocked with fish so that the town would always have food.

Babcia, of course, had argued that God was responsible. Just as she'd claimed it was an angel who'd helped hide her and Kazik's grandfather in the forest during other times of trouble, despite her husband's repeated assertions that it had been the local leszy, the forest's guardian spirit.

"I don't think you're going to find her," Zuzanna repeated a third time.

Kazik clicked his tongue in frustration. Gisela was making a fool of him. He should never have let her out of his sight. All the spirits were growing bolder.

A voice whispered inside his head. *Because they think you're weaker than your grandmother. They're not afraid of you.*

"Why don't we stop by Villa Hyacinth and cool off in the cold pools?" Zuzanna suggested.

Kazik rolled his eyes. She wasn't even trying to be subtle now. A visit to Villa Hyacinth was guaranteed to magically improve your mood. Soaking in the bathhouse's waters summoned back pleasant long-forgotten memories and washed away bad ones. But Kazik preferred to visit the bathhouse in the low season, when it wasn't overrun with tourists, or in the dead of winter, when you could soak in the steaming outdoor pools while the snow fell all around you.

"You go," he said. "I'll join you later. Maybe." He couldn't let Gisela escape again. "There's one more place I want to check."

8

LOOKING FOR LOVE

GISELA

TRACKING DOWN HER SAVIOR was surprisingly difficult. Gisela questioned half a dozen spirits—two drowners, a field spirit, and a barn devil, among others—before she found someone who claimed to have seen a human boy with eyes of two different colors.

"His family owns Villa Hyacinth," Nadia said in her soft flutelike voice. She was a spirit of the air, one of the wiły, sister spirit-maidens of the rusałki. They were often mistaken for water nymphs because they sometimes made their homes by the water and in the forest, as well as in glittering, floating sky castles built upon the crests of clouds.

"They own the whole bathhouse, really?" Gisela was impressed. *This boy must be rich.* Villa Hyacinth was one of the most popular bathhouses in Leśna Woda. What had brought a boy like that to Kazik's house? "And that's where you saw him last?"

Nadia nodded. Her pale skin was almost transparent in the sunlight. Her long blonde hair floated in a nonexistent wind. But aside from that, and the luminous feathery wings sprouting from her back, she looked like an ordinary young woman in her early twenties. "He walked by here this morning."

Here was a shady corner of the vast perfumed gardens outside said bathhouse. They stood half-hidden behind a tree because Gisela didn't want to look like a crazy person talking to herself. A lot of spirits couldn't be bothered to assume a form humans could see; they were invisible to mortal eyes. If she wished to, Nadia could drift through town unnoticed, unless, of course, she was spotted by someone with Kazik's gifts. When a family of three passed by the tree, they glanced at Gisela but not her companion.

Gisela shooed away a honeybee that had mistaken her for a flower and wondered if she'd lose the ability to see spirits when she regained her humanity. The thought left her feeling oddly sad.

"Why are you so interested in this boy?" Nadia asked.

"I'm going to get a kiss from him and become human."

"A kiss from *him*?"

"You don't think he'll want to kiss me?"

"I think . . ." Nadia's feathers ruffled. "He could be trouble. Possibly."

Gisela cocked her head, intrigued, but Nadia failed to elaborate. She was staring after the family that had walked past them with a strangely intense look on her face.

Or, to be precise, she was staring at one member of the family: a sullen dark-haired woman.

Gisela's skin prickled with unease. She tried to remember Great-Aunt Zela's stories; like rusałki, wiły were famous for bewitching unsuspecting young men and leading them to their deaths, but they were often kind to young women. At least, she *thought* they were.

"It's just a feeling I have," Nadia said, turning back to her. "Just be careful. The exorcist is still running around."

"Oh, I know, I've been keeping an eye out for him." That was another reason why they were sequestered in this shady corner behind the tree. If Kazik caught either of them, there'd be trouble. Gisela had already spotted him once this morning, when she'd crossed the Wishing Bridge into the gardens. She'd had to dive under a hedge to hide and was *still* picking leaves and twigs out of her hair half an hour later.

Seriously. He was *such* a pain. She wasn't even doing anything wrong. She simply wanted to thank a human boy who had helped her. It was only polite to say *thank you*. If she got a kiss out of the bargain, well, that was just a bonus.

"I'm so glad you knew who I was talking about," she said. "I've been searching for him everywhere. I owe you."

Nadia gave her a long look. "I'll remember that, and remember what *I* said."

Gisela swept her waist-length tresses over her shoulder; droplets of water sprinkled onto the footpath. "Don't worry. I'm *always* careful."

She said goodbye and left Nadia to whatever mischief she was cooking up—hopefully nothing too nefarious—then followed the loosely curving path that wound through the flower beds and between the garden's neat green hedges. Every time she turned a corner, she held her breath, half expecting to stumble upon Kazik lying in wait. As much as she liked to make light of him, the truth was, he *was* dangerous. He had the power to destroy her, if he chose to.

A few minutes later, she pushed through an iron gate in a hedge, skirted a swan-paddled pond, and stopped. Before her loomed Villa Hyacinth. Red fairy-tale turrets crowned the bathhouse's lemon-yellow walls. Voices carried past her ears: eager chatter and awed exclamations. She watched a group of tourists make their way inside, each figure pausing to exchange coins for a ticket issued by a crimson-suited doorman. She had no money to pay the entry fee—spirits, she'd learned, traded mostly in favors and shiny trinkets.

Still, that was a problem easily solved.

After retracing her steps, Gisela ducked behind an arched trellis of flowering rose vines, inhaling the honeyed scent of the sun-warmed blossoms. Even the air smelled different here on the mainland. She missed the sharp briny scent of the sea, the salt-sweet breeze. She even missed the tide's voice, that soft but hungry *shusha-shusha*, and the ever-constant chorus of the seagulls.

Shoving aside thoughts of home, she took ten deep breaths and focused until her skin tingled. Her body folded into itself. In a flash of silvery light, Gisela vanished once more. Her white baby doll dress slumped to the ground. For the second time in two days, a small green frog emerged from a puddle of clothing.

From there it was only a matter of waiting until the doorman was distracted reaching into his satchel for another ticket. Bracing herself as she crossed through the wards, Gisela hopped inside.

She felt a slight resistance in the air. It was nothing like trying to push through the chalk circle's invisible barrier, but her senses flooded with sudden inexplicable fear. *Get away from here*, something whispered in her mind. *Turn back. Turn around. Leave this place.*

Gisela's skin prickled as she forced herself to move forward regardless. *It's all in your head*, she told herself. *There's nothing to fear here.*

Another hop—and she was through. The effect of the wards faded. Villa Hyacinth wasn't as well protected as some of the other bathhouses. After all, if a spirit snuck in here, they'd only end up in a good mood. Hardly a disaster. Exorcists like Kazik were more concerned with keeping creatures like her away from places like Villa Violetta. The spring water there was imbued with a special energy, and it boosted a spirit's strength every time they bathed in it.

Careful to avoid being crushed by careless feet, Gisela sprang from one blushing marble floor tile to the next, crossing the grand foyer, passing the enormous reception desk. Like all the bathhouses, Villa Hyacinth was a castle-like complex. It had separate women's and men's areas. There were multiple indoor and outdoor pools, soap rooms, steam rooms, saunas, guest rooms, rooms for massage, halls for resting, and gaming rooms where you could play chess while sipping kefir or herbal teas mixed with honey. There was even a restaurant that served the best earthy young-beet soup and a spa orchestra that played every day throughout the summer.

A door swung open, and lavender-scented soap bubbles wafted out, followed by a flock of rosy-cheeked girls, their hair damp and frizzy from the steam. Through a second door, Gisela spied an enormous pool-sized tub bubbling like a cauldron. She wasn't sure where to start looking for the boy with two-colored eyes, but the men's area seemed like a good place to begin.

A short time later, she ended up in what she was pretty sure was a changing room. It was hard to read the shiny signs on the walls when she was this close to the ground.

Gisela quickly hid herself beneath a wooden bench and squeezed her eyes shut, her breath quickening as a bunch of naked boys scampered past. And okay, maybe she cracked *one* eye open. Just to make sure none of the boys was her savior. She had no choice but to peek. How else was she supposed to find him?

She hopped forward, peering past a bench leg, her gaze skimming up and up and up, past toes and ankles and calves and the smooth muscles of thighs, and . . . really, even if she didn't find her savior, there were some boys in here with *very* nice . . .

Sudden motion drew her eye, but she had no time to react as the bench screeched backward and a great shadow fell over her with a deafening crash. The world went dark. Something—a wicker basket, one used to collect wet towels—had slammed over her like a cage.

"Is there no end to your wickedness?" hissed a too-familiar voice.

Gisela let out an offended croak. Kazik. Why couldn't he leave her alone?

The wicker weave of the basket strained to near breakage as

he leaned his weight on it. "Don't think you're getting away this time."

Gisela let out another croak—a frog's version of a very explicit curse. The sound was drowned out by someone calling Kazik's name. Gisela fell silent. She recognized that surprisingly deep voice. It belonged to *him*. The boy who'd rescued her! She was almost sure of it.

"Need some help?" he asked Kazik.

Gisela tried to peer through the weave of the basket. She couldn't see much: only the vague shape of bare legs, the pale flash of a towel.

"It's nothing," Kazik said, sounding choked. "I knocked over the towels. I'll take care of it."

"You can leave it for the maids to clean up."

"It's fine. I'll do it."

"Really, they'll—"

"It's *fine*," Kazik bit out. "I said I'll take care of it." He made no effort to stand nor shift from his awkward crouch, holding the basket over her.

There was a very lengthy pause.

Gisela hoped the boy was giving Kazik a really weird look. Half the town, especially the younger generation, thought he was mad, chasing after creatures they couldn't see or didn't believe were real.

Finally, there was movement, the patter of footsteps slowly moving away. Frustration raked its nails across her skin. The continued quiet told her that she and Kazik were likely alone.

Without so much as a thought to what she would look like, she transformed back into human form.

There was a silvery flash of light. The sound of a bubble bursting. It was always easier to shift back than it was to become something else. Her body unfolded, her limbs lengthening, stretching.

Kazik let out a strangled yelp as a very naked Gisela grew out from under the wicker basket. "You—you *degenerate!*" he sputtered, scandalized, his face cycling through at least five shades of red.

Heh. It was so easy to aggravate him.

Kazik scooped a towel off the floor and flung it at her. Gisela caught it with a smirk. Taking advantage of his embarrassment, she grabbed the wicker basket next and threw it at his head.

In the span of a breath, she was on her feet, wrapping the towel securely around her body and making a desperate dash for the door.

She didn't make it far.

Kazik lunged, tackling her around her middle. They went down in a messy tangle.

"Ow, ow, ow! Let go of me!" Gisela drove an elbow backward, trying to buck him off. She twisted and grabbed a fistful of his hair.

Kazik grabbed a fistful of hers and rolled them over, pinning her beneath him and not in a fun, sexy way. His knee pressed into her stomach. "Do you want to die?" He panted.

"I'm already dead!" Gisela said in a singsong.

"Then die properly this time." Kazik raised his arm. His voice filled the changing room. "Oh, Prince of Heavenly Hosts, grant me the strength to usher this insufferable, exasperating—" His palm filled with searing golden light. White flames knifed between his fingers.

Gisela's heart lurched with genuine fear.

"—evil spirit into the afterlife!" He flung his hand toward her chest, channeling Heaven's wrath in a lethal blast of holy magic.

9

A DEAL WITH THE DEVIL

GISELA

GISELA SQUEEZED HER EYES shut, bracing for the end. For the searing heat, the agonizing pain.

It didn't come.

She cracked an eye open. The heavenly fire Kazik had summoned, the power he'd called down, had snuffed out like a candle extinguished by a gust of wind.

He stared at his palm in slack-jawed disbelief.

"Did—did your exorcism just"—Gisela's voice dropped—"fail?"

Mortification warred with shock for control of Kazik's face. Fresh color crawled up his neck. The tips of his ears burned a furious red. His glasses, which had been knocked askew in their fight, hung from one pierced ear.

"Do you want to try again?" Gisela offered kindly.

The glare Kazik shot her could have melted stone.

"Oh my God! Are you losing your magic?" She sat up and shoved him off her, scooting backward, carefully adjusting her towel. "I knew something was off when you seized up like that yesterday! Is this why you've been so broody lately? Did you do something bad, something terrible?" Wojciech had told her how Kazik's mother had lost her powers.

"Nothing as terrible as what I'm going to do to you," Kazik hissed, shaking out his wrist and glaring at his hand as if he could summon his magic back through sheer force of will.

Gisela beamed when nothing happened.

"This is all your fault," Kazik said, pushing to his feet.

"My fault? How is it *my* fault?"

"Because I never had trouble with my powers until I met you!" Kazik made another frustrated gesture. He shoved his glasses back onto his nose and rubbed his jaw where she'd elbowed him in the face. His shirt was half unbuttoned. He must've been in the process of stripping off himself when he'd spied her in the changing room. It was just her luck that they'd been in here at the same time.

"The saints have probably lost faith in me because I've failed to punish you. They've decided I'm not worthy of their gift because I've let you run around and prey on innocent people. I'm being punished because *you* keep causing trouble!"

"Huh. Really? That seems kind of harsh." Gisela climbed to her feet. She shot a glance over her shoulder at the door. This was her chance to say something suitably mocking and flirtatious before she made a triumphant exit.

Or . . .

A dangerous idea stirred in the depths of her mind. A wild idea. A half-desperate one.

But she *was* desperate. All her clumsy efforts to make someone kiss her had so far been in vain. A part of her was starting to think maybe she was just too repulsive to love, too strange.

What if nobody ever wanted her?

She'd tried luring boys and girls in with flirtatious looks and words, tried becoming human all on her own, and each time she'd failed—or Kazik had interfered. So it only made sense to try something new, didn't it? It couldn't hurt to take a gamble.

Kazik was watching her warily. His hair was sticking up in every direction, and there were dark circles beneath his eyes. She was tired of having to fight him. And maybe, just maybe, he was tired of fighting her.

"Don't think that I need Heaven's help to end you," he bluffed. "I'm perfectly capable of strangling you all by myself."

Gisela smirked. Emboldened by his failed attempt to take her out, she took one step forward and then another, relishing the way he tensed even as he refused to retreat.

He reached into the pocket where she knew he kept his prayer beads. They were standing eye to eye now, almost nose to nose. It was an endless source of amusement to Gisela that Leśna Woda's fierce exorcist was a mere five-six—the exact same height as her.

Kazik had the nerve to heave a great dramatic sigh as if *she* were the one creating problems for him and not the other way around.

"What if—" Gisela bit her bottom lip. "What if there's a way to guarantee that I wouldn't cause any more trouble?"

Kazik stared at her like she'd grown a second head.

"Help me."

"What?"

"Before summer's end, help me get a kiss from a mortal. There's this boy—set me up with him. Play matchmaker. I told you, all I want is to be human again. I'm just trying to get my life back."

Kazik laughed, the sound harsh and ugly. "That story again? You're still dreaming. It's not possible."

"It *is* possible," Gisela insisted. "Wojciech told me. The water goblin is a lot of things, but he isn't a liar."

A small furrow appeared between Kazik's brows, his skepticism wavering before her unrelenting certainty.

"Hear me out. If I regain my humanity, then I'll have no reason to cause trouble. No reason to bewitch anybody. You can get yourself back into Heaven's good graces. Maybe your saints even *want* you to help me. That's why your magic failed when you attacked me."

Kazik was not impressed by this logic. "That's ridiculous."

"You offered to help me yesterday."

"I offered to *exorcise* you."

"And look how that worked out. You know . . ." Gisela tapped a thoughtful finger to her chin. "I wonder what all the other spirits and devils would do if they learned you were having trouble performing a simple exorcism, hm?"

Kazik's jaw clenched. Gisela hoped he understood just how vulnerable he was without his God-given powers to protect him.

"Are you threatening me?"

"Why would I threaten the person who's going to help me? Oh, come on," she added at his dark expression. "This all ends the same way, doesn't it? You help me, you get rid of me, and this way we're both happy. We both win. Don't you *have* to help anyone who comes to you?" she wheedled. "Isn't that one of your saintly rules?"

Kazik looked annoyed that she knew that much. "It doesn't count if the person asking isn't human."

"And who decided that? That isn't fair. I was human once. I can be again. All I want is the life that was stolen from me. It's not like I asked to end up like this. I didn't just wake up one day and decide to drown myself so I could haunt your stupid town. I have a home. A family. I didn't *want* to die."

Kazik's eyes narrowed behind his glasses, some unreadable emotion flashing through their depths. There and gone in an instant. He sucked in air through his teeth. Exhaled through flared nostrils. A beat passed where he said nothing, and Gisela's breath caught as she realized he might actually agree to this.

He'd never, *ever* hesitated to shoot her down before. Silence meant he was chewing on the idea, actually considering helping her out. He was actually tempted to accept her proposition.

"You truly wish to recover your humanity?"

"Yes!"

"And all you need is a kiss?"

"Yes!"

"And if I agree to help you, you'll stop harming people? No more going around seducing innocent townsfolk. No luring anyone down to the river. No *tickling*."

"Yes, yes, *yes*. I already said I wouldn't." Gisela held out her hand to seal the bargain. "So, we have a deal?"

Kazik grimaced, frowning at the offered hand like it was a venomous snake. He sent a glance heavenward, as if praying for divine intervention, but must have received no response, because eventually, grudgingly, he steeled himself, took her hand, and shook it.

10

THE UNCLEAN DEAD

KAZIK

KAZIK WENT STRAIGHT HOME from the bathhouse and prayed to every saint he could name.

For guidance.

For answers.

For an explanation as to why his magic had abandoned him when he'd tried to exorcise Gisela.

He couldn't understand it. It didn't make sense. He wasn't like his mother. He hadn't been misusing his powers—as far as he knew. He knew he wasn't completely free from sin. He'd been dragged to confession often enough and frequently felt guilty about even the smallest thing. But even if Heaven *was* displeased with him, he didn't believe he'd done anything terrible enough to deserve this brand of divine punishment. His gift was such an intrinsic part of him that he couldn't imagine losing it.

He liked having the power to help people. He liked knowing he could make a difference, that he was keeping people safe.

So what was going on? Was it just a temporary loss of his

abilities? Maybe he was just tired. Or was it like Gisela claimed, that the saints *wanted* him to help her?

They were suspiciously silent on the matter. They offered him no answers that night nor the next. Maybe this was a test, and he had to prove himself worthy of the magic they allowed him to wield. He definitely felt like he was being tested, like he was standing on the edge of a precipice and one wrong step here would send him plunging into fiery damnation.

His grandmother would have said this was what it meant to have faith, to believe a higher power had a plan for you even when your life was falling to pieces. His grandfather, on the other hand, may very well have encouraged him to help Gisela. Kazik finally remembered the old folktale Zuzanna had mentioned, the one about the monk who'd saved a water nymph's soul and helped her regain her humanity by tying his cross around her neck and promising to marry her.

It all sounded very unlikely and vaguely blasphemous. A holy man turning his back on the church and choosing to love a monster? A wicked spirit transformed by love? Love seemed to be a common theme. In other tales, the water nymph became the water goblin's bride and ruled the river alongside him for all eternity.

Kazik wished he knew what to do. He wished someone would *tell* him what to do, tell him what the right move was here.

He dragged a hand through his hair and grimaced. His hand—and now his hair—was covered in grave dirt. Normally this wouldn't matter. He often frequented the old cemetery by the park. He'd played house here with Zuzanna as a child amid the graves and greenery while Babcia collected flowers and earth to use in her rituals like he was doing now.

But right now, it was Green Week, a time to honor life and death, and the cemetery was the most crowded he'd seen it since All Souls' Day, when everyone turned out with armfuls of candles and chrysanthemums to tend to their ancestors' resting places. Today colorful picnic rugs blanketed the grass among the monuments and headstones. People had come to eat with the departed, to share drinks with those who'd passed on.

He felt the stares as a family walked by, as if he hadn't elicited enough strange looks when he'd dragged Gisela from the market square the other evening. Ducking his head, Kazik desperately tried not to blush as Adam, a cute boy from church, who'd made out with him once as an experiment, raised both eyebrows at the sight of Kazik scrabbling in the dirt beside a mossy headstone.

Why was this his life?

Some days Kazik consoled himself with the thought of how boring and ordinary everybody else's lives must be. Other days he was so jealous of their ability to live normal lives that the feeling threatened to consume him.

At least this corner of the cemetery was relatively empty. The headstones here were worn and crumbling, shrouded with vibrant green moss and shaded by trees. Weeds sprouted from the damp soil where he was kneeling. There were no bouquets of decaying flowers. No grave candles enclosed in beautiful lantern-shaped candleholders. No vaguely ominous signs as there were in the newer sections of the cemetery, with warnings written in cursive: *This is your place in the future, so take good care of it.*

There was no one left to visit and clean these graves, and there hadn't been for a long, long time.

Kazik traced his fingers over the inscription on one of the headstones, brushing away a layer of dirt and lichen. The hair on the back of his neck prickled, and he ground his teeth together against a sudden rush of paranoia.

He tried to shake off the feeling of wrongness, the crawling sensation of being watched. It could be nothing. Someone else might've spotted him—one of the boys who used to laugh and call him a girl for picking herbs and flowers with his grandmother.

So why did he suddenly feel so on edge?

He reached into his pocket for his rosary. "Stop lurking," he said quietly, "and show yourself before I get angry."

For several moments nothing happened. He could hear the distant blissful chatter of the picnicking townsfolk floating on the breeze. Then a rustling sounded somewhere behind him.

No.

Above him.

Kazik's head whipped up, and he nearly departed the living world for good when he spied a pale face gazing down at him from among the leafy branches. He sprang backward with a shameful yelp, his shoulders knocking against another crumbling headstone.

Gisela laughed. "Wow. You need to lighten up." She was reclining on a sturdy branch with her back resting against the tree trunk. As always, her long black hair and ghostly white dress looked slightly wet, as if she'd just been walking in the rain. She was stringing together a lapful of buttercups to make a flowery green-and-gold crown. "Was I too obvious?"

"What are you *doing* here?"

"Always so hostile. Would you believe me if I said I missed you?"

"You're not my type."

"Shame. What are *you* doing here?" Gisela peered curiously at Kazik's little pile of grave dirt.

"None of your business."

"Aw, don't be like that. I know you like it when I come to see you. I'm practically your only friend. You need to relax and loosen up, Kazik. When was the last time you did something fun? You can't spend all your time brooding and feuding with wicked spirits."

Kazik didn't dignify this with a response. Mostly because he did spend the majority of his time brooding and feuding with wicked spirits. His brows drew together in a frown.

Gisela swung her legs over the branch, kicking her bare feet in front of her with lazy unconcern, showing off far more smooth-skinned thigh than should have been allowed.

Kazik hastily averted his eyes. It annoyed him that she could be so at ease around him. It was like she didn't consider him a threat.

But he wasn't a threat to her right now, was he? Not with his magic acting up. The realization stung.

"Did you think I was a forest spirit?" Gisela asked. "A bies? They must love you. A mortal with divine power in your blood. You're like a delicious snack. Just think of the chaos one of those demons could wreak if they devoured you or possessed your body."

Kazik scoffed, but he pressed a hand to his collarbone, where an oval medallion rested warm against his skin. A reflexive movement. The Saint Hyacinth medal was only one of the spiritual protections he wore that guarded against such a possession.

"Don't worry," Gisela reassured him. "I have your back. We're a team now. With me here, no one else will dare to touch you."

Kazik gave her a flat look. "Are you sure about that? From what I've heard, water nymphs aren't exactly powerful."

The spirit world had a hierarchy. The strongest, most dangerous spirits and devils were nature spirits like the wodnik and the leszy, ancient beings once worshipped as gods. They were powerful beyond imagining and ruled over the lesser creatures that dwelled within their realms. Mid-ranked devils included the vicious biesy and fiendish czarty. The lowest-ranked creatures were those that had once been human—the unclean dead: the bloodsucking strzygi; fiery ogniki; and of course, the utopce and rusałki, the drowners and the water nymphs.

"Isn't this"—Kazik gestured at the encroaching forest beyond the hallowed grounds of the cemetery—"technically Leszek's domain?" Leśna Woda's resident leszy, the ruler of its forests, was territorial and capricious by nature, as likely to lead hikers astray as to help a child lost among the trees. "Maybe you should worry more about protecting yourself."

Gisela sniffed. "*Certain* spirits might look down on us because we were once human, but that doesn't mean we're weak." She drew a bone-white comb from her pocket and carved it through the air, calling forth a great plume of crystalline water, which she made dance like a ribbon.

Kazik was impressed despite himself. Gisela commanded the water as if it were an extension of herself, another limb.

Sometimes he forgot how beautiful the magic of the spirits could be.

She lowered the comb, letting the water fall like rain. "We have our own magic. I could summon enough waves to flood this entire cemetery. As for whose territory this is . . . Wojciech and Leszek have a truce. I can go where I like."

"And you came here. Why?"

"Why do you think? Why are you collecting grave dirt?"

"Because a concerned mother asked me to get rid of the undesirable young man her daughter is seeing."

Gisela's wine-red eyes widened. "You're going to kill him?"

"What? *No.* I'm— The grave dirt is for a charm to make the girl lose interest in him."

"That's hardly as effective. But since you're sharing, I guess it's only fair I do the same. I'm here because *somebody* has been avoiding me."

Kazik had the grace to act guilty.

Damn his conscience. And damn Gisela.

"I hope you haven't forgotten our bargain. You promised to play matchmaker for me, or are you going back on your word?"

If Kazik was entirely honest, he'd only really agreed to help her to buy himself time so he could figure out why his magic had failed when he'd tried to exorcise her. So he *could* exorcise her the next time. He was shocked she was actually keeping up her end of their unholy bargain. Two whole days had passed without incident: No more girls had been found wandering dazed along the riverbank. There'd been no reports of near drownings.

This wasn't how it was supposed to work.

He didn't negotiate with wicked spirits. It was his duty to eliminate them, to punish them, and to prevent them from causing harm. He wasn't supposed to *help* a creature like Gisela.

But maybe there was an inkling of humanity left in that dark heart of hers. He was starting to feel almost honor bound to uphold his end of the bargain too. He *was* a man of his word.

"You said you'd help me," Gisela pressed. "You can't go around making deals with spirits lightly."

Part of Kazik was tempted to keep fighting her just for the sake of it—he still didn't believe a simple kiss would turn her human—but it was easier to humor her. With a sigh, he resigned himself to his fate. It was worth it just to keep her out of trouble, and as she'd pointed out, the consequences of breaking off their deal might be fatal. Gisela might go telling tales to the water goblin. Kazik wasn't in the habit of backing down from a fight, but he also wasn't foolish enough to start one with Wojciech when he could avoid it.

He had to trust that Heaven had a plan, that there were bigger things at work here.

"So, who's the unfortunate victim of your affections this time? This gullible idiot you want to kiss you."

From what he'd gathered, Gisela was incredibly shallow and went after tall pretty boys with broad shoulders and cool girls with boyish haircuts. She didn't discriminate when it came to gender, but neither did Kazik.

"He has a gentle heart," Gisela said, turning the flower crown she'd been weaving between her fingers.

Kazik's eyebrows lifted.

"And he's tall and built, and has these really nice shoulders . . ."

There it was.

"You probably know him. He rescued me from the chalk circle you trapped me in."

"He what?"

"Granted," Gisela continued blithely, "he did think I was a frog at the time."

Kazik was disturbed. If this boy had been at the house . . . did that mean Kazik *did* know him? Wait, if he'd freed Gisela from the chalk circle in the living room, how had he gotten in? Had he forgotten to lock the front door again? Zuzanna was going to murder him.

"I don't know his name," Gisela said, "but if he comes to see you again . . ." She brandished the flower crown at Kazik. "You can introduce me. Talk up all my best points. This is my dear sweet friend Gisela. She's so nice. So pretty. She's—"

"A cold-blooded demon."

"Someone might find that appealing, actually. It's like when the other spirits say things about you. Oh, that wicked exorcist. So dangerous. *So sexy.*"

Kazik kept his expression furiously blank but knew by Gisela's smirk that he didn't quite manage to the quell the blush that seared his cheeks.

God, that smirk. A blast of holy fire would wipe it off her face. He was mouthing a prayer before he could think, the magic within him igniting at the words. The heat of it curled through his veins, but a heartbeat later, just like last time, it slipped away, evading his grasp. It took all his self-restraint not to scream at the sky.

Why? Just, *why*?

Why have you abandoned me?

Kazik gritted his teeth. "I didn't realize you required that kind of assistance. Aren't you an expert at seducing people?"

"Oh?" Gisela batted her lashes. "Have you fallen victim to my charms?"

"Don't flatter yourself."

"See? Clearly my methods aren't enough. Hit me with your best tips, the ones you use to seduce tourist boys."

Kazik choked on air. After a burst of red-faced hacking, he said, "How do you even *know* about—"

"Your shady hookups?" Gisela finished with a cackle.

"Never mind. Don't answer. I don't want to know. Don't you dare tell anybody."

"Kazik?" A voice spoke behind him.

Kazik felt his soul attempt to leave his body. Gisela squinted, peering down from her branch at the speaker. Her face lit up with excitement, in a way that indicated this could quite possibly be the very human she'd set her sights on.

No.

Oh God, please, no.

Maybe he'd misheard the voice? Maybe he was imagining things? It was all the stress from this whole disastrous situation. Maybe it wasn't *him*.

Kazik turned and saw the last person he wanted to see—Aleksey, standing a few paces away, watching them with a smile.

11

THE BOY CALLED ALEKSEY

GISELA

GISELA LEAPT DOWN FROM her branch, dropping to the ground beside Kazik with unearthly grace. It was *him!* The boy who'd released her from Kazik's magic circle. His eyes were as bewitching as she remembered: the right, a perfect sky blue; the left, a brilliant forest green. He was wearing a loose linen shirt tucked into brown trousers, and his unruly honey-blond hair was perfectly tousled. It was hard not to stare.

She wasn't mentally prepared for this. She hadn't *dressed* for this. Saints, did she look okay? Did she look human? Had she dusted enough powder and blush on her skin? Was the unnatural red tint of her eyes hidden by the shadows of the cemetery's trees? She couldn't do anything about her perpetually damp hair. Would he believe she'd just come from visiting one of the bathhouses?

Shit.

She wasn't even wearing shoes!

"Aleksey." Kazik barely even glanced at the gorgeous Heaven-sent figure who had graced them with his presence, greeting the boy in the most lackluster manner possible. If Gisela's very fate didn't depend on her making a good impression, she would've kicked him.

She placed the flower crown she'd been weaving on his head instead, using the movement to draw him close and whisper, "Introduce me."

Kazik tensed. Their faces were close enough that their noses almost kissed. *Don't ruin this for me*, Gisela telegraphed silently.

"I'm not interrupting something, am I?" Mismatched eyes flicked back and forth between them.

"What? No! *God no!*" Gisela and Kazik chorused, springing apart in horror. Kazik started to tear the flower crown off his head.

"Aw, but it looks so cute!" The words were out of Gisela's mouth before she could stop herself. "Don't you think he looks cute?" She cast a playful glance sideways, testing the waters.

Aleksey—his name was Aleksey!—didn't miss a beat. His eyes gleamed with mischief. A dimple appeared in his cheek. "Very cute. So cute, you just want to gobble him up."

Gisela blinked, startled by the fondness in his voice. Kazik, for his part, turned as red as a beetroot. Heh. It was so easy to get a rise out of him.

"You were in my house," Kazik said through gritted teeth. "You let the damn frog escape."

"Oh? How did you find out?" Aleksey's grin was unrepentant. He was like the sun, bright and beaming beside Kazik's glowering storm cloud. The height difference between them was almost comical: Kazik short and slight where Aleksey was tall and solid.

"It was a very kind thing to do," Gisela cut in. "I'm sure the frog was ever so grateful."

"I was worried what Kazik might do to it." Aleksey sauntered closer, his hands in his pockets, stepping around a headstone so he could join them. He leaned down toward Gisela and feigned a whisper. "Kazik and his grandmother used to sacrifice frogs to summon rain."

"No!" Gisela gasped theatrically, pressing a hand to her heart. "Those poor creatures!" She shot a narrow-eyed glare at Kazik. They had better have been real frogs and not some *other* creatures in disguise. "If you wanted it to rain, you could've just asked a wiła to—"

She caught herself. Was that a normal thing to say? Would an ordinary human girl know about the nymphs who lived in the clouds? She had to remember to hide her true nature. "You could have just prayed for rain," she finished hastily.

Luckily, Aleksey seemed not to notice her awkward self-correction. Gisela was almost positive she heard Kazik exhale in relief.

"Some of the girls call him 'Frog Killer,'" Aleksey told her.

"As they should." Gisela crossed her arms.

Kazik looked like he was trying to decide which of them to strangle first. The flower crown sat forgotten and crooked on his head. "Are you both finished?"

"Are you doing more magic today?" Aleksey asked. "Oh, you're collecting grave dirt."

"He's casting a curse to get rid of someone's undesirable boyfriend," Gisela said.

"That's not— I don't *curse* people." Kazik scowled.

Aleksey shared a conspiratorial look with Gisela. "He's also cute when he's angry, isn't he?"

"Right?" Gisela twirled a strand of hair around her finger. This time she was the one leaning in close. Aleksey smelled as sweet as spring, like something green and growing. "You seem to know a lot about him."

"Oh, I know all of Kazik's embarrassing secrets."

Kazik let out a choked sound.

"We went to school together," Aleksey explained.

Oh.

Oh, that was perfect! Gisela mentally congratulated herself. It had been a stroke of genius recruiting Kazik to her cause. He could tell her all about Aleksey: what he liked to do for fun, his favorite color, the types of people he was attracted to. He could tell her exactly how to charm him.

"But I'm being rude," Aleksey said. "I don't think we've been introduced?" His tone lifted at the end, making the phrase into a question. His gaze flicked to Kazik.

Gisela cleared her throat meaningfully.

A mildly pained look crossed Kazik's face. For a second, she wondered if he was about to go back on their deal.

"This is Gisela," he finally said. "She's my—"

"Friend." She was less excited to claim the title now that she knew of the exorcist's crimes against frogs, but it was worth it to see the way his expression soured. "A very dear friend," she added, just to make him squirm.

Aleksey's eyebrows rose. He seemed on the verge of saying something more, but someone called out his name.

All three of them turned. A pale, slender wisp of a girl stood at the end of the overgrown path that ran between the graves. She was carrying a wicker picnic basket and a lacy parasol. Dressed in a floaty white gown, she could've been mistaken for another water nymph.

"Ah," Aleksey said.

Gisela smoothed her dress, conscious of the way the other girl was studying her and Kazik, her eyes narrowed against the sun. She made an impatient beckoning motion with her parasol.

Aleksey tugged at his collar. "I think my friends are keen to start eating."

"You're having a graveyard picnic?" Gisela said with envy.

"I'd invite you both to join us, but I know how much Kazik hates to socialize." Aleksey lingered a second longer, his feet rooted to the ground as if he were reluctant to leave them. Finally, he seemed to shake himself. "It was nice to meet you, Gisela. I hope we see each other again." Walking away, he gave Kazik a small nod, which Kazik returned.

"I hope we see each other again too!" Gisela called after him.

Aleksey glanced back, his expression wavering between curiosity and confusion, his gaze lingering on her like she was a puzzle he couldn't quite piece together.

"I think he likes me," Gisela whispered to Kazik.

He wasn't listening. He was still staring after Aleksey, looking unusually broody even by his standards.

Silently, they watched Aleksey insist on carrying the picnic basket for his pretty friend. His *very* pretty friend.

"Is she going to be an obstacle for his attention?" Gisela asked, at the same time as Kazik said, "She's just his friend. Don't you dare try and hurt her."

They looked at each other.

Kazik let out a deeply put-upon sigh. "How did I know that's what you were thinking?"

"Can you read minds now? Ooh! Are you getting your powers back? See, I knew Sky Daddy would forgive you if you helped me."

"Please never call God that." Kazik dragged a hand across his brow. "Gisela, I don't think—"

"Tell me later," she said. "I need to go rehydrate."

"What, now?"

"Yes, now."

The midday sun was a hot kiss on the crown of her head. There was a reason water nymphs preferred to emerge from the river in the late and early hours, at dawn or dusk. Gisela was feeling slightly dizzy from the heat, and her hair was starting to feel a little too dry. She had to return to the river or find water to bathe in elsewhere.

"Sad to see me leave? Fear not, I won't go far. Don't go thinking this is over. We need to plan what to do next!"

12

A GRAVEYARD PICNIC

ALEKSEY

"WHO WAS THAT GIRL with Kazik?"

"No idea." Aleksey sank down across from Roza on the picnic blanket; she'd spread it over the grass beneath a chestnut tree planted to guard the gravestones. "She said she was his friend."

"He has friends now?" Roza smoothed the ruffles on her dress. "I thought you said he was above making such lowly human connections. You said he was hard to get close to."

"He is."

It was rare to see Kazik with anybody other than his cousin. He gave off such strong *don't talk to me* vibes that most people were too intimidated to approach him. He avoided parties and dances, any kind of social gathering. His guard was always up. Even Aleksey, who'd crafted a reputation as someone friendly and approachable, hadn't managed to befriend him. All his attempts had fallen flat.

But victory wasn't a thing achieved overnight, and Aleksey was willing to wage as many battles as required to achieve his goals, to get what he wanted.

Who he wanted.

He'd always enjoyed a challenge.

"Maybe I'd have better luck," Roza said, tucking a wispy strand of white-gold hair behind her ear. "I can help. I can approach him for you."

Aleksey didn't have a chance to reject the offer before the rest of the usual crowd joined them: Kana and Kamil from Villa Jasmin. Adam from Villa Violetta. Hanna from Villa Lilia. The well-fed, carefully nurtured, hopelessly spoiled sons and daughters of the families who owned Leśna Woda's magical bathhouses.

Aleksey smiled out of reflex and was immediately smothered in hugs and kisses. The boys unpacked the wicker picnic baskets. The girls fussed over the food. Brown paper crackled as the goods were unveiled to "oohs" and "aahs": fresh-baked bread and lavender cookies and fluffy honey-lemon cake. There was cucumber-and–sour-cream salad, boiled potatoes, and cute little sandwiches cut into triangles. Cold sausage. Wheels of smoky cheese. The branches of the chestnut tree danced, shedding pale blossoms with the breeze. Flowers spiraled down, fragrant and soft as snow, falling over the feast.

"You're ruining it," Hanna complained, playfully batting Adam's hands away as he tried to steal some of the berries she was artfully arranging on a silver platter.

Aleksey caught his own face reflected in the metal and blinked, failing for a moment to recognize himself.

"There!" Hanna said.

"Can we eat now? Let's eat," Adam urged, helping himself to a juicy red raspberry.

"Would you like a pillow, Aleksey?" Kana asked, drawing cushions with silk tassels out of another wicker basket for them all to recline on. She wedged herself in beside him, sitting so close, their arms brushed.

Roza wrinkled her nose in disgust.

Aleksey usually found Roza's possessive streak endearing, but he wished she'd try a little harder to hide what she was feeling. They couldn't afford to get careless.

He propped a cushion behind him and leaned back on his elbows, staring up at the branches casting shade over the picnic. Normally, he'd be right into it, playing along, delighting in the game, the deception, trying all the different foods, and savoring each new flavor and texture. He'd always had a ravenous appetite. But today he was distracted. His mind was back among the untended graves in the oldest corner of the cemetery, with Kazik and the strange girl who'd been with him, who'd declared herself his friend.

Gisela.

It wasn't a name he was familiar with, and yet he was almost sure they'd met before. He'd seen her somewhere. She hadn't seemed to recognize *him* though, which was odd.

"Saw Kazik digging up a grave earlier," Kamil said conversationally around a mouthful of cake.

Aleksey stirred from his musings.

"Oh?" Roza looked up. "Is that what he was doing? Why?"

"Oh my God!" Hanna waved a half eaten sandwich, her thick auburn hair tumbling over her shoulders. "Do you remember that time he put grave dirt under Aśka's pillow? Because her mother wanted her to break up with some boy?" She nudged Roza. "Don't you remember?"

Roza pasted a deliberately thoughtful expression on her face. Aleksey could tell she was concentrating, trying to call up the memory. "Of course, I remember. Aleksey, aren't you going to eat?" she asked, deftly changing the subject.

Aleksey sat up and took a handful of cherries to satisfy her. Around him the conversation continued, a half dozen voices chiming in:

"Who's digging up graves?"

"Kazik. Who else? That family's all kinds of strange."

"My parents say they're frauds taking advantage of vulnerable people."

"Father Paweł says they're no better than witches."

"They're not witches. Nor frauds."

Aleksey's eyes narrowed a fraction. It was Adam who'd spoken last. The boy sat up, a curl of night-black hair falling across his brow. To say Adam was attractive was an understatement. He was lanky and long-limbed, and his eyes were a honeyed shade of amber, a sharp contrast to the deep brown of his skin.

If anyone had gotten close to Kazik, it was Adam. He wasn't shy about his conquests.

"They don't take money for their services," Adam said. "They know all sorts of folk remedies and facts about the spirits. Kazik's just intense."

"Just intense?" Kamil cut in. "He gives off this vibe like he thinks we're all beneath him. Like he's too saintly for us."

Adam ignored him. "Plenty of people believe in that old stuff or are simply superstitious. My father had Kazik's grandmother bury amulets around Villa Violetta to keep evil forces out. She hung consecrated herbs beside all our doors for protection. Didn't your parents ask her to do the same thing?"

Kamil didn't reply, but Hanna piped up. "My uncle's supposedly seen some strange things while hiking. He always leaves an offering for Grandfather Forest when he goes hunting. Bread and grain on a tree stump. He's always warning me not to curse nor whistle too loudly when we forage for mushrooms so we don't offend anything."

"Clever," Roza said. "The leszy isn't kind to those with no respect for nature."

"Our nanny used to say there was a little skrzat, a gnome, who lived behind our stove," Kana added. "She said it would burn the house down if Kamil and I didn't clean up after ourselves and say our morning prayers."

Aleksey smiled around a cherry, tucking the pit into his cheek as he spoke. "Did you ever see it?"

Kana laughed. It was a pretty sound, just like a bell. "She was just making things up to scare us into being good. But you've been inside Kazik's house, haven't you? Didn't your mother take you for a healing last year when you were ill?"

Last spring, Aleksey had been stricken by a sudden sickness that had left him bedridden with fever and fatigue. Even the best doctors had been mystified.

Kana squinted at Aleksey through the thick of her lashes and wriggled her eyebrows. "What was it like? I hear Kazik can steal your pain away with a whisper."

Aleksey shrugged. "I wouldn't know. Mother wanted to take me for a healing, but Kazik's grandmother was unwell at the time, so they weren't taking patients."

And Aleksey's fever had broken. Eventually. He'd recovered slowly but steadily. A new life had taken root inside him. Afterward, his mother said he was like a different child—faded thin and pale from the fever, but with a new determination in his eyes.

"I doubt they would've been able to help you," Kamil said.

Aleksey hummed in agreement. He doubted that too. He bit into a second cherry, sinking his teeth into the crisp bloodred flesh. "They're not all-powerful."

"They're not doctors," Kana said. "I mean, faith healing is a fascinating subject, but like Adam said, it's mostly just superstition, right?"

This launched the group into a full-on discussion: Hanna jumping in to disagree, while Kamil concurred with his sister's statement. There had been a push after the war to embrace the rational over the mystical. Technological advancements were doing away with the need for faith and a belief in spirits and witches. The old traditions and customs didn't have a place in the modern world. Only uneducated and childish individuals believed in such things, Aleksey had been told. Even the mystical properties of Leśna Woda's sacred springs could be explained with science. It was something to do with all the minerals in the water.

He couldn't understand exactly why they were so eager to explain away all the magic of the world, but he refrained from arguing. As the discussion droned on, he spat a cherry pit into the grass and leaned back on his elbows again, rapidly losing interest. He let the chatter wash over him, not even bothering to nod along with the conversation, listening instead to the voices of the branches swaying overhead.

Sunlight blinked through the shifting green leaves. A glass-winged dragonfly alighted on the brim of Hanna's straw hat. Aleksey inhaled, relishing the fresh air and the scents of soil and loam and sun-warmed grass. He imagined sinking his roots deep into the earth, imagined letting this fragile body decay until the weeds grew up through its skeleton.

Again, his mind drifted back to the untended corner of the cemetery, where the moss grew over the grave markers, to the girl Kazik had introduced as his friend.

He'd been almost reluctant to introduce her. Aleksey remembered the pointed way she'd cleared her throat, the sharp look she'd given Kazik before he spoke. Her eyes were the oddest shade of brown. Almost a deep red. The color of old blood or wine.

It was all very mysterious and slightly concerning. There was something happening here, something he needed to get to the bottom of fast.

13

BATHHOUSE PREMONITIONS

GISELA

IN THE END, GISELA decided not to return to the river. She didn't want to risk running into Yulia nor getting roped into playing nursemaid again nor doing some other tedious chore for Wojciech. There were other ways to stay hydrated, like visiting one of the spa town's magical bathhouses. Or at least the only bathhouse that didn't mind a few spirits sneaking in.

Villa Lilia was famous for its flower-milk baths and the beautifying properties of its steaming waters; bathing in them daily would enhance your beauty tenfold and leave your skin shimmering like stardust. It had been a favorite haunt of Gisela's in the first few days of her stay that she could remember.

Originally, she'd hoped her father would spend more time with her and Hugo, but he'd been busy with business as usual. Gisela didn't think he was a bad parent, exactly. He wasn't intentionally unkind. He'd never hurt her in a way that left a physical mark. He was just absorbed in his work, in his own life, so frequently absent that he barely acknowledged her existence half the time, save for when he checked in to make sure she was taking care of her little brother. Things might've been different if their mother had been alive, but she'd passed away birthing Hugo. Gisela barely remembered her. Her father had spoken little of the woman he'd married and looked so sad when Gisela brought up the subject that she'd stopped asking, not wanting to cause him any further grief.

She nibbled on a thumbnail. She needed to hurry up and become human again. If any more time passed . . . She didn't want to be like one of those girls in Great-Aunt Zela's stories who returned home hundreds of years later to find their world changed and everyone they'd known and loved dead or aged beyond recognition.

A twinge of pain lanced through her. She wasn't sure if it was heartache or just the overly enthusiastic ministrations of the bathhouse spirit currently slapping her back with a handful of birch twigs.

"Ow! Saints, really? Can't you do it gently?"

"It's good for you!" he declared in a voice like the hiss of water poured over hot coals. The wizened little man, no taller than Gisela's knee, glowered up at her. He was a wispy creature. His plump naked body and long cloudy beard formed not so much from flesh and bone and hair as steam.

Banniki lived mostly in the mainland countries farther east. It was amusing to think this one might've traveled here simply to sample the waters the same way human tourists did.

But not so amusing to think he'd been skulking about in the steam room the last time she'd been here, when she was still mortal, completely invisible to her and everybody human.

Or maybe not everybody.

She wondered what it was like for Kazik, being able to see things most people couldn't. Was that why he was always in such a bad mood?

The spirit blinked its coal-red eyes. Gisela crossed her arms over her naked chest and turned away, scowling at the floor and wincing as the birch twigs lashed the backs of her legs this time.

Beads of moisture trickled down her spine, and a spell of light-headedness made her head spin, but she knew she would feel heavenly afterward, and her skin would be all supple and glowing.

Maybe she should also have a honey massage or a candlelit milk bath scented with wildflowers? She needed to do whatever she could to make herself more appealing, to improve her chances with Aleksey.

She thought she had a decent chance. She'd had a feeling about him from the moment she'd first seen him. They had chemistry, a similar sense of humor—they both liked teasing Kazik. Aleksey had said he hoped to see her again. Which meant he hoped to see her again. Probably. But maybe he'd only said that to be nice? Because he was being polite?

Gisela replayed their conversation in her head, trying to remember exactly what she'd said to him and what he'd said to her, and *how* he'd said it, and how he'd *looked* when he'd said it, trying to decipher any possible hidden meanings.

Her little companion set down his birch switch and clambered onto the wooden bench along the wall. Wisps of vapor wicked off his body like the steam curling off a piping-hot bowl of soup. His scraggly white beard floated up like a cloud with his every breath. It was said that the bathhouse guardians were gifted with the ability to predict the future. Often, all it took to gain a spirit's help was to address it respectfully and directly, although a bribe was always helpful.

Gisela ladled water over the hot stones of the wood-fired stove in the center of the room. Steam billowed up, filling the air with smoky fog so thick, she could barely see through it.

The bannik let out a contented sigh.

Gisela perched on the bench beside him in companionable silence, breathing in the heat, jiggling one foot with impatience before she shifted nearer. "Grandfather," she addressed him. "Will you grant me another favor? What do you think? Will I find love with a human boy this summer? Will you tell me what you see in my future?"

The spirit stroked his cloudy white beard and considered her through half-lidded eyes. His gaze grew distant until it seemed he stared straight through her. Then he beckoned at her with a hooked finger.

Eagerly, Gisela leaned in. His crackly voice, speaking so close to her ear, sent a shiver across her skin. "Silly little water nymph. How can a dead thing have a future?"

Gisela recoiled.

"What mortal man would be mad enough to take a dead girl as his bride?" The spirit cackled loudly, rocking back and forth on the wooden bench, his wispy little body seizing with mirth.

Gisela was so offended that she stormed straight out of the steam room, pausing only to douse herself with a bucket of icy water and shrug on a fluffy white robe. Her slippers slapped the floor as she stalked past a crowd of women with wet hair and rosy skin, past a liveried attendant standing by a golden cage-lift. Like all the bathhouses, Villa Lilia was a grand palatial complex.

She didn't stop until she reached an empty resting hall. A lone marble figure stood in the center, pouring plumes of crystal-clear water into a round ornamental pool. Gisela perched on the lip of the pool and cursed her fellow spirits. What did the stupid old bannik know anyway? She'd show him she still had a future!

Dipping a hand into the pool, she raked her fingers back and forth, creating angry ripples. The water was near scalding, hot enough to hurt. She left her hand in until it was numb and tingling, latching on to the sensation to calm herself down.

The marble statue regarded her with its soulless stone eyes. Glossy green lily pads and a beautiful blush-pink water lily floated past its feet. Gisela reached for the bloom without thinking.

The flower writhed in her grip like an eel.

Gisela let out a startled shriek and let go.

The water lily vanished with a burst of light and an audible pop, making way for an unnervingly handsome young man with black-green hair and wine-red eyes, wearing a fancy silk robe and a self-satisfied smirk.

Gisela gave Wojciech her best deadpan stare. "Of course, it's *you*."

Water spirits were notorious shape-shifters, and unlike Gisela, who could only transform herself into a fish or a frog, Wojciech was perfectly capable of disguising himself as an inanimate object.

It was how wodniki lured in their victims: tempting them with gifts. Girls and boys would reach for shiny trinkets floating innocently upon the river's surface—flowers and bracelets, ropes of pearls and gold pocket watches—only to find themselves dragged into the depths by a creature plucked from their nightmares.

"Such impertinence," Wojciech scolded. "Do the humans from your island have no respect for their elders? Back in the day, I would've eaten someone alive if they dared talk to me the way you do."

Gisela rolled her eyes. She knew Wojciech was more amused by her impertinence than he was offended by it—so much so that he'd even once jokingly offered to make her his bride when she was older. After living for so long, he must always be searching for fresh entertainment. He let her get away with so much that she couldn't resist the temptation to keep pushing her luck just to see if he'd push back.

It was oddly reassuring when he didn't.

He climbed out of the pool and settled beside her on its marble lip, dripping water all over the floor.

"You're leaving puddles everywhere."

Wojciech shrugged. "It's hard to human today."

And wasn't *that* a whole mood. "Should you even be here?" Gisela groused. "I thought Kazik's grandmother forbid you from bathing in Leśna Woda's holy springs on pain of death."

"Why should mortals be the only ones to enjoy the magic of such things? We laid claim to this place long before any humans did." Wojciech blinked. Then he flicked an impossibly long tongue out like a frog and snagged an unfortunate fly that had flown inside the bathhouse.

"Besides," he said after he'd swallowed the fly whole, "Kasia's gone from this world now. She can no longer stop me."

He sounded smug yet also sad, as though he regretted that the witch, his longtime adversary, was no longer around to curse at him and chase him out. The water goblin had been a little in love with Kazik's grandmother, who'd been as fierce and pretty as Kazik when she'd been younger. Gisela suspected this was why Wojciech hadn't dealt with Kazik himself. He had a soft spot for the family.

"You sound like you miss her."

Wojciech didn't respond. "The wards she placed around this town are weakening. I can only feel the echoes of her presence now."

"So I should expect to see hordes of spirits here in the future, lounging in the steam rooms and enjoying the flower-milk baths?"

"Perhaps." Wojciech turned his head.

Gisela followed his gaze. A gaggle of chattering middle-aged women were pouring into the resting hall. Their eyes lingered appreciatively on Wojciech, one or two even offering him an inviting smile. Gisela resisted the urge to gag. All they saw was a deceptively handsome young man. They had no idea who he was, *what* he was, what *she* was. Wojciech's attention wasn't even on them but on the small czart that had crept in after the group. Unseen. Invisible. The devil's feet were a bird's raptor-sharp claws. It was wearing one of the bathhouse's complimentary bathrobes.

Catching her watching, it raised a taloned finger to its lips.

Gisela bit back a grin.

"Perhaps one day these bathhouses will cater exclusively to spirits, and humans will be the ones forbidden from entering," Wojciech mused. "I am surprised more of our kind haven't taken advantage of Kasia's absence. It's been close to a year now since she died. The balance of power has shifted. I thought Leszek would've snatched up the chance to devour her grandson and expand his territory."

Gisela hadn't met the leszy who ruled the forest surrounding the spa town. Mentally, she pictured him as a leafier version of Wojciech, a great godlike being as old and tall as the trees.

She was familiar with some of the forest spirits though: the fearsome child-snatching mamuny and the adorable little ogniki, the wandering fires who manifested at night as orbs of flickering blue and green flames. Ogniki were famous tricksters and liked to lure lost travelers astray, but if you behaved politely or offered them bread or money, you could gain their aid. They might even lead you to hidden treasure—to ancient burial mounds and places where people fleeing war had buried their prized possessions in the hope that they'd return for them someday.

And then there were the biesy.

Vicious all-devouring forces of nature. Cunning forest demons who reeked of calamity and death, of freshly spilled blood, who devoured humans just for the fun of it. Gisela had never come face-to-face with a bies, as far as she knew. They could be difficult to spot even for spirits like her. They liked to play dress-up, to possess human bodies and stroll through the streets, masquerading as mortals.

"So, Yulia tells me—" Wojciech began.

Of course, it was Yulia, Gisela thought, letting out a huff of breath.

"—that you abandoned Tamara at the first opportunity and have been running off on your own and antagonizing the exorcist." His wine-red gaze was heavy with disapproval. "I *asked* you to look after Tamara."

"I did look after her," Gisela protested. "I showed her around and warned her not to stray too far from the river. I told her how to use my comb to conjure water. I didn't *abandon* her. Kazik showed up and we got separated. It wasn't my fault. And afterward she was with the other girls, so . . . so I knew she'd be safe if I left her. And you *know* what I'm busy doing. You promised you wouldn't interfere."

"Did I? Strange how *I* don't recall ever promising that."

"That's because you're old," Gisela said sagely. "Your memory's failing."

Wojciech shut his eyes and sighed. The sound was like water rushing through reeds. "Pray tell, then, my sweet, deranged summer child, how is the search going?"

Sometimes, talking to Wojciech really was like talking to someone from another century. Old-fashioned phrases snuck into his speech at random, mixing with the more casual slang of people her age.

"Have you found a human willing to kiss you?"

Gisela kicked her legs out in front of her. "I'm working on it."

"I warned you at the beginning not to get your hopes up."

"You're always so negative."

"As you take great pleasure in reminding me, I've lived a good deal longer than you have, and if I can say one thing with certainty, it's this: entanglements with humans always lead to heartbreak. Nothing lasts in the mortal world. Humans are judgmental, fragile creatures who—"

"So, I'm supposed to what?" Gisela burst out, her earlier anger at the bannik flooding back. "Just give up?"

Give up and accept her life was over before it had even begun?

She hadn't even *lived* yet. She was only sixteen. She'd only *been* sixteen—though she no longer aged in the mortal way. There were so many things she'd missed out on, things she'd never get to do nor see. She still hadn't figured out what she wanted to do for a career nor even who she really was.

"*You* were the one who told me there was a way to become human again."

"I expected you to give up after the first few attempts," Wojciech admitted. "Like the others before you did. You're not the first girl unwilling to accept what happened to her."

Gisela gripped the edge of the pool. "I'm not in denial. I—"

"The others weren't half as stubborn as you are though. I didn't think you would keep at it this long. I didn't think you would wish to return to your old life. I thought you had started to enjoy your time with us."

Gisela couldn't hold his gaze. Because it was true that once the initial shock and fright of awakening in his underwater realm had faded, she had started to enjoy herself.

She didn't enjoy the ever-present threat of drying out nor the feeling of being trapped here, but . . . she liked the powers she'd gained as a water nymph. The magic. Conjuring and controlling water with her hair comb. Shape-shifting if she chose to. She liked how quickly her cuts and scrapes healed and how she could see as clearly at night as she did during the day. She liked being able to see spirits.

She was something more now—and something less.

And the Crystal Palace was undeniably enchanting, and she liked being a part of Wojciech's strange found family. . . .

She liked it so much that she'd started to feel guilty. Because she already *had* a family. Who loved her. Maybe. Her father wasn't an affectionate person, but her little brother adored her. What kind of person would she be if she said she never wanted to see them again? If she didn't want to go home just because she was having more fun here?

What kind of daughter would that make her? What kind of sister?

They depended on her. Her father had said so. Repeatedly. *I'm so busy with my work, Gisela. If you don't look after Hugo, who will?*

She bit her lip. "I have to go home. My little brother—"

"Is not your responsibility. You're not his mother. You have a father."

"I know that, but my father's always so busy, and Hugo's all by himself. He's only twelve."

"And did you not manage to look after yourself at that age?"

"Well, yes." After their mother had died, Gisela and Hugo had been raised by Great-Aunt Zela until she'd passed away too, after which Gisela had been deemed old enough to look after the home while their father was away. "But—"

But if she wasn't there, who would make sure Hugo was eating? Who would run his bath and get him to bed? Who would do the laundry? Who would make sure he went to school?

"Maybe you're underestimating your brother," Wojciech said. "And maybe you should let your father do his job."

Gisela lifted her chin defiantly. "You don't understand. And why does it matter so much if I leave? Why do you care?"

"Because Heaven knows why, but I've grown rather fond of you. We all have. And I believe I can provide a home for you where you can be happy, where you can live at ease. I can ensure this new life of yours is filled with all the happiness your last one lacked."

Gisela was rendered momentarily speechless.

"I know you care fiercely for your brother," Wojciech said softly. "I admire that. But you deserve to be taken care of too. Have you considered what it will even be like to return to your human family after living like this for so long? Can you be sure that once you are home again, you won't yearn just as passionately for this place?"

After having a taste of this world, would she find her old life bland?

Gisela swallowed to dislodge the sudden knot in her throat. Her island had its own magic—plenty of it, she reminded herself. "I'm grateful for all you've done for me, but this isn't where I belong. And if you're not going to help me, fine." She'd handle her problems herself, as she'd always had to. Standing, she pulled the sash of her fluffy bathrobe tightly around her waist. "Stay out of my way. Don't try and stop me."

Resignation etched itself into Wojciech's ageless face. "I won't stop you if you wish to keep trying. However—" He motioned with his hand. Ribbons of water lifted out of the marble pool and danced through the air.

Gisela let out a squeak as one dipped into the pocket of her bathrobe and pinched her hair comb. "Hey! Give that back!"

The ribbon of water dropped the comb into Wojciech's lap. "I'm confiscating this."

"What?!"

"If you insist on behaving like a disobedient child, then I'll be forced to treat you like one. I am fond of you," Wojciech repeated, standing tall. "But I am not nearly so forgiving as you seem to think. When I ask you to do something, like look after one of your sister rusałki, I expect to be obeyed."

Gisela gaped at him.

"Be grateful I'm not confining you to your room in the palace."

"B-but what do I do if I'm trapped somewhere with no water?" Like Kazik's magic circle. "How will I leave the river? Keep my hair from drying out? How will I defend myself?"

"Perhaps you should've thought of that before you selfishly abandoned Tamara," Wojciech said, sinking into the puddle at his feet and vanishing.

14

A GUEST IN THE HOUSE IS A GOD IN THE HOUSE

KAZIK

OF ALL THE PEOPLE in Leśna Woda, of all the people in the world, was it so much to ask that Gisela not set her sights on Aleksey?

It was like someone up there had it out for Kazik. Had he murdered a saint in a past life or something? He kicked the bedsheet off and stared unseeingly at the shadows creeping across the slanted beams of his bedroom ceiling.

It wasn't as though Gisela hadn't gone after one of his childhood classmates before, and it wasn't that he had anything against Aleksey—far from it. Ask anybody, and they'd tell you Aleksey was perfect.

Friendly and easy to talk to, he was the kind of boy who helped grandmothers to cross the street and carry their groceries. His family was one of the richest in town. And then there were those eyes and those shoulders and that waist that tapered just so. . . .

Kazik pulled his pillow over his face.

Aleksey was one of those boys you daydreamed about while knowing deep down that they'd never be with someone like you. Kazik didn't have a high opinion of Gisela's taste, but this time he couldn't fault her.

He rolled onto his left side and then his right side and then sat up. He struggled out of his shirt and flung it across the room before collapsing back onto the mattress with a groan. The house was still warm from the sun the walls had drunk during the day. Even the tiny breeze blowing through the open window did little to lessen the heat.

He shut his eyes and tried to will himself into unconsciousness. Physically, he was exhausted, but his mind just kept on turning. One moment he was thinking of Aleksey, and the next moment, Gisela. Eventually, at some point, he must've slipped over the edge into sleep, because the next second he knew, his eyes were snapping open.

Kazik bolted upright, his breath coming fast. His skin crawled with the panicky, prickly feeling that something wasn't right. Something had disturbed him. Some . . . noise?

Sweat beaded on his brow while he held as still as he could in the dark, straining his ears and senses for what had startled him awake. He tried to breathe shallowly so that the sound didn't carry.

Was he only imagining things? Being paranoid?

He stretched an arm out, his fingertips feeling for his glasses and for the holy knife, the consecrated blade he kept on his bedside table.

A ghoulish face swam out of the shadows. "Bad dream?"

"Mother of God!" Kazik recoiled and threw himself sideways.

The edge of the mattress disappeared beneath him. He rolled off the bed before landing on the hardwood floor with a bruising thud. "How did you get in here? What are you doing in my house?"

His shoulder throbbed. He was incandescent with fury. There were very few places where he felt safe, where he knew he wouldn't be attacked by wicked spirits. His room was his sanctuary.

"You sleep so early," Gisela complained, peering over the edge of the mattress with an exaggerated pout. In the darkness her wine-red eyes had a catlike shine.

Kazik wanted to strangle her. He pushed himself up onto his elbows. Bathed in the moonlight spilling through the window, Gisela looked ethereal, even more like the spirit of a drowned girl than usual. Her long green-black hair dripped water onto his sheets. The wet fabric of her white dress was scandalously see-through, clinging to her skin like sin. He could discern every line and curve of her body.

For an unforgivable moment, Kazik's body betrayed him, his heart racing at the sight. He was ashamed to feel the blood rushing to his face. But then again, at least it wasn't rushing anywhere else.

Small blessings.

Gisela smirked and leaned over the edge of the mattress, clearly relishing the way Kazik shuffled back in discomfort. She was having way too much fun with this. And he . . . he was feeling very exposed suddenly, shirtless and dressed in only a threadbare pair of sleeping shorts.

"You shouldn't leave your bedroom window open, Kazik. You never know what kind of wicked creature might crawl in."

"Like you?" Kazik retorted, grabbing his shirt off the floor and yanking it over his head in one quick motion. He didn't understand. There were magical protections surrounding the house, invisible wards he and his grandmother had created by burying pages of holy scripture at all four corners of the property.

How the devil had she gotten past them?

Of course, those wards were only supposed to deter spirits with ill intentions from entering. They didn't stop benevolent creatures like the domowiki, the house spirits that looked after people's homes, from coming in. Theoretically, this meant Gisela had no wicked intentions toward anyone here.

Theoretically.

Kazik's instincts screamed at him not to let his guard down. She was still a rusałka. An abomination. A girl who refused to stay dead. He couldn't forget who he was dealing with. This had to be an intimidation tactic. It was like the flirting; she was trying to throw him off-balance, trying to prove she could get to him.

"Wait." A thought occurred to Kazik. "My bedroom is on the second floor."

"I'm good at climbing," Gisela said, like this was a normal explanation. She flopped onto her side with a sigh, getting comfortable on the bed. *His* bed. "I didn't want to go back to the Crystal Palace. The vain old toad is being so annoying today."

Kazik blinked, his sleep-addled brain struggling to keep up. Vain old toad? Was she referring to the water goblin? He fumbled atop the bedside table, reaching for his glasses. "So you decided to grace me with your presence instead?"

"Don't pretend you're not happy. I know you're head over heels for me, really. It's my undeniable charm." Gisela sat up and swept her hair back. "I told you I'd be back. You're not off the hook yet. Let's talk boys—or rather, a boy. How do I charm Aleksey and make him want to kiss me?"

"How should I know?" Kazik said. He and Aleksey weren't friends. They moved in different circles, lived in different worlds. He actively tried to avoid the other boy because it was hard to function in the same space as someone that attractive.

Although, thanks to his godforsaken luck and because he seemed to attract what he tried hardest to avoid—spirits, demons, Gisela—somehow, he always seemed to be running into Aleksey. In the street and at the bathhouse, while walking home or on his way to church, even once while he was getting groceries. He couldn't shake him off.

"Didn't you learn anything when you were stalking him the other day?"

"I wasn't stalking him," Gisela said. "I was merely attempting to observe him from afar. It's only stalking when you follow them home."

"You would know."

"He said you went to school together. You have to know something. Does he like anyone? Has he liked anyone before? What were they like? Were they cute? Quiet? Funny?"

Kazik slid his glasses onto his nose. "Pretty. Probably. Like the girl you saw him with at the cemetery." Aleksey was always surrounded by admirers, girls who'd do anything to please him. He tolerated the attention with good humor but had never seemed overly enamored with anyone in particular. "It's hard to tell who he likes because he's friendly and nice to everybody."

Unlike Kazik, who was ill-tempered, unsociable, and tended to always assume the worst of people.

"What is he interested in, then?" Gisela pressed. "What does he do for fun? What does he like?"

"Hiking and animals, I guess." Kazik had seen Aleksey rescue injured hedgehogs and a hatchling that had fallen from its nest once. "And sketching. He's one of the few people our age who believe in spirits."

Gisela perked up.

"Which is only going to make him harder to fool. He's more likely to figure out what you are."

Gisela deflated comically, her shoulders drooping.

Kazik's lip twitched with something like laughter. "I've seen him leave offerings for the leszy. He's asked me questions about magic before and what I can do." And he hadn't lost interest even after hearing the answers like most boys did when Kazik explained his power had more to do with faith and healing than summoning bolts of flame and lightning.

Not that he *couldn't* do those things, necessarily.

"And you said you didn't know anything about him."

Kazik rolled his eyes. "This is stuff everybody knows."

"Do *you* like him?"

"What? No." The words came out too quickly, too loudly. Damn it. "No," Kazik repeated more steadily. "Of course not. I think he's good-looking—doesn't mean I like him."

It was a pointless waste of time pining for somebody who would never look at him that way. It was oddly freeing admitting to his attraction out loud though, knowing he didn't have to brace himself for Gisela's judgment nor worry she'd react badly. Unlike Aleksey, Gisela was also attracted to people of more than one gender. In this single regard, Kazik felt safe with her.

Gisela smirked. "Aw, we have the same taste."

Kazik snorted.

"Are we bonding? I feel like we're bonding."

Kazik ignored the question. "I already introduced you to him as my friend. Wasn't that enough?"

"That was just the beginning! Our deal was that you play matchmaker." Gisela rubbed her hands together. "We need to strategize."

"What?"

"Strategize. We need to come up with a plan. We need to engineer another chance encounter. Arrange things so Aleksey and I are thrown together until he falls madly in love with me and wants to kiss me. I was thinking you could invite him to go rowing on the river with you, and then I could swim underneath the boat and capsize it and pretend to rescue him from drowning so that he'll think of me as his savior."

"Or . . ." Gisela continued at the appalled expression on Kazik's face. "The three of us could go walking in the forest, and you could pretend to sense a dangerous spirit so that Aleksey and I are forced to run and hide somewhere for safety. Preferably in a small dark space, like the hollow of a tree, so we're pressed all close together. You know what would be even better though? If he got hurt somehow. Just a little. Then I could tenderly minister to his injuries."

"I'm beginning to understand," Kazik said slowly, "why you

haven't been successful at making anyone want to kiss you in the past."

"I wasn't successful," Gisela corrected him, "because *somebody* kept interfering with my plans. But we can keep it simple to begin with. Let's arrange it so that I coincidentally show up somewhere he's also going to be. You invite him out, and I'll just happen to be there too, and then you can make some excuse and slip away to leave us alone together."

Kazik opened his mouth to argue and froze. He held up a hand to shush Gisela. "Did you hear that?"

"Hear what?"

He could've sworn—

The sound came again: the warning groan of the stairs leading up to his bedroom as someone made their way upstairs. Kazik swore and yanked Gisela off the bed and onto the floor. There was no time to shove her back out the window.

"Quick! Get under—"

Gisela squeezed herself under the bed.

Kazik stood, whirling to face the door just as it burst open to reveal his cousin, who would've been shocked but thrilled to find someone in his bedroom at this hour.

Less thrilled, of course, when she realized Gisela wasn't human. She'd probably try to exorcise the water nymph. For a second, Kazik wondered why that thought worried him.

"Wh-what?" he stuttered, his voice cracking.

"Kazik? You're awake?"

"I am now."

"Did you sense that?" Zuzanna lifted the candle she was

holding. Its light flickered over her face and sent shadows dancing over the walls. "I could've sworn I sensed . . . I thought I heard voices."

"Voices? No. I mean, I didn't hear anything?" Kazik's throat ran dry. "It must've been the wind. A branch falling?" He glanced at the open window.

Zuzanna was across the room in an instant, yanking the panes closed, double-checking the latch. "You shouldn't leave it open while you're sleeping! Any evil thing might try and crawl in," she scolded.

"Too late for that."

"What?"

"Nothing." Kazik perched on the edge of the bed, jiggling one leg restlessly, praying she would just leave. Instead, Zuzanna picked up a discarded piece of clothing and folded it slowly. She was always trying to tidy everything up. Afterward, he could never find anything. "Zuza," he said, hating how his voice became a whine.

"You know, if you keep drying your underwear on the radiator, you're going to burn the house down."

Kazik's face heated. "I wasn't— I haven't had time to put the laundry away." He only dried his underwear on the radiator in winter, when he wanted it all nice and toasty.

Zuzanna raised a disbelieving eyebrow. But Kazik's thoughts were focused elsewhere. Saints, had Gisela seen his—

"Are you having trouble sleeping? Do you want some chamomile tea?"

Kazik dragged a hand through his hair, turning it into even

more of a ruffled mess. "I'm fine. It's just hot. Why are you still up? Don't you have to catch the early bus home tomorrow?"

Zuzanna regarded him with a seriousness that made her look far older than her years. "I told you. I thought I sensed something. It woke me up. And . . . and I had another dream."

Oh.

"Like—"

"Like the dreams Babcia used to have about you. I was walking barefoot through the forest. It was dark, almost completely black, and petals were falling all around me like rain. I saw you lying at the foot of a great tree, strangled in the roots."

"It was just a dream," Kazik said quickly.

Zuzanna gave him another look. He knew what it meant. Sometimes, dreams were messages from above.

His cousin lingered for a minute longer, haloed in the candlelight, then sighed and turned toward the door. "Be more careful with the windows, okay?"

Kazik grunted. He watched to make sure she closed the door fully, counting to ten silently in his head just in case she decided to come back. He prayed Gisela hadn't been paying attention to their conversation, but his hopes were dashed when the water nymph's smirking face reappeared.

"Don't worry, I didn't peek at your underwear."

"You know what?" Kazik said. "I take back our deal. Get out of my house."

"Too late," Gisela sang, clambering back onto the bed. "Just help me get a kiss, and then you can go back to your boring broody life."

"My life is not boring."

The mattress dipped with Gisela's weight. A pale hand landed on Kazik's thigh for balance.

He flinched violently. There was not a single spark of warmth in that touch. Gisela's fingers were shockingly cold.

It was like being touched by a dead thing.

She *was* a dead thing.

A shudder of revulsion ran through Kazik. He was sharing his bed with the ghost of a girl.

Gisela yanked her hand back and curled her fingers into a ball. For the first time since Kazik had known her, she looked embarrassed. Even ashamed. She didn't blush though. But how could she when she had no living heart pumping blood through her veins?

She retreated until she was sitting amid the tangled sheets at the very foot of the bed with her knees pressed close to her chest. She looked smaller suddenly, vulnerable, her usual flirtatious mask abandoned. A better exorcist would have leapt at the chance to attack her now when her guard was down, but Kazik didn't move.

Zuzanna's voice echoed in his head.

They're sad things, really. Lost souls who weren't able to travel to the afterlife. The spirits of maidens who died before their time. Girls cursed to haunt the bodies of water where they suffered violent ends.

Gisela was roughly the same age as himself. She'd only been his age when she—

"That was your cousin?" Gisela wound a strand of hair around a finger. "She's nicer than I expected. I've heard about her from the other spirits. She has quite the reputation. I think they're even more afraid of her than they are of you."

Envy knifed through Kazik. He didn't doubt it. Zuzanna was a force to be reckoned with when she got serious. "I've watched her take on a strzyga single-handedly. I don't think she's afraid of anything. Do you . . . Did you have—"

"I have a little brother. Hugo. He's twelve. Well, thirteen now. I missed his last birthday after I . . ." Gisela's gaze fell to her lap. She was still twisting the strand of hair 'round and 'round her finger.

Kazik held his breath, waiting for her to continue, to reveal what had happened to her, how she'd become a water nymph, how she'd died. A morbid part of him desperately wanted to know.

"I don't remember it," she said finally. "What happened. It's like there's this great big hole in my memories. One moment I'm arriving in Leśna Woda; the next I'm waking up as a spirit."

Kazik frowned. "You don't remember anything at all?"

"I have nightmares sometimes where I feel like I'm being chased, like I'm running from some nameless horror, but I'm not sure if that's actually a memory." Gisela rubbed idly at the base of her skull. "And sometimes I'll feel like I've been somewhere or seen someone before. I'll hear a voice that sounds familiar. Feel afraid for no apparent reason. But there's no context. I never know why I'm reacting that way. Even Wojciech doesn't know what happened to me, and he knows *everything* that goes on in his river. The other water nymphs said he was distracted that night because he'd heard your grandmother had been attacked."

Kazik's frown deepened.

"But it doesn't matter. I'm kind of glad I can't remember. I don't need to know what happened. All I care about is regaining my humanity, getting my life back. My family—" Gisela bit her lip. "My father's not— He's away a lot, traveling and doing business. He relies on me to look after things. I'm the one who takes care of my brother. That's why I really need a kiss, so I can stop haunting this place and go home."

The moonlight wrapped around them.

Kazik tried to tell himself that he didn't care about this latest revelation regarding Gisela's motives. Spirits were manipulative. They were liars. They took pleasure in confusing and deceiving humans. But what she'd said about her family made him think of his mother—always busy with work or a new boyfriend, uncaring and uninterested in his life. A part of him had always wondered what would've happened if his grandparents hadn't been there to take him in, if there'd been no one to look after him.

Gisela sighed into the silence. "You don't have to believe me. But I feel guilty, like I've escaped to a magical new world and left Hugo behind to fend for himself. I'm scared he's all alone. I'm worried no one is checking on him."

"You shouldn't feel guilty," Kazik said, the words spilling out even as the rational part of his mind whisper-screamed at him in protest. "You didn't ask for this. You . . . can check on him when you're human again."

Gisela looked up.

"I'm still not *entirely* convinced." He still had his doubts. Would a kiss truly be enough to restore Gisela to life? "But I promised I'd help you, didn't I? So let's talk boys."

15

MAKEOVER

KAZIK

THEY STAYED UP MOST of the night talking, which was strange in itself, because talking to people usually tired Kazik out. He told Gisela about his various trysts with hot tourist boys—the good ones and the hilariously bad. He explained to her what boys were like and what they liked. In the morning, after Zuzanna left, he even ended up giving her a mini-makeover. Honestly, it was a miracle Gisela had ever managed to fool anybody into thinking she was human running around like a barefoot ghoul in her ghost-white dresses with her long dripping-wet hair.

"I can't let it dry out," she protested.

"Then at least braid it back or tie it up or *something*."

He let her borrow one of Zuzanna's hair ties, a pair of her old sandals, and a wide-brimmed straw hat with a strawberry-red ribbon that his cousin had left behind at the house. Alas, he couldn't lend her any of Zuzanna's colorful velvet dresses—his cousin made most of her clothes herself and would murder him if he let a creature like Gisela wear them. The next closest person to the water nymph in size, as much as it pained Kazik to admit, was him.

He was *not* lending her his clothes.

"Why not?" Gisela complained, trailing after him through town. "I bet I'd look good in them." She leered.

Kazik scoffed and walked faster. Why did she even want to wear boys' clothes when girls' clothes were so much cuter? At least it was easier to deal with her when she was being flirtatious and annoying than when she was being all soft and sad and vulnerable.

He wiped the sweat from his brow. It was another sun-kissed day. The sky was disgustingly beautiful—a perfect powder blue. The air smelled like honey and apple blossoms. The tree-lined, petal-strewn avenue winding past the shops down to the farmers market looked like something out of a storybook. Kazik was usually so busy rushing from place to place that he was oblivious to the beauty around him. It had been a long time since he'd stopped to soak it in, since he'd taken the time to really look at everything.

He only made it another few steps before Gisela swerved into his path. She spun, turning to skip backward in front of him, smiling wickedly beneath the shadow of her straw hat. Her skin still gleamed faintly green blue in the sun—but so faintly, it might easily be dismissed as a trick of the light.

An odd flash at the corner of Kazik's vision had him turning, then removing his glasses and cleaning them just to make sure a smudge wasn't to blame. But he hadn't caught so much as a glimpse of any other unholy terror, hadn't felt the spine-tingling sensation of being watched. He supposed it was because Gisela was with him. For the most part, spirits tended to avoid poaching one another's prey.

"You could buy me something more colorful to wear," she said, peering wistfully through the glossy windows of a fancy dressmaker's shop at a mannequin on display. It was dressed in a floaty mint-green gown with short puffed sleeves and a low scooping neckline. A creamy silk ribbon cinched the gossamer fabric below the bust and tied into a sweet bow at the back.

It looked like something an angel might wear.

Gisela let out a soft sound of longing. The unclean dead were always thirsting for the things they'd lost, for the trappings of the lives they'd once lived. Rusałki, in particular, had a healthy appetite for pretty and frivolous things: hair ribbons and headscarves and sparkly beads—all the treasures people left out as offerings. Kazik didn't even want to think about how much a dress like the one in the window might cost. "You wouldn't look good in it," he said, walking on.

Gisela kept pace. "That wasn't exactly a no."

"It definitely wasn't a *yes*." Clearly, their habit of bickering would take more than one night together to break. "Doesn't the water goblin provide you with clothes?"

"Of course he does. But they're impossible things: dresses made from mist and moonbeams or swirls of watery foam and bubbles. You can't wear them in the mortal world, so when we come here, we just wear the clothes we died in or rags we snatch from clotheslines."

Kazik cut a sharp glance sideways, but Gisela didn't seem particularly bothered by what she'd just said.

She peered through another shop window, admiring a bakery's mouthwatering selection of cream cakes and sweet-cheese buns nested on beds of decorative flower petals. "So, what's next?"

"Like I said, I'll approach Aleksey. See if I can find out what kinds of girls he likes and feed you the information. Then I'll ask him if he'll come hiking with us. I'll say you're visiting for the summer, and I don't know the trails well. I'll stop by Villa Hyacinth later. I have errands to run at the market now."

"Right now?"

"Right now. Look," Kazik said seriously, slowing. "I can't drop everything for you. I have responsibilities. There are other people who also need my help." He had to meet Mrs. Mróz and collect the altar candles she'd acquired for him so he could perform a ritual.

And he wanted to see Mrs. Mróz for another reason. Something Gisela had said last night was niggling at him.

Even Wojciech doesn't know what happened to me, and he knows everything *that goes on in his river. The other girls said he was distracted that night because he'd heard your grandmother had been attacked.*

A premonition of unease swept through Kazik. It was just the mystery of it, the timing, he told himself, that had him concerned.

"I'll let you know afterward what Aleksey says. Then we can rehearse what you'll say to him and how you should act."

It was better to take things slow. Even with his many hookups, Kazik wasn't exactly an expert at this. Romance—especially between a boy and a girl—wasn't something he was well versed in. A tiny part of him worried he was setting Gisela up for failure. But then, she had about as much chance with Aleksey as Kazik did with or without his help, which was to say not much of a chance at all.

It wasn't that he didn't find her attractive. Unfortunately. Kazik didn't think *he* was completely unattractive either. But Gisela was, well, the lecherous spirit of a dead girl, and he was the grandson of a witch, a boy who communed with demons. Neither of them was exactly . . . prime kissing material.

It wasn't as though Aleksey would want either of them when he could have literally anyone else.

But when Aleksey *did* inevitably reject Gisela, that would be the end of it. Kazik could redirect her attention toward someone more suitable. In the meantime, she wouldn't be off causing trouble. Maybe this would even be enough to get him back into Heaven's good graces. Kazik cheered slightly at the thought.

"But what am I supposed to do until then?" Gisela groused.

"Whatever you like. What do you water nymphs usually do when you're not trying to trick unsuspecting humans into falling in love with you?"

"Sometimes we entertain ourselves by capsizing the little rowboats the tourists take out on the river to scare them."

"Don't do that," Kazik said immediately. He raised a hand to shield his face as a breeze swept down the road, snatching loose leaves and blossoms from the surrounding trees. He caught a petal on his palm. It was light as air. A deep bloodred.

"I'll come with you," Gisela said. "To the market. I can help you run errands. It'll be faster. I'm not letting you ditch me again. You know, it's almost suspicious how you keep trying to delay setting me up with someone. Are you sure you're not secretly in love with me? You know, *you* could always kiss me."

"You'd like that, wouldn't you? Never going to happen."

"You like me—admit it."

"I cannot wait for the day when I am free of you at last."

The cheerful ringing of a bicycle bell had them leaping apart as a girl on a blush-pink bike with a basket zipped by perilously close. The damn tourists rented them from the bus station to pedal about town. The sound frightened a fat tabby cat from the stoop of a nearby shop.

It slunk across the footpath to greet them—only to streak away with a furious hiss, every hair on its body bristling the moment it sniffed Gisela and realized what she was.

Gisela pouted. Animals were always more sensitive to a spirit's presence than humans. Some devils were even afraid of cats and dogs.

"Just wait for me," Kazik said.

"But what do I do while I'm waiting?"

"I could keep you company," someone offered in a deep voice.

Kazik stiffened. Gisela whirled around.

Aleksey stood a few paces behind them, bloodred petals swirling at his feet. He nodded a casual greeting, his cheek dimpling with a grin.

Kazik's traitorous heart skipped a beat. He didn't need to look at Gisela to see her melt. He knew what that dimpled grin did to people, himself included. Sometimes he resented Aleksey's ability to cast a spell over everyone, but he could never hold on to the resentment for long.

Still, people shouldn't be allowed to just go around smiling like that.

"You're here again," Aleksey noted, his gaze settling on Gisela.

Gisela beamed. "Can't get rid of me that easily, right, Kazik?" Her voice was all high and breathy.

"Not for lack of trying," Kazik said.

Gisela elbowed him in the ribs.

Kazik winced.

Aleksey looked like he was trying not to laugh. "You know, I think I'm jealous of you, Gisela. Kazik's practically a hermit, but this is the second time I've seen him out with you. You must be a very special person." His eyes lifted to meet Kazik's for a beat before his attention returned to Gisela. "Or he must really like you."

Kazik choked on his own spit.

"I was just saying that!" Gisela said.

"Oh?"

"But we're just friends. Kazik is *so* not my type," she added, so quickly and adamantly that Kazik's temper sparked.

"Really?" he said. "Back in the cemetery, I thought you said I was dangerous and sexy."

"Th-that was just—" Gisela floundered.

Kazik couldn't ever remember being the one to fluster her before.

It was deeply satisfying.

She glared at him. He didn't even try to hide his smirk.

"Didn't you have errands to run?" Aleksey asked, before things could escalate. "At the market? I'm heading that way too. I couldn't help overhearing."

Kazik wondered just how much of their conversation Aleksey had overheard, how long he'd been there.

Gisela looked equally uneasy, but it didn't prevent her from saying, "That's right, Kazik, don't you have errands? You better hurry up and go do them."

"I'll show Gisela around," Aleksey said, looking at her. "I was hoping to get the chance to talk to you again."

Gisela's eyes widened. If she were human, she'd probably be blushing. Kazik wanted to snap at her not to act so desperate. *Surely*, Aleksey couldn't find that attractive.

He looked back and forth between them, feeling oddly, unreasonably betrayed.

"Fine. You do that." He rolled his shoulders, stamping down a jolt of pointless jealousy, trying to shake off this odd, misplaced sense of possessiveness. It wasn't like he had any claim on Aleksey—or Gisela for that matter. "I won't be long. I just have to check in with Mrs. Mróz." He started to stalk away.

"Take your time," Aleksey called after him.

16

THE FOOD OF THE GODS

GISELA

DESPITE HOW EAGER GISELA was to talk to Aleksey again, a ripple of anxiety ran through her when Kazik left them alone together. She probably shouldn't find so much comfort in the exorcist's presence. But she had to give him credit: wearing the straw hat and braiding her hair really was helping to keep it from drying out so quickly—which was lucky because she didn't have her comb to conjure emergency water at present.

She tilted her chin to peer up at Aleksey, holding the brim of her hat to keep it from blowing away in the breeze. She racked her brain for something clever to say. What had Kazik said last night? How had he told her to act? How was she supposed to charm Aleksey? They'd both agreed that laughing loudly at all his jokes and doling out compliments was probably a good place to start.

Aleksey was watching her intently, almost expectantly, like he was waiting for her to say something to him now that it was just the two of them. His eyes narrowed with curiosity.

Or was it suspicion?

Gisela swallowed. Kazik had warned her that Aleksey believed in spirits, that he'd be hard to fool. She fought the urge to squirm self-consciously.

"Are you hungry?" Aleksey asked, when the silence threatened to stretch into awkwardness.

"Yes!" Gisela said, relieved. Kazik hadn't bothered with breakfast. She didn't know if he was fasting for the good of his soul or something equally saintly, or if he'd simply forgotten to eat; either way it explained why the exorcist was so thin. "I'm absolutely starving."

"Me too." With a disarming smile, Aleksey guided her down the path to Leśna Woda's bustling farmers market. The place was packed with people walking shoulder to shoulder, haggling and bartering, complaining about the heat and the government and the price of meat. Stalls set up on either side of the street were selling all sorts of treats: pint baskets of juicy wild berries and herbs picked from the forest and fields, rhubarb and giant cabbages, chanterelles and bottles of birch-tree juice, even hand-knit house slippers and great wads of tart goat cheese.

The mouthwatering fragrance of roasting meat and onions wafted on the air. To Gisela's left, a food cart was hawking smoked sausage; on her right, a stall shaded by a striped awning displayed a sign claiming to serve the best dumplings in the region.

Aleksey left her side and returned moments later with forks and two plates piled high with dumplings stuffed with fresh blueberries, each serving topped with a generous dollop of sour cream and sprinkled with crunchy sugar.

Gisela was in heaven. Dumplings were the food of the gods.

Aleksey must've thought so too, because he was practically inhaling his portion. "Divine, aren't they?" he said, watching her swallow, looking pleased by her reaction. "There's another stall too, farther on, where they serve the best crispy potato pancakes with goulash. But these are my favorite. Have you tried sweet dumplings before?"

Gisela licked her fork clean and nodded. "My great-aunt used to make them for us. She had a stall at the floating markets back home."

"Floating markets?"

Just to be cautious, Gisela avoided talking about herself when she was trying to charm a human—there were too many things she couldn't tell them. But when she *did* have to talk about herself, her island home was a safe topic, one that instantly made her seem more interesting. After all, Caldella was a mystery, a magical island-city where humans lived under the rule of a wicked witch-queen. Outsiders had been forbidden from visiting the isle for over a decade now. Its very existence was disputed.

"They're markets where everything is sold from little boats. I'm from Caldella originally." She cast the name out like a hook, and as expected, Aleksey took the bait.

His voice rose. "You're from the witches' island? What's it like there?"

So, between delicious mouthfuls of dumpling, she told him.

About the half-moon bridges that arched over the canals that twined through the city. About the broom boats, the little magicked skiffs that sailed you down those canals with only a rap of your knuckles. About the row houses painted in pastel colors and the witches who caught falling stars and brewed cocktails in teapots. About the gruesome sacrifices the queen made to keep the city from sinking and the great stone pillar engraved with the words OUR LOVE KEEPS US FROM DROWNING.

She told him about the rock pools where she'd take Hugo to catch tiny orange crabs, about how in winter, when the witches froze the sea solid, they would traipse onto the icy waves and feel the dark tide pounding like a heartbeat beneath their heels.

Aleksey hung on her every word with a flattering childlike fascination.

Gisela smiled to herself.

The more she talked about the island, the closer to it she felt. It felt like she might look up right now and see the glitter of the sea and the dark spires of the witch-queen's palace rising out of the depths. She'd hear the crashing of the ravenous ink-black waves and the lilting melodies floating from the windows of the famous Conservatoire.

"You sound like you miss it," Aleksey said, returning their empty plates to the woman running the dumpling stall.

She did. She missed the salt-sweet air and Hugo so fiercely, it was like an ache. She craved familiarity and the things she knew inside and out. But there were some things she *didn't* miss too. Like having to go to school, where she'd always been in trouble for being late or not finishing her homework because she was busy helping her brother finish *his* homework. And her father . . . She'd tried to make his constant absence into a game. The first time she'd been left in charge, she'd been so proud that he trusted her to look after everything while he was gone. She'd felt important, valued, and oh, so grown up. None of her classmates had that kind of responsibility nor freedom. She and Hugo could go to bed as late as they wanted, eat whatever they liked—dessert for every meal—and no one would even care.

"I do miss it," she said, truthful for once. Kazik had responded better to her sincerity, to her fears, than he had to her flirtations—much to her discomfort. Gisela wasn't used to being so honest about what she was feeling. But maybe Aleksey would react the same way. It was worth a try. "But I really like it here too. It's just . . . different." She fell into step beside Aleksey. They ambled aimlessly through the market stalls. "It's been a lot to get used to."

"I think I know what you mean."

Gisela raised an eyebrow. "Haven't you lived here your whole life? Kazik told me you have."

A peculiar expression crossed Aleksey's face. His gaze settled on her even more curiously than before. "You and Kazik talked about me?"

Shit.

"Uh—"

"You two seem *very* close."

"I told you we're just friends."

"Just friends?"

"*Just* friends," Gisela stressed.

Aleksey grinned. "Don't protest too much. I might get the wrong idea."

"Why does it matter anyway?" Gisela challenged. "Why are

you so curious if we like each other? Did you bring me here just to question me about our relationship?"

Aleksey held his hands up in mock surrender. "You caught me. I wanted to see what kind of person you were and make sure you don't have any wicked intentions toward Kazik. He tends to attract nefarious types."

Oh.

That . . . well, it was disappointing, obviously. She'd hoped he'd wanted to spend time together simply because he'd taken a liking to her. But it was also kind of sweet, the way he was looking out for his childhood classmate.

Aleksey really was a nice person. No wonder even Kazik found him attractive.

"So how did you become 'just friends' with him?" Aleksey asked. "Kazik doesn't usually allow anyone to get close to him. It's hard to find a hole in his armor." His gaze slid across her again, those beautiful eyes searching hers, oddly intense. "He's not here. You don't have to pretend. I can understand why you're drawn to him. Leśna Woda's famous exorcist *is* very pretty and perfectly bite-size."

"You make it sound like I want to eat him."

Aleksey's grin widened. "Don't you?"

Gisela was too distracted to answer. They were passing a stall selling jars of homemade jam and artisanal honey. The grumpy-looking stall owner was speaking with a customer. Neither human took any notice of her, but the same couldn't be said for the invisible little czart lounging beside the jars. It was the size of a cat, with a vaguely human-shaped body and cloven black hooves. Curling horns poked through its miniature beekeeping hat and veil. It was clutching a tiny smoke pot.

Great-Aunt Zela whispered in Gisela's ear, *Devil beekeeper.*

A type of domestic spirit that inhabited the human world. Gisela had seen them guarding the hives some of the local families kept in the forest. She'd heard them singing to the bees. Miray had shown her how to sneak past them to pinch honeycomb when she was feeling peckish.

The little devil was staring straight at her.

She tried to pretend like she couldn't see it. The absolute last thing she needed right now was for it to recognize what *she* was, then make a scene and give her away. Hopefully with the straw hat and her hair braided, it wouldn't . . .

With an excited hiss, the devil leapt to its feet, knocking over a jar of honey. The stall owner spun toward the crash. Stopping, Aleksey started to turn too.

If he believed in spirits, did that mean he could also see them? See the little devil angrily waving its smoke pot at her?

Panicking, Gisela froze. But then, thank all the saints, a loud bark cut through the market.

A fluffy white dog flung itself at her knees. She stumbled against Aleksey. He pressed a hand to her back to steady her. As he did so, Gisela saw the beekeeper devil retreat behind the honey jars.

"I'm so sorry!" A lisping voice cried an apology. A flaxen-haired girl in a frothy peach-colored sundress melted out of the crowd. "He keeps running off."

Standing very still, Gisela peeked down at the little dog

sniffing at her legs. Its leash trailed behind it across the path. There was always a fifty-fifty chance an animal would react badly to her presence—which was probably why the beekeeper devil was hiding.

Cautiously, she crouched to pat the dog on the head, almost slumping in relief when he snuffled at her palm with his cold wet nose, his tail wagging madly.

That had been way too close.

She risked a glance at Aleksey, praying he hadn't noticed anything amiss. But he was busy frowning at the girl. Something clicked in Gisela's head—this was the girl who'd been with him at the cemetery the other day.

"Don't worry about it," Gisela told her, and then she addressed the dog. "Yes, yes, I'm very glad to see you too." *Very, very glad.* "Aren't you adorable? Yes, you are!"

"He's a terror," the girl said. Up close, she was even prettier than Gisela had initially suspected. Her eyes were the color of smoke, and her lips looked as soft and pink as petals. "Sometimes," she said, "I just want to pinch his little ears until he yelps."

Realizing she was staring, Gisela quickly looked back down at the dog. Maybe she could offer to walk him so she could use him to scare off any more spirits that appeared?

The dog finished sniffing her and scampered over to inspect Aleksey. "I wasn't expecting to see you here, Roza," he said. "I thought you had a piano lesson this morning."

"I'm on my way there now," Roza said, her attention still centered on Gisela. "You're the girl Kazik was with the other day. His friend." She gave Aleksey a questioning look, then pivoted in place, scanning the market with ravenous interest. "Where is our delectable exorcist today? I should say hello."

The dog barked at Aleksey, then bounded back to Gisela before flopping onto his back at her feet and pawing at the air, signaling he wanted his belly rubbed. Frowning, Gisela obliged. Something about Roza's tone irked her—she didn't like hearing this girl describe Kazik as delectable. It seemed to affect Aleksey the same way.

"He had errands to run," he answered shortly.

"Of course, he did. He's so hard to pin down." A faint furrow appeared between Roza's pale brows. "How did you get tangled up with him?" she asked Gisela.

"It's a long story." Not wanting to go into details, Gisela gestured at the dog. "What's his name?"

"Poppy. What's your name? How come you're hanging around Aleksey? You know, you look kind of familiar. Have we met before?"

"I don't think so?" Gisela couldn't remember ever having done so.

"Really? Because I feel like—"

A deep growl rumbled from Poppy's throat. The dog was on his feet again, sniffing the air for a threat. Gisela glanced at the honey stall; the devil beekeeper had poked its hatted head out from behind the jars.

"What's the matter with you now?" Roza scolded, when Poppy started to bark. "Be quiet!"

Aleksey scooped the dog up and bundled him into Roza's arms. There was an edge to his voice that Gisela hadn't heard before. "Take him out of here. He's causing a scene."

"But—" Roza said.

"And you're going to be late for your lesson. People are going to talk."

Poppy squirmed in Roza's arms, snapping at her chin. She hissed and bared her teeth at him. She and Aleksey traded an indecipherable look, holding eye contact for a disconcertingly long time before Aleksey's focus returned to Gisela.

"Come on, Gisela. Let's go."

Eager to get away from the honey stall, Gisela hurried after him. She cast one brief look over her shoulder. The devil beekeeper was hiding again, but Roza's eyes were fixed on her, keen and assessing.

Gisela studied Aleksey next, but nothing in his profile gave away what he was thinking. "So," she said, "you and Roza?"

"She's a friend," Aleksey said.

"*Just* a friend?"

Aleksey's steps slowed. His gaze slid sideways.

Gisela smiled up at him innocently.

Aleksey let out a bark of laughter. "Just a friend. She's someone I've known for a very long time. She likes to follow me around and insert herself into whatever it is I'm doing. In some ways, she's like an annoying younger sibling."

"Ah." She was like Hugo, then. Not that Hugo was *super* annoying—except for when he was throwing tantrums and calling her *bossy* and refusing to go to bed. In any case, Gisela was relieved to know Aleksey wasn't interested in Roza as anything more than a friend. She might've joked to Kazik about the other girl being an obstacle, but she had no desire to compete with anyone for Aleksey's affection.

A breeze set the ribbons on her hat dancing. “Earlier, you said something about potato pancakes?”

Aleksey’s face lit up. “You want to try them?”

“We should get something for Kazik too,” Gisela said. “He doesn’t eat enough.”

“That sounds like an excellent idea.”

17

CHURCH CANDLES

KAZIK

KAZIK MIGHT NOT FIT in with anyone his age, but older people adored him. Mrs. Mróz started smiling and fussing the second she saw him approaching the little stand where she sold flowers.

"Kazik! I was wondering when you would come by. Your face looks thin. Have you been eating properly?"

"Do you have any candles for me?" he asked, stepping sideways to make room for a possible customer. A handsome bearded man had paused to admire the array of ready-made bouquets displayed in silver buckets: dewy bunches of lilacs and daffodils; sprays of pink and orange tulips; pale blue hyacinths; and primroses in every color.

Mrs. Mróz winked at Kazik. "Of course! Come." She was a stout woman with snow-white hair who always wore the same faded floral shawl no matter the weather. "Maria! Kazik is here."

A second, nearly identical, woman emerged from the shadows of the stall's green cloth awning. Her white hair was covered by a kerchief tied into a knot beneath her chin. She was holding a giant bouquet of lilies done up with yellow ribbon.

Kazik signed hello with his hands the way Babcia had taught him. Mrs. Mróz's younger sister hadn't spoken a word since the war. She put a hand on his arm and shepherded him behind the front bench. The sisters' shoulders were hunched with age, but they still managed to stand taller than him. Saints, he hated always being the shortest person in the room.

Mrs. Mróz cast a furtive glance over her shoulder before she stooped to rummage through a wooden crate for what Zuzanna liked to call *the illegal goods*.

In other words, beeswax altar candles pinched from the church.

"David made soup," Mrs. Mróz said, pushing a warm thermos into Kazik's hands. "It's your favorite." Which meant it was tangy sorrel soup thick with young carrots and potatoes.

Kazik took the flask only because he knew Mrs. Mróz wouldn't take no for an answer. She was always trying to feed him. The way the elderly women from Babcia's rosary circle insisted on taking care of him always left him feeling both loved and suffocated. Some days, he felt like he'd never run out of grandmothers.

"How is he?" he asked. David was Mrs. Mróz's second husband. "Is he still having trouble sleeping?"

"The lemon-balm tea you recommended is helping. I keep telling him that he needs to tire himself out, but he refuses to go hiking." Mrs. Mróz sighed. "He avoids the forest now. He won't admit it, but I know he's afraid."

Last spring, David Mróz had gone hiking with a friend. The two men ventured off the usual trails, traipsing far deeper into the forest than was generally advised. They'd heard a child crying. Really, living out here, they should've known better than to follow the sound. There were at least a dozen horrors capable of mimicking human voices, spirits who could assume the likenesses of loved ones. And so, later that night, they'd returned home with something else inside them.

There was a particularly devious type of forest demon that liked to play at being human. Biesy were cunning creatures known to possess mortals and cause mayhem. They were hard to fight and even harder to catch because when they possessed someone, they could take knowledge from their memories, making it easier to impersonate that person. When they wanted to, they could blend almost seamlessly into human society.

It was usually only a trail of bodies that gave them away.

Kazik could still recall the way his skin had crawled when he'd looked at Mr. Mróz and seen something else—something wretched and hungry—looking out at him from behind the mask of that familiar sun-weathered face. He remembered the sheer malevolence emanating from the old man and the unnatural speed with which he'd moved, the way the demon had mocked Kazik when he demanded it leave the body it was controlling.

Or what? You can't hurt me, exorcist, without hurting the man I'm wearing.

The look in those eyes, so confident, so full of contempt.

Kazik's lip curled. It had underestimated him. He'd ripped that *thing* out by its roots, banished the demons from both men's flesh. But the more powerful of the pair had wounded his grandmother in retaliation before it fled back into the forest to lick its wounds. Kazik should have chased the creatures down and finished them off, but he'd stayed with her. She'd passed away not long after, from an unrelated fall, but a part of Kazik blamed the biesy for her death. If she hadn't been recuperating from her wounds, she might've had the strength to recover.

His brows knit in a frown, Gisela's story popping back into his head.

Even Wojciech doesn't know what happened to me . . . The other water nymphs said he was distracted that night because your grandmother had been attacked.

A burst of laughter jolted him out of his thoughts. He turned his head to watch two of his childhood classmates wander past the stall arm in arm. Stefan, who used to poke fun at Kazik for picking flowers with his grandmother, and Anna, who, when they were eleven, had invited Kazik to an all-girl tea party and asked him to teach them how to summon a demon. They still looked like children, carefree in a way he knew he would never be. Sometimes he felt so disconnected from the people around him that it was like he was living in a completely different reality. The world they moved through was not his world.

Kazik wondered what it was like to have no worries, no responsibilities, no evil spirits actively trying to ruin your life. What did ordinary people even do?

With a sigh, he carefully stowed the thermos of soup inside the brown paper bag full of candles that Mrs. Mróz handed him. "Do you remember ever hearing anything about a tourist girl drowning in the river or going missing?" he asked. She would know something; the local grandmothers made it their business to know everything.

"A tourist girl?" Mrs. Mróz's brow furrowed. "You don't mean that poor maid from Villa Lilia? They're saying she was involved with one of the guests, a man engaged to be married, and we all know how that ends. They hire those girls from anywhere these days."

"No, not her." That death had occurred more recently. A suicide, apparently. There had been an inquiry, but the officials had ruled out any foul play, though Kazik had heard rumors to the contrary. It wouldn't be the first time a rich tourist bribed their way out of trouble. "This would've happened last spring, on the day you came to Babcia because your husband wasn't acting like himself."

Frowning, Mrs. Mróz glanced at her sister, who was spraying the ready-made bouquets with water so that the flowers glittered. The other woman signed something too fast and complicated for Kazik to catch, but Mrs. Mróz nodded vigorously.

"Ah yes, yes, of course. That foreign girl who went missing. They had search parties out looking for her everywhere."

Even as she said it, Kazik was remembering he'd heard something about that back then too. He just hadn't connected it with Gisela. All his attention at the time had been focused on his grandmother. He'd never seen her wounded before. Never seen her look so frail. He'd been terrified.

Mrs. Mróz clicked her tongue. "I'd forgotten about it until now. My memory isn't what it was. The girl's father was so broken up about it. Poor man. Apparently, she'd gone for a walk alone in the forest after dark."

A chill traveled down Kazik's spine.

The biesy had fled back into the forest that night. If one of those demons had come across Gisela . . .

It was probably just a coincidence. There was no reason to connect the two events if not for the timing. He could be jumping to conclusions.

But if he *wasn't* . . .

It might mean it was his fault she'd ended up the way she was.

He clenched his jaw against a pang of guilt. Was that why he was unable to exorcise her?

"Is this about the new guesthouse?" Mrs. Mróz eyed him eagerly. "The one on Hydrangea Lane? Is this foreign girl the one haunting it?"

Kazik stared at her blankly before it hit him. Inwardly, he groaned; with everything going on with Gisela, he'd forgotten the promise he'd made to Mr. Haase, the owner of one of Leśna Woda's guesthouses.

He quickly thanked the sisters, who reminded him to eat the soup—"David will feel badly if you don't. He made it specially for you!"—and left the stall, debating whether he had time to take a quick detour before he found Gisela.

He needed to talk to her. Question her. Grill her about her lost memories.

And, after listening to her describe her previous matchmaking schemes last night, he didn't trust her to be alone with

Aleksey for long. She might get some mad plan into her head. Might try and poison him or something just so she could gently nurse him back to health and earn a kiss.

They were supposed to take things slow. Knowing her, she'd say the wrong thing if Kazik wasn't there and give herself away. Really, they should've gone on a practice date themselves first.

A minute later, Kazik finally spotted Aleksey's tall figure over by a food stall. His steps sped up then slowed. Aleksey looked like he'd walked out of a daydream—the kind that made Kazik douse himself with cold water and pray for forgiveness. His honeyed hair was windswept, brushed back off his brow, bringing all the focus to his bewitching two-colored eyes, and the crisp white shirt he was wearing only brought attention to his broad chest in a way that made you want to grab him by his suspenders and just . . .

Kazik's throat ran dry.

Aleksey leaned down to whisper something in Gisela's ear. They were so absorbed in each other that, for a moment, neither of them registered his presence. Kazik didn't miss the way Gisela's face lit up as she covered her mouth, giggling at whatever Aleksey had said that couldn't be *that* funny.

She really did flirt with everybody, didn't she? Kazik wasn't special. And Aleksey . . . Kazik hadn't expected him to make the first move. He hadn't expected Aleksey to make any move at all.

Kazik's stomach twisted with something . . . He wasn't sure what he was feeling. He had the sudden mad urge to throw his body between them like a shield. Really, what was he doing, agreeing to set Aleksey up with a demon? A dead girl. A love-starved thing masquerading as a human.

It was wrong.

It was *unnatural.*

In his cousin's straw hat, with her damp hair neatly braided and her feet tucked into borrowed shoes, Gisela looked like she belonged here, but she wasn't an ordinary sixteen-year-old girl dropping by for a visit, as much as she might want to be.

This shouldn't have been happening. Alarm bells should've been ringing. Kazik should've been in fight mode. He should have had a consecrated knife pressed to her throat and his prayer beads binding her wrists.

So what if she'd shown a flash of vulnerability last night?

So what if they had a deal?

So what if she only wanted a kiss because she was desperate to return home to her little brother?

The thought sobered him.

Gisela hadn't asked for this either, and if a spirit *he* had failed to destroy had somehow had a hand in her death, then . . . then he owed Gisela his help.

"Kazik!" Gisela called, catching sight of him. She was at his side in an instant, sweeping a deathly cold arm around his shoulders in a move too fast to counter.

Damn her inhuman reflexes.

"You're just in time," Aleksey said, holding out a soft round bun filled with sweet cheese curd and sprinkled with crumble. It was wrapped in a square of paper. "We got you something. Gisela thought you might be hungry."

"She—what?"

"You don't eat enough," Gisela scolded, stealing the brown

paper bag from Mrs. Mróz and peering inside. "Are these the magic altar candles? Are you finished running errands?"

"Almost." Kazik took the offered sweet-cheese bun from Aleksey. He wasn't hungry, but he wasn't about to pass up free food, and he was oddly touched that they'd thought to buy something for him. "I need to drop by one of the guesthouses."

"The one on Hydrangea Lane?" Aleksey guessed.

Kazik's eyebrows shot up.

Aleksey faced Gisela and dropped his voice. "Everyone's saying it's haunted by a vengeful spirit. Doors slam when no one is near them. Candles snuff out unexpectedly. People say they've heard crying and footsteps running from room to room. All the guests are too spooked to stay. The owner's throwing a fit. The place has only just opened."

"And let me guess, you promised to help cast the spirit out?" Gisela leaned into Kazik's side. Her corpse-cold lips ghosted against the shell of his ear, making him shiver as she whispered, "Funny how you're so eager to help *some* people while the rest of us have practically to beg you."

Because, of course, that was what she was concerned about.

"That's because—" he hissed back, his mouth full of pastry.

"How are you going to handle this if you can't even, *you know*?"

Kazik bristled.

"Everything all right?" Aleksey asked.

Kazik and Gisela jumped.

Aleksey grinned. "You want to go look at the place? It's only a short walk from here." He didn't look to see if they were following before he started shouldering through the crowd.

Gisela raced after him, still clutching the bag of candles to her chest. "You believe in spirits, don't you? Kazik told me."

"He told you that too?" Aleksey raised an eyebrow at Kazik. "How often *do* you two talk about me?"

Kazik shoved more sweet-cheese bun into his mouth so he wouldn't have to answer.

"I don't have Kazik's holy gifts," Aleksey said. "But I always thought there must be some truth in the stories that the old folk tell. And then I got really sick last spring. I've been able to see spirits since then."

"You have?" Kazik couldn't keep the shock from his voice. He barely knew anyone his age who could. There was another boy, in a village several hours north, but his grandmother was a healer like Kazik's had been.

"They say it can happen after a brush with death," Aleksey said.

Kazik hadn't realized Aleksey had been that ill. He read the worry on Gisela's face; Aleksey really would be hard to fool. Had he noticed anything odd about her already?

They turned down a side street and then another and another, taking a twisting route past a churchyard and the small corner store where Kazik's grandfather used to send him to buy cigarettes. Gisela and Aleksey started to theorize about what manner of creature might be haunting the guesthouse.

"It could be licho," Gisela said, referring to a demon that brought misfortune upon a household.

"Or a poltergeist," Aleksey suggested. "Some of the guest-houses here are so old, their rooms come with their own ghosts."

"It could be a cranky kikimora." A fearsome female house spirit. "Or—"

"Or it could just be the gurgling of hot water pipes or the wind making noise," Kazik finished. "Old houses creak." Half the time that was all these cases amounted to.

"Oh, but where's the fun in that?" Aleksey glanced sideways at Gisela. "You know an awful lot about spirits too."

Gisela's gaze flickered to Kazik in panic.

Kazik manfully resisted the temptation to roll his eyes. "I've told her a lot," he said, coming to her rescue.

Aleksey smiled.

It didn't take long to reach their destination. Brilliant pink, blue, and purple hydrangea bushes bloomed on either side of the eponymous lane. It was quieter here after the crush and bustle of the market. There was only the gentle patter of their footsteps and a distant warble of birdsong.

At the very end of the road stood a grand old house clad in slatted wood with a peaked roof, bay windows, and a spacious front porch held up by carved pillars. During the war, most of Leśna Woda's large residences had been converted into convalescent and military hospitals. Now they just functioned as boutique guesthouses for wealthy tourists.

"It doesn't look like anything out of the ordinary," Aleksey commented.

Kazik crumpled the sweet-cheese bun's paper wrapping into a ball and shoved it in his pocket. He turned his focus inward, to where that spark of divine fire normally waited and felt . . . his magic sputter like a dying flame.

This was driving him crazy.

Gisela tilted her head at him in question.

Kazik avoided eye contact. He shook the tension from his shoulders, annoyed at himself for feeling so on edge. He wasn't totally powerless. Even if something was haunting this place, he could still defend himself, if less effectively. He reached for the medallion around his neck, drawing strength from it. "I'm going to take a quick look inside. Stay here."

18

PETALS RED AS BLOOD

GISELA

IF KAZIK THOUGHT GISELA wasn't going to take advantage of this situation, he was an idiot. Venturing into a potentially dangerous, purportedly haunted house gave her the *perfect* opportunity to shriek and throw herself into Aleksey's arms in fright if things got scary. Like hell they were staying outside.

Seizing Aleksey's sleeve and tugging him into motion, she hurried up the front steps and slipped silently into the guesthouse after Kazik. The front door swung shut behind them with an echoing crash. Gisela jumped.

Kazik spun around. "What do you think you're doing?"

"What do you mean? We can't let you walk into this alone, right, Aleksey?"

"Definitely not," Aleksey said. "Friends watch out for one another."

Gisela dumped the bag of candles beside a hatstand in the shadowy foyer.

"I've never been inside a haunted house before," Aleksey said, turning in a circle, taking in their surroundings: the marble floor, the crystal chandelier hanging like a spider overhead, the ornate staircase curving upward, leading to more floors upstairs. "How do you think we lure the spirit out? Should we speak with the owner first?"

Kazik caught Gisela's elbow, digging his fingers into her forearm hard enough to bruise. He lowered his voice. "This isn't a game. If there's really something in here, someone could get hurt."

"Aw, are you worried about me?"

"I'm not talking about you. I know you can handle yourself."

Gisela was oddly flattered.

"I'm talking about Aleksey," Kazik said. "You of all people should know what a malevolent spirit can do to an ordinary human."

"So? I'll keep him safe." Gisela reached into her pocket for her hair comb—and found it empty. Because, *of course*, wretched Wojciech had confiscated her comb back at the bathhouse. She was as disadvantaged as Kazik was without his holy magic right now.

A sliver of doubt pierced her confidence. But it wasn't like she was completely helpless, and she couldn't let this chance slip through her fingers. She wouldn't have been able to use her comb in front of Aleksey anyway without revealing herself.

"It's not fun unless there's a *little* bit of danger," she told Kazik with a smirk guaranteed to incense him. "And this spirit has only been scaring people, right? You didn't say it had actually harmed anybody."

They'd be fine. Hopefully.

“Hello?” Aleksey’s voice carried back to them. “We’ve come about the ghost.” He was moving toward a stretch of hallway on their left.

Wrenching her arm free, Gisela chased him. Kazik was forced to follow.

“Did the owner say they’d be home?” Aleksey asked him.

“The front door wasn’t locked,” Kazik said grimly.

Gisela wasn’t sure if it was her imagination, but she swore she could almost feel a hostile chill emanating from the walls as they ventured deeper into the guesthouse. It was as though the building itself were not pleased to have visitors.

They passed a fancy office and a private library, then peered into a bedroom, a bathroom with a massive claw-foot tub, and a sitting room with a glossy black piano.

The sight made Gisela think of her little brother and the lessons they’d taken together, the two of them sliding their hands over the cold ivory keys as they sat side by side on the piano bench.

Unconsciously, she drifted toward the instrument.

The chill in the air grew, seeming to leak from the walls like mist, seething with hostility. Gisela felt something whisper against the back of her neck, but when she whirled around, the space behind her was empty. There was no one there.

Aleksey and Kazik stared at her from the doorway.

“Did you feel that?” she said.

“Feel what?” Kazik said.

A ripple of unease chased down Gisela’s spine. Her skin prickled with goose bumps. “Nothing.”

She turned, tailing them out the door. They made their way upstairs to the second floor, wandering through more rooms that seemed just a little too dark now, too full of shadows and places for someone or something to hide.

There was still no sign of the guesthouse's owner. Most of the curtains were drawn, and some of the furniture was covered by sheets. Empty room after empty room conjured a sense of melancholy.

Kazik stopped suddenly and cursed beneath his breath.

"You lost it too?" Aleksey asked quietly.

"Lost what?" Gisela said. "Were you following something?"

"I thought I could sense something." Aleksey glanced over his shoulder.

"Stay close," Kazik warned. "And keep quiet." He moved; they followed.

Edging closer to Aleksey, Gisela reminded herself that she was, or should be, the scariest thing in here, even without her hair comb. She had to focus on the real task at hand. Namely, finding a way to win Aleksey over.

The creak of a floorboard made her halt midstep.

All three of them tensed. The ensuing silence was that of an indrawn breath, the pause before a scream. Gisela watched Kazik draw a vial of holy water from his pocket.

Rounding another corner, they entered a musty book-lined study with an open fireplace and a solid mahogany desk. Dust danced in a fall of pale sunshine spilling through a gap between the curtains. The air smelled of wood polish and old leather. Gisela snuck a glance at Aleksey out of the corner of her eye, only to catch him doing the exact same thing—sneaking a curious sideways glance at her.

Gisela blinked. So did Aleksey.

A sudden loud *bang* sounded overhead.

Aleksey's head snapped up. Gisela leapt three feet in the air but still managed to seize her chance, letting out a fake-terrified shriek as she grabbed his hand.

Aleksey nearly jumped out of his skin. He yanked his hand free and grabbed at Kazik, who let out a shout like he was being murdered.

"Mother of God! Don't just suddenly grab—"

"Your hand—" Aleksey gasped at Gisela. "It's like *ice*. I thought you were—"

The ghost, Gisela finished silently. She wanted to sink through the floor. It was just like when she'd touched Kazik and he'd flinched and recoiled in horror. How stupid she'd been to think she could hold hands like an ordinary person.

"Stay right here," Kazik ordered breathlessly, racing out of the study, likely going after whatever had made the noise.

Aleksey spun, staring after him.

"Don't worry," Gisela said quickly. "He's pretty deadly with a vial of holy water."

She was speaking from experience. If anything, Kazik was more of a danger to whatever dark presence was haunting the house than it was to him. At least . . . he should have been. But his magic had failed the past two times he'd gotten into a fight with a spirit, with her. Gisela's mind, always so helpful in these situations, kindly conjured images of all the possible dangers he might face.

Wait, what was wrong with her? This was Kazik she was thinking about. Leśna Woda's brooding exorcist. The bane of her existence. Since when did she give a damn what happened to him?

Though it would be terribly inconvenient, if he was gobbled up by some other spirit before he could finish playing matchmaker for her. It would throw off all her plans. He was no good to her dead. But she couldn't just abandon Aleksey and go after him. And what if *she* got caught alone? She didn't have her comb to defend herself with.

"Oh, I'm not worried," Aleksey said, drawing her from her mental spiral. "I know how powerful Kazik is when he gets serious. He has even more spiritual power than his grandmother, and he doesn't let his guard down. Have you noticed how he never takes off all those protections? He wears that saintly medallion and carries his prayer beads with him even when he visits the bathhouse."

Gisela had noticed. It wasn't surprising. That was Kazik all over—paranoid and overly cautious. And it made sense; if he annoyed her and her fellow water spirits, he was bound to have made other enemies. He was probably surrounded by creatures eager to drink up the drops of divine power in his blood.

"Have you ever seen him take his medallion off?" Aleksey asked.

"Never," Gisela said. "He even wears it to bed."

Aleksey looked at her and kept looking, until she started to feel self-conscious. The intensity of his stare made her stomach swoop. When he spoke again, there was a hint of reluctant admiration in his voice—and more than a trace of mischief. "You keep saying you're just friends, but . . ."

Gisela's eyes widened as she played back what she'd said. "I didn't mean it like that! I've just seen him in his pajamas."

Aleksey hummed, clearly unconvinced. Or maybe he was just enjoying teasing her, watching her get flustered.

"It's not what you think. He's just helping me."

The teasing smile slipped off Aleksey's face. "Helping you? Why would he help *you*?"

Gisela didn't have a chance to reply because a sudden blood-curdling scream rang through the guesthouse. She startled, her elbow clipping and knocking a vase of flowers off a shelf.

"Shit!" Gisela lunged for the vase as it hit the carpet and rolled under the study's fancy mahogany desk.

"That came from upstairs," Aleksey said. "We need—"

Gisela stared into the darkness beneath the desk.

Something stared back. Two eyes that glowed like scorching red-hot embers. The scream ripped from *her* throat this time as she stumbled back into Aleksey.

A howl of wind rushed through the room, tearing the straw hat from her head. The curtains billowed. The door slammed open and closed. Loose papers and fountain pens swept off the desk.

Gisela leapt back as a second vase hurtled through the air. Porcelain shattered to shards against the wall to her left. A howling voice whispered at the edge of her hearing, muttering indistinctly, growing louder, surging until she could make out the words: *Get! Out!*

Get out, get out, get out, get out!

Gisela clapped her hands over her ears, but the voice reverberated inside her head. The house itself was trembling. The windows rattled in their frames. What kind of spirit was this? And where the hell was Kazik when she needed him?

Something flashed to her right.

A heavy bronze candlestick flung itself off the mantel above the fireplace, flying toward their heads.

Gisela moved with unearthly speed, grasping Aleksey and diving out of the way just in time, pulling him with her. The candlestick clipped the edge of her temple. Stars danced across her vision in an explosion of pain. An ordinary human girl would've collapsed to the floor in agony. She gritted her teeth, blinking back tears. But better it hit her. She healed far faster than any mortal did. Without her comb, the best thing she could do right now was use her body as a shield.

She seized Aleksey again, yanking him down with her as heavy books hurtled off the study's shelves. He stared at her, his beautiful eyes wide with shock. Guilt knifed through her. Kazik had been right. She should never have brought him in here.

The shadows thickened, an unnatural night falling over the room.

Gisela shot to her feet, backing up, shoving Aleksey behind her, looking around in desperation.

She had to do something.

She couldn't conjure a flood. Shape-shifting into a fish or frog wouldn't help. She could try singing, try bewitching whatever was attacking them with a water nymph's sweet song, but if she did that, she'd expose herself. Aleksey would know the truth of what she was, know she wasn't human but something else.

A dead thing.

A girl crawled out of a watery grave.

She could wave any chance of getting a kiss from him goodbye.

A hiss of air. A fire poker speared past her ear, past Aleksey. Its sharp iron point embedded itself in the wall. That decided her. Even if he fled from her in revulsion, she couldn't just stand here and do nothing. If she had to reveal herself to keep him safe, then she would. She'd told Kazik she wouldn't let anything happen to Aleksey.

Heart sinking, Gisela sucked in a breath and whirled to face the desk and whatever was beneath it. Soft, ethereal notes bubbled up her throat.

"Gisela!" Aleksey shouted. "Look out—"

With a ferocious crackling roar, a fire flared to life in the hearth. A rush of flame rippled toward her, filling her vision. It moved too fast. She couldn't dodge.

Gisela squeezed her eyes shut.

Heat licked her face. But flames failed to engulf her body. An arm encircled her waist from behind, yanking her back against a firm chest.

She opened her eyes with a gasp. An explosion of bloodred petals filled the air, swirling around her and Aleksey in a protective whirlwind, shielding them, holding the flames at bay. A hundred thousand bloodred petals spun in a violent storm with the two of them at its center.

An anguished wail rent the air.

What . . . what was this?

Smoke curled from the scorched edges of countless petals. Breathing in, Gisela could smell the forest, a scent sweet and dark and earthy. A memory jarred loose, floating to the surface:

A rain of red petals. A clearing circled by towering trees. Heavy branches creaking in the wind. A pained cry and . . . and a golden-haired figure hunched over in the grass.

Aleksey's grip around Gisela's waist tightened, bringing her back to herself, to the present. She blinked rapidly, her head swimming. The strange images faded, slipping away even as she strained her mind to catch them.

"I think it's a domowik," Aleksey said, speaking close to her ear, making her shiver. "A powerful one."

A domowik? Gisela struggled to think. A *house spirit*? She didn't know much about them other than that they could mend things and sometimes did chores. According to her great-aunt . . . "Aren't they supposed to be benevolent toward humans?"

"They are. But I don't think it likes us."

Gisela scowled, her temper fraying.

But why the petals? She knew the creature must've conjured them because she certainly hadn't—water nymphs didn't have that kind of magic—and Aleksey was human. So why would the spirit shield them from its own attack?

It must've had a change of heart at the very last second. Or perhaps it was toying with them. So many spirits did take joy in messing with mortals.

A crash. Her gaze snapped toward the sound; through the

fall and whirl of petals, she could just make out a shadow. A silhouette. A small, child-sized figure cowering against a bookcase.

Aleksey started to say something, but Gisela was already moving. Anger drove her forward; this little demon had very nearly incinerated her. It had almost forced her to expose herself.

She pounced with unnatural speed, seizing the creature by the front of its sooty vest before it could fight back. It was of more or less human form, but hairier, and two small pointed horns poked from its forehead. Its bushy fire-red beard and grandfatherly looks reminded her of the bathhouse spirit.

All at once, the whirlwind dispersed and the shadows lifted, petals fluttering across the rug like bloodstained snow, most disappearing when they touched the floor.

Gisela hoisted the diminutive creature into the air. Red eyes met red eyes. In a low voice, she hissed, "*Big* mistake. You're going to regret attacking us."

A floorboard creaked. The creature shot a panicked glance over her shoulder at Aleksey. The color drained from its ruddy face.

Aleksey smiled with all his teeth. "What she said."

His words were punctuated by the violent crash of the study door flinging wide open. Kazik tumbled back into the room, looking equally disheveled and furious. A blinding flare of light emanated from the silver medallion hanging from his neck.

Instinctively, Gisela cringed away from the radiance, releasing her grip on their assailant. She backed up, the heel of her sandal catching on the edge of the rug. She stumbled and would've fallen if Aleksey hadn't reacted, sweeping an arm around her waist again to steady her, only this time he lost his balance too, so they went down together.

He landed on his back with a hiss, Gisela sprawled across his chest. Their foreheads knocked together. When she lifted her face, wincing, she froze, finding his lips a mere whisper away from hers. Her breath hitched.

So close!

She could feel his hands on the small of her back and the solid warmth of his body beneath hers, see her own startled face reflected in that bewitching two-colored gaze.

Could he see her just as clearly? There was no straw hat to shade her eyes. Wild strands of hair were escaping from her damp braid. Did he see a monster when he looked at her? Could he feel the deathly chill emanating from her skin?

There was a sharp inhale from across the room.

Panicking, Gisela pushed herself up, sitting back on Aleksey's waist. The sound had come from Kazik. He looked from her to Aleksey and back again, his expression unreadable. Then his gaze landed on the stocky little figure she'd been threatening.

He stalked forward with purpose.

The appearance of Leśna Woda's famous exorcist was the final straw. All the fight went out of the creature. It deflated like a pricked balloon. With a pitiful wail, it cast itself face down on the carpet and cried, "Have mercy!"

19

THE MASTER OF THE HOUSE

KAZIK

THE CULPRIT WAS A domowik. A house spirit. They took the form of tiny people or small animals like cats and snakes, and they made their homes beneath thresholds and behind stoves, in the dark corners of kitchens and attics. This one had assumed the guise of a little grandfatherly man. He wore a sooty black vest and had a long, fire-red beard.

"Forgive me!" he wailed, groveling at Kazik's feet. "I sensed an evil presence enter the house. I didn't know you were a powerful witch with demon servants. Don't let them eat me!"

Evil presence? Demon servants? Kazik cast an alarmed glance sideways. The creature could only be referring to Gisela. House spirits had keen senses, could identify other spirits at sight, and were protective by nature. They guarded the home from outside forces, sometimes even warning their chosen family of impending danger.

Had Gisela blown her cover somehow? Did Aleksey know what she was now? He didn't look distressed nor disgusted nor shocked.

No. They'd looked quite *cozy* together if that almost kiss was anything to go by.

Kazik couldn't decide if he was more annoyed at Gisela for directing her charms at Aleksey while all this was happening—while *Kazik* had been running in panicked circles through the guesthouse—or at Aleksey for falling for them. She was right: a little danger was all it took to get him interested.

To hell with them both. They deserved each other. Kazik couldn't believe he'd actually worried something bad might've happened to them. He'd even thought *they* might've been equally worried about him.

"I'm not a witch," he told the domowik with a scowl. "And these two aren't my servants. They're my—" He bit the word out like it tasted bad: "Friends. They're not demons."

The domowik looked like he wanted to argue.

Kazik leveled him with a flat stare. "I don't want to hear another word against them." If Gisela's secret *was* safe, it was best to keep the spirit's mouth shut about her true nature. "They're not going to eat you."

"Oh, I don't know," Aleksey said, pushing to his feet and dusting off his clothes. There was an uncharacteristic edge to his voice. His usual cheery tone was entirely absent. It sent a not-unpleasant shiver down Kazik's spine. "He did attack us."

"He did." Gisela stalked closer, looking murderous.

"Gisela—" Kazik cautioned.

"Relax, I'm just going to bruise him a little."

"Break a few bones," Aleksey added, cracking his knuckles. "I'll hold him down, Gisela, if you'd like to do the honors?"

Kazik raised his eyes to Heaven. Saints above, did Aleksey, a mere mortal with no divine powers, really think he could hurt a spirit? Was he trying to show off in front of Gisela?

In front of Kazik?

"You said they wouldn't hurt me!" The domowik's panicked gaze jumped from Aleksey to Kazik.

"He didn't say that," Gisela corrected. "He said we wouldn't *eat* you. Why are you protecting him, Kazik? He's clearly the one who's been terrorizing all the guests. He nearly incinerated us! He trapped me and Aleksey in a whirlwind of petals." She bent down and picked a blackened petal off the rug. It disintegrated to ash between her fingers.

Kazik's brow furrowed. House spirits worked hearth-and-home-related magic. They could control fire and manipulate the space and objects within their abode, turning hallways into labyrinths, causing the temperature to drop, making belongings move, forcing food to sour and rot. But, as far as he knew, they had no power over plants. It was the forest spirits who wielded petals and leaves as weapons.

Was Gisela exaggerating? The only petals he could see looked like they'd come from the shattered vases of flowers strewn across the floor. The whole study was a mess—books and pens and papers scattered everywhere. He didn't have time to ruminate further, however, because the domowik's temper sparked. The fireplace spat flames.

"The demon's lying! They're the ones who attacked me!"

"Because you attacked us first!" Gisela cut in.

Aleksey came to stand beside Kazik. The domowik shrank back.

"Can you really believe anything he says?" Aleksey asked. "House spirits are manipulative creatures. You should hurry and exorcise him."

"E-exorcise?!" the domowik stuttered. "You're the exorcist?"

"The one and only," Gisela said.

Strangely, Kazik was not as pleased by this display of fear as he'd usually be. In the past he'd felt righteous, justified, when confronting troublesome spirits. He'd savored the giddy rush of power he felt when he removed them from the world, even though, deep down, he knew it was sinfully wrong to feel anything like elation when taking a life.

Right now he just felt oddly irritated.

Steadying himself with a deep breath, he crouched so that he was on eye level with the domowik. He spoke in a voice low enough that only the two of them could hear. "What did I just say about calling my friend a demon? I'm aware of her true nature, and I don't care to hear anything more about it." Clearing his throat, he spoke at a normal volume. "Are you the one who's been scaring away all the guests?"

It made no sense. House spirits weren't malevolent by nature. They liked to be helpful and would often creep out at night when no one was watching to clear away dirty dishes, chop wood, and dust away cobwebs. They brought good luck to a home and could improve a family's fortune.

Sometimes literally.

There was a particularly enterprising barn spirit who lived on a farm just outside town; the little demon was known to pilfer grain and hay from neighboring estates to feed its own family's animals. Kazik's grandfather had told him tales of other household spirits stealing coins and chickens when their families were in need. But he'd never heard of a domowik deliberately sabotaging their family's business.

Though, as well as lacking morals, spirits were temperamental and easily angered. They often caused mischief if they felt they'd been slighted or disrespected.

"Has your family done something to upset you?" Kazik asked.

The flames in the hearth calmed; the question seemed to appease the domowik. Maybe because it was a question, an attempt to understand, not an accusation nor a threat.

The creature puffed out his chest to make himself look bigger. "My family—the family are not at home at present. I am guarding the house until they return. I've scared away all the intruders."

"Intruders? The people coming here are *guests*. Mr. Haase told me so," Kazik said, referring to the guesthouse's owner.

"This house doesn't belong to him. He has no right to invite people in. This house belongs to Emilia and the children."

Kazik's frown deepened. "Are you talking about the family who used to own this place, before it was sold?"

"Why should the house be sold?" The domowik crossed his hairy arms over his chest. "I wasn't consulted! What's so wrong with living here? There's no reason to leave."

Some people believed domowiki were ancestor spirits, souls come back to watch over their descendants. Right now, Kazik could believe it. The little creature sounded exactly like somebody's grouchy old grandfather.

"Ah," Aleksey said. "I think I understand."

Kazik and Gisela turned to look at him.

"They left without you, didn't they? Emilia's children didn't ask you to come with them when they sold the house and moved away. That's why you're still here causing trouble, isn't it? Because your human family abandoned you."

"Oh . . ." Gisela said softly.

The domowik's lips pulled back in a snarl, but his shoulders trembled. "They'll come back for me. They won't forget. Emilia's put out a bowl of honey and groats and cream for me every night since she was a girl."

Which would have been a very long time ago. Emilia, or Mrs. Novak, as Kazik had known her, had been even older than his grandmother. No wonder the creature was so strong—house spirits were strengthened by mortal offerings and gifts; without them they weakened and eventually faded out of existence.

Kazik was surprised this one hadn't started to weaken and fade. "Emilia passed away," he said gently. "You know that, don't you?" That was one of the reasons her children had sold the place. Neither of her sons had wanted to live in such a large house.

The fire in the hearth blackened down to mournful embers. The domowik fisted his hands in his beard. "I tried to tell them she was ill, but the children could not see or hear me." He suddenly looked close to tears.

It was unnerving. Spirits weren't supposed to feel things like humans did. They were incapable of true emotion. They were malevolent beings, creatures of malice and mischief and bloodlust.

A feeling of wrongness welled up inside Kazik. He straightened from his crouch so he could look down on the domowik, so he could feel more in control. He had to keep it together. It was just the healer in him. He'd always hated seeing anyone in pain.

"Were you hoping," he asked, having a sudden epiphany, "that if you chased away the new owner of the house and his guests, your old family would return?"

The domowik was quiet.

Kazik removed his glasses and pinched the bridge of his nose. Why did spirits always have to go about things in the most chaotic manner?

"They deserved it," the domowik blustered. "They were bad guests! They trekked mud on the carpets. They cursed and smoked cigarettes in the library."

"You can't stay here if you're going to cause trouble," Kazik said, replacing his glasses. "You're terrorizing innocent people." Ordinary people. Powerless humans, whom Kazik had a duty to protect. "If you won't leave this place willingly, then . . ." He hesitated.

"Kazik will have to exorcise you," Aleksey finished.

If the saints granted him that power, Kazik thought uneasily.

The domowik's ember-red eyes were round with fear. Kazik half wished he would attack them again so he could viscerally remind himself the creature was a danger. A threat that needed to be eliminated.

It was hard to look at the little creature and see a threat. The domowik's head barely came up to their knees.

Gisela crouched down this time. "Do you have somewhere you can go?" she asked softly.

The house spirit tugged on his beard. Kazik wondered how long he'd lived here, watching over the family. The house had to be at least a hundred years old.

"You'll fade away if you remain," Aleksey said. "With no one to leave you offerings."

The domowik made a protesting noise, but Gisela nodded. "Kazik will help reunite you with your family."

Kazik's head snapped toward her. "I'll what?"

Aleksey and the domowik gaped at Gisela.

"You want him to stop causing trouble here, right?" she said to Kazik. "So find out where Emilia's children moved to and tell them they can't just leave him behind. He's been guarding the house for them, Kazik. He's been waiting for them to return all this time."

Of course, she'd latch on to that. Gisela knew what it was like to wait for family that never came home—so did Kazik. He knew that gutting sense of abandonment. How many hours had he spent waiting for his mother after she'd left him with his grandparents? How many times had he insisted she was definitely coming back for him?

That shouldn't matter. He shouldn't care. And he *didn't*.

"That's none of my concern," he said. "Five minutes ago, you were literally threatening to break his bones."

"That was before I knew the whole story." Gisela faced the domowik. "Don't worry," she told him. "Kazik has to help anyone who comes to him. It's a rule."

"You know it doesn't count if the person asking isn't human."

"He's helping me," Gisela continued, deliberately ignoring him. "He'll help you too. He just likes to complain."

Glaring at Gisela, Kazik caught Aleksey watching them both curiously from the corner of his eye. He really didn't need this in his life.

But it *was* only a domowik. It wasn't like he would be agreeing to help a bloodsucking strzyga or, worse, a bies. And if he did try to exorcise the creature now and failed and word got out . . . Not to mention how mortifying it would be to fail in front of Aleksey.

"Fine," he relented, already knowing this wouldn't, *couldn't*, end well for him. "We'll try it your way." And if it didn't work out, he'd exorcise the creature privately.

Something akin to shock flashed across Aleksey's face, there and then gone so fast, Kazik might only have imagined it.

Gisela shot the domowik a triumphant grin. "See, Grandfather? What did I tell you? Nothing to worry about. Isn't Kazik kind? Doesn't he have a heart of gold?"

The beginnings of a fresh migraine pounded behind Kazik's eyes.

"Leave it all to us," Gisela said. "We'll take care of you."

20

YOUR TYPE

GISELA

LIKE ANYTHING INVOLVING SPIRITS, reuniting the domowik with his family turned out to be easier said than done.

For one thing, Gisela learned that there was a whole ritual for transferring a house spirit from one abode to another. Despite her year here, and all those hours spent listening to her great-aunt's tales, there was still a lot she didn't know about spirits. The head of the family, Kazik told her, was supposed to offer the domowik bread and salt and formally invite him to accompany the family when they moved. Once he'd accepted the invitation, embers from the hearth of the old house had to be carried into the new so that the spirit would know where to materialize.

And on top of that, they soon discovered that both of Emilia's sons had moved abroad for work.

Forced to improvise, they ended up bringing the little creature—whom Gisela had taken to calling *Domek*—into Kazik's home temporarily, only for Domek to grumble that the kitchen was too small and Kazik was a terrible housekeeper.

"Shouldn't you be grateful we're even doing this for you?" Gisela pointed out. But she didn't mind his grumbling too much because Aleksey had insisted on helping too, and all this meant she had an excuse to cozy up to him some more.

It became a group project. They investigated. They brainstormed solutions. She and Aleksey also invaded Kazik's house so they wouldn't have to stop talking. Kazik was, after all, the only one of them who lived alone. Aleksey lived with his mother, and it wasn't as if Gisela could drag the boys down into the depths of the river to visit the Crystal Palace. Wojciech would have a breakdown.

The days slipped by, one day melting into two, two days blurring into two weeks. When they weren't trying to track down other relatives for Domek to stay with, they wandered through Leśna Woda's lush green parks and gardens and ate ice cream. They lay in the grass, picking out shapes in the clouds, and made fun of the spa guests tasting the spring waters from the decorative taps and drinking fountains, laughing at the faces they made at the strong salty flavors.

At times like that, it was far too easy to forget she was doing this solely so she could leave. The truth was she'd missed out on a lot of things growing up because she was always busy caring for Hugo. Things just like this. Mindlessly spending hours with friends or doing something fun with a boy or girl she liked. The few times Gisela had been asked out on a date, she'd gotten weird looks because she'd brought Hugo along too, but it wasn't like she could've left him at home alone.

It was nice being able to do things by herself. For herself.

She and Aleksey even tagged along when Kazik picked magical herbs in the forest, and afterward all three of them foraged for wild berries until their fingers were stained and sticky from juice, until their mouths were as violet tinged as hers without lipstick.

The only really frustrating thing was that she kept having to slip away at the most inopportune moments, returning to the river for a quick dip or ducking into a bathhouse to keep herself from drying out.

Gisela cursed as she slipped behind a tree now to use the new shell-shaped hair comb she'd managed to sneak from the enchanted chest in the palace, conjuring water and letting it drip from the amber-gold tines to soak the strands of her waist-length hair.

The weather was divine today. The unforgiving sun beamed down from a clear milky-blue sky. The air, as always, was laced with the honeyed scent of wildflowers.

Peeking around the tree, Gisela reassured herself that Aleksey was still busy helping Kazik clean the old forest shrine. She still caught him shooting her puzzled glances from time to time when he thought she wasn't looking.

But who *wouldn't* be puzzled by her constant disappearances and awkward excuses? Not to mention what he may or may not have noticed about her when they were up close and personal after that accidental near kiss.

Sometimes, she was almost sure he did suspect something. Maybe he was just too polite to say anything, or maybe he assumed she wasn't a threat because she was Kazik's friend? Maybe he *had* seen her for what she was and didn't care?

Was that too much to hope for?

Gisela winced as the comb snagged in a tangle. She swept a section of hair over her shoulder and tensed as the tree branches rustled overhead.

"So that's your type," someone whispered in a high-pitched voice.

Gisela looked up. Two—no, three—ghoulish faces peered down at her through the leaves. Three pairs of crimson eyes winked like rubies in the sunlight.

"Go away!" Gisela mouthed silently, making a frantic shooing motion with her comb.

It had the exact opposite effect.

Beaming, Miray swung down from her branch. A sheepish Zamira followed her, crawling down the trunk like a bug. Yulia slid down last in a much more dignified fashion. Gisela briefly wondered where Clara and Nina-Marie were and whether Tamara was with them. She hoped someone was looking after her.

All four water nymphs crowded together behind the tree, trying to keep hidden. It was fortunate this particular tree was so large; its trunk was thrice Gisela's width and more than double her height.

"The old toad sent you to spy on me, didn't he?" she said.

Miray slung an arm around her shoulders. "Wojciech's freaking out because you didn't come home again. He sent us to check on you."

A familiar mix of exasperation and warmth filled Gisela's chest. Great-Aunt Zela had told her that while many spirits lived alone, the water goblin was a creature who cared deeply for his chosen family. But honestly, she wasn't a child in need of constant supervision. She'd been looking after herself and her brother since she was ten.

She'd stayed overnight at Kazik's house. They'd had another one of their midnight chats—despite his protests, it was clear Kazik was just dying to complain and gossip with someone.

So she'd been safe. She hadn't even thought to let Wojciech know where she was.

Her father had never worried like this. He probably wouldn't even have noticed her absence. Gisela wondered if this was what it was like to have an overprotective older brother or a parent who genuinely cared about her well-being.

It wasn't an entirely awful feeling.

"And," Miray added, peering around the tree trunk at Aleksey and Kazik, "we wanted to get a look at your newest crush. We're all rooting for you. Well, except Yulia. But she's just jealous."

"Don't put more idiotic ideas in the idiot's head," Yulia said.

"I'm not an idiot," Gisela snapped.

"I want to see the boy too!" Zamira hopped on tiptoe, trying to see past Miray's and Yulia's shoulders. She tipped so far forward that Gisela had to snatch hold of her white dress to keep her from toppling over and exposing them all.

"*Careful!*" Gisela said.

"What do you think they're saying?"

"Shh! They'll hear you, idiot."

Miray nudged Gisela. "So, which one is it?"

"The blond one," Gisela said shyly. In the sun, Aleksey's honey-hued hair looked like it had been spun out of light. He was dressed in corduroy trousers and a loose linen shirt that laced closed at the collar.

Miray's gaze raked up and down his tall, broad-shouldered frame. She must've liked what she saw, because she hummed in approval.

"Oh, he *is* handsome!" Zamira elbowed Yulia. "What do you think?"

"Why do I feel this strange need to remind you that I don't like boys?"

Zamira pursed her lips. "You don't need to be attracted to someone to acknowledge that they're objectively good-looking."

"Forget it," Miray said. "You know how Yulia hates it when we gush over boys."

"I don't hate it," Yulia retorted. "I just don't see what's so great about them." She turned her back to Miray, crossed her arms, and muttered under her breath to Gisela, "Guess you decided you do like boys better after all, huh?"

Gisela flinched. The words twisted like a knife in an open wound. It wasn't like she hadn't heard comments like that before, from other girls back home. From other girls who liked girls.

They had a real talent for making her feel small, for making her feel terribly guilty and like she needed to apologize for the part of her that liked boys.

"I'm not going to defend my sexuality to you," Gisela said, more hurt than she was willing to let on. "Again." She'd defended herself too many times in the past, to Yulia and others, and she was tired of it. "If you don't want to look at boys, you can go inflict your presence on Nina-Marie or Clara or something."

"Where *are* the lovebirds?" Zamira asked.

"Hooking up somewhere." Miray grinned. "They can't keep their hands off each other. That, or they're down at the river traumatizing more tourists. It's Nina-Marie's favorite game."

Gisela could picture that easily enough: Nina-Marie swimming under the little blue rowboats the tourists took out on the water, dragging her nails along the hulls until they screamed in terror, while Clara sat in the grass with a book in her lap, watching her girlfriend with an indulgent smile.

Uneasiness pinched Gisela. "Is Tamara with them?"

"How should we know?" Yulia said. "Aren't *you* the one who's supposed to be babysitting her?"

"She's probably with them," Miray said, before they could start bickering. "So, how's it going with the boy? Has he kissed you yet?"

"Would she be hiding behind a tree desperately drenching her hair with water if he had?" Yulia said.

Gisela scowled and tucked her comb away. "It's going fine. Just . . ." It was annoying having to always slip away like this, and she was nervous to get too physical with Aleksey after their almost kiss and her disastrous attempt to hold his hand.

She remembered the way he'd yanked his fingers from hers in fear. In revulsion. Like he couldn't get away from her fast enough. You would think after so many rejections that one more wouldn't hurt—but it did. It always hurt.

She wouldn't make the same mistake again. She was careful not to even brush fingers with him now. It worried her though: How was she going to progress their relationship if she couldn't even touch him?

She told the girls, and they immediately rushed to console her.

"Cold hands feel nice when it's warm like this," Zamira said. "They're nicer to hold than hot and sweaty hands."

"Just lie and tell him you have bad circulation," Miray suggested. "You could even try wearing gloves."

"Because *that's* not suspicious," Yulia said, "in summer."

"They don't have to be winter gloves," Miray said. "She could wear, like, lace gloves. We could find a really cute pair."

"Or you could try taking Wojciech's potion."

Yulia's and Miray's heads snapped toward Zamira.

She wilted a little under their combined gazes. "I mean, if you're really desperate?"

"Potion?" Gisela said blankly.

The three older rusałki seemed to be conducting a silent argument.

"He has a potion," Zamira finally blurted, despite Yulia's glare, "brewed by a powerful witch. It contains half a drop of Living Water and will restore a water nymph to life, turn her back into a human. He keeps it in a special cabinet in his chambers with all his favorite teacups."

"*He what?* What do you—" Gisela froze, holding her breath. Belatedly, she clapped a hand over her mouth and cast a wary look around the tree.

Kazik and Aleksey were so absorbed in each other that they hadn't even looked up at the sound of her exclamation. Gisela let out a relieved breath. She watched them for a moment longer, her stomach suddenly twisting with a queasy feeling she didn't fully understand. A feeling almost like jealousy—only she wasn't sure who she was jealous of. *She* would've liked to be the sole focus of Aleksey's attention, but she'd also never seen Kazik look so captivated.

It was probably just the strange sight of him deigning to talk to another human being.

Gisela shook herself. She had more important things to focus on, like the secrets a certain traitorous water goblin had been keeping from her. A wave of anger swept through her. This whole time, she'd been struggling to get a kiss. Why hadn't he told her there was a cheat she could use to regain her humanity? The spring of Living Water was legendary. Everyone knew it could restore life to the dying, but the spring's location was a mystery. How had Wojciech gotten his hands on a potion like that? And why hadn't any of them told her about it before now?

She must've voiced the last question aloud because Miray replied, "Because the transformation is only temporary. The potion wears off, and when it does, you don't return to your current form. You would no longer be a water nymph. You'd be a shadow of what you are now. A ghost-thing. A shapeless, formless creature."

They all took a moment to digest this.

"Aren't we already ghosts though?" Zamira ventured at last. "I mean, technically."

"It's different," Yulia said grimly. "You wouldn't have a physical form nor a voice. No one would be able to see you. You wouldn't be able to communicate with anyone. You'd be less than a shadow. Nothing but air. The merest whisper against someone's skin."

Despite the heat, Gisela shivered.

Miray played with the velvet ribbon she was wearing as a choker. "That's why we didn't tell you. It's safer to try and get a mortal to kiss you if you want to regain your humanity."

"But couldn't she take the potion first and then get someone to kiss her?" Zamira looked at Gisela.

"And if they *don't* kiss her before the potion wears off?" Yulia countered.

Gisela chewed on a fingernail. Her gaze drifted back to Aleksey and Kazik. Kazik turned toward the tree, rolling his shirtsleeves up to his elbows.

"Wait," Zamira said. "Isn't that—"

"The *exorcist*?" Miray finished, craning forward. "I didn't see his face clearly before. What is *he* doing here? Is he interfering again?"

Gisela blinked. Then a slow obnoxious smirk curved her lips. "Oh, him?" She twirled a strand of damp hair around her finger. "Kazik's helping me."

It was truly gratifying the way they all turned to gape at her with open mouths. Even Yulia. It was almost enough to make her momentarily forget all about Wojciech's potion.

"I've bewitched him with my beauty and wiles, and now he's playing matchmaker for me."

"No." Miray breathed. "Gisela, you demon! Seriously?"

"Oh my God!" Zamira squeezed Yulia's forearm. "You have to give us all the details. I can't believe you didn't tell us!"

"Are you actually serious?" Yulia said. Her face was like a thundercloud. "You're not making things up? You can't trust him. He's dangerous."

"Why even bother with the other boy," Miray said meditatively, "if you have the exorcist wrapped around your little finger?"

Gisela frowned in confusion. "What do you mean?"

"Have him kiss you. Kazik."

Yulia let out a strangled sound.

"Don't be stupid. No," Gisela said, even though she'd suggested as much to him herself. But that was only teasing. "It's not like that. He doesn't *like* me. He hates me. He's only helping me so that I'll go away." She tried to ignore the sudden pang in her chest. Kazik wasn't helping her because he wanted to; he was helping her because she'd begged and blackmailed him into doing so.

Zamira hummed in thought. "I think he must be sweet on you. You don't see him helping any other spirits, do you?" Her leer was a match for Miray's.

"He's helping Domek. A house spirit," Gisela protested weakly. "He's helping him to find a new home." But that, too, was because of her. Because she'd asked him, insisted. She quickly cut off that train of thought. "He's just . . . There's nothing between us. You'd understand if you knew him. It's more complicated than you think." She turned back toward the shrine, falling silent as she took in the empty clearing.

"Well, don't look now," Yulia said, "but I think your precious matchmaker has made off with the boy you're planning to kiss."

21

PLAYING CUPID

KAZIK

IT HAD BEEN A mistake letting Aleksey and Gisela tag along again today, Kazik decided, trying not to stare as Aleksey stretched his arms above his head. The hem of Aleksey's shirt hiked up, offering the world a tantalizing flash of pale skin.

Kazik tore his gaze away. *Focus,* he told himself. *Think pure thoughts.*

Pure thoughts.

He tossed a decaying bouquet into the surrounding greenery, his fingers crunching on dried petals. This was why he took pains to avoid Aleksey. He didn't trust himself around the other boy; he was too aware of Aleksey's presence, his nearness, every move he made.

Tipping his head back, Kazik stared up at the giant centuries-old linden tree casting dappled shadows over the shrine. It was a humble shrine, like so many that dotted the countryside: a small roofed wooden box housing the timeworn statue of a saint.

Kazik was only able to identify the statue as Saint Barbara by the tower she held in her palms. Each saint had a symbol with which they were depicted—a raven, a bell, a crown, a star—so they could be recognized even by those who were illiterate. Saint Barbara was one of the saints people prayed to for protection from illness. Kazik had come here with his grandmother every week to replace the flowers and tidy the votive candles and small devotional objects left as offerings. They'd sung hymns here together in early spring. This was where he'd always felt most at peace. More so than in any church or chapel. Here, on the edge of the great primeval forest, listening to the soft creak of the branches swaying overhead. Here, where the rustling of the leaves sounded like the whisper of holy words. There was something about this place that soothed his soul.

We're a forest people, his grandfather had told him once.

The sharp sound of a camera shutter startled Kazik from his reverie. He grimaced. Of late, the shrine had become more of a tourist hot spot than a place of prayer and worship, a place that drew the ill and faithful. It was marked on maps as one of the many attractions in the vicinity of the spa town, just like the ruins of the old castle on the far side of the river.

"You look like you're about to bury that tourist's body beneath the shrine," Aleksey commented, coming up alongside Kazik.

Kazik glanced sideways with a start. A breeze swirled through the trees, sweeping fallen leaves and blossoms in a circle around their ankles. It carded through Aleksey's hair, blowing unruly strands into his eyes. How it didn't block his vision was a mystery. A minor miracle.

"Wouldn't be worth the effort. You"—Kazik gestured—"have a leaf."

Aleksey reached up, trying and failing to brush the offending leaf out of his hair. Kazik's hand moved of its own accord, his fingers grazing Aleksey's temple. Aleksey's hair was surprisingly soft.

Quickly, Kazik handed the leaf to Aleksey, who twirled it by its stem.

Definitely a stupid idea to let the two of them tag along. Sweat beaded above Kazik's upper lip. Feeling self-conscious, he asked, "Don't you have somewhere else to be?"

Aleksey raised an eyebrow. "Ouch. If you want me to go, just say so."

Abruptly, Kazik realized how rude the question had sounded. "I just meant this is hardly what people do for fun."

What you *usually do for fun.*

Aleksey had no shortage of people desperate to spend time with him. Gisela and Kazik had their own ulterior motive for wanting to get close to him, but Kazik was still surprised Aleksey was so keen to join them. It didn't feel real, somehow.

"I like being with you and Gisela."

"You do?" Kazik couldn't keep the skepticism out of his voice.

"You're both very entertaining."

Great. Aleksey thought he and Gisela were some kind of comedy act.

"But I get the feeling you don't like being around me for some reason," Aleksey said. "Have I done something to offend you?"

"That's not—I don't *dis*like you."

Saints. Why did everything coming out of his mouth sound so . . . ? Where was Gisela when he actually needed her? *She* was good at talking to people. Kazik knew he came off as cold and unfriendly, and knowing that only seemed to worsen his efforts on the rare times he did try to interact.

"And I like being here," Aleksey said, staring at the branches shifting overhead.

That at least made sense. Aleksey had always liked hiking and being outdoors. Kazik relaxed a fraction. "It's nice here," he offered. "Peaceful."

Aleksey rearranged some of the votive candles. "My mother came and prayed here last spring when I was ill. She believes that's why I recovered."

Last spring . . . That reminded Kazik that he still hadn't managed to properly question Gisela about her death. Aleksey was always around now, and Gisela kept changing the subject when Kazik brought it up. She didn't seem interested in remembering what had happened to her.

The sharp crack of a twig had Aleksey turning to scan the tree line. The tourist and his camera were wandering back along the well-worn path toward town. "Gisela's taking an awfully long time finding water for the flowers."

Probably because she was using that same water to rehydrate.

"She disappears a lot, doesn't she? Should we check on her?"

"She probably just got distracted," Kazik said. "Or stopped to fix her lipstick. You know what girls are like."

Aleksey hummed. "Gisela's not really like any other girl I've met though. She's definitely something else. Something stranger."

Kazik's skin prickled with alarm. Of course, Gisela was

different from the girls Aleksey usually spent his time with. She was a cold-blooded demon for one thing, and way more irritating.

"Of course, she's a bit strange," he said, feeling an irrational need to defend her. "She comes from an island where they literally sacrifice boys to the sea." Now that he thought about it, this really went a long way to explaining Gisela's personality, as well as her disregard for other people's lives. "At least you're never bored with her. Isn't it more interesting if she's not like everybody else? So she has no concept of boundaries nor personal space, and she's probably never taken no for an answer in her entire life, but she's not . . ." Kazik paused, hating the truth of it. "She's not a bad person at heart." Even he had to admit that. Despite her many and numerous faults, Gisela was caring in her own way.

Aleksey eyed him for a long moment. "I meant it as a compliment."

Oh.

Well, now Kazik was just annoyed.

"I like her," Aleksey said.

Something inside Kazik clenched. "Well, good." That was what he wanted, wasn't it? Well, not *wanted*, but what he needed to happen.

"Just want to be clear about it. I don't want to come between you two."

Kazik scoffed.

Aleksey broke into a dimpled grin. "At least you're not worried that she's been gobbled up by a wicked forest spirit."

"They don't often come near the shrine."

"Because if they did, they'd be hunted down by bloodthirsty exorcists?"

Aleksey's tone was only teasing, but Kazik's eyes narrowed. "*Bloodthirsty* exorcists wouldn't have to hunt spirits down if they didn't prey on powerless humans."

"Maybe spirits wouldn't attack humans if humans left them alone."

"Humans aren't the ones constantly attacking—"

"Do you ever get tired being so self-righteous all the time?"

Kazik's mouth swung open.

"Most spirits," Aleksey said, "are the products of human violence, and the rest are constantly being demonized and diminished. Humans clear the land. Cut down forests. Dam the rivers and choke the air with coal smoke. They erect wards to drive creatures away. Human exorcists discourage people from leaving offerings. They teach people to fear and flee from spirits. Is it any wonder that spirits retaliate?"

Kazik didn't have a chance to answer.

"Nature spirits especially," Aleksey went on, his cheeks flushed, "are bound to their homes in ways humans can't hope to comprehend. Think of the water goblin. He's strong because his river is strong. Its currents swift and ever flowing. But he would grow weak if those waters were polluted or diverted. It's no different for other spirits. Even the leszy's stature is determined by the height of the trees in his forest. With his realm constantly shrinking, his very existence is under threat."

Kazik couldn't formulate a response. He'd never seen Aleksey fired up like this, never heard him speak so heatedly. The Aleksey he knew—or thought he knew—was easygoing to a fault. Kazik had written him off as a bit of an airhead. Someone who didn't care deeply about anything.

He had also never considered the unsettling possibility that Aleksey might disapprove of what he did.

"I didn't know you thought like that," Kazik said, trying not to sound defensive. "You were pretty eager for me to exorcise the domowik the other week."

Aleksey opened his mouth, then seemed to catch himself. He pressed his lips together briefly. "I'm not such a fool as to show mercy to a creature that attacks me. I'm not exactly the forgiving type. I just sympathize with the rest. I've heard a lot of stories from the local foresters."

So that was where he was getting his information. Kazik's grandfather had been a forester. He'd been empathetic toward the spirits too.

"But you're right," Aleksey said, his tone carefree once more—Kazik was almost disappointed. "I doubt any demons would risk visiting the shrine. You probably don't even need to worry about wearing *this*." He threaded a finger beneath the chain Kazik wore around his neck and tugged, drawing the silver medallion at the end of the chain into the light.

Kazik froze, too startled to react.

Not that it mattered, because the next second Aleksey yanked his hand back like he'd been burned. "Static shock," he said weakly, shaking his hand out. He bowed his head, the sun streaking his hair every shade of gold as his face slipped into shadow.

"It was my grandmother's." Kazik ran a thumb over the medallion, feeling for the familiar edges and notches in the metal. It resembled a two-sided coin and was engraved with an image of Saint Hyacinth. Wearing it invoked the saint's protection. Babcia had clasped it around his neck before she'd died and made him promise never to take it off. No matter who asked it of him.

It will keep you safe.

He could still feel the ghostly touch of her wrinkled fingers struggling to fasten the clasp.

Kazik swallowed around the knot forming in his throat. Grief was a slow knife to the gut, a pain that wouldn't end. Some days, it was still hard to believe she was gone.

The breeze picked up, swaying the linden tree's branches. Aleksey cocked his head, his brows knitting in an uncharacteristic frown. He left Kazik's side, moving away from the shrine and into the surrounding trees.

"Where are you—" Kazik started to ask. Oh hell. Was he going to look for Gisela like he'd suggested earlier? If he happened upon her while she was in the middle of conjuring water with her comb or something equally damning . . .

Kazik jolted into action. "Hey!" he called, jogging after him. "Hey, we should wait here for Gisela." If they ventured too far into the forest, she wouldn't be able to follow. They were already a good distance from the river.

There was no path he could discern, but Aleksey wove through the trees like he walked this way every day, pressing his fingers against each trunk as if in greeting. "I heard something," he said over his shoulder, vanishing behind another tree. When Kazik stepped around it too, he almost ran into Aleksey's back, catching himself at the last second. "It sounded like—"

A strange haunting cry pierced the air.

"—a child crying," Aleksey finished.

Kazik stilled, but Aleksey picked up his pace.

This idiot. If you thought you heard someone crying or calling your name in the woods, if you heard laughter or felt a sudden prickling desire to turn around while you were hiking . . .

No, you didn't. You didn't turn around. You heard nothing, you felt nothing, and you kept walking. You walked faster.

Hadn't they just been talking about forest spirits gobbling people up?

Wet, hiccupping sobs drew them deeper into the trees. Wind seethed through the branches. An angry cawing reached Kazik's ears. Up ahead, a mob of glossy black crows had cornered a smaller dark-winged bird. It was limping along the ground, dragging a wing through the dirt as the crows swooped and circled.

"Hey!" Aleksey bellowed, surging forward.

Like children caught with their fingers in a cookie jar, the crows froze. Then they took off with a cacophony of panicked shrieks, in a raucous tumble of black feathers.

Aleksey was already kneeling to examine the bird on the ground. It attempted to fend him off with a feeble flap of its wings.

"Is it injured?" Kazik crouched beside Aleksey, only to recoil violently, falling back on his hands with a curse, sitting down hard.

The bird had the face of a human child. A distinctly avian face, but still, impossibly human. Fleshy, beak-like lips made a sound halfway between a child's hiccupping cry and a distressed trill. Kazik could see the small black nub of a tongue.

He shuddered in revulsion.

Latawiec.

One of the air spirits. They were born from the souls of deceased children and, like most souls that did not find their way to the next world, were often harmful to mortals. They weren't as deadly as other demons of the air and wind, such as the nocturnal bloodsucking strzygi, but they were still incredibly dangerous.

"Aleksey. Don't move." Sunlight glinted off the creature's razor-sharp talons. Kazik couldn't afford to provoke it until he'd gotten Aleksey out of the way. "You need to—*for God's sake.*"

Ignoring him, Aleksey took hold of the creature's drooping wing and gently pulled it away from its body, feeling for injury with his fingers. The demon let out a pitiful chirp.

Kazik found himself recalling all the times he'd seen Aleksey rescue hatchlings and other small animals. Aleksey glanced over at him.

"You want to help it," Kazik said sourly.

"And you want to kill it."

"You're making me sound like the villain here."

Aleksey didn't say anything, but his mouth curved up at the corners. The sun yielded suddenly to a bank of cloud, casting them in darkness.

Goose bumps pebbled Kazik's arms with the sudden drop in

temperature. His gaze slid from Aleksey to the demon. Its feathers were fluffed up in stress. Its eyes were partly closed. They were a crow's eyes—impossibly round and blue. The prayer to exorcise the unholy creature played inside his head: *May Heaven grant this child eternal rest. May the Holy Mother fill your heart with peace.*

Instinctively, he felt himself reach for that spark of power at his core. It was still there, deep inside him, waiting. A faint warmth like a dying ember. He could feel it flicker feebly, but for once, he wasn't sure if it was because the saints had shackled his magic or if his own will was to blame. Where was the conviction that usually fanned that spark into righteous flame?

Thunder rumbled in the distance. The creature let out another pathetic chirp.

Aleksey continued to watch him. Kazik knew the other boy was testing him, challenging him, and a part of him hated him for it. Letting sentiment cloud his judgment wasn't just dangerous—it could be fatal. Why couldn't he just do what needed to be done, regardless of what Aleksey or Gisela might think of him?

Why was he being so damn weak?

Before he could decide what to do, Aleksey acted. Peeling off his shirt, he carefully bundled up the creature in the fabric as if it were an ordinary injured bird.

Kazik looked away, but not fast enough. Now the image of Aleksey's naked chest was burned into his mind. He met the latawiec's unnaturally blue eyes. Was it his imagination, or did the demon bird look almost smug?

"If you hurt him," he said, addressing the bird, jerking his chin at Aleksey, "I'll burn your wings off."

Aleksey stared at him in fascination.

Overhead, the clouds shifted, and the sun abruptly brightened again, sending blades of light through the forest. Brushwood and leaf litter crunched beneath approaching footsteps.

Startled, Kazik glanced over his shoulder as Gisela stepped between the trees. He shouldn't have felt so relieved to see her.

She did a double take when she spied Aleksey without his shirt. "I'm not complaining," she said, "but why are you half naked? What are you two doing all the way out here?"

"Debating if we should help or exorcise another spirit," Aleksey said.

Gisela shot Kazik a withering look. "How do I already know what Kazik wants to do?"

Kazik opened his mouth to defend himself, but Gisela went on, striding closer.

"We should help it. Not all spirits are wicked monsters. It's not fair to always assume the worst."

"It's safer if you do," Kazik said.

Gisela ignored him. "Spirits have feelings too. They make mistakes. They deserve empathy and compassion. Look at Domek, he was only— What the devil is *that*?" She leapt back with a shriek as the latawiec poked its head out of Aleksey's shirt.

Aleksey's cheek dimpled with a grin. "Isn't it cute? Haven't you ever seen an air demon before? Here, come pet it."

Gisela backed away. "Don't bring it near me!"

Aleksey rose to his feet, still grinning. Kazik was struck with a weird sense of déjà vu; he felt like he was a child again, watching a classmate taunt a girl they liked with a worm they'd dug out of the soil.

"Come on, Gisela!" Aleksey crooned. "'Spirits have feelings too.' You're making it sad. Come kiss its creepy human face."

Gisela let out another shriek as Aleksey carried the demon closer. "Why does it *have* a face?"

Kazik didn't think he'd ever heard Aleksey laugh so hard. Honestly, Gisela's audible outrage made him want to laugh too. She might claim she wanted to help the creature, but she was clearly as unnerved by it as he was.

He leaned back on his hands, watching the two idiots chase each other around a tree, the tension slowly easing from his body. If he'd been a real matchmaker, a real friend, he might have made some excuse to slip away and leave them alone together. But he felt a strange unwillingness to move.

He told himself it was because he was still worried about the latawiec.

"Kazik! Kazik, don't just sit there!" Gisela gasped. Her chest was heaving from giggles now too. Her eyes were shining in a way he'd never seen before. It was cute.

Really cute.

"You call yourself an exorcist! Come help—" She staggered to a halt. "Oh my God!"

Aleksey stopped next to her in surprise. "What—"

Gisela stabbed an accusing finger at Kazik's face. "He's *smiling*."

Kazik rolled his eyes. "No, I'm not."

"He *is*," Aleksey said, squinting.

"I'm really not." Kazik stood, dusting off his backside, avoiding eye contact. It would be pure madness to admit he was smiling because of an unholy terror like Gisela.

22

GIVE THE DEVIL A BODY

ALEKSEY

IT WAS STORMING WHEN Aleksey finally returned home. In between the growls of thunder, he could hear the soft child-like voices of the plants rejoicing. Rain dripped from the slanting eaves of the two-story cottage, its whitewashed walls and pink shutters nestled within a quiet corner of Villa Hyacinth's grounds.

Aleksey removed his muddied shoes at the front door and dried off his hair with a towel the housekeeper handed him. She informed him that the mail had arrived, that his mother was reading in the sitting room, and that dinner would be ready soon.

Flashing the elderly woman a grateful smile, Aleksey made his way to a bright airy room at the back of the house. The cottage was sprawling, yet cozy. The hardwood furniture shone with polish, and the glossy floorboards were softened by patterned rugs that swallowed your footsteps. Oil lamps illuminated each room, while vases brimming with wildflowers filled the air with sweet perfume.

Occasionally, an odd trick of the light made it seem as though the shadows of leaves danced over the walls, as if branches were waving in a breeze, though no trees stood outside the windows.

"Mother?" Aleksey peered around the door into the sitting room.

Irina was fast asleep in her favorite armchair. A newspaper lay open on her lap, and on the coffee table before her was a scattering of dried violets she must've been pressing into the pages of a journal. A new project.

A rush of overwhelming fondness filled Aleksey. Memories—not his own—crowded his mind. He crossed the room and on impulse kissed the top of her head. There was a dab of blue paint in her smooth brown hair.

He slid the newspaper from her lap and folded it closed.

Irina stirred at the sound of the paper crackling. Sky-blue eyes fluttered open. Aleksey stilled as a pale hand cupped his cheek with devastating tenderness. Another odd feeling bloomed inside his chest, one he didn't understand, so he shoved it away.

It was still a novelty, not being looked at as if he were something monstrous and inhuman. Nobody had touched him like this before. Gently. Softly. No aggression. No nonconsensual grabbing. No veiled threat of violence.

He still didn't know what to make of it. He caught her hand and squeezed it, returned it to her lap.

Irina smiled sleepily. Her eyes drifted closed again.

Aleksey straightened. "And what are you looking at?" he whispered to the potted fern wilting on the coffee table. He brushed his thumb over one of its tightly curled fronds, then smiled as it unfurled and curled around his finger.

He left the sitting room carrying the potted plant, careful to let the door snick shut behind him. With the house practically empty, he could let his mask slip. It was exhausting always pretending to be someone you were not. There were so many things to remember when he was around humans. Not talking to the trees was one; stifling the urge to devour whoever annoyed him was another.

"And why are you looking so pathetic?" he asked the fern. "You were standing tall when I left. Did somebody bother you? Should I scold them? Tell me—" Aleksey halted.

A few paces ahead, a flaxen-haired girl wandered out of the study and into the hallway. She whirled around at the sound of his approach.

"A-Aleksey?" There was a quaver in Roza's voice and a bright red stain on the puffed sleeve of her yellow sundress.

Aleksey's eyes narrowed.

"I don't—" Roza looked around herself in confusion. "Is this your house?" She gave a small shocked laugh, lifting a hand to cover her lips. "I woke up in the study?" It came out as a question. "I can't remember how I got here."

Aleksey studied her for another beat, then set the potted fern down on a hall stand. Reluctantly, its pale green fronds released their grip on his fingers.

He slipped on his most disarming smile—one he'd practiced in the mirror. A smile designed to show off the dimple in his cheek. When he spoke, his voice held the perfect measure of friendliness and a faint hint of worry. "Why don't we go upstairs to my room?"

Roza knotted her fingers together nervously. "No, no, I think I should go home. Do you know what time it is? My mother—"

"Take a moment to sit first. You don't look well."

"No, I'm fine. Really. I just—I'm a bit confused." She came forward, trying to see a way past him.

Aleksey stood in her path. His expression didn't change. "Let's go upstairs and work out what's going on." He held his hands up, his palms open to demonstrate his lack of threat, and adjusted his tone, sweetened it. "It's just me, Roza. You trust me, don't you?"

Roza's lips parted. She let out another weak laugh. But there was still a wariness about her. She was tense as a deer in the forest after hearing a branch snap. "Of course, I trust you. I just—" She gasped, clutching at her chest.

For a split second, her horrified stare met Aleksey's. Then her head dropped forward, and a violent shudder bowed her body inward. Her limbs jerked like they were being manipulated by an invisible puppeteer.

A moment later she straightened, blinking, and rolled her shoulders back. "Sorry." She sounded sheepish. "I lost control for a moment. This damn skin suit is driving me mad."

"Roza," Aleksey said warningly, casting a glance over his shoulder. Roza was not her real name, of course, as Aleksey was not his, but it was easier and safer to refer to each other as such, even in private, because you never knew who might be listening.

"I know, I know." The bies inhabiting Roza's body cracked her neck. "I'll be more careful."

"There's blood on your dress."

"Not all of it's mine."

"Why does that not comfort me?"

"It's not my fault human bodies are such weak, unwieldy things."

"Only because you're careless with them."

Roza picked at the stain on her sleeve. Her fingers came away red. "One little prick and all the life starts leaking out of them. That stupid little dog nipped me and ran off again." She shrugged. "It's fine. If I break this body, I'll just find another. They're not exactly in short supply."

"If you want to get caught and exorcised, then by all means, go right ahead. Hopping from body to body too often is dangerous. It draws attention."

"Says someone who used to change bodies as often as a human changes coats." Gray eyes looked Aleksey up and down. "You haven't been acting like yourself."

"That's because I have my eyes on a very *particular* coat this time."

Roza wasn't impressed by his joke. She blew her cheeks out, visibly frustrated. "You're taking an awfully long time getting your hands on it. I hope you're not getting soft. I know you like to play with your food, but there are easier ways to revenge yourself on Kazik than by possessing his body. You said once you recovered your strength, he would be the first person you killed. You said you would devour his flesh while he was still screaming. You said you would pick his bones out of your teeth.”

He had said that. He’d been a *little* overdramatic.

Aleksey couldn’t keep the edge out of his voice. “I told you before, that would be too easy.” It wouldn’t be enough. He wanted Kazik brought low, like *he* had been. He wanted him on his knees, bent in supplication. “You don’t have to kill someone to destroy them. And the situation has changed. There have been new developments.”

“Good or bad?”

“Too early to say.”

He didn’t elaborate, didn’t explain that Leśna Woda’s famous exorcist was suddenly lowering himself to help spirits—not that Aleksey believed that would last. He’d been burned before. Humans liked to play nice, until they didn’t. They couldn’t be trusted. No, this new development was purely down to Gisela’s influence.

Aleksey was still trying to puzzle out how she’d done it. It was confounding. Fascinating. Infuriating. Kazik wasn’t the type to be swayed by a pretty face. He’d rebuffed *Aleksey’s* every attempt to get close. Gisela though . . . Gisela had managed to slip past his defenses and wrap him around her little finger without so much as a visible effort.

It had been a long time since anyone had piqued Aleksey’s interest like this. How had a mere water nymph . . . ? And she *was* a water nymph. No matter how hard she and Kazik tried to hide the truth. And that, too, was puzzling. Did Kazik just not want anyone to know he’d been bewitched by a spirit?

Aleksey had so many questions and not only about Gisela—was she competition or a potential ally? Kazik was also turning out to be something of an enigma. He was so different from what everyone had made him out to be. From what Aleksey had thought him to be.

He couldn't figure either of them out, and it was driving him to distraction.

Gesturing for Roza to follow, Aleksey started to make his way upstairs.

He would never forget his first face-to-face encounter with Kazik—that fatal chase through the night-blooming gardens encircling Villa Violetta. He remembered it like it was yesterday: the cool bite of the evening air, the sweet scent of jasmine, the searing heat of the holy flames summoned to exorcise him.

Even now, the memory was enough to make his heart skip a beat.

The leszy had given Aleksey strict instructions: *Possess a mortal. Infiltrate the town of Leśna Woda and observe the old witch and her grandson. Learn what you can about him. Determine his strengths and weaknesses.*

Do not get distracted.

Do not get attached to any mortals you meet.

Do not get caught.

Aleksey had been overconfident to the point of boredom. He was a prince among his kind. He devoured exorcists for breakfast. The old witch was supposed to be fading, and no one had expected her grandson to be so powerful.

He remembered the way Kazik had held his ground, refusing to show fear even as his hands trembled. How furious, how utterly sublime he'd looked, like something stepped out of a holy painting. A saint with blood on their fists. A divine weapon made flesh.

He remembered the touch of Kazik's magic reaching past the frail form he was inhabiting, through blood and bone and muscle. He remembered the rap of the old witch's walking stick, the gravel of her voice, the snick of prayer beads running through Kazik's fingers, and the pain—the blistering, agonizing pain.

Aleksey didn't often feel fear, but that . . . that had been one of the rare times when he'd actually felt afraid.

He'd thought long and hard about how to repay Kazik for that—he was going to make a puppet of that saintly body, make it do such terrible things that Kazik would be too ashamed to face his grandmother in the afterlife. Kazik was the only mortal who had ever succeeded in evicting Aleksey from a host. It was because of Kazik that Aleksey had been forced to hide inside *this* body while he recovered his strength. The indignity of it all was a constant itch, but at least the experience didn't grate on him the way it did Roza.

"I don't know how you stand it," she complained, as they reached the second-floor landing. "Don't you feel wrong inside that skin? Even the feel of these teeth in my mouth is just—ugh!" She raked her nails down her forearms. "I can barely keep myself from cringing at the sound of my own voice. *Her* voice."

"Keep that voice *down*," Aleksey snapped.

Pouting, Roza brushed past him through a door on their left. Aleksey's bedroom had windows looking out onto the garden and the little studio behind the house, where his mother would paint. There was a bed in one corner, an oak wardrobe, a handsome writing desk, and cluttered bookshelves.

A flower had sprouted between the floorboards.

"We've been here for a whole year," Roza said. "I don't understand why you're not more—" The searching gaze she cast his way felt like it was trying to pry him open. "I hate seeing you reduced to this." She bit her lip, suddenly emotional.

Maybe his lack of discomfort should worry him more.

Aleksey caught a lock of her pale hair and smoothed it between his fingers, gently tucking it behind her ear.

Roza stiffened in surprise but leaned eagerly into the touch.

"I can't possess him while he's wearing that medallion," Aleksey said soothingly. "The leszy originally sent me to spy on him. I want to learn more about his holy gifts. I want to know more about him." Aleksey wanted to know *everything* about Kazik. "I'm still gathering information."

"While picking berries together and eating ice cream?"

Aleksey stamped down on a flare of irritation. There were times when he regretted having ever let her tag along with him. "I told you before that it's hard to get close to him. I'm doing what I have to."

"That girl managed it easily enough," Roza groused. "His new friend. Gisela. She got close to him. She must be as bewitching as a damn rusałka."

Aleksey blinked, then started to laugh.

Roza looked up, startled. "What?"

Aleksey shook his head. "Nothing. It's unimportant."

"I still think she looks familiar, but I can't for the life of me remember where I've seen her before." Roza hissed in frustration. "It's so hard to think when I'm like this."

It *was* hard to think sometimes, crammed inside someone else's flesh, inside their mind, assailed by the constant echo of their thoughts and emotions. While having access to a host's memories made it easier to impersonate them, it was also a danger. It was so easy to lose yourself.

"It'll come back to you," Aleksey said. "In the meantime, I have a task for you."

Roza perked up.

Gisela was so busy hiding what she was that she hadn't yet realized what *Aleksey* was, despite the hints he'd dropped. Most spirits couldn't recognize a bies in human guise unless they gave themselves away using their powers. Aleksey hadn't intended to use his in front of Gisela. The urge to protect her took him by surprise. But she'd defended him too, back at the guesthouse. No one had ever taken a blow for him before. No one would think they needed to.

He should have found it insulting—that she saw him as someone weak enough to need shielding. Who did she think she was, to think he needed her to defend him? But instead, a fierce protectiveness had surged through him.

Thankfully, Gisela seemed to believe Domek had conjured the whirlwind of petals. Her knowledge of what certain spirits were capable of was clearly patchy. She hadn't known what the latawiec was either. Aleksey didn't think she'd been a water nymph for long. He had an uneasy feeling he knew how she'd become one, but he'd cross that bridge when he came to it.

The immediate threat was the little domowik. The house spirit had very nearly outed Aleksey in front of Kazik. Domek seemed to have taken Kazik's assurance that they were friends to heart, but Aleksey couldn't guarantee the creature wouldn't let something slip.

"There's a domowik residing in Kazik's home," he told Roza. "He knows what I am. I want you to get rid of him. The house is warded, but not to the level of the bathhouses. You'll feel some discomfort but should be able to force your way through. Eat the little devil or chase him away—do whatever you like. Just be subtle about it."

"A house spirit?" Roza grumbled. "That's all? I thought it would be something exciting."

"You can't handle it?"

Roza scowled. "Of course, I can."

"Good. Take care of it, then."

"And you'll take care of Kazik?"

"When the time is right. I have it handled."

"I hope you do," Roza said, concern creeping back into her voice. "Remember, *Aleksey*, we can't play house here forever. You know what they say about biesy who live too long as mortals. They start to develop human emotions. They start to forget that they were ever monsters."

23

NO REST FOR THE WICKED

GISELA

"DARLING, I'M HOME!" GISELA called out, waltzing into Kazik's house without knocking, knowing it would annoy him. She kicked her borrowed sandals off by the front door, curious to discover what her reluctant partner in crime was up to now. The last time she and Aleksey had burst in here during the day, they'd caught Kazik in the middle of one of his witchy rituals. A dozen candles were burning. Kazik was pouring wax into a bowl of icy water held over an elderly man's head.

Gisela had been impressed at his ability to retain his composure. Kazik jumped but miraculously managed not to drop the bowl and burn the old man's face off with hot wax. He'd glowered at them, but it was his *not you again* glower as opposed to his deadlier *I am going to end you* murder glare. She was beginning to recognize the difference. There was a particular twist to Kazik's mouth. A scrunch to his nose. It was like learning the words of a secret language. She liked that she was getting to know a side of Kazik that very few people knew.

Later, once his patient left, he explained that he could

diagnose a person's illness by reading the shapes the wax formed. He could read fortunes that way too, dripping wax through the eye of an old skeleton key stolen from the church, divining meaning from the shape of the shadows the cooling wax cast over the walls.

It was all so different from the magic she'd seen worked on the island. So deeply rooted in faith and ritual. The way visitors to the house watched Kazik with awe and hope made her think he really *was* something special. Something out of the ordinary. Kazik might instruct a woman to light three votive candles in the church every day for three days to cast off the evil energy surrounding her, or he might help lessen a person's pain by whispering prayers in their ear for an hour. He might just as easily send them off to the hospital. Because he wasn't a replacement for a doctor—something a lot of people didn't seem to understand; he couldn't cure diseases with a touch nor mend a broken bone with a snap of his fingers. But he could give the sick the strength they needed to recover naturally and, of course, deal with spirits and curses no modern medicine could combat.

There had been something about seeing him in his element, commanding and confident, looking oh, so responsible, so incredibly adult . . .

Neither she nor Aleksey could keep their eyes off him.

Gisela spared a glance into the living room, where smudges of chalk on the floorboards still marked the faded remains of the magic circle he'd bound her in. She inhaled the now-familiar scent of incense and burnt flax.

Today Kazik was standing at the kitchen bench with a

dishrag slung over his shoulder, ladling cold beet soup into a bowl hand-painted with flowers. He looked up at the sound of her footsteps and let out a long-suffering sigh. "How do you keep getting in? Do you waltz into everyone's house uninvited?"

Gisela shrugged, unrepentant. "I can't help it. I'm a wicked, ill-mannered demon. What did you expect? It's like you don't know me. Besides, your door wasn't locked."

"That's not an invitation."

Gisela drifted closer. Kazik had even prepared side dishes. There was a plate of creamy mashed potato topped with crispy bacon bits, and a loaf of dark rye bread sat cooling on the windowsill.

Stomach growling, she dipped a finger into the soup and licked it clean, then danced out of the way when Kazik threatened her with the ladle.

"That's my food!"

"Wow! It's actually good."

The soup tasted like summer. Like home. Like the soup Great-Aunt Zela used to make. Gisela had tried to recreate her recipe—her father expected a good meal the rare times when he was home—but her great-aunt had cooked by taste and feel, so Gisela could never get it quite right. She watched Kazik garnish the rich pink broth with halves of a boiled egg, edible flowers, and a sprinkling of sliced radish.

"You're going to make an excellent housewife," Gisela told him.

Kazik scoffed, but the tips of his ears turned pink. "And you? Here to brag about your success with Aleksey? I should've known you two would hit it off. You're both equally annoying. Is he everything you hoped he'd be?" He asked the question like he couldn't care less about the answer but didn't quite meet her eyes.

Gisela bit her lip. "I don't know that I'd call it a success. He hasn't kissed me yet."

And if he'd started to suspect what she was, maybe he never would.

She quickly shoved that thought away, refusing to let her mind spiral to darker places for once. In any case, things were moving too slowly. It was already nearing midsummer. Time was ticking by. Water nymphs didn't fare well in the cold. They spent the autumn and winter months hibernating in the depths of the river and didn't return to the world of the living until the earth began to warm. If Aleksey didn't kiss her soon . . .

"I suppose we're making progress. But then, I do have an excellent matchmaker. He's so knowledgeable about boys. Handsome too."

"Flattery will get you nowhere," Kazik said.

"So, you really think Aleksey likes me? Did he say something to you? He hasn't, like, asked you if I'm a demon or anything, has he?"

Kazik snorted and shook his head. "I think your secret's safe for now."

Gisela let out a relieved breath. "I like him," she admitted softly, leaning back against the kitchen bench. "I don't think I truly *like* liked any of the people I tried to get a kiss from before." Not this much. She probably would've wanted to kiss Aleksey even if she hadn't had an ulterior motive.

Kazik regarded her from behind his wire-rimmed glasses, his expression unreadable. "Don't get too attached," he warned.

"You're doing this so you can leave Leśna Woda. So you can go home and take care of your little brother, remember?"

"Of course, I remember," Gisela snapped. If all went to plan, she'd get her kiss and go. She'd regain her humanity and put all this behind her. She hadn't forgotten Hugo. She'd always had to put her brother first. Sometimes, she secretly resented that he'd been born. If Hugo didn't exist . . .

She immediately felt horribly guilty for even thinking that.

Gisela opened a cupboard, peered inside at the jumble of plates and cups, and closed it with a *bang*. "Always so eager to get rid of me, Kazik."

"That was our deal from the beginning."

Gisela resisted the urge to rake her nails down his face. It shouldn't hurt that he was still keen to see the back of her. She'd gone into this knowing it was only a temporary arrangement. Afterward, whatever uneasy trust, whatever bond had grown between them, would die. They would go their separate ways. She'd probably never see nor talk to Kazik again. He'd probably forget her the second she stepped out of his life. She'd return home. He would resume his role as Leśna Woda's merciless exorcist, no longer forced to consort with wicked spirits. It was foolish to think anything between them had changed. She'd let Miray's and Zamira's teasing go to her head.

"Don't worry," she said, feeling embarrassed. "Once I have my kiss, I'm going to leave even if you try and stop me." With a huff, she opened and closed another cupboard at random, deliberately making noise and taking up space while Kazik complained about her getting her unholy germs on everything.

Hurt morphed swiftly into anger. Swanning past him, Gisela reached for an old walking stick propped against the wall beside a mop and a broom.

"*Don't!*" Kazik grabbed her wrist, his grip tight enough to bruise.

Gisela flinched, less from the violence of his touch than the crash of the walking stick falling to the floor. "What have I done now?"

"It—it was my grandmother's stick."

Oh.

"She wouldn't like you touching it."

Fresh annoyance bubbled inside Gisela, but Kazik sounded almost apologetic, and he didn't release her. With surprising gentleness, he turned her wrist this way and that, inspecting her palm, each of her fingers, the back of her hand. A little shiver ran up Gisela's spine; his palms were ember warm.

"It's carved from bladdernut shrub wood. We make rosaries of bladdernut seeds. The wood protects its wearers from witchcraft. Spirits are supposed to be afraid to touch it." Kazik looked up. "Does it hurt you anywhere?"

Flustered, Gisela shook her head.

Kazik let out a soft sigh of relief.

"Look at you, all worried about me. Careful, I might start to think you care."

Kazik's expression darkened. He dropped her hand. "I'm not as heartless as you and Aleksey seem to think." Turning away stiffly, he set the walking stick back against the wall.

Gisela stared.

After a second's hesitation, she pulled out a chair at the kitchen table and took a seat, tucking a leg beneath her, watching as Kazik carried his bowl of soup to the table. She expected him to sit, too, but he returned to the bench and prepared a second bowl, then set it before her with a sharp *plunk*, shoving aside a dish of the sticky-sweet berries they'd foraged in the forest with Aleksey. The table was crowded with odds and ends—scatterings of wild strawberry leaves left to dry and glass jars of pickling vegetables.

Gisela bit back her surprise. A thought occurred to her, and she voiced it before Kazik could fall into one of his brooding silences. "I've heard stories about that walking stick. From Wojciech. Apparently, your grandmother used to smack him with it whenever she caught him trying to sneak into the bathhouses."

Kazik barked out a sharp, genuine laugh.

Gisela smirked. It did paint a comical picture. The famous all-powerful water goblin fleeing the wrath of a cranky old witch.

"She used to smack *me* with that stick when I misbehaved." Kazik's voice softened. "She raised me. She and my grandfather. My mother fell apart after my father left. My grandparents taught me everything I know."

"You're lucky to have had them."

"I was." Kazik raised an eyebrow. "You and the water goblin seem . . . close. You're always talking about him." He sounded openly curious.

Gisela rolled her eyes. "He likes to act like we're all one big family." A strange dysfunctional family that she had never agreed to be a part of. "He's always nagging me about something or complaining I stay out too much. He's maddening."

"Most families are." Kazik touched the medallion hanging from the chain around his neck. "My grandmother rescued her best friend's soul from his clutches. Wojciech had her soul trapped in one of his teacups. Babcia dove into the river and stormed into his palace of crystal and demanded he return her. My grandfather used to tell us the story when he put me and my cousin to bed."

Gisela's smirk widened. She'd heard that story, too, from Yulia and Miray, who'd actually witnessed it happen all those years ago. Gisela wished she could've seen Wojciech's face when he'd realized a mere human had managed to force her way into his watery realm uninvited.

Kazik carried the side dishes to the table. "She passed away last year after a bad fall. She was trying to pick sour cherries off the tree in the garden. Even though I *told* her that I would do it."

Gisela could hear the mix of pain and exasperation in Kazik's voice.

"She never listened to anybody. She was still recovering from what happened with . . ." He veered into his own thoughts.

Gisela tilted her head at him in question.

"You haven't remembered anything more about how you became a water nymph?" Kazik asked.

Gisela picked at the wild strawberry leaves drying on the table; Kazik had told her wild-strawberry-leaf tea was good for arthritis. "No. Nothing."

Nothing aside from the usual nightmares, the familiar

phantom pain at the base of her skull, and those strange flashes of memory she'd had when Domek had attacked them—scattered images, a blur of colors and sounds and shapes, that feeling of dread. They were like pieces of a dream, and like with any dream, the harder she tried to grasp the details, the faster they slipped through her fingers.

"And you're absolutely sure Wojciech doesn't know anything?"

Gisela looked up sharply. "What are you getting at?"

For a moment, it seemed like Kazik wouldn't answer. Then he squared his shoulders as if preparing for a fight. "Do you know what a bies is?"

A forest demon. One of those spirits that devoured humans just for the fun of it.

"Of course, I know what a bies is," Gisela said.

"Be-es." Kazik corrected her pronunciation. "Not bees."

Gisela scowled. She knew she mispronounced things sometimes. This wasn't her first language. Wojciech had told her that her accent was *adorable*, that it had an old-fashioned lilt he hadn't heard in decades—likely because she'd learned from her great-aunt.

"Biesy like to possess humans," Kazik continued. "A pair of them managed to infiltrate town that way a year ago. Last spring."

A chill prickled Gisela's skin.

"I exorcised them from the bodies they were inhabiting, but I couldn't destroy them fully. One of the demons even wounded my grandmother. You said Wojciech was distracted the night you died because he'd heard she'd been attacked."

Gisela's mind was spinning. "And you think—"

"I don't know," Kazik said quickly. "I've just been thinking about it since you told me when you died. The timing could be a coincidence. I've been trying to find out more."

"You have?" He kept surprising her today. A month ago, Kazik would've been the last person she'd expect to care enough to look into her past, to worry about who or what might have hurt her.

"Mrs. Mróz, the woman who gave me the altar candles, told me you'd gone for a walk in the forest before you disappeared, and the biesy fled back into the forest, so . . ." He sounded apprehensive, almost guilty, as if he blamed himself for what might have happened to her, which was utterly ridiculous.

Gisela ran a finger around the lip of her bowl of soup. She'd never actively tried to remember what had happened that night nor pressed Wojciech for what details he knew of her death. She'd told herself she was lucky not to remember. It was better that way.

"One of those demons hurt your grandmother?"

Kazik nodded tightly.

He'd want revenge for that, obviously, and if there was something in her past that might help him discover what had become of the demons, if she could do that for him . . .

Gisela pushed the loose waves of her damp hair behind her shoulders. "I'll ask Wojciech if he knows anything more."

Kazik let out a soft exhale.

"He was in love with your grandmother, you know," Gisela added. "I'm pretty sure he snuck into the bathhouses just so he could see her. He's always talking about how exceptionally fierce and beautiful she was. He said you look just like her."

Kazik's horrified expression really helped to lighten the moment.

As did the sudden appearance of Domek—a blur of orange fur streaked into the kitchen and leapt onto Gisela's lap. Lately, the house spirit had taken to assuming the form of a fat soot-streaked cat with grandfatherly whiskers. He spent most of his time napping beneath the stove or snuggled up in one of Kazik's old knit sweaters.

Kazik turned his eyes to the ceiling and muttered something less than holy, but Gisela stroked a hand along Domek's back, smiling when he arched into the touch. "Still here, Grandfather?"

"Can't get rid of him," Kazik said. "Not unlike somebody *else* I know."

"If you want me gone so badly, *you* need to put more effort into playing matchmaker," Gisela retorted. "While I interrogate Wojciech, you can strategize. We need to spice things up. We have to give Aleksey an opportunity to kiss me. We have to set the mood. Create the perfect romantic atmosphere." She snapped her fingers. "I know a wiła. Maybe we could convince her to conjure a storm so we could get caught in a romantic downpour together? Or is there a dance or a party we can all go to? I could dress up all pretty."

Kazik's gaze flicked over her. She was dressed in her usual ghostly white attire, in a flowy slip dress of pale cotton with straps that tied into little bows atop her shoulders. She'd snatched it from a random clothesline a while ago. There was a small hole in the hem.

Self-conscious, Gisela shifted the fabric to hide the tear. She scratched Domek under the chin. "Grandfather, feel free to throw in suggestions."

Suggestions? The domowik's gruff voice spoke inside their heads rather than their ears. He sounded half asleep.

Gisela stopped petting him. "We're trying to come up with ideas for a romantic evening. I want to give Aleksey a chance to kiss me."

Domek yawned and leapt onto the table to inspect Kazik's bowl of soup. *The humans always hold a festival to celebrate Saint John's Eve. But why do you want to be kissed by that—*

"Don't put your nose in there!" Kazik snapped at him.

"Saint John's Eve," Gisela repeated, her eyes wide.

"Do you even know what that is?" Kazik said skeptically, moving his soup away from Domek.

"Why do you keep thinking I don't know anything?" Gisela might not come from a very devout family—her father only attended church on major feast days to keep up appearances, and half the time, she'd had to nudge him awake when he fell asleep and started snoring—but she knew her saints, and she knew how they celebrated Saint John's Eve on the mainland.

The festival coincided with the summer solstice. It was a night when the veil between the mortal and living worlds was thin. A wild night when witches and spirits were at their most powerful. A night when humans lit bonfires along the riverbanks and girls floated enchanted flower wreaths on the water to divine if they'd find love.

It was the *perfect* opportunity.

"Grandfather," she said, clapping in delight, "you're a genius!"

Domek twitched his whiskers. *Does that mean I can eat the soup?*

"Yes," Gisela said, at the same time as Kazik said, "No. That's mine. How are you still hungry? You already ate all the blueberry yeast buns I got as a thank-you gift."

I left the last one for you, Domek said.

"Aw, that's so sweet!" Gisela exclaimed. "Isn't that sweet, Kazik?"

"How is it sweet if he's the one who ate the rest of them?"

Gisela opened her mouth to reply, but before she had the chance, there was a jangle of keys and the sound of the front door creaking open on its hinges.

Kazik twisted to face her, his expression panicked.

There was the tread of approaching footsteps. A voice called Kazik's name. Gisela recognized those dulcet tones from the night she'd first snuck into Kazik's bedroom.

The voice belonged to his cousin.

"Quick, get out! She can't find you here!" Kazik caught Gisela by the shoulders and bundled her toward the back door before wrenching it open.

"Wait, *wait*, my shoes!" Gisela grabbed at his sleeve as he shoved her outside into the fading afternoon light. "I left my sandals at the front—" With a curse, she stumbled down the back steps into the unruly garden behind the house. Grass bristled between her toes. She stubbed her heel against an overturned flowerpot.

Kazik made shooing motions at her as if she were a misbehaving pet.

"Wait, Kazik!"

He pulled the door shut.

"I didn't even get to eat my soup!"

24

MIXED BLESSINGS

KAZIK

"SO, MAMA'S MADE YOU, like, a week's worth of her rhubarb-and-strawberry soup," Zuzanna said, sweeping into the kitchen already talking, "and—what are you doing?"

Kazik wheeled away from the back door.

"I'm not interrupting something, am I?"

"Yes?" Kazik tried, hoping she'd take the hint and go so he could call Gisela back inside.

His cousin didn't take the hint. She started dumping her bags and a parcel wrapped in brown paper on the kitchen table. She'd returned to the university for the past few weeks, but here she was back again. Clearly, he wasn't going to be able to eat in peace today.

"Hello, Zuza," Kazik muttered under his breath. "How nice of you to visit. Would you like to come in?"

"What did you say?"

"Nothing."

"You're looking especially brooding today."

"I'm not brooding. This is just what my face does."

"No." Zuzanna shook her head. "Those eyebrows are definitely pulled into a deeper frown than usual, and you were all jumpy when I walked in." She played with one of the rosaries around her neck. The glossy wooden beads clicked between her fingers. "What's wrong?"

"Nothing's wrong."

"Nothing?" Zuzanna repeated, unconvinced.

Kazik wished his cousin weren't so damn perceptive. Babcia had always said she had a talent for seeing into others' hearts.

"Is that water nymph still giving you trouble?"

Sweat beaded at Kazik's temple. "I've got it handled."

"Oh?" Zuzanna pulled a chair away from the table and settled into it. "I heard that you've been busy—" She cut off abruptly, finally noticing the fat grandfatherly cat frozen on the table behind the dish of wild berries. Domek's ears were flat against his head. In his rush to hide Gisela, Kazik had forgotten all about the other demon in the house.

Zuzanna leapt to her feet, fumbling to catch her chair as it tipped backward. "*That* is not a cat!"

Kazik wondered what had given it away—were Zuza's senses just that keen, or was it the house spirit's slitted ember-red eyes? If Kazik were a better person, he might've confessed to everything then and there, but he tugged on an earring, stalling for time, half-afraid to explain himself. "He was causing trouble at one of guesthouses," he said in a rush. "It was easier to remove him than to exorcise him. His family moved away and left him behind. We're trying to track down some relatives for him to stay with."

Domek licked his nose.

Zuzanna pinned Kazik with a look. "*We?*"

Kazik cursed internally.

"This wasn't exactly what I was envisioning," Zuzanna said, "when I heard you'd been busy making friends."

"Friends?"

The corners of Zuzanna's mouth quirked up. "Mrs. Mróz and her sister reported that they've seen you running around with a pretty girl."

Reported? Heat surged up the back of Kazik's neck. "Would it kill them to mind their own business?"

"Probably. You know what the old women here are like. They have their own whisper network."

Zuzanna was right. They'd probably been speculating about him and Gisela from the very second they'd spied them out and about together. Kazik dragged a hand through his hair. He should've been more careful.

Zuzanna tapped the parcel she'd dropped on the table. "Mrs. Grigoryan also gave me this to give to you. She was so curious about who you were buying a gift for. Are you going to tell me what it is?"

Kazik's face was on fire. "No."

Cackling, Zuzanna picked up a jar of baby cucumbers he'd left to pickle on the table. She wrested the lid off.

"Those aren't ready yet."

"Mm, still tastes good," Zuzanna said, after taking a crunching bite. She smacked her lips. And then, to Kazik's shock, she offered a second small cucumber to Domek. "So, you're living here now?"

"Temporarily," Kazik stressed as Domek sniffed eagerly at the offering.

"It'll be good for this house to have a domowik again." Zuzanna nodded to herself. "I was so angry when you let the last one leave." She stroked one of Domek's ears. "Can I leave the house in your care, Grandfather? You'll give any trespassers a good fright and keep Kazik safe? I'll give you all the food offerings you could possibly wish for."

Domek sank his pointy little teeth into the cucumber's tangy green flesh and pushed his face against her hand as if in acceptance of this bargain, then leapt down from the table and scurried under the stove with his prize as if he feared someone might take it from him.

"*Zuza*," Kazik complained.

"*Kazik*," she retorted, mimicking his tone. "The wards surrounding this house are designed to discourage spirits with ill intentions from entering. But that doesn't mean they can't be breached by a truly powerful demon. It's not going to hurt to have a little insurance. House spirits employ powerful magic to guard their homes, and they can sense when something unearthly crosses the threshold."

That only reminded Kazik of all the trouble Domek had caused at the guesthouse and of something their grandfather had once said: *Spirits are hard to win over, but if you earn their loyalty, you have it forever. Sometimes the best way to defeat a strong enemy isn't to destroy them, Kazik, but to turn them to your side. Then you have one less enemy and a powerful ally.*

Dziadek had been less devout than their grandmother and

more cynical of the church's teachings. He'd left offerings of food and other trinkets for a lot of the creatures in these parts, and in return they'd loved and looked out for him. The last house spirit to make a home behind this kitchen's stove had even gone so far as to sneak the cigarettes out of his pockets, replacing them with random pebbles and odd buttons, because the little creature knew they were bad for his health.

That same spirit had thrown a great tantrum, threatening to burn down the house, before it vanished last summer because Kazik had stopped leaving out food for it. He hadn't been in a mood to leave offerings for a spirit after losing his grandmother.

A soft, contented crunching sounded from beneath the stove.

Kazik watched Zuzanna select a sun-ripe strawberry from the dish on the table. "So, you're not angry, then?"

"About what?"

Kazik dropped into the seat across from her. "That I'm helping him. A spirit. A literal demon."

"Since when do we get to be picky about who we help? It *is* one of our rules. We help anybody who needs help. Even our greatest enemies."

"Doesn't that only apply to humans? Babcia said—"

"Babcia used to tell us to keep chestnuts in the pockets of our coats as protection against the dangerous newfangled waves that radios emit."

Kazik choked on a laugh.

Zuzanna smiled. "You didn't always hate them the way you do now. I feel like they've been an easy target for your anger since she died. Even Babcia didn't actively seek out and go hunting for spirits to exorcise. She just dealt with those that caused trouble, and she wasn't right about everything. She grew up in a different time. Maybe always fighting the spirits isn't the only—nor best—way to protect this place. You have a softer heart than she did. Stop thinking about what she would do and think about what *you* want to do. Make your own choices."

"And if it all goes up in flames?"

If he let everybody down? The waters drawn from Leśna Woda's sacred springs often had a greater effect on spirits than they did on mortals. Villa Violetta was just one example: the heavily warded bathhouse drew its steaming water from the Violetta Spring, which was famous for its restorative powers. A visit there would revitalize Kazik after an illness or a long night out, but if a demon bathed in or drank from the same water, it would boost their magic, increase their strength. With repeated visits, a powerful demon would become almost impossible to kill.

"I have more faith in you than that," Zuzanna said. "Have more faith in yourself. You're just as strong and skilled as Babcia was. Even more so."

"You really think so?"

"I think the only difference between you two is that you lack conviction. And even if it does all go to hell, I'll always come and help you fix things."

Kazik slunk lower in his seat. "When did you get to be so wise?"

"I've always been this wise. You're finally noticing. Personally, I think if you're in a position to help someone, you should."

Kazik wondered if she'd still apply that logic to more

dangerous spirits like the wounded latawiec he had brought home the other day—or even Gisela. Though lately even he'd been finding it hard to remember Gisela was dangerous.

And that frightened him.

"I just don't know what to think anymore." He pushed his glasses into his hair and pressed the heels of his hands into his eyes. "Everything used to be simple."

Cut-and-dried.

The time he'd spent with Gisela wasn't enough to fully change his mindset—he wasn't about to abandon his entire belief system so quickly. But without his grandmother's guidance, without her example to follow, his viewpoint was shifting. Apparently, a few midnight heart-to-hearts with an insufferable water nymph was all it took to have him questioning things he'd never let himself question before.

Was he truly that gullible, that wretchedly lonely?

It was his own fault. Like Zuzanna was always lecturing him, if he made more of an effort, if he didn't close himself off to people, he wouldn't latch on to the first person to stick to him like glue.

Kazik cleaned his glasses on his shirt before putting them back on.

He needed to remember that Gisela was only hanging around him because of the unholy bargain that they'd struck. That was the extent of their relationship. She was only using him to get close to Aleksey. All this was just a means to an end.

Zuzanna nudged the bowl of cold beet soup he'd made earlier toward him. "So, are you going to tell me about this girl everyone's seen you with? And why there are *two* bowls of soup on the table?"

Kazik should've known she was only lulling him into a false sense of security before she grilled him. "The other bowl is for the domowik."

"Sure, it is. Come on, I'm dying to know! It's all I've been able to think about since I heard."

"Maybe you should get a hobby."

Zuzanna turned toward the stove and raised her voice. "Grandfather, do *you* happen to know who Kazik's mystery girl is?"

"She's just someone I'm helping," Kazik said quickly, praying Domek wouldn't reappear. He looked around for a spoon.

Zuzanna slid one across the table for him. "If you say so. I'm just . . ." She twirled her rosary around a finger. "A girl?" She sounded both relieved and faintly skeptical.

Kazik tensed. "I do also like girls, Zuza."

Zuzanna blinked slowly. Then she smiled and reached over the table to ruffle his hair condescendingly. "Of course, you do," she said, in a way that made it clear she didn't fully believe him. "I just hope nothing I've said— I hope I haven't pressured you nor done anything to make you feel as if you have to act like something you're not."

"Because when I told you I might like boys you said, 'It's fine with me, but don't tell Babcia or your mother or anyone else, all right?'"

Zuzanna winced.

Kazik knew it had come from a place of caring, but that hadn't made it hurt any less. And he'd listened to her because he couldn't afford to be cut off nor kicked out of the house. The church had shitty views on such things, and though he liked to think his grandparents would've loved him regardless, in the end it had been easier and safer to keep his mouth shut. He hadn't wanted to upset them after all they'd done for him.

For the thousandth time, he reminded himself that his sexuality wasn't something to be ashamed of; liking people regardless of their gender didn't mean he was broken nor unlovable. There were a lot of things wrong with him, but that wasn't one of them.

Zuzanna didn't apologize out loud, but she did start acting all sweet, fussing over him the same way Babcia had when she felt bad about something she'd done to him. She urged him to start eating the soup; she got up and cut him a generous slice of rye bread from the loaf cooling on the windowsill. Zuzanna was better with words than he was, but when it came down to it, they both preferred to rely on their actions to speak for them.

"I heard she's cute," she tried. "Are you going to ask her to the festival on Saint John's Eve?"

"Don't be ridiculous. I don't even *like* her. I tolerate her."

"With you that's practically the same thing."

"She likes someone *else*, Zuza," Kazik said, cringing a little at the hint of a whine in his voice.

Zuzanna's eyebrows lifted. "Okay. But I'm still happy you've made a friend. Now you just have to make more."

"Isn't one enough?"

"Nope. It's dangerous to build your life around one person alone. What happens if things don't work out or they leave?"

Kazik supposed she had a point. His mother had built her entire life around his father and had unraveled spectacularly when he'd walked out on them without a word. And then she decided she didn't even want Kazik and left him with his grandparents. And then his grandparents had left him, stolen away by death.

Even Gisela was ultimately going to leave him. He'd just reminded her of that. She'd get her kiss and go, and that would be the end of it. They'd be out of each other's lives for good.

The thought didn't fill him with the joy it usually did.

Maybe, a tiny treacherous voice whispered inside his head, *none of this will actually work. Maybe she'll be forced to stay and haunt the river. Haunt me.*

"That old story grandfather used to tell us." Kazik toyed with his spoon. "About the monk who helped a water nymph rejoin the living world. Do you think something like that could actually happen?"

Zuzanna raised an eyebrow, clearly surprised at the abrupt change of subject.

"I know it's just a fairy story," Kazik said quickly. "I mean, a spirit regaining their humanity just because someone kisses or promises to marry them is—"

"Ridiculous? Unlikely? Impossible?" Zuzanna's eyes crinkled at the corners when she smiled. "Maybe. But why not? Why couldn't it happen? There's a special, powerful kind of magic in the connections we make with other people."

A loud knocking distracted Kazik before he could give this thought. He set down his spoon. Zuzanna started to stand, but Kazik got there first. "I've got it."

She followed him out of the kitchen anyway. The person on the other side of the front door rapped their knuckles impatiently. Whoever it was, they were in a hurry. Saints, he didn't think he could handle much else at the moment.

Frowning, Kazik opened the door to an agitated Mrs. Mróz. Her wrinkled face was flushed from exertion. She let out a sigh of relief at the sight of them. "Kazik, do you have some time this evening? We might have trouble."

25

THE PALACE IN THE DEEP

GISELA

SINCE KAZIK WAS BUSY with his cousin, Gisela decided now was as good a time as any to get some answers from Wojciech. The Crystal Palace was always deserted after dusk; everyone left the river at moonrise to haunt the earthly realm, but she hoped she might still catch the water goblin before he went off to moon bathe.

The central atrium and the great hall were empty, and when she peeked inside the dining room, there was only a frog-faced water hag clearing away a towering stack of empty plates. Now that was something Gisela definitely didn't miss about her old life—doing dishes—having to clean up after Hugo and her father.

The hag glanced up at the sound of footsteps, her long river-weed hair and gown billowing in that strange watery gravity unique to this place, but she made no comment.

Clutching a ribbon-tied box to her chest, Gisela continued on her way. The walls, floor, and ceiling all had a luminous glow after dark, as if the moonlight from the world above shone directly through the crystal. It made the palace as a whole seem like nothing more than a ghostly conjuration. A fitting home for the souls of those who had drowned.

Slipping down a corridor lined with pillars, making her way into the north wing, Gisela passed a sparkling indoor waterfall and a pond filled with moon-white water lilies before arriving at her destination: the imposing pair of golden doors leading into Wojciech's private chambers.

She knocked once. Twice. Three times.

Silence. No voice bid her to enter.

Gisela shifted her weight from foot to foot, then shot a quick furtive glance over her shoulder. She'd never been invited into these rooms, and barging in felt wrong. Still, she clutched the gift box to her chest, at least she'd come with a peace offering. If she'd learned anything this past year, it was that all spirits, no matter how old and powerful, were weak to bribes and offerings. Knowing how annoyed Wojciech had been with her lately, she'd thought it best to come prepared.

Before she lost her nerve, Gisela pushed through the golden doors. "Hello? It's me! I come bearing gifts."

More silence.

Damn it. He must already be off frolicking in the moonlight with the others or doing whatever it was senior citizens did to entertain themselves.

Gisela puffed her cheeks out in annoyance. Her gaze slid around the room. Glowing amber lamps, the kind that came from her home island of Caldella, hung from the ceiling like teardrops, illuminating a cluttered space. Wojciech's chambers looked like they belonged to a hoarder or a disorganized magician. They were crowded with antique furniture and every kind of shiny trinket and sparkly oddment he had amassed over the ages: stacks of waterlogged books, strings of coral beads so heavy that it would hurt her neck to wear them, ancient bone-handled daggers, opera glasses, tobacco pipes, violins, gilt-framed paintings, and pocket watches on long golden chains. Moving forward, Gisela nearly tripped over a hatbox and a great spool of hand-dyed silk.

And, of course, there were more teacups.

Stored inside a tall glass-fronted cabinet against the far wall, imprisoning Wojciech's most treasured human souls. The pride of his collection. The souls of those he couldn't bear to let go. The souls he was driven by love or spite to keep with him forever and always, for all eternity.

Gisela shivered. He had some *serious* attachment issues.

The sighs of those souls filled her ears as she edged closer—a desperate ethereal tinkling as the teacups rattled softly upon their saucers. Among the more modern pieces of crockery were several small earthenware pots with lids, which she supposed he must've used to trap souls before the invention of fine porcelain. It was easy to forget that Wojciech was one of the monsters from her bedtime stories when he was always acting like such a nag, when he acted like he cared about her. Sometimes she wondered how different their relationship might've been if they'd crossed paths when she was an ordinary human girl.

She was tempted suddenly to set all the souls inside the glass-fronted cabinet free. She'd accidentally released one once. A rose-gold teacup had slipped from her fingers as she was replacing it on a shelf and dashed to pieces upon the floor. The resulting explosion of light had almost blinded her. She could still remember Wojciech's anguished shouts. The freed soul had taken the form of a brilliant white dove. It had soared heavenward with a piercing trill before it vanished, leaving only feathers floating in its wake.

Shaking the memory from her mind, she started to turn away from the cabinet, but something caught her eye. On the very bottom shelf, beside a jade-colored teacup hand-painted with peach blossoms, was a small heart-shaped perfume bottle with a flame-shaped stopper.

Zamira's voice echoed in her head. *He has a potion brewed by a powerful witch. It's made with half a drop of Living Water and will temporarily restore a water nymph to life, transform her into a human. He keeps it in a special cabinet in his chambers with all his favorite teacups.*

Gisela bit her lip. A second later, temptation got the better of her. Setting down the box she was carrying, she opened the cabinet door—it wasn't locked. Wojciech probably arrogantly assumed no one would dare intrude on his private space uninvited.

She reached inside before a whisper of doubt made her hand still.

The transformation is only temporary. The potion wears off, and when it does, you don't return to your current form. You would no longer be a water nymph. You'd be a shadow of what you are now. A ghost-thing. A shapeless, formless creature.

Her fingers twitched.

She was already an undead spirit. An abomination. Already a monster people recoiled from in horror. Did she really want to risk becoming something worse?

But . . .

This potion might give her the edge she needed. How was she ever going to progress her relationship if she was too scared to touch Aleksey? Taking it would dispel any niggling suspicions he might have about her. She wouldn't have to keep running back to the river in a panic like some girl in a fairy tale when the clock struck midnight. Even if the transformation was only temporary, *surely* she could get him to kiss her before its effects wore off. Kazik had basically declared their efforts a success. This was the closest she'd ever come to regaining her humanity, and time was ticking away.

Gisela caught her torn reflection in the cabinet's glass doors. She bit deeply into her cheek, latching on to the pain to keep herself calm. It wasn't like she had to drink the potion right this second. She would just take it with her now, in case she decided to use it later. A chance like this was too good to pass up. She sincerely doubted Wojciech would hand it over without a fight. Or worse, another lecture. This way she wouldn't have to pester him for it.

The tiny heart-shaped bottle was cold as ice against her fingers. Gisela lifted it toward the light, studying it closely. The liquid inside was the color of moonlight. Curious, she popped the flame-shaped stopper free.

A wisp of pale smoke snaked from the bottle toward the ceiling. She quickly replaced the stopper, but not before she'd breathed in the heady scent of honey and rain-soaked roses.

It made her head spin. She gripped the edge of the cabinet to steady herself, then slipped the long glittering gold chain attached to the stopper over her head and tucked the bottle down the front of her dress.

With her throat running dry now that she'd actually done it, Gisela fled the room like she was fleeing the scene of a crime, as quickly as she could.

The halls of the palace were still blessedly deserted, so it was a rude shock when she sped around a corner and nearly slammed face-first into a drowner. A willow-thin boy with a deathly blue cast to his olive skin. His long auburn hair tumbled like waves over his shoulders. Staring at his bare feet, Gisela could see the frog-like webs between his toes.

Inwardly, she cursed. She usually got on well with the male water spirits, but Akiva was the sole exception. Of all the drowners to run into now.

"What are you doing here?" he demanded. "This is our wing of the palace. No thieving rusałki allowed."

Gisela rolled her eyes. Akiva had been sore with her ever since she'd tried to kiss a human girl he'd had his eye on. Not that she knew he liked her at the time. And nothing had come of the flirtation; Kazik had interfered as usual and warned the girl against her.

"I told you before," she said, falling back a step. "I didn't know you liked Helena, and it's not my fault if she thought I'd make a better boyfriend than you."

Admittedly, this wasn't hard. Akiva's idea of romance was leaving shiny river rocks and dead things on his crushes' windowsills. Pebbles and fish bones. Stunned lizards and little birds. He was like a cat leaving presents on its owner's doorstep. Gisela didn't know how many years Akiva had been a spirit, but clearly, he'd been down here long enough to have forgotten how to woo people in the human way.

"If you'd like some tips," she offered magnanimously, "I'd be happy to share my wisdom."

Akiva let out a growl. "You think you're *so* special, don't you? Just because Wojciech likes you." With a flick of his wrist, he drew moisture from the air, condensing the droplets into an orb that floated ominously above his palm.

"Seriously? You want to fight about this?" Gisela dug a hand in her dress pocket for her replacement hair comb.

"Maybe you should've stayed out of our territory."

Spears of water jetted toward her. Quicker than Akiva could blink, Gisela sliced the comb through the air, redirecting the liquid.

The drowner's eyes widened as the water answered to her will, not his. He scrambled backward as she sent a miniature waterspout whirling after him. But her triumph was short-lived as, just like that, *her* hold on the water was severed—control wrested from her like an object ripped from her grip.

"Children!" A perpetually exasperated voice bellowed.

Before the shock could fully register on Gisela's face, the water snaked into ribbons, coiling around her and Akiva's ankles, yanking their feet out from under them and lifting them off the floor. Gisela let out a shriek as she was dangled upside down, suspended in midair.

Dropping the hair comb, she grasped at her dress with one hand, trying desperately to keep the fabric from falling down over her face. Her other hand clutched the potion bottle to her chest.

Wojciech stalked around a bend in the hallway. Handsome and youthful as ever, he looked like he'd been swimming in his fine clothes; his forest-green trousers were sopping; his linen shirt was so wet, it was sheer and clinging to the lean planes of his chest.

"If you must fight," he snapped, "have the intelligence to do so in a place where I don't have to listen to you."

"She started it!" Akiva protested. "She's not even supposed to be in this wing of the palace!"

Wojciech's eyes narrowed on Gisela. For a fleeting second, she wondered if she'd finally irked him enough that he'd drop his caring act. "Ah, Gisela, how kind of you to finally grace us with your presence, to what do we owe this pleasure?"

Oh great, he was in one of his *sarcastic* moods.

"Finally decided to come home? Didn't feel like worrying us all by not telling us where you were? My palace is not a hotel you can waltz in and out of as you please."

"Tch, okay, *Father.*" There wasn't a rule that they had to be back at the palace by a certain time or anything. At least she'd never been told there was.

"What's that you have there?"

Gisela's fingers clenched around the potion bottle. "What do you mean?"

Wojciech prowled closer. "What's that chain around your neck? You don't usually wear jewelry."

Gisela swallowed. "It's just a—a—"

"It's probably something she stole," Akiva piped up unhelpfully.

Gisela twisted in the air to face him. "Nobody asked you, fish face! It's just a necklace," she lied. "A trinket from Green Week left on a tree branch. I thought it was pretty. I'm wearing it to impress a human boy I like."

"A human boy," Wojciech parroted sourly. "He wouldn't happen to be a certain exorcist Yulia tells me you've been hanging around?"

Shit.

"You've been hanging around the exorcist?" Akiva exclaimed.

Gisela didn't say anything. She was too busy mentally planning how she would murder Yulia.

Wojciech's expression darkened. Saints, what punishment was he going to dream up for her now? Would he forbid her from leaving the palace like he'd threatened to last time?

"Kazik just wants to know how I died," she said quickly. "He thinks it's strange that I can't remember what happened. He even thinks the forest demons who wounded his grandmother could have been involved."

Wojciech blinked, caught off guard.

Gisela didn't give him time to recover. "Do you think that could be true? Do you think a bies could've hurt me?"

"Those monsters are capable of anything," Akiva chimed in.

Wojciech shot him a look. "I'm sure they say the same thing about drowners. Those *monsters* were not always so bloodthirsty. Mortals demonize them, and exorcists drive them from their homes, so they assert their strength by attacking weak humans or one another. Fighting over the scraps of what's left of their territory, lashing out in frustration and anger. But that's neither here nor there, the matter at hand . . ." His attention sliced back to Gisela. "I see you've even managed to acquire another hair comb, after I went out of my way to confiscate your old one."

Gisela gulped, but the harsh rhythmic slap of wet feet interrupted them before he could decide her fate. A figure rushed around the corner. Stocky. Blond. Hans. Another drowner.

Hans spared Gisela and Akiva a brief bewildered glance and stopped in front of Wojciech. Droplets of water slid down his round cheeks like rain. "Grandfather," he said breathlessly. "It's Tamara. The new water nymph. She's gone and dragged a man into the river. Drowned him."

Gisela's stomach plummeted.

Akiva hissed. "It's always the shy ones."

The watery ribbons holding him and Gisela dissolved with a splash, dumping them unceremoniously on the floor. Only Gisela's quick, inhuman reflexes saved her from landing flat on her face.

If she'd thought Wojciech looked angry before, it was nothing to how he looked now. The water goblin's eyes glowed a deep bloodred. "This is exactly why I wanted you to keep an eye on her. Where?" He snapped the final word at Hans.

"The riverbank near Villa Lilia's boathouse."

Wojciech craned his head back, looking up, as if he could see the scene in the world above through the ceiling. He strode past Gisela. Anger dripped from his words like poison. "You had better pray we find her before your new exorcist friend does."

26

THORNS

KAZIK

"WE'LL HAVE TO HANDLE this very carefully," Zuzanna said, striding ahead.

Kazik followed his cousin through Villa Azalia's night-blooming gardens. Despite the late hour, people still thronged the public paths. They passed a tired-looking maid carrying laundry from the bathhouse and a group of street musicians tuning their instruments by a fountain shooting sparkling jets of water at the sky.

"Don't confront her alone," Zuzanna continued. "I'll go with you."

"So, you think Mrs. Mróz could be right?"

"What do you think?"

Crossing a bridge arching over a pond, breathing in the fragrant scent of jasmine, Kazik cast his mind back.

Mrs. Mróz had brought them to an ornate wooden pavilion in the center of the garden's manicured lawns. There, she'd introduced them to a plump, flaxen-haired woman with round blushing cheeks and sharp gray eyes. Kazik thought she looked familiar, but it wasn't until she started speaking that he made the connection.

"It concerns my daughter, Roza," she said. "She hasn't been acting like herself."

"Like my husband," Mrs. Mróz interjected, crossing herself. "She could be possessed by another one of those forest devils."

Roza's mother clasped her hands in her lap. Kazik could tell she didn't truly believe her daughter was possessed by any kind of spirit—it was the skeptical purse of her mouth. His grandmother had had a hard time convincing Roza's family to let her place protections around Villa Azalia. Which was vexing because the bathhouse's waters blessed those who bathed in them with luck. Not exactly a quality Kazik wanted to gift any spirit.

"It's been worrying me for some time now," Roza's mother said, clearly so concerned for her daughter that she'd even confide in Kazik. "But lately it's gotten worse. I first noticed a change in her last year. We've always been close. Roza used to tell me everything. Now she barely talks to me. At first, I thought, 'Well, she's growing up. Maybe she doesn't want to spend so much time with her mother.' But there have been other things. She's always been such an accomplished pianist. She plays beautifully. She loves music. Always has. But she's been skipping her lessons. She dresses differently and disappears at odd hours. Comes and goes without a word. She treats us, her family, as if we're strangers. Even her little dog, Poppy, has been behaving strangely. The other day he bit Roza and ran off, and he's adored her from the moment we first brought him home," she'd said.

Kazik stopped before a gate tucked between the garden

hedges; the iron bars were nearly lost behind a veil of flowering vines. "I think I need to talk to a friend of hers."

This wasn't the first time an anxious family member had come to him convinced there was something not quite right about their loved one. He'd dealt with more than one mother convinced her offspring had been spirited away by a mamuna and replaced with a changeling. Often there was nothing wrong with the child in question. They were merely a little quiet or didn't adhere to society's strict standards of behavior.

None of the things Roza's mother had accused her of was overly damning. It was only odd that her dog had taken such a violent dislike to her.

"I know someone she's close to," he said. "If she's been acting strangely, Aleksey will have noticed."

"Aleksey?" Zuzanna said. "Isn't that the boy you like?"

"You're seriously bringing that up now?"

Zuzanna looked torn. But she must've decided the possibility of Roza being possessed by a bies was slightly more important than who he liked, because she said, "And if he has noticed something?"

Kazik's expression was grim. "Then we'll handle it carefully like you said."

It was risky to tackle this head-on. Like any spirits, biesy had their weaknesses, but they were extremely powerful. Second in strength only to the leszy, the lord of the forest, and they had no qualms using the humans they possessed as shields. It was incredibly difficult, as Kazik had learned, to separate an unwilling bies from their host.

The gate in the hedge clanged angrily as he pushed through it. It always came back to those demons. He would never, ever forgive them. "You head back to the house," he told Zuzanna. "I'll see if Aleksey's home."

His cousin waggled her eyebrows at him. "Don't get distracted."

Kazik made a rude gesture at her with his hand. Zuzanna cackled. But he was in no mood for teasing. Turning on his heel, he changed direction, stalking through the shadows of the park separating Villa Azalia from Villa Hyacinth, his senses on high alert just in case anything came at him from the darkness. The full moon cast an otherworldly glow over the grounds. Spirits always got a little moon drunk on nights like this, especially water spirits.

It had been a moonlit night when he'd gone to confront Mr. Mróz too. Hadn't his chasing away those last two demons been enough to scare the forest spirits off? It couldn't be one of them returning for revenge, could it? They'd have to be fools to try him again.

Or perhaps not—Kazik wasn't confident he could even summon the power to fight them right now. Could they know that? Had Gisela told the other spirits how he'd failed to exorcise her?

No.

Troubling as it was to admit, he trusted her to have kept his secret. More spirits would've come after him before now if she'd let something slip.

His gaze drifted heavenward. Couldn't the saints see this was the worst possible time to punish him or teach him a lesson or do whatever it was they were trying to do?

Why have you forsaken me?

How can I redeem myself?

Do you not want me to protect people?

The path rounded a curve, a cluster of neatly pruned trees, and then his destination came suddenly into view: a white-washed cottage with pink shutters in the corner of Villa Hyacinth's sprawling gardens. The house sat back from the path, covered in honeysuckle and climbing rose vines. A warm glow emanated from the windows. Two figures stood silhouetted in the light not far from the front door.

Kazik halted midstep, catching the murmur of their voices. He'd recognize the deep pitch of Aleksey's voice anywhere. He also recognized the girl he was with—Roza. Her hair gleamed like white gold in the fall of light.

What was she doing here so late?

Kazik dug a hand in his pocket, his fingers brushing rosary beads. They were speaking too softly for their words to carry clearly, as if they didn't want anyone to overhear their conversation. Pulse quickening, Kazik edged forward, trying to get close without revealing himself.

"They're not your friends, Aleksey."

"I know that."

"Do you?" Roza's voice rose in pitch. It was sharp with agitation.

Kazik's eyebrows lifted. Aleksey's face was half shadowed, but Kazik could see the tension in the broad line of his shoulders. It sounded like they were arguing.

"You could have—"

"I *know.*"

"Why haven't you, then?"

"I told you before, I'm waiting for the right moment. I—"

Somewhere in the dark, a nightingale sang.

Aleksey and Roza raised their heads and froze, looking like two startled deer. A beat later, Aleksey muttered something that Kazik didn't catch. Abruptly, Roza spun away from him, moving so fast, Kazik barely had time to sink into the dark at the side of the house before she stormed past. He glanced back and saw Aleksey run a hand roughly over his jaw.

Kazik brooded for a moment, unsure what to make of it all. Finally, he stepped out of the shadows and rounded the corner of the house. A rock crunched beneath his heel.

Aleksey whirled around with a curse. "*Kazik?*" he exclaimed, taking such a sharp step back that he tripped over a flowerpot and had to clutch comically at the rose trellis against the wall to catch his balance. "Where the devil did you come from—" He jerked his hand away from the trellis with a pained hiss.

Kazik was at his side in an instant. "Let me see." He caught Aleksey's wrist, holding tightly as Aleksey tried to yank his hand free. "Hold *still*. You're bleeding." He peeled Aleksey's fingers away from the cut flesh and angled their hands toward the light from the window.

"I always knew you'd be the death of me," Aleksey said faintly.

Rolling his eyes, Kazik pulled a clean handkerchief from his pocket and dabbed gently at the wound. Aleksey was being dramatic. It was an ugly gash, weeping crimson. Aleksey had probably caught it on a thorn. But the cut was shallow, thankfully, and would likely heal on its own without stitches. It shouldn't even leave a scar.

Aleksey had a small white scar already, in the center of his palm. Kazik traced his thumb over the raised flesh unthinkingly, stilling, when Aleksey's breath hitched.

Kazik was suddenly acutely aware of how very close they stood. Every muscle in Aleksey's body was tensed, as if poised to flee or fight.

"So," Aleksey said. There was an odd note in his voice. "What's the verdict?"

This close, his mismatched eyes were even more arresting than usual.

Kazik swallowed but managed to keep his face completely deadpan. "I'm afraid," he said, "that we're going to have to chop it off."

Aleksey blinked and then barked out a startled laugh, his chin dipping toward his chest, his honeyed hair falling into his eyes. "Did you just make a *joke?*"

A small, rare smile pulled at Kazik's lips. Dropping his gaze, he concentrated on wrapping the handkerchief tightly around Aleksey's palm to staunch the blood flow. *Get a grip on yourself. He likes Gisela.* Aloud he said, "You should clean it and put some ointment on it. If you have gauze inside, I can bandage it up properly."

"You're not going to kiss it better?"

Kazik didn't trust himself to answer.

Slowly, Aleksey drew his hand back, running the fingers of his uninjured hand over the makeshift bandage. The night breeze gusted between them, cool and smelling of jasmine and sweet green things.

"You're really . . . not what I expected, you know," Aleksey said suddenly.

Kazik's brows lifted.

Aleksey shook his head. "What brings you by here so late? Are you keeping tabs on me now?"

"You're close friends with Roza, aren't you?" Kazik said. "Her mother approached me earlier. She said Roza's been behaving strangely. She's been skipping her lessons. Sneaking out. Apparently, her dog bit her and ran off. I wanted to ask if you'd noticed anything . . . off about her recently?"

Aleksey was slow to answer. "It's a little complicated," he said after a lengthy pause.

"Complicated?"

"Yes. Roza's been having a hard time lately. It might not seem like it, but her mother's really strict and controlling. I don't know what else she told you, but she has Roza's whole future planned out for her, and lately Roza's been feeling like that isn't the life she wants for herself." Aleksey shrugged. "She's rebelling. It's just family drama. Nothing for you to be concerned about."

The knot of worry in Kazik's chest loosened a fraction. "I thought it could be something like that." Even so, he made a mental note to talk to Roza himself as soon as possible. Most spirits were adept at disguising their true natures in order to better deceive humans, and biesy were particularly clever and cunning. "If you do notice anything, you'll let me know?"

"Of course. Why? Are you worried she might've been possessed by a demon?"

Kazik felt the heat climb up the back of his neck. The teasing arch of Aleksey's brows made him feel like a fool for even entertaining the idea.

With a knowing grin, Aleksey jerked his chin toward the house. "You coming in? Mother will have my head if I don't at least offer you a drink. And I think we do have gauze." He moved toward the front door, gesturing for Kazik to follow.

Kazik hesitated. In the back of his mind, he could hear Zuzanna reminding him not to get distracted. But he *had* offered to patch Aleksey up properly, and any chance to spend time with him was an opportunity to gather more information for Gisela to use in her quest to win his affections.

"Just for a second," he said, following Aleksey inside.

27

THOSE WHO HAUNT THE EARTH

GISELA

THEY FOUND TAMARA BY the riverbank not far from Villa Lilia's boathouse. A mist was rising cold off the water, unusual for summer. Gisela assumed Wojciech had conjured it as a kind of smoke screen. The milky pall veiled the scene like a funeral shroud. Tamara was alone, thankfully, sitting amid the roots of a willow tree with her knees drawn up to her chest and her back resting against the trunk.

There was no sign of Kazik. No sign of anyone, aside from . . .

Aside from the figure lying face down in the shallows, entangled in the reeds and rushes. The man's pale skin and crumpled white dress shirt were illuminated by the light from the moon.

Gisela approached slowly, moving like someone caught in a dream. She could feel her breath coming fast. The world felt like it was slowly tipping sideways.

Wojciech overtook her. Hans and Akiva brushed past on her other side, wading into the inky water. Together they hoisted the limp, dripping-wet figure onto the bank and rolled the body over so the man's face turned toward the sky. His eyes were open and staring at nothing, his features frozen in a mask of terror. Muddy water trickled from the corners of his lips.

Gisela clapped a hand over her mouth. A wave of nausea hit her, and she doubled over, emptying the contents of her stomach onto the grass. She knew the stories. She'd grown up with them. She knew rusałki were famous for drowning men. But she'd never seen an actual dead person before. Not a dead person who was really, *truly* dead.

Was that how *she'd* looked when they'd found her? Had Hans or Wojciech fished her bloated and lifeless body out of the river?

The horror hit her all at once. Gisela crashed to her knees, watching Akiva crouch beside the man and, with a strange tenderness, gently stroke the hair back from his brow.

A small sob ripped out of Gisela. This was all her fault.

Water lapped against the riverbank. She could hear the distant haunting warble of a nightingale and Wojciech speaking quietly. "Take the body into the forest and burn it so that the man's soul moves swiftly to the afterlife. Ask the fire spirits for their help if you must. Tell them I'll owe them a favor. We need to cover this up. I don't want to give the exorcist a reason to come after any of us."

It took a beat for the words to fully register. Fear bloomed anew inside Gisela's chest. How would Kazik react if he discovered Tamara was responsible for this man's death? Would he hunt her down, trap her inside a magic circle, and attempt to exorcise her?

It was probably a blessing that he couldn't use his magic right now.

"Hans," Wojciech said. "Make sure you perform the proper funerary rites. Wrap the body before you burn it. Drive a stake through the heart. We want to prevent him from coming back as a drowner. It would only cause more trouble."

Gisela sucked in a deep shuddery breath, wiped her mouth on the back of her hand, and rose slowly to her feet. Trembling, moving like she was still caught in a terrible dream—she wished this were a dream; she wanted so badly to wake up at home in her own bed and find this was all just a nightmare—she made her way over to the girl beneath the willow tree.

Tamara hadn't moved. She looked like a ghost in her floaty white dress, all soft edges, her skin aglow with a strange and ethereal light.

Gisela knelt across from her. Tamara hugged her knees close to her chest. The mist roiled as Wojciech moved to join them.

"I'm sorry," Gisela blurted, addressing them both, her head bowed. "I'm so, so sorry."

"But you weren't the one who—" Tamara interrupted.

"No, but if I had . . . if I hadn't left you alone . . . if I hadn't been so focused on getting a kiss . . ." Gisela buried her face in her hands. If she hadn't been so wrapped up in herself, if she hadn't been so selfishly absorbed in her quest to regain her humanity, if she'd listened to Wojciech, she might've been there to stop Tamara from harming anyone.

Now . . . now someone was *dead*.

She was just like her father: entirely consumed with her own pursuits, only thinking about her own needs and feelings.

"Oh, Gisela." Tamara reached over and drew Gisela's hands

away from her face, clasping them tightly between her own. "You couldn't have talked me out of it," she said, as if she could read Gisela's mind. "What I've done, it had nothing to do with you. You aren't responsible for my actions. I told you once, didn't I? That after I started working as a maid at the bathhouse, I fell in love with somebody I shouldn't have. He—" Tamara swallowed. "He hurt me. He ended *my* life. And no one was going to punish him for it. I overheard Villa Lilia's groundskeepers talking. They said I threw myself into the river because I was heartbroken when I discovered he was engaged to be married. I wasn't heartbroken. I was *angry* that he hadn't told me. I was going to tell his fiancée."

All the hairs on Gisela's arms rose.

"After I came back like this, I still wanted to tell her. I wanted her to know what kind of man he was. I think that's why I came back. I couldn't rest until I'd paid back the person who'd done this to me. So I snuck away while I knew you and the other girls were busy. I came to the riverbank several times—we used to meet here—and tonight I saw him standing by the water's edge. He was so shocked, you know, to see me. It was easier than I'd thought to pull him into the river and hold him down. It felt so good to finally have the power to hurt him back. I was just so angry. I—I'm not sorry for what I've done," Tamara said in rush, but she looked a little fearful when she glanced at Wojciech.

"If he was the one who took your life," the water goblin said, "then you had every right to be angry. He deserved his fate."

Tamara's lip wobbled, but she straightened slightly, sitting up taller, clearly bolstered by his words of validation. "Thank you, Grandfather. I'm sorry to have worried you. I know this will probably cause you trouble with the exorcist."

Wojciech lifted his shoulders in a helpless shrug. "This is hardly the first time I've had to cover for one of you girls. I only regret . . ." Gone was his earlier anger. There was only sorrow on his face now. "I wish you could have stayed with us a little longer."

Gisela glanced at him sharply. "What do you mean? You just said—you can't punish her for—"

"It's not a punishment." Tamara squeezed Gisela's fingers. Something about the weight and feel of her grip was off. The touch was too light. That strange glow suffused all of her now, from her skin to her short brown hair, turning it silver.

It was similar to how Gisela glowed when she shape-shifted. "What's happening to you?" she whispered.

It was Wojciech who answered. "Water nymphs are maidens who died unnatural deaths," he said, echoing what Gisela had once told Tamara, what he had once told her. "You're bound here by your grief and grudges to live as restless spirits, unless you find a way to rejoin the mortal world or your deaths are avenged."

Because if they managed to revenge themselves on those who had wronged them, they could move on to the afterlife.

"Don't be sad," Tamara said, clearly sensing Gisela's growing alarm. "I feel like I can let it all go now, all the rage and regret, everything that was anchoring me here. I feel lighter. I did what I needed to do." Her gaze drifted back to the water. "I don't think I was even the first girl he hurt. But he can't harm anyone else now. I'm relieved, really, to leave this all behind me."

"But—" The words stuck in Gisela's throat. "Do you have to move on now? Don't you want to stay? I'll do it right this time," she promised. "I'll show you around properly. We'll relax at the bathhouse together. Take milk baths. We'll explore the parks, and I'll braid your hair with flowers. You won't have to clean up after any guests. I'll introduce you to all the spirits. Not just the ones like us. There's beautiful wiły who live in the clouds, and ogniki, fire spirits, who guard hidden treasure. I'll even introduce you to Kazik. The exorcist. He's not as scary as everyone thinks. And you can meet Domek. His fur is so soft and—and—" Gisela was forced to pause for breath.

Tamara smiled at her softly. "Are you certain you're not the one who wishes to stay?"

Gisela's mouth opened and shut.

"I'm ready to move on," Tamara said. "I'm kind of excited to find out what comes next. Whatever *you* choose to do, I hope you find happiness. I hope you find peace. And I hope . . ." Her voice choked slightly.

Tears blurred Gisela's vision.

"I was brought up believing in the old ways," Tamara said, "believing that after souls spend time in the afterlife, they return to this world and are reborn again. So I hope we can find each other in our next lives and have the chance to become friends."

Tamara's hands still gripped Gisela's own—but Gisela could no longer feel them. The glow emanating from Tamara's skin grew so blindingly bright, Gisela was forced to close her eyes. When she opened them again, it was to watch Tamara take the form of a bird. A beautiful gossamer-winged creature. It shook out its brilliant white plumage and unfurled two radiant wings.

A breeze blew, sighing through the willow tree's branches. Gisela blinked stars from her vision as the bird let out a joyful trill and took off, soaring toward the night sky, up and up and up, following a starlit path and vanishing into the dark.

28

BEING HUMAN

GISELA

GISELA HARDLY REMEMBERED THEIR return to the palace. Afterward, she only vaguely recalled Wojciech silently helping her to climb the atrium stairs and guiding her through the arched door behind the waterfall that led to the water nymphs' quarters. Each girl had a room to herself, with a reflective pool for a mirror, a carved chest full of impossible dresses, and a four-poster bed curtained by billowing canopies. Gisela pressed her face into her bed's feathery pillows until she ran out of tears.

She didn't sleep that night. She couldn't. Her mind wouldn't stop reliving that moment on the riverbank. She couldn't stop seeing that pale body tangled in the reeds. She couldn't stop seeing Tamara disappearing.

Grief and guilt poured over her like a wave and swept her under.

She didn't get up at first light. She didn't answer when Miray and Zamira knocked softly on her door. She didn't move when night fell once more. She didn't leave her bed until a whole day later, once she heard the other girls go down to the dining hall for the midday meal.

She couldn't bring herself to face them.

It took all her will just to dress and wash her face. Her hands. There was dirt, mud from the riverbank, crusted under her nails. She scrubbed at her fingertips until they throbbed, then worked the tangles out of her ever-damp hair with the comb she'd discovered on her bedside table.

It was her hair comb. The first she'd been given. The one she'd lent Tamara that Wojciech had confiscated. Bone white with glossy black river pearls embedded in the handle. Wojciech must've left it there for her. She didn't understand why he would have returned it. He had to be furious with her after everything that had happened.

But maybe he thought she'd finally learned her lesson. Maybe he thought losing Tamara was punishment enough.

Gisela set the comb down. He was probably wishing she'd never ended up in his realm, that she'd never become a water nymph. All she'd ever done was cause him trouble.

Well, not anymore.

She'd been right from the beginning—this wasn't the place for her. She didn't *deserve* to be here. Gisela's hand drifted to her throat, to the chain around her neck. The chain on which hung the tiny heart-shaped bottle containing Wojciech's potion. The sight and sparkle of it reminded her that she didn't have to remain here if she was only willing to take a risk.

She held the bottle up to the light. All the other water spirits probably wanted her gone now too. She was doing them a favor. She couldn't cause anyone any more grief if she left.

Slowly, she popped the stopper free and lifted the bottle to her lips.

She had to think of Hugo; she'd failed Tamara, but she wouldn't fail her brother. She needed a kiss from a mortal now more than ever, and if Aleksey was too repulsed by her in her current form to touch her, then—

Before she could think twice, she swallowed the potion in one quick, deep gulp. Her mouth twisted at the taste: coppery like blood, yet strangely sweet like honey.

For a split second, nothing happened. Gisela stood with the tiny bottle still raised to her lips, feeling foolish. Maybe this wasn't even the potion the other girls had talked about.

A bolt of searing heat speared through her center. She let out a gasp as the magic took hold. It felt like she'd been gutted by a fishhook. No one had warned her that drinking the potion would *hurt*.

Gisela bent almost in two, clutching at her belly when the pain spread outward, lighting up every nerve in her body. It felt like flames were licking at her insides. The pain was all-consuming, all-encompassing. It was devouring her alive.

Fear seized her. Had she made a mistake? This felt like dying, not coming back to life.

Gisela staggered and collapsed against her bed, clawing her fingers into the sheets. She lost awareness of her surroundings, of time. The world spun into blackness.

***

The cold woke her hours later, making her shiver. The cool, moisture-laden air raised goose bumps on her skin.

Her strangely warm skin.

Gisela sat up so fast, the world spun a second time. The chill down here had never affected her like this before, and there was an odd feeling in her chest. A frantic, frightened drumming. A pounding that, at first, she couldn't identify. It had been so long.

Her heart, she realized with a jolt. Her heart was *beating*.

She pressed a hand to her breast, to the soft skin below her jaw, to her throat, to her wrists, relishing each pulse. The rhythm of her heart was the most tantalizing song. She'd done it. The potion had worked. It had refashioned her into something human.

Or something almost human.

An eager glance at herself in the room's reflective pool confirmed her complexion had lost its deathly green-blue pallor. Her skin was the color of summer-ripe peaches. But her eyes were still a shade too red. A sign, perhaps, that some magic still lingered within her.

She experimented with her hair comb, drawing ribbons of liquid from the pool, then stilling the surface so that it did not so much as ripple, finding she could still manipulate water. Yulia had told her tales of humans hunting water nymphs for their combs, hoping to steal that power for themselves. But they would only discover that as mortals they couldn't wield the combs' magic after all. So she wasn't fully mortal—yet.

Concealing her hair—her *dry* hair—beneath a scarf embroidered with little rosettes she'd borrowed from a clothesline some time ago, Gisela snuck out of the palace. The empty heart-shaped bottle swung from its chain around her neck as she left the river and made her way to Kazik's house.

She neared the cottage, coincidentally, just as his cousin was leaving. Zuzanna's brows furrowed slightly, as if in recognition, but a pair of storks flying overhead drew her attention away while Gisela hurried past her.

She let herself in without knocking, sweeping through the front room and into the kitchen. "Darling . . ." She trailed off.

Kazik was sitting at the kitchen table, his arms folded on the wood, his head pillowed on his forearms. His eyes were closed. His mouth was slack, his lips just slightly parted.

Asleep, Gisela realized.

His wire-rimmed glasses rested on the table before him. He looked strangely vulnerable without them. Younger.

She tiptoed closer, stilling when Kazik stirred, his dark brows pulling into a frown even in slumber. He muttered something inaudible.

Gisela smothered the sudden irrational urge to reach out and smooth away the worried crease between his brows with the pad of her thumb. "Kazik," she said softly.

His lashes fluttered and his frown deepened, the muscles in his shoulders bunching. She wondered if he was having a nightmare.

"Kazik." Gisela laid a hand on his arm, intending to shake him awake.

His eyes flew open at her touch, his hand catching hers in a punishing grip. He surged to his feet so fast, his chair crashed to the floor.

"Saints, it's just me!"

"Gisela?" Kazik blinked in obvious confusion. "What—" He

released her, his eyes focusing on her face. "Where have you even *been*?"

"Why?" Gisela tried, attempting to recover her composure. Her heart was racing. "Did you miss me?"

"Of course not!" Kazik snapped, his cheeks going from tan to red in a flash. "I just—" He raked a hand through his hair. It was such a mess, it looked like he'd run his fingers through it several times already. "You were gone all yesterday. I didn't know what to think. You're always around. I thought something might've happened to you. Especially with a bies possibly running around."

"A bies?" Gisela said sharply. "Did something happen?"

Kazik didn't answer. His attention had snagged on a note left folded on the kitchen table. He picked it up and cursed when he read it.

"What is it?"

"A note from my cousin. A young man is missing. He was seen walking in Villa Lilia's gardens the night before last but never returned to his hotel."

A shiver of dread traveled down Gisela's spine.

"Zuzanna's gone to try and determine if a spirit is involved." Kazik pressed both hands to his face and inhaled deeply. "This is what happens when I let my guard down. This is because none of you fear me, isn't it? That's why things keep happening. None of you see me as a threat. Even the saints have lost faith in me." His voice splintered. "If something's happened to him, it's my fault. I'm the one who's supposed to guard the town. I promised . . ."

"It's not your fault!" Gisela burst out. She couldn't stop herself from stepping closer, from laying a hand on his chest. She felt him stiffen, but he didn't pull away. It rattled her, seeing him look so defeated. "It has nothing to do with you. Whether you're a threat doesn't matter. Spirits have reasons for acting the way they do. They have their own fears and desires and grudges, just like humans. It's not your fault if—if a spirit was responsible for that man's disappearance."

She bit her lip. Surely even Kazik couldn't say that man's fate was undeserved. He'd hurt Tamara first. It had been the consequences of his own actions that had led to his death at Tamara's hands.

Gisela wanted to tell Kazik what had happened, but she couldn't, not with Wojciech's warnings echoing in the back of her mind. Tamara had already moved on, and Gisela didn't want Kazik hunting down any of her fellow water spirits in retribution.

She swallowed the impulse to confess. "It's not your fault," she repeated. "*I'm* a spirit, and I'm telling you this, so you have to believe me. You're trying your best, even without your powers."

Kazik snorted softly, but Gisela was relieved to see some of the anguish leave his face. "It's hard not to blame myself," he admitted quietly. "When something like this happens, I feel like I'm failing everybody. I feel like I should've done more or done things differently." He ground a knuckle into his eye; his gaze had gone a little glassy. He turned away, clearing his throat, clearly embarrassed. He probably hated anyone seeing him be vulnerable.

He stepped away from her, picking his glasses up from the table. He slipped them on. "Did you have a chance yet to ask the water goblin about your death?"

Gisela unwound the scarf from around her head. "No. Not in detail. We—we were busy with other things." She twisted the scarf between her fingers. "What did you mean earlier when you said one of those forest demons could be running around?"

"Do you remember Aleksey's friend?" Kazik said. "The pretty girl from the cemetery."

"Roza?"

"Her mother said she's been acting strangely. I'm not certain she's been possessed. I talked to Aleksey, and he thinks it's just family drama."

"He would know," Gisela said reassuringly. "He said she's like a younger sister to him."

"I hope that's all it is. I still want to talk to her myself. I couldn't track her down yesterday. It's like she's avoiding me." Kazik frowned. "Not that confronting her is going to do any damn good if I can't summon the power to perform an exorcism."

"I'll help you deal with her," Gisela said before he could start to fret again. She could still use her hair comb after all.

"You think you're strong enough to take on one of those demons?"

Gisela scowled at the hint of amusement in Kazik's tone. "You need to stop underestimating water nymphs. We're not weak."

"Neither are biesy. Just be on your guard, all right?" After crossing the kitchen, Kazik picked a parcel wrapped in brown paper and tied neatly with string off the bench. The sound of his footsteps must've roused Domek from a nap, because the house spirit poked his whiskered head out from beneath the stove.

With a great yawn, he padded closer, slinking between Gisela's ankles.

Kazik dropped the parcel into her arms. "That's for you."

"For me?" Gisela looked at him in surprise. "What is it?"

"Just something I got for you." Kazik rubbed the back of his neck, looking more embarrassed by the second. "You don't have to wear it."

Carefully, curiously, Gisela unknotted the string and unfolded the layers of brown paper to reveal a dress—a long, floaty mint-green dress with short puffy sleeves and a low scooping neckline. A wide cream-colored ribbon cinched the whisper-soft fabric below the bust and tied into a large bow at the back.

It was the dress she'd admired in the shop window all those weeks ago.

Gisela was too stunned to do anything but stare. "You bought it for me? From that shop? Wasn't it expensive?"

"Never mind that. The dressmaker is an old friend of my grandmother's. She was happy to do me a favor." Kazik shrugged, avoiding eye contact.

"But . . . why?"

"Didn't you say you liked it? You'll need something to wear tomorrow night. It's Saint John's Eve. You thought it was the perfect opportunity for you to dress up all pretty and get a kiss, didn't you? Aleksey's sure to attend the festivities."

Warmth bloomed inside Gisela's chest.

"There's even this tradition," Kazik continued, "where girls weave wreaths from wildflowers and magic herbs and cast them upon the river as night falls. If your wreath floats and is carried calmly by the water, it means you'll find love. If your wreath tangles in the reeds or is stolen by the current and sinks, it means love has forsaken you. And, if your wreath drifts toward a certain person, it means they're fated to be your future lover or lover for the night. You can make a wreath. I'll make sure Aleksey is standing at the river's edge when you place it on the water. Then you can give the wreath a little push with the help of your enchanted comb and direct it toward him. We'll create the perfect romantic moment."

He'd come up with a whole damn plan.

Gisela looked down at the dress—the dress he'd remembered she'd liked, that he'd gone out and bought specially for her—and quickly dropped back into her usual flirtatious persona to cover the unwillingly jolt her heart gave. "Aw, Kazik, you really know how to make a girl feel special."

Kazik blushed scarlet. "Like I said before, you always go around looking like a ghost in your funeral-white dresses with your wet hair dripping everywhere . . ." He trailed off abruptly, staring at her with an expression of growing horror. "Y-your—"

Domek let out a panicked yowl, his body arched in alarm.

Kazik grabbed a pitcher of water and, before Gisela could react, upended its entire icy contents over her head.

29

REVELATIONS

GISELA

GISELA SPLUTTERED, SPAT, AND blinked water from her eyes. “What the hell?”

“Y-your hair!” Kazik stuttered.

It was dry, Domek finished.

Gisela looked from the house spirit to Kazik, taking in their identical horrified expressions. Oh, of course! She swept a strand of wet hair off her brow and sighed, playing the whole thing off like it was nothing, while a tiny mischievous smirk curved her lips. “Well, that’s because I’m human right now.”

Kazik stared. “Wait, what do you mean? Did—” His eyes were wide as saucers. “Aleksey hasn’t already kissed you, has he?”

Gisela had forgotten what it felt like to blush. The sudden excruciating rush of heat to her cheeks made her want to cover her face. “No! Not yet.”

“But how?” Kazik set the water pitcher down.

Gisela patted her skin dry with her scarf. “The older girls told me Wojciech had a potion that could transform a water nymph. So I, uh, drank it.”

Domek let out a loud feline wail. *Why would you ruin yourself like that?*

Gisela rolled her eyes at the house spirit's dramatics. "Because I *want* to regain my humanity. Not all of us are content to be spirits, Grandfather."

Domek's whiskers twitched disapprovingly. With a huff, he nosed his way inside a kitchen cupboard left slightly ajar.

Gisela expected Kazik to protest, but he pulled out his chair at the table and sat back down. He hadn't stopped staring at her for even a second, his expression slowly morphing from shock to a kind of awe.

Gisela smirked again and took the chair beside his. "Want to feel my pulse? I have one!"

Wordlessly, Kazik took her hand in his, encircling her wrist with unexpected care, as if he were worried that she might dissolve to nothing beneath his touch. Heat radiated from his fingertips as he traced the inside of her wrist, feeling for the life in her, for the beat of her heart. A look of pure childlike wonder crossed his face.

"You're a witch," Gisela teased, "and you're shocked by the effects of a little potion?"

"It's like something out of a story," Kazik confessed. "I'm always dealing with magic and spirits, so sometimes I forget what it's like to witness a true miracle. I'm not sure I even believed this was possible until now." He let out a breathy laugh and smiled so radiantly, Gisela's heart skipped a beat.

Kazik had a very nice smile when he remembered to use it.

It was almost worth the risk of taking the potion, to have made him smile like this.

"Why didn't you take the potion before?" Kazik asked. "Why bother with—"

"I didn't know it existed, and the transformation is only temporary. It won't last. I still need someone to kiss me to make this permanent."

Kazik pushed up his glasses. His eyes moved over her face, drinking her in like he was trying to memorize her as she was now, seeing the ordinary human girl she could've been. The girl she *had* been. Once. Her pulse sped up beneath his fingers. She wondered if he could feel it. The world narrowed to the gentle pressure of his thumb against the soft skin of her wrist and the wonder in the dark of his eyes, the brush of his knee against hers as he leaned forward in his chair.

His gaze dipped to her mouth, and for a single impossible moment, Gisela thought *he* was going to kiss her.

For a single guilty moment, she wanted him to.

Kazik's lips were a little chapped, but they looked incredibly soft, the bottom lip so captivatingly full. Time slowed; Gisela's breath stuttered to a stop as Kazik leaned even closer.

The distant *bang* of the front door slamming and the sound of Aleksey calling out a greeting brought reality rushing back. The spell broke.

Gisela froze in place, while Kazik flinched back so violently, his side struck the table. He knocked his chair over again in his haste to stand.

It fell to the floor with a crash.

A fever-hot flush of embarrassment swept Gisela from head to toe. It wasn't just her cheeks burning now. Her whole body was on fire. She felt a powerful need to look anywhere but at Kazik. She could still feel the warmth of his fingers like a ghostly echo against her wrist. "A-Aleksey!" she stammered as he entered the kitchen.

Kazik reached down to pick up his chair. Gisela couldn't see his face, but his ears were a searing red.

Aleksey did not seem bothered by this—if anything, he looked supremely entertained. "Did I come at a bad time? Do you two need a moment alone?"

"*No!*" Gisela blurted.

Kazik set the chair on its feet. "I need to—to hang the laundry out," he said, grabbing a wicker basket of clothing by the back door and fleeing into the garden.

"I—I should get home too," Gisela said with a shaky exhale. Her heart was still beating wildly. She tried to think of something madly unattractive—Wojciech naked, in his true form.

That helped.

Aleksey was still staring after Kazik, but he turned when she stood from the table. "Do you have an umbrella? It's raining."

"It is?" It *was*. Straining her ears, Gisela could make out the soft patter of rain on the roof and the faint croaky refrain of frog song somewhere in the distance. What was Kazik doing outside in the rain, then? She quickly shook that thought from her head. She didn't care. "I don't have one."

Water nymphs didn't own umbrellas. They were inordinately

fond of walking in the rain. The other girls were likely out in the downpour already, rejoicing and catching droplets on their tongues, drinking the rain directly from the sky.

"You can share mine, then," Aleksey said.

"But you just got here," Gisela protested. "Did you need something?"

"I was just passing by and thought I'd poke my head in. I didn't see either of you yesterday." Aleksey swept a bandaged hand through his hair.

Gisela's eyes widened.

"Just a scratch," Aleksey reassured her. "Nothing serious. I've had worse." He dropped his arm to his side. "My mother's waiting for me at home anyway. I can walk you to the bridge if you like."

"Um, yes, yes, I'd like that." Gisela hesitated, then grabbed the dress Kazik had bought her from the table. She hastily folded it back up in its brown paper wrapping.

Aleksey's eyes narrowed as he watched her. He canted his head to one side. "You look—"

Terrible! Domek wailed, popping back out of the cupboard. *Look what she's done to herself. She's gone and—*

Gisela cut the house spirit a look that told him he'd better keep his mouth shut in front of Aleksey or else.

"I think she looks beautiful," Alekscy said.

Gisela almost dropped the dress parcel.

Domek feigned hacking up a hair ball in disgust. *Of course,* you *would think that. All your kind—*

"Shall we go, Gisela?" Aleksey interrupted, holding out his hand.

Gisela desperately wanted to leave before Kazik came back,

so she nodded and let him lead her out of the house. If she stayed in the kitchen for a moment longer, she'd dissolve into a panicked mess.

Outside, Aleksey opened a crimson-red umbrella over both their heads. They walked in silence. Gisela's thoughts raced.

She'd always flirted with Kazik, but that was just habit. It didn't mean anything. Originally, she'd just wanted to throw him off-balance. It was fun seeing him get annoyed and worked up and flustered. He was so easily embarrassed. In the kitchen they'd just—just gotten swept up in the moment, in the excitement of her transformation. That was all.

Wait, if he'd been about to kiss her . . . shouldn't she have let him? Wasn't that what she'd been aiming for this whole time? It didn't matter who she got a kiss from, as long as they were mortal.

Gisela bit back a groan. She wanted to slap herself. If she'd just leaned in, she would've gotten exactly what she wanted. She could've stopped haunting this place. She could've returned home, returned to where she belonged. Left all this behind.

For some reason, her heart sank a little at the thought when she should have been elated.

And she *was*. She'd decided this was for the best. She'd come so close to getting her old life back, to seeing Hugo again. Hugo, whom she missed so fiercely. So why did she also feel so inexplicably sad?

She wondered if her brother was even still hoping or expecting her to make her way back to him, or if he had already grieved her and moved on.

The light summer rain pattered against Aleksey's umbrella.

"Are you . . . okay?" he asked softly. "You're kind of quiet."

"What? Yes, of course! I'm great. I actually really love walking in the rain." Gisela smiled brightly. She just needed a moment to sort through all her muddled feelings.

Aleksey mirrored her smile. "Are you just telling me what I want to hear?"

"Like you don't do that all the time."

Aleksey's eyebrows shot up.

Damn it. She hadn't meant to say that. But it was something she'd noticed the more time they spent together. He was always so cheerful, so even-tempered. His responses were so quick and almost always what the other person wanted to hear. She'd yet to see him upset. He seemed to have endless patience with everyone and everything.

"It's hard to tell what you're truly thinking and feeling sometimes," she confessed. There was something guarded about Aleksey despite his easygoing attitude. "I just get the feeling you're not always comfortable being yourself around other people."

"Oh?" Aleksey hummed. "I think you're the only one who's noticed."

That wasn't surprising. It was simply because she did it too: masked and hid things about herself. A lot of the time, the parts of themselves people showed you were only what they felt safe to share.

Aleksey twirled the umbrella. The panes cast a bloodred shadow over the top half of his face. "I guess I worry people won't see me the same way, if I'm completely myself around them. I think they only like the person they perceive me as. The person I present myself as. I wonder if they would still like the real me."

"Is the real you so awful?"

A hint of mischief caught in the curve of Aleksey's lips. "Oh, terrible. You have no idea. I'm a real monster." He bared his teeth at her.

Gisela laughed.

"Maybe I'll show you my true face one day, Gisela, if you promise not to recoil in horror."

"Promise," Gisela said immediately. Maybe one day she'd be able to share a more honest version of herself with him too. "I think everyone has a side to themselves they keep from other people for fear of being rejected. It's not just you. Everyone's putting on an act of some kind. The right person will accept every part of you. I won't reject you—the real you."

"I'll hold you to that."

They turned a corner, and Aleksey tilted the umbrella. Gisela realized abruptly that it wasn't big enough to cover the two of them; Aleksey was letting one of his shoulders get wet in order to shield her completely.

Really, sometimes he was just too good to be true.

Gisela hugged the dress Kazik had given her to her chest and gathered her courage. "Are you—are you going to the Saint John's Eve festivities tomorrow night? I thought it could be fun if we went together." The words came out in a rush.

"I'd like that."

"Really?"

"Kazik will come, too, won't he?"

Gisela's stomach twisted with that same odd mix of jealousy and possessiveness she'd felt watching Kazik and Aleksey at the forest shrine. "You know, sometimes I think you like Kazik more than you do me."

"I like you both. For different reasons. I like you equally."

Gisela pouted. "That does not make me feel any better."

Aleksey laughed. "I'm never bored with you. You always surprise me. And you're the first person who's ever tried to protect me."

Gisela glanced at him in surprise.

"Back at the guesthouse when Domek attacked us."

She did remember pulling him out of harm's way. Shielding him behind her. Aleksey was so tall and powerfully built. She supposed most people looking at him wouldn't think he would need, or even might like, to be protected and treated softly.

She hopped over a puddle, feeling pleased with herself.

"So, are you going to tell me what's going on between you and Kazik?"

"Nothing," Gisela said quickly.

"Did you fight?"

"Fight?" Gisela shook her head. "We weren't fighting. We—" She really did *not* want to explain what had almost happened to Aleksey. "Kazik's just upset about some forest demons. He doesn't know how he's going to deal with them now that he's lost his magic."

Aleksey halted midstep. "Now that he's lost his *what?*" His voice was sharper than Gisela had ever heard it.

She suddenly felt guilty for saying anything. But she'd

needed to say something, and that was the first thing that had popped into her head. "He's just having trouble exorcising spirits at the moment. He thinks the saints have lost faith in him."

"Does anyone else know about this?"

"I don't think so." She hadn't told anyone until now. "I don't think he's even told his cousin. You'll keep it a secret, won't you?" Gisela asked anxiously.

Aleksey stared straight ahead. His expression was uncharacteristically troubled. "Of course. I won't tell a soul."

Some of the tension left Gisela's body. She let out a breath. They were following the cobblestone path that ran along the river's edge until it curved sideways to cross the Wishing Bridge. She'd told Aleksey a while ago that she was staying at a guesthouse nearby. This was where they always parted ways, but today . . .

She had the urge to say something more, anything, that would draw this moment out a little longer. She didn't want to return to the Crystal Palace just yet. She wasn't ready to face the other water spirits after everything that had happened with Tamara.

But the rain was falling harder, and Aleksey had said his mother was waiting for him. He looked like he was deep in thought. She drew a circle on the pavement with the toe of her sandal.

"Do you ever"—Aleksey paused—"just not want to go home?"

Gisela looked up.

"You want to walk around some more?" he asked.

"Yes! Yes, let's do that."

30

KNEW YOU WERE TROUBLE

ALEKSEY

THERE WAS SOMETHING SOOTHING about spending time with Gisela. Aleksey liked their banter. He liked how easy she was to talk to. He liked the faint greenish sheen to her long black hair; it reminded him of the deep shadows of the forest. He liked the way she could shock a genuine laugh out of him. He was so used to planning his every reaction—his every smile calculated, brought out to elicit a specific response in whoever he was with.

So, despite the rather alarming revelation that Kazik had somehow lost his ability to exorcise spirits, Aleksey was in a good mood when he finally returned to the rose- and honeysuckle-covered cottage that he currently called home.

A ray of sun broke through the gray billows of cloud floating overhead. A puddle mirrored a sudden snatch of blue sky. The breeze had torn so many blossoms from the trellis that the path was a shifting sea of pink snow. Petals rose and swirled around his ankles.

What terrible sin had Kazik committed to make the saints lose faith in him? Were they displeased he'd grown so close to

Gisela? To Aleksey? Or was it merely a matter of conviction? Had Kazik simply lost his resolve?

Aleksey should celebrate. Gisela had found a crack in Kazik's armor, and now all he had to do was drive his sword in. This was going to make possessing the exorcist's body that much easier—so long as no other spirit gobbled him up in the meantime. He and Gisela would have to stick close to Kazik. They would have to protect him. There were still traces of divine power in his blood. He was still a tasty soul for any spirit to feast upon, especially those eager to grow their power.

Aleksey paused as he pushed open the front door. He should probably send word to the leszy and tell Roza. Yet he felt curiously reluctant to do so.

He wondered if the feeling belonged to Human Aleksey; it wasn't like *him* to be so hesitant.

The housekeeper greeted him as he stepped indoors, then informed him that he had a guest. What remained of his good mood abruptly evaporated. He found Roza in the sitting room, perched demurely in his mother's favorite armchair, reading a novel—a clearly curated pose. Aleksey wouldn't have been surprised to find she was holding the book upside down.

The housekeeper placed a tray with two teacups and Aleksey's favorite gingerbread cookies down between them, then took her leave. The rich aroma of coffee filled the room.

"I told you to choose a new host," Aleksey said. "Kazik's suspicious. I thought you'd be delighted to get out of that body at last. You said it felt like a cage."

"It does feel like a cage." Roza scowled and slammed her

book shut. "I've been avoiding Kazik, and I've chosen a new host. I'm going to possess his girlfriend. Gisela. I finally remembered why she seems so familiar." She watched him for his reaction. "You already recognized her, didn't you?"

Aleksey kept his face expressionless. He *had* had an uneasy feeling that he'd seen Gisela before, an uneasy feeling that he knew just how her human life had ended. But he'd only glimpsed her briefly that night last spring, and he hadn't been in his right mind. A part of him had hoped he might be mistaken, but the fact that Roza remembered her, too, only confirmed his suspicions.

He crossed the room to stand before the windows and ran his fingers along the wooden sill, feeling the faint echoing heartbeat of the tree from which it had been crafted.

"Why didn't you say anything?" Roza said. "She saw you take possession of that body you're wearing. She saw *us*. She—"

"Doesn't remember. Clearly."

Roza blinked. "She doesn't? That's so strange." She pursed her lips thoughtfully. "It's all so strange. I remember chasing her right to the edge of the river. She slipped off the edge of the old pier. Sank like a stone. Honestly, I thought she was dead."

A muscle ticked in Aleksey's jaw. He tugged on his collar to loosen it. The sitting room windows looked out onto the lawn. He could see the old oak and the tree swing that he—no, that *Aleksey*—had fallen from and broken his arm. He shook his head, trying to shake free from this body's memories. They were surfacing more and more often lately.

"Anyway, what I don't understand," Roza babbled on, "is how that girl is still walking around."

"Haven't you heard what can happen to humans who die unnatural deaths?"

Roza was silent for a beat before understanding dawned. "So she's a—"

"Water nymph." At least . . . Aleksey's brow furrowed as he recalled Gisela's changed appearance today. "She's one of the local rusałki."

"So that's how she managed to bewitch Kazik. Huh." Roza twirled a strand of white-gold hair around her finger. "I've never tried to possess a water nymph before."

"Do you think you can?" Aleksey said dryly. "You didn't even manage to get rid of the domowik like I asked you to."

"I did try. I went to the house, but Kazik's cousin was there. What was I supposed to do? I'll possess Gisela's body, and then I'll deal with it."

Aleksey turned away from the window, wrestling down the irritation blooming inside him. "Gisela is off-limits. Do *not* touch her."

Roza stared.

"She may have once been a creature of the mortal world, but she's one of us now." And Aleksey liked her. Far more than he should. Letting Roza possess Gisela felt like a violation.

Like a betrayal.

"*Is* she one of us?" Roza said. "Rusałki aren't true spirits. They're just undead humans. Girls too stubborn to move on to the afterlife."

"Even so, they're the water goblin's precious granddaughters. Gisela could be acting on his orders. If you hurt one of his wards, he'll turn you into a fish. Even the leszy won't tolerate you starting a fight with Wojciech." The alliance between the forest and the river was tenuous at best.

"And if she does remember us?" Roza pressed. "You were so worried about the domowik. What if she recovers her memories and tells Kazik a demon is inhabiting his dear friend Aleksey's body? That a bies is manipulating his flesh like some kind of meat puppet?"

Aleksey grimaced.

"Plus, I'd be better positioned to help you. I can get nice and close to Kazik while wearing her face. I bet I could even get him to remove his saintly medallion. Isn't that what you want? That's almost worth getting on the water goblin's bad side. Come on, let's go stir up some trouble like old times! Let's end this."

Aleksey's gaze dropped to the bandage on his palm—a vivid image of Kazik's fingers trailing bloody over Aleksey's skin flashed before his eyes. That painfully gentle touch . . . "I'm not ready to end this yet."

Roza shrank back as if he'd slapped her.

"Don't you find it interesting how Kazik is hanging around Gisela, even knowing what she is? And I still don't know what her goal is. She said he was helping her. There are so many things . . ." Aleksey raked a hand through his hair. There were so many things he didn't understand. So many questions he wanted answered.

Roza's face was white. "Next you'll be telling me you've lost your taste for blood and have decided to make peace with him."

"Don't be foolish."

"I'm not being foolish." Roza closed the distance between them. "This isn't like you. At the very least, tell me your actions are all part of your revenge. Tell me you're only doing this in order to make Kazik trust you so you can break his heart when you reveal yourself." Her face pinched. "Tell me, how much of this is *Aleksey's* thoughts and personality bleeding into yours? How much of you is in control right now? Can you even tell?"

Aleksey was assailed by two conflicting feelings then: his own rising irritation and a foreign sense of guilt at seeing Roza so upset—not his emotion, Human Aleksey's. His heart squeezed as he looked at her.

He crushed the feeling, but a tiny seed of uncertainty sprouted. Would he be acting differently if he were not in this body? When *had* this desire to understand grown stronger than his hunger for vengeance?

Roza's gaze was so sharp, it seemed to slice him open. "I hardly recognize you right now. You need to snap out of this. You need to remember who you are. Can you imagine what the others would say if they could see you now?" She stepped closer, backing him against the window, crowding him in. "Are you afraid? Is that it?"

"Afraid?" Fury sparked hot in Aleksey's chest.

"Of Kazik? Of things turning out like they did last time? Is that the real reason you're dragging your feet? I haven't followed you around all these years to see you reduced to this. *You* may be losing yourself to human emotions and cowardice, but I. Am. Not." Roza stabbed a fingertip into his chest as she spoke, emphasizing each word.

Aleksey's pulse roared in his ears. "That's enough."

"And I'm not going to stand here and let you make a fool of yourself—"

"I said that's *enough!*" Instinct took over. One second Aleksey's hands were clenched at his sides, and the next second, they were closing around her throat.

Roza gasped.

Aleksey choked the sound off, tightening his hold. Step by step, he walked her back until her spine slammed against a bookshelf, leaning down until their eyes were level. She was so much smaller than him in this form—which wasn't necessarily a bad thing. Aleksey had worn girl-shaped skins before and enjoyed it. The fit hadn't felt quite right, but it had been fun being underestimated.

Roza clawed at his hand, trying to pry his fingers loose.

"You forget yourself," he told her. "Who do you think you're speaking to? I'm still myself. I might wear this form and another's face, but what I am, *who* I am, at my core has not changed. I know who I am. I'm in control."

If he seemed different, it was simply because he was putting on an act. No matter whose body he wore, his mind—his thoughts and wants—remained his own. And maybe these days he didn't always daydream about killing Kazik, but he still wanted to punch that self-righteous look off the exorcist's face when he talked about spirits. He still wanted to eat him alive, to consume him and chew him slowly. He wanted to force his way under his skin and live inside him. There were no human words to describe that feeling.

"I'm not afraid of him." If what Gisela had revealed was true, Kazik was even less of a threat at present. "And I don't care if you think I'm dragging my feet. I'm enjoying myself here." He hadn't felt this alive in a long, long time, and things just kept getting more and more interesting.

He was putting off the inevitable—so what? What was the harm in drawing this out a little longer? Why was Roza so impatient to end things? What was time to beings like them? The ticking of timepieces, the ringing of church bells determining each hour, the frantic rush of minutes and seconds, those were mortal constructs.

"Talk to me like that again, and I'll rip your roots out of that flesh with my teeth."

Roza's eyes were so wide, he could see the white all around her irises. Another gasp left her lips. Aleksey smiled.

But that smile faded when an answering grin crept onto Roza's face, fear morphing into something closer to relief, to outright adoration. She dropped her hands from his and let her arms dangle at her sides even though every instinct within her must be screaming at her to fight back.

She started to giggle.

Unnerved, Aleksey let her go.

"Now that's more like it," Roza rasped, holding her throat. "There's the real you."

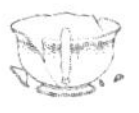

31

SAINT JOHN'S EVE

KAZIK

SAINT JOHN'S EVE WAS always madly busy. There were particular healing roots and grasses that had to be foraged from the fields before the day was finished, and half the girls from town and the surrounding villages turned up on Kazik's doorstep to ask which the best flowers were to weave into the wreaths they'd cast upon the waters to divine if they'd find love. Even with his cousin there to help, Kazik barely had a moment to breathe.

Zuzanna hadn't learned anything more about the man who'd gone missing—he'd vanished without a trace—but neither had she uncovered any signs that a spirit was involved in his disappearance. Kazik could only hope that was the case. He was also hoping Roza might drop by the house so he could have an answer to that question too.

But the hours ticked on, and she didn't appear, and none of the other girls he asked had seen her—a fact that was making him distinctly uneasy.

"Oh my God," Zuzanna exclaimed, jerking him out of his thoughts. "Why are you all dressed up? Is it for a date?"

Kazik reddened and hastily finished knotting his necktie. "Don't be ridiculous."

He was only joining tonight's festivities to play matchmaker. Even so, Gisela and Aleksey would be dressing up, so he wanted to look halfway decent. He'd unearthed one of his grandfather's old vests, shaved, and slicked his hair back with wax. He'd even left his glasses off. He could see better with them, but not so much that he had to wear them all the time.

Though he regretted it now, watching Zuzanna smirk at him.

"It *is* for a date," she said.

"You're not going out?" he asked.

Zuzanna's expression turned mournful. "I have to take the night bus back to the city. I have a paper to write for one of my professors. It's weeks late already."

"Maybe you'd have finished it earlier, if you weren't always coming here."

Zuzanna made a face. "I'll be back to check on you in a few days."

"You *really* don't have to do that."

"As your cousin, it's my duty to check if you're alive." Zuzanna stepped forward, opening the front door for Kazik to step through. "Have fun on your *date*."

"Go catch your bus already."

Zuzanna grinned and closed the door behind him. The cool evening air hit Kazik's over-warm cheeks. He started down the garden path.

He wasn't the only one making his way to the river as dusk fell. He ended up trailing behind a loud group of girls until they reached the riverbank. Strings of twinkling lanterns cast a warm romantic glow over the gently sloping stretch of grass where the festivities were taking place. Billows of blue smoke drifted up from a huge bonfire, sweetening the air with the herbs thrown onto the flames: wormwood, mugwort, nettle. Plants burned as a protection against the evil forces, the witches and spirits, who'd be at their most powerful tonight.

Watching the crowd gather, Kazik blanched at the sheer number of bodies. Just the thought of being dragged into that crush gave him a headache. There were people everywhere. More girls dressed in flowy white dresses, their hair braided with red ribbons and their necks adorned with strands of blood-coral beads. Boys with their hair slicked back and their crisp white shirtsleeves rolled up to the elbows. Adults gossiping and laughing. They were feasting at low wooden tables or dancing to traditional folk tunes played by a score of musicians armed with flutes, fiddles, and accordions.

As with Green Week, the festivities seemed to have lost some of their authenticity; this was all for fun, the rituals treated as something cute and a little silly. The more cynical part of Kazik wondered if it was worth preserving these traditions if no one was going to take them seriously. But the thought that people had been celebrating this same night—leaping over bonfires by this same river, casting wreaths upon the same water—for thousands and thousands of years made him feel like he was a part of something much bigger than himself, something ancient.

Perhaps everyone else here felt the same way.

As always, his presence caused something of a stir. He

caught several faces shooting him curious looks. Everybody was here: The old women from Babcia's rosary circle. His childhood classmates. The rich tourists, easily identifiable in their fashionable foreign clothing—a good number of them had clearly paid a visit to Villa Lilia's baths beforehand because their skin glittered like starshine.

Feeling self-conscious, Kazik swept a hand through his hair, only to grimace and abruptly remember he'd waxed it back. The rings on his fingers caught the light as he tried to subtly wipe his hand on his carefully pressed trousers.

Squinting, he tried to spy Gisela among the festivalgoers. He hadn't seen her since their moment in the kitchen—but she'd taken the dress with her when she'd left, so he had to assume they were still going ahead with his plan. He fought to keep the memory of their near kiss from his thoughts, tried not to think about the way her pulse had stuttered beneath his fingers, about the way her mouth had hovered mere inches from his own, about what might have happened if Aleksey hadn't interrupted them.

For a terrible second there, he'd wanted to be the one who gave her what she wanted. He'd wanted to be the one to kiss her. To restore her life to her. She'd come to *him* for help. He'd been with her from the beginning. He knew her better than Aleksey did.

In fact, wouldn't it be better for him to kiss her? There was that whole story about the monk and the water nymph. They had to make sure this worked. Gisela would be crushed if it didn't.

Kazik's stomach turned over. God in Heaven, it was bad enough that he'd let himself become comfortable with having her around, but this?

He must be losing his goddamn mind. He had almost kissed a *rusałka*. A demon. A wicked undead creature. Even if she'd taken a potion to temporarily transform her into a human, she still wasn't *fully* human.

And he'd promised to set her up with someone else.

It was a good thing Kazik was so used to burying his feelings. He'd just suffer through this for one more night, and then he could kiss this whole sorry affair goodbye.

Lost in thought, he nearly missed the familiar figure as it entered his periphery. Kazik pivoted on the spot. "Took you long enough—" His breath caught.

Gisela looked like a summer daydream. Like a fairy. An adorable rosy blush stained the apples of her cheeks. Her lips were glossy strawberry red. She was wearing the floaty mint-green dress he'd bought for her. A wreath of wildflowers crowned her head, and there were more flowers blooming in the darkness of her hair.

Her dry hair that had lost its oddly greenish sheen. Kazik found himself almost missing that hint of otherworldliness. He swallowed thickly.

Gisela seemed to be having trouble not staring at him too. Heat surged up the back of Kazik's neck. Was it the tie? The tie was too much, wasn't it? Or maybe he'd used too much hair wax.

By some miracle, he managed to unstick his tongue from the roof of his mouth. "You're late."

"I had to find the right river grasses and flowers for the wreath." Gisela reached up, her fingers brushing Saint John's wort, buttercups, and a sprig of rue. She gave a little twirl that made the skirt of her dress flare out. "So, what do you think? How do I look?"

Kazik grunted and looked away. "You look fine."

"You're not even looking."

"I don't need to. You look good in anything."

There was a heartbeat of silence. Kazik stiffened in horror, realizing what he'd just said. It was too late to backpedal, too late to save himself.

Even Gisela was rendered momentarily speechless, but she recovered quickly, falling back on her usual over-the-top flirtatiousness. "Aw, Kazik!" She poked him playfully in the side.

Kazik smacked her hands away. The tips of his ears were burning.

"I think that's the nicest thing you've ever said to me. I could've sworn you didn't like me."

"Whatever gave you *that* idea?"

A man jostled Gisela as he pushed past them. Kazik moved to steady her, catching her against his chest. They both froze. For a beat, an excruciating awkwardness poured over them.

Kazik drew his arms back, stuffing his hands in his pockets. "Have you seen Aleksey anywhere?" he said at the same time as Gisela burst out with "your tie's crooked!"

"I-it is?"

Gisela grabbed the offending tie and pulled it straight. "Honestly, how are you going to survive without me?" Her tone wasn't quite right, but Kazik rolled his eyes anyway, glad for the familiar banter.

"You should be thinking about how things are going to go

with Aleksey, not worrying about how I look," he said. "I'll make sure he's standing at the river's edge so you can float your wreath toward him. This is your best chance to get a kiss. Don't screw it up."

"Thank you for your vote of confidence."

"You wanted my help," Kazik said unsympathetically.

He expected her to shoot back with a retort. But Gisela was silent. She let go of his tie. Then, before he could react, she leaned in and pressed a kiss to his cheek. Nothing more than a featherlight brush of lips, a brief second of contact, but Kazik felt his entire body lock up.

"Thank you. For helping me. For everything. I wouldn't have gotten this far with him without you."

Kazik's skin tingled where she'd kissed him. He could still feel the silky smoothness of her cheek against his own. "Gisela, I—"

As if on cue, the crowd shifted, and his gaze slipped past her, falling on Aleksey surrounded by his usual admirers. His gaze lifted and found Kazik's across the sea of people.

A bolt of mortifying guilt went through Kazik.

Aleksey shouldered his way through the crowd with barely a parting word to his friends. "Sorry to keep you waiting," he said, joining them. He looked as handsome as the devil in a freshly starched shirt unbuttoned enough to reveal a tantalizing glimpse of collarbone.

It was maddening how developing these new feelings for Gisela hadn't seemed to lessen Kazik's long-held crush on Aleksey.

This must be what Hell was like. Some people might think

being attracted to more than one gender was a blessing because there were more chances for you to find love. But for Kazik, all it really meant was more suffering.

He didn't miss the way Aleksey's eyes widened as he took Gisela in. "You look as pretty as a wood nymph," he told her softly. "Doesn't she, Kazik?"

"What?" Kazik said stupidly. He felt like he was on the verge of a panic attack. Sweat pearled at his hairline. He didn't know where to look.

"You don't clean up so badly yourself," Gisela said, drawing her eyes up and down Aleksey in a slow, unsubtle sweep. She winked.

Laughing, Aleksey produced a beautiful bloodred flower with a theatrical flourish and gently tucked it behind Gisela's ear, slotting it beneath the circle of her wreath. Kazik wondered if it was a learned skill or if being effortlessly charming just came naturally to them both.

"Shall we?" Aleksey said.

Gisela took his proffered arm.

"You should hold on too," Aleksey called over his shoulder to Kazik, "so we don't lose one another."

That was the absolute last thing Kazik wanted to do, but Gisela grabbed his hand before he could argue, entangling her fingers with his. He felt so out of his depth, so out of place, dragged along behind two of the most beautiful people here like some awkward, ungainly gremlin.

Maybe he should just go home. Bail. Gisela would probably get angry, but it didn't really matter. It wasn't like she even needed him anymore. Clearly. They were never supposed to be friends, and after tonight . . . after tonight, if all went well, he might never see her again.

Saints, why didn't that thought please him the way it used to? Why couldn't he just feel the way he did at the beginning of all this?

It occurred to him suddenly that Aleksey, too, would have no more reason to hang around him after tonight; it was Gisela who had brought them together. This was probably the last time they'd be together like this. The three of them.

It's not like I haven't survived losing people before, he reminded himself. *I'll get over it. Life will go on.*

Maybe.

"Oh no," Kazik said, digging his heels in when they neared the makeshift stage where the musicians were playing. "You and Gisela go ahead. I don't dance."

"Liar," Gisela said. "I've seen you shimmying along to the radio."

"Well, if you don't want to dance," Aleksey cut in smoothly, sweeping his arms around both Gisela's and Kazik's shoulders before they could start bickering. "We can always go search for the fern flower together."

A wash of feverish heat hit Kazik's cheeks.

"The fern flower?" Gisela asked, confused. "Isn't that a fairy tale?"

She didn't know. *Of course*, she didn't. It was easy to forget that she hadn't grown up here.

"The fern flower," Aleksey explained, casting a mischievous

grin at Kazik, "blooms at midnight on Saint John's Eve in the farthest reaches of the forest, in the dark corners where mortals and even some spirits fear to tread. If you can find it, it will grant your heart's desire. You'll be gifted with magic and riches beyond your wildest imaginings—so long as you never share those gifts with anybody. If you do, you'll lose everything."

Which was true, but *asking* somebody to go look for the fern flower with you was also a sly way of asking them if they wanted to hook up. For centuries couples had used the excuse of searching for the magical flower to sneak off into the forest together for some alone time.

"Let's do that!" Gisela said.

"Let's *not*," Kazik said.

"Aw, don't you want to join us, Kazik?" Aleksey laughed. "In some tales, they say the fern flower is guarded by a witch."

"Witches aren't the only ones said to guard it," Kazik countered. "Evil spirits deliberately frighten away those who try to take the flower out of the forest. Dangerous spirits, like the forest demons."

He and Gisela exchanged a look.

"Forest demons?" Aleksey said softly.

"They're the worst kind of spirit," Gisela said. "Vicious and bloodthirsty."

"Ah." Something flashed behind Aleksey's eyes, but then his usual carefree expression slotted into place. "Really? Personally, I think the worst spirits are the rusałki. The way they go after human boys. It's utterly shameless."

Gisela's mouth fell open. Smirking widely, Kazik stepped on her foot before she could respond with something she'd regret.

"I guess we have no choice, then." Aleksey squeezed Kazik's shoulder, locking eyes. "I promise it won't kill you to dance with me."

It might.

Gisela clicked her tongue. "You're doing it wrong, Aleksey. If you want Kazik to do something, you can't ask him *nicely.*"

"Oh? You think we should just drag him in?"

"What?" Kazik took a step back when Gisela grinned. "*Wait.* I said I don't—"

Aleksey's arms hooked around Kazik's middle, crushing him against his broad chest. As always, the scent of green things, of the forest, seemed to cling to Aleksey's clothes, to his skin and hair. Kazik's feet left the ground. Gisela grabbed a fistful of his carefully ironed vest. "This way!"

"*Wait!*" Kazik shouted, half struggling, half laughing now as he was forcefully hauled into a whirling, swaying sea of sweaty bodies. The band struck up another tune. The music swelled, rising to a breathless fever pitch.

"Why are you both like this?" Kazik had no idea what to do with his arms nor his legs. He didn't know where to look—at the swell of Gisela's breasts, at the sweat beading into crystals above Aleksey's upper lip. He was trapped between them, with Gisela's hands on his shoulders and Aleksey's hands gripping his waist. The way they moved together made him ache for more. It kindled a hundred thousand wants he wasn't supposed to have.

He was going to spend hours on his knees at confession.

Spinning dizzily, with Aleksey's chest pressed firmly against his back, Kazik put his hands on Gisela's hips and pulled her in closer, leaning in and shouting over the music: "You are such a nightmare."

Gisela's lips ghosted over the shell of his ear. "You like it though."

Heaven help me, I think I do.

A shiver racked Kazik's spine as Aleksey's laughter brushed warm breath against the back of his neck. Gisela's eyes gleamed wicked red in the firelight. That small glimpse of lingering monstrosity should've repulsed Kazik, should've had him reaching for a flask of holy water. Instead, the sight made something in his chest clench.

"Just think how boring your life would be," she shouted, "if I'd never dragged you into this."

32

FIRE, WATER, AND LOVE

GISELA

THE FOLLOWING HOURS SPED by in a dizzying blur. They danced until their feet ached. They sang along with the songs the band was playing until their voices were hoarse. They nibbled on sausages straight out of the fire, grilled on sticks until they were black and crunchy on the outside and soft and juicy inside, then quenched their thirst with shots of homemade cherry liqueur.

The drinks left Gisela so tipsy that Kazik had to prop her up, cackling at her as he did so, making her suspect he wasn't nearly sober himself. She was partly annoyed, partly disappointed, and partly relieved that he was playing off their almost kiss like it had been nothing. It was better, she told herself, than him acting weird or avoiding her. They'd finally gotten to a place where they weren't actively trying to strangle each other. She didn't want to ruin that. If he wanted to continue with their plan of having Aleksey kiss her, then *she* wasn't going to be the one to say anything.

Even so, there was something in his expression when they danced, something soft but also sad when he looked at them.

Spying Nina-Marie from the corner of her eye, Gisela pushed away from his side. The other water nymph was making an anxious beckoning motion with her hand. Gisela was half tempted to pretend she hadn't seen her. She was still avoiding the other girls. But guilt needled her insides. "I'll be right back," she said, trying not to slur the words. Her thoughts were a little fuzzy. Her body felt all floaty.

Moving away from the delicious crackle and snap of the bonfire, she spotted even more mystical beings enjoying the festivities. Mortals weren't the only creatures having fun tonight. Nadia, the beautiful wiła who'd told her where to find Aleksey all those mornings ago, was lounging at a long wooden bench, playing a drinking game with Hans and another drowner.

Even Yulia was here, looking unfairly attractive in a pair of high-waisted pants and a dress shirt unbuttoned halfway down her chest. She was flirting with a short-haired human girl also wearing trousers, literally sweeping her off her feet, lifting her into a princess carry like she was nothing, showing off her preternatural strength. The girl looked half in love with Yulia already.

Gisela shook her head, amused. Before she could identify any more of her fellow spirits, wheat-blonde hair filled her vision, and Nina-Marie caught her elbow and pulled her into a tipsy embrace. Gisela returned the hug, managing to sway only slightly on her feet.

"Gisela!" Nina-Marie steadied her. "Your dress is so pretty!"

Gisela preened. "Isn't it?" She leaned in to whisper in Nina-Marie's ear: "The exorcist bought it for me."

"What?"

Gisela leaned back, giggling. She hoped she looked okay in it—Kazik's reaction had certainly been gratifying. The dress fit perfectly but emphasized her chest in a way she wasn't entirely comfortable with. Gisela liked breasts on other people, not so much on herself. Which was why the next thing to come out of her mouth was "Your dress is pretty too! It makes your chest look *amazing.*"

It really did. Nina-Marie's dress of shimmery blush-rose chiffon had lantern sleeves, and the diaphanous fabric clung to her in all the right ways, accentuating her waist and the rise of her breasts. A sudden wave of drunken affection swept through Gisela, and she hugged the other girl again.

She was so giddily relieved that Nina-Marie didn't seem to be angry with her. "I'm so glad you're not—" Gisela swallowed. "I'm so sorry about Tamara."

Nina-Marie squeezed her close. "I'm sorry she couldn't stay with us longer too. I wish we could've gotten to know her better. But no one blames you for what happened. Not even Yulia."

"Really?" Gisela said skeptically. She couldn't help searching Nina-Marie's eyes for any hint of accusation, for any resentment she might harbor toward her.

"*Really.*" Nina-Marie pulled back. "Don't beat yourself up over it. We're all different. Some girls are happy to live as water nymphs. Some long to find a way to rejoin the mortal world." She poked Gisela gently. "And others just want to get revenge and move on."

"Which are you? Do you wish you could've revenged yourself on—"

"Who says I didn't?" Nina-Marie cut in with a sharp grin. "For Tamara that was enough for her to find peace. To get closure. I'm happy for her. Me? I'm not finished having my fun here. I resent the fact that I didn't get the chance to live the life I wanted, so I'm doing so now. In this beautiful, dreamy world where I can stay a girl forever, where I don't have to grow up, nor grow old and marry a man I'd never truly want and be mother to his children. I can live openly as myself here with all of you. With my beautiful solemn Clara."

"You've never missed your old life, worried about your family?"

Nina-Marie chewed her cheek, then shrugged sheepishly. "Not like you do. But my family didn't treat me in a way that made me long to return to them, so I don't think they could blame me. Some of us were born into supportive families. Some of us have to find or create our own. If that makes sense?"

Gisela nodded, thinking of her father, always absent, dropping in only now and then to comment on how she and Hugo had grown before he drifted back into his own world.

A loud shout interrupted their heart-to-heart; a middle-aged woman was calling for any girls who wished to float their wreaths on the river to come forward. Gisela's skin prickled with nerves. This was her moment.

This could be *it*.

If Aleksey kissed her tonight . . . she was so close to saying goodbye to all this.

Uncertainty gripped her. "I should—wait." She paused. "Did *you* need something from me?" Nina-Marie had beckoned for her to come over here, hadn't she? Gisela had gotten all distracted.

"Oh yes!" Nina-Marie said, remembering too. "I had to warn you! Wojciech's here. Somebody stole a valuable potion from his chambers. He's been questioning everyone, asking us if we told you about it. Um, I'm pretty sure he thinks you took it?"

The news was like a bucket of icy water turned over Gisela's head. It sobered her instantly.

Shit.

"Did—did he look angry?"

"I don't know if 'angry' is the right word." Nina-Marie twisted a strand of damp hair around her finger. "More like disappointed? And worried."

Somehow, that was worse.

Gisela sank her teeth into her bottom lip. "Thanks for the warning."

"Don't mind him too much," Nina-Marie said. "Wojciech always gets all grumpy and weepy when a girl wants to leave him. He's lived so long; he's had to say goodbye so many times. I think it's hard for him."

Gisela had never really thought of it like that before. Leaving Nina-Marie's side, she retraced her steps, debating if she should find Kazik and Aleksey first or head straight down to the river and trust Kazik would bring Aleksey to stand at the water's edge?

A screaming child ran past her, waving a sparkler, pursued by their anxious parents. A familiar pang of emotion choked her throat. A feeling like homesickness that wasn't homesickness at all, but a longing for the type of home and family she'd never had. Tonight's festivities reminded her a lot of how the island celebrated the feast days of other saints. Saint Sebastian and Saint Walpurga. It was fascinating noting the similarities and the differences, recognizing the traditions and beliefs that immigrants from the mainland kingdoms had brought with them to Caldella.

A minute later, hopelessly lost, Gisela gave up battling through the crowd and made her way down the grassy slope to the river's edge, where, because her luck was like that, she almost crashed right into Wojciech.

Tonight, the water goblin was dressed in a verdant three-piece suit, and if not for his dark waterlogged hair, he'd look like someone her father might've met at an art gala or the opera. He was speaking with a boy her brother's age. For a heartrending moment, an impossible hope flared in Gisela's chest, only to flicker out when she saw that, no, the planes of the boy's face were sharper than Hugo's. His skin was paler, and his hair was an odd blue-black that shimmered like a raven's wings. Gisela had also never seen her little brother wear a feathered cloak.

The boy who was not her brother said something to Wojciech, and they both stared out at the river.

Gisela followed their gazes and gasped. Orbs of teal-blue phantom fire darted to and fro above the current, bobbing in time to the distant music, dancing together like fireflies. Only, these weren't fireflies.

Squinting, she could just make out the tiny faces on the fire spirits' flickering bodies. One little spirit came to hover before Wojciech in silent greeting. Another flitted over to her, flaring brightly with excitement. Ogniki spoke their own wordless language of light, their flames blazing to signal happiness and wavering when they were sad.

Gisela giggled at their antics before she remembered herself. Hastily, she attempted to retreat back up the grassy slope unnoticed, but Wojciech's head whipped around, and she froze in her tracks. Her hand flew to her chest, guiltily covering the glittering heart-shaped bottle hanging from the gold chain around her neck.

"Well, look who it is." Wojciech waved a hand, and the fire spirits scattered.

Gisela felt a pang at watching them vanish. She caught the boy in the feathered cloak shooting her a curious look, his head tilted to the side, birdlike, but then Wojciech's shadow fell over her.

"Hello, Gisela. You're looking awfully *human* this evening."

"And you're looking as youthful as always, Oh Ancient One. What's your secret?"

"I moisturize."

Gisela couldn't help it. She snorted out a laugh.

Wojciech's mouth curved into the ghost of a smile, but it waned as he eyed her up and down. His expression turned rueful. "You're so desperate to leave us that you'd take the potion even knowing the risks."

"I'm not . . ." Gisela clenched her fingers around the necklace. Why was there always this strange hollow feeling in her chest when she thought about leaving now?

Why couldn't Wojciech just be angry with her? That way she wouldn't feel so—so . . .

"You left something in my chambers," he said. With a gesture from him and a soft bubble-like *pop*, a square ribbon-tied box materialized between his palms.

It was the gift she'd brought to butter him up when she'd ducked into his rooms the other evening. She'd set the box down when she'd picked up the potion bottle and had forgotten all about it. How Wojciech had even noticed it amid all his disorganized clutter was anyone's guess.

He'd already acknowledged the change in her appearance. She doubted he'd believe her if she lied and said the box wasn't hers. And anyway . . .

"It was for you. A gift."

"A gift? Why?"

"Does there need to be a reason? If you don't want it"—Gisela reached for the box—"I'll take it back."

Wojciech wrested the gift out of her hands. "No take backs! It's impolite to refuse an offering." Lifting it to his ear, he gave the box a tiny shake.

Gisela swallowed another laugh. It was hilarious watching a thousands-year-old being act like a child on their name day. "It's fragile," she warned.

Wojciech grunted. The red ribbon tied around the box came loose with a tug. Genuine surprise painted his ageless features as he lifted the lid off and peered at the object inside: an antique teacup and saucer stamped with gold leaf in a delicate pattern of waterlilies.

She'd spotted it at the night market and had talked a couple of the ogniki into leading her to some hidden treasure in the forest so she'd have money to buy it. Even before it had occurred to her to use it as a bribe, she'd thought it might be nice to do something for him after all he'd done for her. He'd given her so many things. In some small way, she'd wanted to return the gesture. It would even the scales.

"In all my years," Wojciech said hoarsely, "no water nymph has ever gifted me a teacup."

That did not surprise her. Most girls wouldn't want to actively encourage his habit of collecting human souls. After all, they'd once been human themselves. Gisela was trying hard not to think about what he'd do with her gift.

"It will make an excellent prison for a soul."

Gisela made a face. "Don't you have enough already?"

"One can never have too many souls. Nor teacups." Wojciech held her gaze. "Thank you."

Heat flooded Gisela's cheeks. Embarrassed, she started to duck her head but froze when Wojciech's fingers brushed the flower tucked behind her ear. He frowned. "I thought these only grew in the heart of the forest."

"Aleksey gave it to me."

"And who, pray tell, is Aleksey?"

"The boy who's going to help me regain my humanity permanently!"

Wojciech raised his eyes heavenward, much like Kazik did when he was praying for strength. "Has he kissed you yet?"

"He will."

"And if he *doesn't*?"

"I'm willing to take that risk."

Wojciech let out a soul-deep sigh.

Gisela reached into the pocket of her dress. "Here." She held out the hair comb he'd returned to her. The comb he'd given her when she'd first awoken in his Crystal Palace. "I won't be needing it anymore. And I—I'm sorry. For always causing you trouble and for taking the potion without asking. I knew you wouldn't want to give it to me. But you should be relieved. You won't have to put up with me anymore."

Wojciech looked at the gleaming bone-white comb for a long moment. In the dark it seemed to shine with its own light, with a ghostly pearl-white glow. "As exasperating as you can be, I have never once forced myself to 'put up' with you, Gisela." Gently, he closed her fingers back around the comb. "Hold on to it for a little longer. It's yours. A gift. A keepsake to remember us by. This world is full of monsters; you never know when you might have need of it." His attention returned to the flower behind her ear.

A lump formed in Gisela's throat. Kazik had been right that time he'd warned her not to get too attached to Aleksey—she shouldn't have let herself get attached to *anyone* here, to anyone she'd only miss once she was home again.

"You'll get wrinkles if you keep frowning like that," she said, trying to make a joke, trying desperately to change the subject so she could stop feeling so vulnerable.

Wojciech huffed. "Have you spoken more with the exorcist about your death?"

"No. No, not really. I haven't been able to remember anything new. I should—I should find him." Gisela looked back up the slope at the crowd. "We have a plan. I need to get ready. I don't want to miss out on getting my kiss before the potion wears off."

Wojciech caught her elbow as she started to move away. "How long ago did you take it? If it starts to wear off before—"

"It won't. You worry about me too much."

"Because restoring the dead to life is no simple feat. What you're trying to do, I've never seen it done. Not in all the years of my existence."

Gisela pulled free. "There's a first time for everything. You'll see. It'll all be fine."

33

TEMPTATION

KAZIK

STUMBLING AWAY FROM THE jostling crowd, Kazik slapped at his forearm, trying and failing to kill the mosquito that had been slurping his blood for the past half hour.

"They're murderous little vampires tonight, aren't they?"

Kazik looked up, closing his eyes briefly to stop the world from spinning. Adam—whose family owned Villa Violetta, who sung in the parish choir and had the voice of an angel, whom Kazik had made out with once behind the church—blinked back at him, startled. A moment of mutual astonishment stretched between them.

"You look like you've seen a ghost," Kazik said finally.

Adam recovered his composure. "I didn't realize it was you. You're not wearing your glasses." He scrapped a hand through his carelessly styled black hair. "I didn't think you'd be here."

Kazik raised an eyebrow. "It's Saint John's Eve. Haven't you heard? All the dangerous witches and spirits come out on nights like this."

Adam snorted a laugh. "No, but I mean, you don't usually

come out for *this* part of it." He gestured at the dizzying whirl of dancers that Kazik had stepped back from to catch his breath and the bonfire beyond. The flames splashed them both with light. "You always find some excuse to escape."

Both of Kazik's eyebrows rose now. He wondered suddenly if his constant insistence that he didn't fit in had become something of a self-fulfilling prophecy. "It's just not . . ." He faltered. "I don't dance."

"You sure?" Adam grinned. "I saw you out there. Like I said, I didn't even realize it was you. It's nice seeing you like that. You look good when you're having fun."

Heat surged up the back of Kazik's neck. This was the trouble with hooking up with someone you knew and would see again—you would see them again.

Adam glanced over his shoulder briefly as someone called his name before his attention returned to Kazik. His amber eyes traveled from Kazik's face, down his body, then up again to hold his gaze. A different kind of heat kindled low in Kazik's stomach.

"A few of us are going to search for the fern flower in the forest. Care to join us?"

Kazik almost laughed. *Do I want to pretend to search for a magical flower and hook up?* How many boys were going to ask him that question tonight?

He went to adjust his glasses, only to remember he wasn't wearing them.

A part of him was tempted. He missed the thrill of making that physical connection with someone. Adam was a damn good kisser, and he'd been so pent up the past few days, tormenting himself with pathetic fantasies about people he couldn't have—Aleksey, Gisela, the two of them together.

And he was flattered. Surprised but flattered. He'd written off the thing with Adam as a one-time deal. He knew that, for a lot of his hook-ups, he was someone they felt they could safely experiment with, someone they used to sate their curiosity. Nothing more than a temporary fling.

He was used to it. He didn't mind it *too much*. Sometimes it even made him feel kind of powerful.

Adam canted his head in question.

"I wouldn't want to intrude."

"You wouldn't be," Adam said quickly.

Kazik hesitated, then shook his head. Hookups were fun in the moment, but a lot of the time, he just ended up feeling empty afterward. And right now his heart wasn't in it. Adam wasn't who he really wanted. "Had too much to drink," he added, to soften the rejection. "My head's not in the right place."

Adam shrugged, as if to say, *Your loss*. "If you change your mind, you know where to find me."

"Be careful out there. You don't want to get eaten by a hungry forest spirit."

Kazik couldn't hear Adam scoff over the music, but he was pretty sure the other boy did. He shot Kazik a rueful smile, lifted a hand in farewell, then turned and jogged past the tree line.

Sparing a moment to admire Adam's backside, slapping at another mosquito, Kazik almost regretted his decision. Adam really did have a very nice—

"What did Adam want with you?" Aleksey asked, materializing behind him, sending Kazik's heart racing.

"Saints, do you always have to appear like that?" Kazik stepped away reflexively, swaying a little on his feet as he did so. He hadn't lied about drinking too much. He could feel the warmth of the alcohol pulsing through him. He hoped Aleksey wouldn't notice. *He* didn't seem to be affected at all. Because Aleksey was too perfect for that. Too perfect to be true. His eyes were aglitter with the light from the bonfire—a hypnotic mix of blue and green.

"See something you like?" Aleksey teased.

Kazik was glad for the cover of night, otherwise the flush in his cheeks would've been unmistakable. This was why he didn't drink. Once he started, he found it hard to stop. It made him careless, and he couldn't afford to be careless nor to let his guard down. It also dredged up unwanted memories, ugly echoes of the racket his father used to make stumbling home, red-faced and swearing, in the early hours of the morning.

Kazik shook his head to clear it. What were they talking about? "He wanted me to help him find the fern flower," he said, remembering he hadn't answered Aleksey's first question.

Those beautiful eyes narrowed.

"Jealous?" Kazik took another unsteady step sideways. At least he wasn't the only tipsy person falling over themselves tonight. Someone else tripped by, knocking into him and spilling beer on both their shoes.

Aleksey should've been able to steady Kazik with ease, but

maybe he wasn't as sober as he appeared after all, because he staggered trying to pull Kazik upright. Somehow, Kazik ended up with his arm around Aleksey's narrow waist—for balance, he told himself; not because, not because he wanted—

God, he couldn't even follow the torrent of his own treacherous thoughts.

"I have you. Let's go this way," Aleksey said, tugging him toward the river.

"Where's Gisela?"

"Not sure. But the girls are starting to float their wreaths on the water."

This was it, then.

"Are you going to kiss Gisela if her wreath floats toward you?"

"Are you, if it floats toward you?"

Kazik didn't answer. There was an ugly feeling in his chest. He didn't know how to articulate what he was feeling. He had no way to explain that yes, *he* wanted to be the one who jumped into the water and retrieved Gisela's wreath, while at the same time he wanted to *be* Gisela floating a wreath on the water for Aleksey to retrieve.

He was so confused by his own desires that he wanted to scream.

Aleksey's mouth curved in a grin. "Shall we fight over it?"

A rush of unreasonable anger surged through Kazik. He wanted to grab Aleksey and smash his face against something solid. He breathed hard through his nose. "Here." Stepping away, he shoved aside a swathe of river reeds. Dark water lapped against the toes of his shoes. If Aleksey stood just here, where the bank curved, Gisela should have a good view of him from where the girls were gathering. With a little magic, she'd be able to float her wreath straight toward him.

All that was left was for Kazik to make himself scarce. To leave them to their love story.

"I'm going to get another drink. You stay here. Do *not* move." Kazik stabbed a finger at Aleksey, then stumbled unsteadily back up the grassy bank. He wondered if he should find Gisela and make sure she was ready. Would she have joined the other girls already, or would she come looking for him first?

Kazik was halfway up the slope when he saw Roza—a pale vision backlit by the bonfire, her white-gold hair aglow.

She was walking away from the festivities, heading into the forest like Adam had.

It was like a sign.

This was what Kazik should be focused on. He shouldn't be letting himself get distracted. His steps quickened. He felt the heat emanating from the bonfire as he swept past the flames.

Wiping sweat from his brow, Kazik slipped into the dark space beneath the trees. Thick trunks shot up around him, reaching toward the moon, their tangle of branches casting black shadows across the forest floor. The music and sounds of revelry faded into the background, leaving only the crunch of his steps through the underbrush. He felt the fingerlike brush of fern fronds against his trousers.

"Roza!" he called out.

A low-hanging branch lashed out like a hand and caught on the chain around his neck.

Kazik jerked away in frustration, struggling to disentangle himself, his alcohol-addled mind grinding to a halt as more hands reached to help.

Aleksey's fingers traced the stinging red scratch the branch had left on Kazik's neck. There was an edge to his voice. "Don't you ever take a break from hunting spirits?"

Kazik's pulse stuttered. His gaze skipped past Aleksey, watching Roza vanish between the trees with a flare of irritation. "I—"

Aleksey pressed his thumb into the hollow dip at the base of Kazik's throat, drawing his attention back. "I know I can think of things I'd rather do tonight."

Before Kazik could move, before he could say anything, before he could even think, Aleksey closed the distance between them and brought his mouth down to Kazik's.

Shock rippled through him. He went as still as if he'd been bewitched. That was what it felt like, like he'd been bewitched, like he'd fallen under a spell. Because this couldn't be real. This wasn't actually happening.

Firm hands cupped his jaw. Teeth nipped his bottom lip. His mouth opened beneath Aleksey's, a shudder of desire ripping through him. Kazik felt a tree hit his back as Aleksey walked him backward. He could taste the cherry liqueur they'd both been drinking.

The kiss was everything his traitorous heart had ever dreamed of. Aleksey's lips were soft, his mouth wet and so agonizingly hot—a thousand times hotter than the summer night.

He was licking fire into Kazik's mouth. A low needy sound rumbled at the back of his throat.

For a moment, nothing existed beyond this. It was all he was aware of until a sharp gasp cut the air.

The spell shattered.

Kazik broke away with a start. He turned . . . and looked straight into Gisela's pale face.

34

BETRAYED WITH A KISS

GISELA

IT FELT LIKE HER chest was caving in.

She felt so stupid. Why hadn't she seen this coming? She should've known from the ravenous way Aleksey looked at Kazik—like he wanted to eat him with his eyes.

But she'd thought Aleksey liked her too. He'd *told* her he did. And she'd thought Kazik was on her side. She'd believed him when he said he harbored no romantic feelings for Aleksey. This whole time, had he just been lying to her face?

The betrayal was like a punch to the gut. She felt more betrayed by *that* than she did the actual kiss. She didn't think she'd feel half so devastated if it had been anyone other than Kazik with Aleksey. Had this all been a joke to him? Had he been secretly laughing at her behind her back? Laughing at the water nymph foolish enough to come to him for help?

Damn it. *God damn it.*

Tears blurred Gisela's vision, and her sandal caught on a fallen branch as she fled through the trees, trying to put as much distance between herself and them as she could.

She kept trying to fit the pieces together, to make sense of it all, but her mind kept blanking. She didn't want to believe Kazik would do this to her. She'd trusted him. She'd even started to *like* him. She'd thought Kazik had started to see her as more than just a wicked troublemaking spirit, to see her as a friend, and possibly something more . . .

She should have known better. She shouldn't have let her guard down. Kazik despised creatures like her. He was still her enemy, still the heartless exorcist he'd been this whole time. But somewhere in between their midnight heart-to-hearts and boy talk and helping spirits together, she'd forgotten that. He'd looked so sincere when he'd given her this dress.

Again, Gisela stumbled and caught her balance—barely. She slowed, bracing one hand against a birch tree to steady herself. Up ahead, rosy lantern light and the orange glow of the bonfire knifed between the trees, flickering as the silhouettes of happy couples and joyful festivalgoers danced past the flames.

It wasn't fair. *Tonight wasn't supposed to go like this.* She scrubbed the tears from her cheeks with the back of her hand, only for more to well up in their place. Why did it feel like she was forever fated to have her heart broken? Was she destined to be unloved in both life and death?

When she was close enough to make out the faces of individual dancers, she thought she heard someone call her name. Her breath caught in her throat.

But it wasn't Kazik's voice calling her back.

Or Aleksey's.

She turned her head and saw Yulia.

Of course, it was Yulia. She was as interfering as Wojciech. The older water nymph's eyes widened when she met Gisela's tearstained gaze.

Yulia was the last person Gisela wanted to see right now. She'd warned her not to trust Kazik. She'd warned her that the living would always choose to be with the living, that no one would ever want to kiss a dead girl.

She was ridiculous for even thinking Aleksey or Kazik might want her when they could have each other. When they could be with someone who was actually alive.

She couldn't bear to hear any of Yulia's *I told you so*'s.

Before Yulia could reach her, Gisela bolted back through the trees, running faster now, running so fast that she swore she could feel her bones rattle inside her skin. She ran until it hurt to breathe, ran until every nerve in her body was begging her to stop, heading for—heading where she didn't know. She just needed to get as far away from *here* as possible.

Her feet carried her farther and farther. The moonlight turned the trees into skeletons. Low-hanging branches snagged at her dress, at her arms, and at the side of her neck. A wave of déjà vu swept over her; she'd done this before. She'd run like this before.

This was the path she took in her nightmares.

A prickle of remembered terror raced over her skin. The crash of pursuing footsteps filled her ears—real or memory, Gisela couldn't tell. Her arms and legs pumped faster still. Her own voice screamed inside her head: *Don't look back!*

Twigs snapped beneath her sandals. She stumbled blindly over an exposed tree root.

Bursting past the tree line into a sudden wash of moonlight, she found herself back at the river's edge, at a muddy bank overgrown with reeds and rushes. A rotting wooden pier, a small jetty, jutted out into water as black and bleak as a broken heart.

Gisela staggered to a halt, her chest heaving for breath. This, too, was distressingly familiar. Something was writhing at the back of her mind, a memory trying to claw its way to the surface. What had she been running from? Why did this feel so, so . . .

A sharp twinge of pain tingled across the base of her skull. Gasping, she gripped her head in both hands. Anger surged. Why couldn't she remember?

She tottered forward, and something fell to the ground at her feet. Something bone pale and gleaming.

Her hair comb.

The enchanted comb that all rusałki carried, that they used to conjure and control water. The comb Wojciech had insisted she keep.

Hold on to it for a little longer. This world is full of monsters; you never know when you might have need of it.

Slowly, Gisela bent down to retrieve it.

But her fingers wouldn't take hold. They slipped straight through the comb, straight through the grass, without so much as rustling it.

At first, she didn't understand. She stared at her hand, bewildered. At her pale palm and four fingers and thumb. In the moonlight they looked oddly insubstantial, almost ghostly, as if all it would take were a breath of wind to dissolve her flesh.

Cold horror speared through Gisela as she remembered.

The potion wears off, and when it does, you won't return to your current form. You'll no longer be a water nymph. You'll be a shadow of what you are now. A disembodied spirit. A ghost-thing.

The warnings of the other water nymphs echoed in her ears, drowning out the sudden frantic pounding of her heart, pushing aside all her other worries and heartache. Surely, *surely*, the potion couldn't be wearing off. Not now. Not so soon. Her luck couldn't possibly be that cruel.

How long *was* the transformation supposed to last?

The phantom pain at the back of her skull surged into a red-hot ache. Gisela's knees struck damp earth as her vision tunneled. Her limbs spasmed.

She bit off a gasp. The edges of her hand were wisping into the air like smoke, as if the very essence of her were evanescing.

Fear pooled in her belly. In denial, she grasped for the comb a second time, willing her flesh to hold together, willing her hand to close around it.

Again, her fingers passed straight through.

Gisela let out a small helpless croak of a sob—a low animal sound of horror.

What am I becoming?

On the third desperate attempt, she felt the silky touch of the river pearls embedded in the comb's handle and the coldness of the bone it was carved from. She clutched the comb with all her strength, letting out a ragged cry of relief when she managed to lift it off the ground. Maybe she still had time before she faded to nothing.

A flicker of blue light pulled her attention to the left. A dozen ogniki flashed across the dark surface of the river like a warning, the bright blue orbs of flame just skimming the water.

She was about to call to them for help, but they raced away as suddenly as they'd appeared, vanishing into the dark.

Fleeing.

Behind Gisela, a branch snapped.

She jerked toward the sound, and in that moment, her focus broke, and the comb slipped through her fingers. She bit down on her lip hard enough to draw blood to keep herself from screaming in frustration.

A slender figure emerged from the shadow of the trees.

Roza.

Aleksey's pretty friend with the white-gold hair. She wore a crown of wildflowers just like Gisela's. One of the dainty straps of her pale dress was sliding down her shoulder. She canted her head to the side. "Oh, what have we here? Well, isn't this a coincidence. Gisela, isn't it? You're just the person I wanted to see."

35

FLOWERS THAT BLOOM IN THE DARK

KAZIK

KAZIK WAS GOING TO Hell.

If he'd resented the saints for taking his magic before, now he felt that such a punishment was only justified. If anyone should have their powers stripped away, it was him. He deserved to be punished. He felt filthy with shame.

He shoved through the throng still crowding the grassy riverbank, shouldering his way through the crush of sweaty bodies, elbowing past tipsy festivalgoers and curious tourists, searching everywhere for Gisela. When she'd run from him in the past, she'd always escaped into places bustling with people, and yet there was no sign of her now.

He had to find her. He had to fix this. He had to explain. He had to—

How are you going to face her with Aleksey's kiss still cooling on your lips? A voice inside his head taunted him.

Kazik's stomach roiled. He wished he could blame it all on pure drunken stupidity, but that would've been a lie.

He circled the bonfire, briefly considering if he just should throw himself into the flames. He felt like he'd traveled back in time to when he and Gisela were still enemies. He felt like he'd spent half his life chasing after her.

It really didn't help that he wasn't wearing his glasses. Half the faces were a blur.

He cursed his eyesight. He cursed God. *Why did you have to go and make me so shortsighted? Why did you have to make me so incredibly stupid?*

"Kazik! Kazik, wait!"

He ignored the voice calling his name.

Wherever she'd disappeared to, it felt like she'd taken his heart with her. There was an aching empty cavity inside his chest, as if she'd ripped the organ right out of him. He wanted to fold himself around the wound. He felt so incredibly small.

He'd try the forest again. Maybe she hadn't attempted to disappear into the crowd this time. He headed back toward the tree line and stumbled through a cluster of ferns, oblivious to his surroundings. The worst kind of demon could have flittered out of the dark right now and tried to eat him, and he would have let it.

An exposed root reached out like a hand and snagged his ankle. The ground rushed up to meet him. In a cruel echo of earlier, it was Aleksey who gripped him by the shoulders to keep him from falling.

This time, Kazik shoved him away, lashing out before he could think. "Don't *touch* me!" He felt the impact of his fist against Aleksey's jaw and a sudden shocking burn in his knuckles.

There wasn't much strength behind the blow, but Aleksey's

head snapped back, his lip splitting beneath the force. Kazik heard his teeth meet with a *click* and tasted something hot and metallic in his own mouth as if he'd taken the hit himself.

Shock widened Aleksey's beautiful eyes. His chest heaved. His breathing was harsh in the silence that fell between them.

He looked utterly debauched. Wild. Like temptation personified, with his mouth swollen and leaves caught in his crown of honey-gold hair. His expression darkened, and for a second, Kazik wondered if Aleksey hid emotions as intense as his own behind that easygoing mask.

Goose bumps swept over his skin. He felt like he was looking at a completely different boy, at someone he'd never met.

Slowly, Aleksey raised his hands in a gesture of surrender. A drop of blood welled at the corner of his lips. Kazik tried but couldn't look away. He couldn't forget what that mouth felt like pressed hot and hungry against his own.

As penance, or torture, his mind immediately called up the look of shock and hurt on Gisela's face.

"Why would you do that?" Kazik's gut roiled with self-loathing. He wanted to hate Aleksey for dragging them into this mess, for instigating the kiss, but he hated himself more.

"Because—because I wanted to," Aleksey said, the words coming out as a choked confession.

"You want to kiss me?" Never in a million years had Kazik thought . . . He hadn't thought Aleksey liked boys. It had been easier to believe he didn't—that way Kazik wouldn't hope.

He clasped both hands behind his neck and hung his head, squeezing his eyes shut. "You were supposed to kiss Gisela." He'd sworn to play matchmaker, promised to help her regain her humanity. Aleksey wasn't supposed to want *him*. "She likes you. You said you liked her."

"I do like her," Aleksey said.

"You can't like us both."

"Can't I?" Aleksey's mouth curved in a humorless smile. "Why not?"

"Because—" Kazik gritted his teeth. That was like asking him to explain why the sky was blue, why demons and spirits were evil. That was the way the world worked. Everyone knew you were only supposed to fall in love with one person. You were only supposed to want to kiss one person.

Yet Kazik's own heart betrayed him. Because he'd fallen in love with and wanted to kiss countless people. The boys he'd been with in the past. Aleksey. Gisela. He had feelings for them both, and he couldn't separate them.

And that was the terrifying part, God forgive him, because he knew that, if given the chance to travel back in time and redo the past hour of his life, he'd choose to do it all again, consequences be damned. Even knowing what would happen, he'd still kiss Aleksey back.

Kazik pressed the heels of his hands into his eyes. He'd long since stopped beating himself up about his sexuality. He knew, deep down, that there was nothing wrong nor shameful about having many or multiple partners so long as everyone involved was happy. There wasn't a right or a wrong way to love.

But at the same time, a part of him was still deeply afraid of disappointing his grandmother.

"I didn't want this either," Aleksey bit out. "It would be far easier if I felt nothing for you both. Can't we just . . . continue as we have been, the three of us?"

He couldn't really think it was that simple.

Could it be that simple?

It was far too easy a solution. Things in Kazik's life weren't ever that easy, and they were still keeping secrets from one another. Aleksey didn't know Gisela was a water nymph. He didn't know Kazik had made a deal to set him up with a literal demon.

"Is it such a terrible sin, liking more than one person?" Aleksey came closer, each tentative step a hiss in the grass. He moved like he was approaching a cornered animal that might lash out with claws and teeth.

"You don't understand," Kazik said, "Gisela and I— She isn't— She's—"

"A water nymph?" Aleksey finished for him.

Kazik stared.

"You really thought I wouldn't notice?"

"You didn't care? You never said—"

"That sort of thing doesn't matter to me."

"I really can't with you both," Kazik whispered. If it wasn't Gisela turning his world upside down, it was the boy before him. It would be a thousand times easier if Aleksey and Gisela would just run off into the sunset together.

And just imagine how boring life would be if they did.

Kazik sucked in a deep breath. He just needed a moment to breathe. A moment to piece himself back together. He still needed to find Gisela. Needed to talk to her. Needed to apologize. He wanted to hash this all out, make sense of it, like they were having one of their whispered midnight conversations.

He was so terrified that he'd ruined things between them for good.

"We'll find her," Aleksey said, his voice embarrassingly gentle, like he was soothing a child. "I'll talk to her. I know you like her too. We'll fix this."

Kazik so wanted to cling to the hope that they could, that there was still a way to salvage things. He dragged a hand through his hair, feeling wretchedly guilty. No matter what Aleksey said, it still didn't seem right, didn't seem fair, to ask Aleksey to help him go after someone else. "What if she hates me?" Kazik's voice cracked on the final word.

"She—" Aleksey's head snapped toward the trees as a furious heartrending shriek split through the forest.

Kazik's blood turned to ice. His hand flew to the medallion around his neck. What unholy abomination made a sound like that?

It was only then that he realized how eerily quiet it had become. No night birds called through the dark. No nocturnal animals scurried through the undergrowth. There was no rustling of foxes nor hedgehogs, no soft hum from the crickets. Not even a mosquito's whine.

The forest had fallen silent. The sound of his and Aleksey's breathing was obtrusively loud.

Hairs rose on the back of Kazik's neck as the branches of the surrounding trees quivered, producing a sound like chattering teeth. He scanned the gloom between the trunks for movement, searching for shadows amid shadows. The longer he stood there listening, the more convinced he became that the trees were actually speaking, the rustling of the leaves trying to impart some kind of message.

Or warning.

Aleksey cursed beneath his breath, almost as if he understood. He met Kazik's gaze briefly, his expression dark with worry. "The river. That's where she'd go. We have to hurry."

Kazik stared at him, his skin prickling with unease, but he didn't have time to focus on why because Aleksey was already sprinting into the trees. Kazik chased him, following at his heels.

36

BIES

GISELA

ROZA WADED THROUGH THE grass, stopping just short of where Gisela stood. Her pretty face contorted in a strange, wrong-feeling smile. There was something about the look in her gray eyes, a cold kind of amusement, that triggered something deep inside Gisela. She felt on edge all of a sudden but couldn't put her finger on why. It was only Roza, Aleksey's friend.

Aleksey's friend whose mother thought she was behaving strangely.

Aleksey's friend whom Kazik had warned her about.

A breeze raised goose bumps on Gisela's skin. Somewhere nearby, a frog croaked in the dark. Saints, she didn't have time to deal with this right now. She had far more pressing matters to contend with—like the fact that she was dissolving into nothing. "If you're looking for Aleksey, he's . . ."

She didn't want to think about where Aleksey was and what he might be doing, with whom.

"Oh, I don't think we need to involve him," Roza said. "He doesn't seem to understand that there are greater things at stake here than his amusement. And I think he's grown a little too attached to you. It's not good for him."

Gisela frowned in confusion. Was Roza jealous Aleksey hadn't come to the festivities with her?

"You don't remember me, do you?"

"We met at the farmers market."

Roza looked Gisela up and down and continued as if she hadn't spoken. "I suppose it has been a while, and I did look very different then."

"I don't—"

"You haven't worked it out yet? I heard you're a water nymph now. You can't recognize what *I* am?"

Gisela's senses flared, her skin prickling. Roza's smile was all teeth. Something shifted in her eyes, and it was like something *else*, some other presence, was peering out at Gisela. That face suddenly seemed like nothing more than a pretty mask.

The sight jarred something loose. The sour taste of fear crawled up Gisela's throat. The scent of the forest filled her lungs. Memories swam before her vision, bubbling up from the murky depths of her mind, finally dredging to the surface. Time stood still. Then it wound rapidly backward, transporting her back to an evening last spring.

***

She'd fallen into one of her melancholy moods, feeling down because her father was as distracted and distant as always, consumed with his own affairs, too busy to make time for her and Hugo even on holiday. It was her birthday tomorrow, and she knew he'd forgotten. She'd put her brother to bed at the hotel and afterward, she'd slipped out alone as the sun sank, wanting to disappear for a moment and escape from everything.

A small part of her even hoped that her father might worry about where she was. She'd taken one of the lonelier walking paths, following the trail into the forest until it brought her to a clearing circled by towering trees.

There, a boy knelt, hunched over in the grass.

He was breathing hard, struggling to stand. His hands clutched at his arms, almost rending and ripping the fabric of his sleeves. A pained moan tore through the air. A gust of wind creaked through the trees.

Gisela rushed forward through a rain of leaves and petals. "Hey, are you all right?"

The boy's head whipped up. She inhaled sharply. His eyes—the left was summer blue, the right spring green. Shadows crept across his irises like wisps of smoke. For a split second, something else seemed to stare out at her from behind that beautiful gaze, something not of this world.

A dark shape rose behind him. An enormous monstrous silhouette.

It resembled a wild boar walking on its hind legs. Mottled green fur covered its beastly body. Tusks curled from its mouth. Great branching antlers protruded from its skull.

Bies.

One of the forest demons from her great-aunt's stories.

Blazing eyes of solid, unbroken gold fixed on Gisela. Falling back, helpless with terror, she turned and ran.

And ran and ran. Ducking beneath branches, scrambling over roots and rocks and the slipperiness of fallen leaves, skidding on patches of mud and moss as the beast smashed through the trees behind her.

Ahead, the glint of something. Darkly rushing water. The river! The ground gave way to a slope, and she came out upon the bank.

How deep was the water? Could she wade to the other side? Gisela looked frantically around. There was no bridge. The current was flowing fast but—there.

Hidden amid the reeds and rushes was a pier. A wooden jetty stretching out over the water. Maybe there was a rowboat tied to the posts? Like the ones tethered near the hotel.

A hideous high-pitched giggle spurred Gisela forward. Reeds whipped her legs. Planks of rotted wood warped and creaked beneath her weight.

But there was no boat tied to the pier.

There was no boat.

She felt the tremor of steps behind her. A touch like breath on the back of her neck. Spinning in panic, Gisela stumbled and lost her footing. The world tilted. The darkening sky flashed overhead. Her head slammed against something hard—the back of her skull clipping the edge of the pier as she fell—dazing her even before she sank like a stone into the water. Too stunned to even struggle.

***

"You know, you're the first human I've met who's come back as a spirit." Roza's voice seeped into Gisela's consciousness, bringing her back to herself, to the present.

Gisela stared blindly at the girl before her, her mind still awhirl with memories.

The bies. That was what she'd run from. That was what had chased her. That fall was how she'd died. Here, by that rotting wooden pier, in that ink-dark water. This was where she'd been transformed into something else.

A tear rolled down her cheek.

And that was why Aleksey had felt so familiar to her. She'd seen him . . . she didn't understand what she'd witnessed back then. Had the demon attacked him too?

There was no time to sink into the revelation because Roza was stalking closer.

Run, something whispered inside Gisela's head. *Run, now.*

But her legs refused to listen. Her feet were rooted to the ground. Terror, and a kind of horrified disbelief, held her in a viselike embrace. She couldn't move. She couldn't *breathe*. It was like she existed in a place outside her own body, like she was looking down from a great height, watching herself the way the moon would, watching her end unfold.

"I was going to use you as a host back then, but you fled so quickly. Second time's the charm, I guess." Roza—no, not Roza. This wrctched *fiend* wearing Roza's skin reached out and grabbed Gisela's wrist.

The shock of that unwanted touch sent a rush of adrenaline through her. Gisela recoiled, ripping her arm free, stumbling clumsily backward. Twisting on her heel, she broke into a sprint, fighting through the grass as the long green blades tangled around her legs.

"Why are you running?" Roza called, sounding unconcerned. "We have so much to catch up on!"

An upturned root seized Gisela's ankle. She pitched forward and went down hard, her chin, palms, and knees scraping raw as she hit the ground. She tasted dirt and blood.

Roza clicked her tongue. "Now, look what you've done. You've gone and hurt yourself. You're going to ruin that body before I have a chance to—"

Gisela pushed herself onto her hands and knees.

The root she'd tripped over tore itself from the earth and hooked around her calf. She cried out as she was dragged back to where she'd stood, toward Roza's feet.

She clawed at the ground, fighting the pull, her fingers digging frantically through the grass for a stick, a rock, for something—anything—she could use to defend herself.

Her hand closed on her hair comb.

Her grip was solid enough to grasp it.

The root flipped Gisela onto her back. She lashed out, slashing blindly with her comb as Roza leaned over her. Fine bone teeth gored through flesh, slicing open Roza's cheek.

Roza let out a shriek that shook the forest, staggering back with her hands cupped over her face. But to Gisela's horror, no sooner had she regained her balance than she started to giggle, throwing her head back in glee.

Gisela scrambled to her feet. She risked a glance over her shoulder.

"Looking for help? For your exorcist friend? For *Aleksey*?" Before Gisela could react, Roza lunged, sailing straight through Gisela's body, tripping through her as if she were made of mist. As if she were nothing but a ghost.

"What the hell?" Roza whirled around, her eyes wide. No longer laughing.

"Surprised?" Gisela brandished her bloodstained comb and tried not to let her voice tremble. "Like you said, I'm a monster now too."

Roza's lips peeled back in a snarl. "A monster? Hardly. You're just a human girl too stubborn to die properly." Blood trickled down her neck and pooled in the dip of her collarbone. "Good thing this isn't my body, or I'd really be angry."

The realization hit Gisela like a blow—that was an innocent girl she'd just wounded. A girl who'd been possessed. A girl who was Aleksey's friend. Someone he thought of like a sister.

"Why?" Gisela demanded.

"Why what?"

"Why are you doing this?"

"To get close to the exorcist, of course."

To Kazik?

"If you're going to be angry with someone," Roza said, "be angry with him. It's because of Kazik and his grandmother that we came here in the first place. It's because of him that we had to flee into the forest, where you stumbled upon us. It's because of *him* that I was forced to hide inside this cursed body for a year. And it's because of him that you're going to suffer now." She stepped forward.

Gisela's fingers clenched around her comb. She raised it, praying it wouldn't slip through her fingers, but hesitated at the very last second. She wanted to hurt the bies, not the girl it was wearing, who was as much a victim as Gisela had been.

That pause was her undoing.

Roza swatted the comb aside. In the span of a breath, a pale hand closed around Gisela's throat with horrifying strength and lifted her off the ground.

Gisela's feet dangled uselessly. She tore desperately at the hand that held her, trying to pry Roza's fingers free.

"What happened to your little ghost trick? I've never seen a water nymph do that." The hand on Gisela's throat forced her head to the left, then the right, examining her face, the strange insubstantiality of her flesh. There was a hint of grudging respect in Roza's voice, "Maybe Aleksey was right to see something in you. You really have become something interesting. You should thank me for that."

Gisela's breath stuttered. Dark spots bloomed at the corners of her vision. A familiar feeling of hollow despair came sweeping in. Maybe she should just give in. Give up. Let it end. What was the point in fighting?

Even if Roza didn't choke the remaining life out of her and steal her body and she somehow miraculously managed to tear herself free, Gisela was still going to dissipate into nothing. Either way, she was going to die here. For good this time.

And who would miss her?

She'd never known her mother. Great-Aunt Zela was no longer here. Her father didn't have it in him to care for her. He couldn't even be bothered to come home half the time. Kazik had always wanted her gone. She'd failed to make Aleksey like her enough to want to kiss her. She'd failed to regain her humanity. She'd failed her little brother.

She'd left Hugo all alone.

Gisela's heart wrenched. All she'd wanted was to ensure he didn't grow up feeling unloved. She'd wanted to protect him, to make sure he never felt lonely nor isolated nor as hurt as she'd felt tonight. Now she'd never see him again, and it was because of *this* monster, this monster that had separated her from him in the first place.

Searing, unbridled rage blazed through her veins. Gisela kicked out with all her might, connecting hard with Roza's shin.

Roza grunted and staggered, her grip slipping enough for Gisela to suck in a frantic breath. "Why are you being so stubborn?"

Because I'm not going to make this easy for you.

Because for all her dark thoughts and bouts of melancholy, she didn't *want* to die. Because she wasn't *done* yet. She hadn't had the chance to fight last time, but this time was different. The desire to live, to tear this creature limb from limb, burned through Gisela's entire body. She kicked out again and again. Squirming. Thrashing. Refusing to give in.

If she couldn't have love nor her humanity back, then she wanted *vengeance*.

She clawed at Roza's forearms, no longer caring who she hurt. Her nails shredded skin until her hands were slippery with blood.

But Roza merely grinned.

The grip on Gisela's throat tightened. Her vision slipped in and out of focus. Her limbs grew numb. Her hands fell limply to her sides. She didn't have the strength to lift them.

Behind Roza, the cold black surface of the river rippled.

Then it surged.

37

RUSAŁKI

GISELA

WATER CRESTED IN A giant wave, arcing over their heads and smashing against their bodies. Gisela hit the ground on her back. Roza landed on top of her, but she was only down for a heartbeat.

With a hiss, she rolled off Gisela and scrambled to her feet, her white-gold hair plastered to her face.

Looking up, gasping for breath, Gisela saw Yulia standing in the shallows. The moonlight painted her in a pool of silver, highlighting the drowned pallor of her skin. Her eyes burned a brighter, more deadly shade of red than usual. In that moment, she truly looked like a rusałka from the stories. A creature both alluring and terrifying.

A golden comb flashed in Yulia's grip. Her gaze darted uncertainly between Roza and Gisela, and then all hell broke loose.

Wicked black thorns ripped through Roza's skin, erupting along her forearms in a spray of blood. The ground tore open, and a viciously pointed tree root speared toward Yulia.

Yulia spun out of the way. With a sharp flick of her comb, the river came alive, streams of water striking sharply at Roza like a many-headed snake.

"Wait!" Gisela rasped, breaking into a painful coughing fit.

Hands grasped her shoulders. "Gisela? Gisela, are you hurt?"

Gisela shook her head, her vision swimming, holding one hand against her throat as Miray helped her stand. A hail of dirt and water rained down on them.

Roza let out a furious shriek as one of Yulia's attacks landed, a swell of water slamming into her side. "Ooh, little water nymph thinks she has *teeth*. Careful, you might hurt the human I'm wearing."

"You say that like you think I care," Yulia shot back.

The trees along the riverbank shuddered, their great branches swaying, their trunks groaning. Squirming gnarled roots wormed out of the heaving soil.

Miray hauled Gisela along the riverbank, away from the fight.

"Don't think you're getting away," Roza snarled. At the flick of her wrist, roots streaked toward their heads.

Swiftly, Miray brandished her comb, pulling water from the river and throwing it up as a wall. It froze into a shield.

The roots slammed against the barrier with a deafening *crack*. Splinters of wood and ice flew in every direction.

A shard sliced Miray's forearm. Gisela cried out in panic.

Cursing, Yulia charged forward, only to duck and jump back as a tree branch whipped down at her.

But the river swelled as the crowns of three heads emerged slowly from the water, followed by three pairs of glowing red eyes. Moonlight danced off Nina-Marie's glasses. It dripped from Clara's and Zamira's dark ringlets. Ribbons of water snaked through the air, glinting darkly.

They shot toward Roza, coiling tightly around her torso, yanking her toward the river's edge. "Little pests," she spat, struggling madly, her heels digging furrows in the mud. "You'd better run while you still have the chance!" She let out another heartrending shriek.

Then, for a split second, her body went utterly slack. Her eyes rolled back in her skull until only the whites were visible. Shadows crawled across her sclera. Her back arched so violently that Gisela feared her spine might snap in two. Dark smoke poured from her mouth and nose and ears, forming a writhing, twisting black cloud that condensed into a truly grotesque shape.

An all-too-familiar shape.

The horror that had chased her.

Yellowed tusks jutted from the demon's jaw. Mottled green fur covered its massive boar-like frame. The jagged branch-like antlers protruding from its skull added a half meter to its height. It towered over them.

"Mother of God," Miray whispered.

Even Yulia blanched, falling back a step. Was this the forest demon's true form? Gisela had heard they were monstrous or so inhumanly beautiful that they could beguile even the holiest of saints.

Roza's body slumped lifelessly to the ground beside the beast's cloven feet. Its voice spoke inside their heads. *You're out of your depths, rusałki. You may have shed your humanity, but you're not true spirits—at heart you're still just dead human girls.* The ground quaked as it stalked forward. *You should know your place. I'm going to lay you to rest for good.*

"Do you really think you can?" Nina-Marie's voice piped up.

Gisela's head snapped toward her. She wanted to shout at the other girls to run, but her throat burned furiously from where Roza had choked her.

"I wouldn't write us off so soon," Nina-Marie said. "You're outnumbered six to one, and this is *our* territory."

The bies's golden eyes blazed with amusement. *I'll give you points for bravery. Leave Gisela, and I'll spare the rest of you. Don't go picking a fight you can't win.*

"I think that's our line?" Clara twirled an amber hair comb between her fingers. "You're going to regret challenging us in our own waters."

With a gurgling roar, another dark wave arced up from the river.

The older girls moved so fast, Gisela could barely follow their motions. They didn't give the demon a moment to breathe. They were ruthless. Relentless. Grinning and feinting and lunging in, cleaving at the bies with the sharp teeth of enchanted combs, with water sharpened into frozen shards, into knives of jagged ice. They attacked with inhuman speed, dodging the swipes of claws and tusks with eerie unearthly grace, matching their opponent blow for blow, without once tiring.

It was all the forest demon could do to deflect and evade their attacks. Its movements grew more and more frantic as they struck again and again and again. The beast might be larger than them, but that just meant it was a bigger target. Watery whips lashed around tusks, around those monstrous branching antlers. Its desperate shrieks shuddered through the air. *I am going to kill all of you!*

The rushes along the bank came to life, ensnaring Zamira and Clara in the shallows, wrapping around their limbs like living nets. Nina-Marie screamed in outrage, hacking at the reeds with her comb as they wound tighter and tighter around her girlfriend. Miray raced to help them.

Gisela surged forward, grasping for a shard of ice. It slipped through her ghostly fingers. In that case—

"You can't kill," she rasped, drawing the demon's attention away from the others, "what's already dead!"

With a furious bellow, the bies turned and charged her, slashing madly with its claws. Gisela stepped into the strike as if she welcomed it. Voices cried out, but the claws swiped straight through Gisela's body as if she were made from nothingness.

The motion threw the demon off-balance, and in that split second before it could recover, Yulia brought a massive wall of ice, a frozen wave, crashing upon its head from behind.

The bies staggered, its eyes rolling wildly, then crumpled to the ground with a thunder that shook the earth.

For a moment, no one moved.

No one spoke.

No one could tear their eyes away from the demon, as if none of them could believe they'd actually managed to incapacitate it. The reality of what they'd done hit them all at once.

"Is—is it dead?" Zamira whispered, tearing a now-lifeless reed from around her waist.

"Look at its chest." Clara pointed. "It's still breathing."

"I don't think it's getting up anytime soon though," Yulia said grimly, nudging its side with her toe.

Gisela's knees gave out. The relief was so potent that tears spilled down her cheeks. She shut her eyes against the carnage and sucked in a deep shuddery breath.

"What do we do now?" Clara asked uneasily. "Yulia? If it wakes up and tells the other forest spirits we attacked it, there could be real trouble."

Gisela opened her eyes and saw Yulia bend over the prone form of the real human Roza, putting a finger to her pulse, searching for a hint of life.

"She's alive." Despite Yulia having said she didn't care, she sounded awfully relieved. "Zamira, go catch some human's attention and lure them over here. They can look after her."

Zamira took off at speed.

"Should we tell Wojciech?" Clara asked.

"What if he gives us up to Grandfather Forest to keep the peace?" Nina-Marie protested.

"He won't," Yulia said firmly, dusting her hands on her trousers. "Wojciech would go to war for us. Don't doubt that for a second. And the demon attacked us first. We'll take it below for now, before it regains consciousness." She glanced at Miray.

Miray nodded. "I have an idea for where we can hide it."

Yulia, Nina-Marie, and Clara pulled more water from the river. Ribbons of liquid roped around the bies, dragging its body through the mud and into the shallows with a splash.

Miray wrapped a comforting arm around Gisela's shoulders. "Come on, let's get you out of here too."

For a second, Gisela fought the pull of the embrace; too much adrenaline was still thrumming through her veins, and too many thoughts were racing through her head. She bit her lip hard, latching on to the pain to ground herself. It was a sign she was still alive. Still here. For now.

They walked into the rippling black water together, sinking slowly beneath the surface.

38

HEAVEN-SENT

KAZIK

"GISELA!" KAZIK'S DESPERATE SHOUT rent through the night. "Gisela, wait!"

Ahead, past the willowy reeds that lined the shore of the river, a familiar ghostly figure was sinking into the rushing water, slipping below the surface. Kazik's heart stuttered in his chest. The grass swished and whipped at his calves. He could hear the thunder of Aleksey's footsteps beside him, his long legs easily keeping pace as they reached the water's edge.

Kazik tossed aside his vest, kicked off his shoes. They landed in the mud. He sucked in a breath and plunged into the dark water, following Gisela into the depths.

A month ago, such an act would've been unthinkable. A month ago, he would've been glad to see her go, would've rejoiced to see the back of her. But somehow, impossibly, Gisela had become somebody he cared about.

And something in his heart told him that if he didn't go after her now, he'd lose her forever.

The water was cold enough to bite.

Kazik kicked hard against the current as it attempted to sweep him downstream. It flowed faster and stronger than he'd thought it did. He dove deeper, dragging his body through the water with desperate strokes, reaching, raking his fingers blindly through the dark. She had to be here somewhere. The murky water burned his eyes, but he forced them open.

He couldn't make out a thing.

Despite the brightness of the moon, there was only endless blackness below the surface. The river swirled around him. His chest burned for air.

He looked up, not even sure where the surface was anymore. It was then that something jerked at his leg. Kazik kicked out in panic. A flash of icy fear speared through him.

He and Gisela weren't alone down here.

A glowing figure materialized from the swirl of water before him. A boy with bone-pale skin and wine-red eyes and lips as blue as death. His white shirt billowed away from his lean torso. Auburn hair tangled like silk across his cheeks.

Utopiec.

Drowner.

A male water spirit.

Kazik's lips parted in shock, and he was suddenly choking on a mouthful of frigid water. Precious air escaped in a rush before he clamped his lips shut.

The drowner grinned widely, revealing teeth as pointed as an animal's. Teeth so sharp, they could rend flesh and splinter bone. In a flash, he'd locked his arms tightly around Kazik's waist, pinning his arms to his sides.

He dragged him down, down, down.

Kazik thrashed and kicked. Twisted, summoning every ounce of strength. But the spirit's arms only squeezed tighter and tighter, until he felt his ribs might crack, his lungs might rupture.

He couldn't get free. They were sinking deeper and deeper. Far deeper than the river was supposed to go. His chest strained with the fierce need to breathe. His vision was going spotty. What were a drowner's weaknesses? Every devil had a weakness, and Kazik had been trained from childhood to memorize them all. But right now, his mind was appallingly, terrifyingly empty.

He reached frantically for that spark of divine fire at his core.

Please.

Wasn't it Saint John's Eve? Wasn't tonight a night when a witch was supposed to be especially powerful?

Those saints who watch over me . . .

He needed air. He needed *air.* Any second now he was going to give in to the fatal temptation to part his lips and take a breath of liquid.

Kazik gagged, fighting his own body. His heart screamed in protest, beating like a drum.

Had Heaven truly abandoned him?

It couldn't end like this. He had to find Gisela. Had she felt like this when she'd drowned? Had she felt this same vise around her chest? This same terrible sense of helplessness?

He had to reach her.

He needed to tell her . . . He had to make things *right.*

Light bloomed in the darkness.

Startled, the drowner looked up. His grin slipped as the silver medallion at Kazik's throat pulsed with flickering light.

The light grew, enveloping them, blazing bright in every direction.

Kazik reached for the spark at his center, and instead of the magic skittering away at his summoning, it came at his call, filling his veins with molten heat. Strength flowed into his limbs. Power swelled within him. The feel of it thrumming through his blood once more was so overwhelming, it made him want to weep.

He smashed his forehead against the drowner's. The boy reared back with an agonized shout that reverberated through the river. His grip came loose.

Kazik's hand rose, his fingers spreading wide. He slammed his palm into the drowner's sternum. Searing light exploded from his hand, hurling the demon backward.

At the same time, something heavy plowed into the river behind Kazik, as if someone or something had jumped into the water. The force buoyed him forward. The drowner wore a look of shock as he stared over Kazik's shoulder. In a flash, the boy's body dissolved and vanished in a swirl of bubbles.

Kazik stared into the murky darkness where he'd been, struggling to make sense of what was happening. Why had he fled? Was there something else in the water? Another monster? Something horrifying enough to make a drowner flee?

He twisted this way and that, trying to see, still desperately seeking any sign of Gisela. His chest grew tight again, his borrowed strength already waning. The glow from his medallion flickered urgently.

He was out of time. He needed to return to the surface for air. His heart sank as he started to swim upward, but then, down in the deep below, he saw it—an answering flicker.

Kazik blinked, squinting, trying to focus as a hazy fog filled his head. At first, it was nothing more than a glimmer. The gleam of a lost ring buried in mud and silt.

A near-death hallucination?

The vision seemed to grow before his eyes, revealing a place he'd only ever visited in his dreams, lulled to sleep by stories of ghosts and goblins. He felt a phantom hand ruffle his hair. The echo of his grandfather's gravelly voice rumbled in his ears:

And when your grandmother's feet finally touched the bottom of the river, before her rose the water goblin's home—a great palace adorned with glittering domes and gold-tipped spires, crafted from the purest crystal, clear and shining as glass.

The surreal apparition rippled like a mirage. Kazik reached a desperate hand toward it, his fingers clawing and closing emptily on watery darkness. It was an effort to move, to keep his eyes open. His fingertips felt numb. But if he could just . . .

A new pair of arms encircled his waist from behind, pulling him down. He couldn't fight this time.

Darkness stole across his vision, blotting out everything as he lost consciousness.

39

THE WORLD BENEATH THE WATERS

ALEKSEY

"KAZIK?" ALEKSEY SAID, SHAKING him gently. "Kazik?"

Kazik's eyes fluttered beneath their lids, but he remained unconscious, sprawled in a puddle on a crystal floor inlaid with intricate gold patterns of waves and crescent moons. But at least he was breathing. His pulse was steady.

Aleksey sighed heavily, running his fingers through his wet hair. "I shouldn't be so relieved," he said softly, "that you are so hard to kill." His gaze lingered briefly on Kazik's lips. Just remembering how it had felt to have Kazik's mouth and body pressed against his own was enough to rekindle a treacherous heat in his gut. There had been a thousand ways to distract Kazik and keep him from following Roza; Aleksey still didn't know why kissing him had been the first thought to pop into his mind.

The second after he'd pressed his lips to Kazik's, he'd known it was a mistake. A terrible dread had filled him when Kazik froze, until his mouth opened beneath Aleksey's, kissing him back. Aleksey's entire body had responded then, certain parts with absolutely mortifying enthusiasm.

He blamed it on the effect alcohol had on a mortal body. That was the only reasonable explanation. He was starting to think maybe, just maybe, Roza was right. His control *was* slipping; Human Aleksey's emotions must've filtered into his own. There was no other reason he would have reacted like that. *Enjoyed* that.

Shaking the memory away, Aleksey staggered to his feet.

And that was another problem—Roza. He should've known she'd ignore his threats. Trusting a bies was like trusting a cat that would look you right in the eye and then deliberately knock a glass off a shelf just to watch your reaction. There'd been a fight by the riverbank. Who had won? He hadn't had time to ask the trees for details. If Roza had laid a finger on Gisela . . .

Anger surged through Aleksey as he scanned their surroundings. The Crystal Palace was as grand as the rumors boasted. Moonlight speared through the domed ceiling, rippling over the clear jewellike walls. In the center of the cavernous atrium rose a glittering pillar honeycombed with shelves housing what could only be drowned souls.

The sound of those souls trying to escape their teacup prisons, an ethereal chime-like tinkling, was audible even above the distant roar of the river's current. There was a scent in the air like rain-soaked roses.

Aleksey turned his head, spying a crystal urn full of freshly cut rosebuds. A knot in his chest loosened. He'd thought there would be no greenery down here, that he'd been cut off from the forest.

Now he wouldn't be defenseless. Even so, they needed to find Gisela and get out of here quickly before any more water spirits discovered them.

The nervous tinkling of the teacups suddenly increased in volume. Aleksey moved toward the pillar. Were the souls trying to raise the alarm? "Hush," he whispered.

If anything, the teacups' rattling only grew louder.

Aleksey raised a hand.

"I wouldn't touch those, if I were you."

The words were the only warning he got. Even as Aleksey spun on his heel, the water puddled on the floor was coming alive, rising, cresting into an impossibly colossal wave. It broke over him with all the force of a cannon, throwing him back until his body slammed against a wall. His bones screamed at the impact. His head cracked against the crystal, and for a chilling second, his vision went dark.

"In all my long years, only one other person has dared to force their way in here."

Aleksey's vision cleared just in time to watch an impeccably dressed figure descend one of the stairways on either side of the chamber, advancing on him with slow, even strides.

Another drowner? Like the boy who'd attacked Kazik? This young man didn't share that boy's deathly blue pallor, but he had the same hooded wine-red eyes as Gisela, the same green-black hair.

Aleksey's gaze flicked to Kazik. He was still out cold. Aleksey would have to finish this lowly creature off quickly before the exorcist woke.

He stood, a hand pressed to his ribs, the other reaching to the back of his head, checking for injury—he was going to have a nasty bruise. The drowner would pay for that. Aleksey was going to grow flowers in his lungs and have him choke on petals.

Across the chamber, the urn of rosebuds burst into vicious bloodred bloom. Aleksey flexed his fingers. Briars snaked over the floor, growing thick and fast, twining themselves into an impenetrable cage of thorns around the advancing figure with a sound like the scratching of claws.

The water spirit stilled, his wine-red eyes narrowing as a single sharp-tipped thorn froze inches from his face. "And here I was wondering who would be so foolish as to trespass into my palace."

Aleksey smiled widely. It had been some time since he'd let loose. Thorned vines rose up like snakes about to strike. "Surpri—" He stopped short, his thoughts finally catching up with the young man's earlier words.

Wait, *my* palace?

The man moved faster than Aleksey could follow. One second, he was standing in a puddle across the floor, caged in by briars; the next he was gone, before reappearing directly behind Aleksey, rising out of the puddle at his back as if it were a portal.

But of course, to a *water goblin*, a puddle was nothing but a door. He could transport himself instantaneously between bodies of water, sinking into one puddle and rising from another as easy as breathing.

Long webbed fingers plucked ribbons of liquid from the air. They whipped around Aleksey's wrists, around his ankles. He yanked a foot loose and twisted violently, slashing at the restraints.

Droplets of water flew everywhere as he ripped the ribbons apart, but for each one he tore through, two more materialized, lashing around his legs, his arms, his torso. A hiss escaped his lips as he struggled to break free, fighting until a final rope of liquid noosed around his neck.

The air choked from his lungs at the sudden pressure on his throat.

This was . . . not good. He had never officially met this river's water goblin, but he'd heard the stories. Every monster in these parts knew the ruler of the water spirits by reputation alone.

Wojciech came to a halt in front of him, his hands clasped behind his back. "You're limited by that mortal flesh you're inhabiting. You'll have to abandon that body if you intend to put up a real fight."

He was right. Aleksey had no chance against him in this form. Wojciech was as old and powerful as the leszy—which was why Aleksey hadn't expected him to look so young.

But Wojciech could take any form he desired, couldn't he? In that regard he and Aleksey were not so different.

Aleksey's mind raced. One wrong move here could spell the end. He could feel *Human Aleksey's* fear eating away at his courage, making him timid.

That was unacceptable.

He met the water goblin's assessing look with a snarl.

In response, the watery ropes yanked his legs askew and pulled his arms wide. With a horrifying *pop*, his left shoulder wrenched out of its socket. His head fell forward with a strangled gasp.

Hot sparks of agony shot like lightning up his arm. He couldn't move his fingers. He panted through the pain, his chest rising and falling. Mentally, he tried to separate himself from this body, tried to go to a place where the pain couldn't reach him. *This is nothing. I've taken worse.* "Do you treat all your guests like this?"

"Only those who arrive without an invitation—and you've tracked mud all over my floor."

"Sorry," Aleksey bit out, his tone anything but apologetic.

The watery ribbons jerked his arms farther and farther apart. He wondered idly how long a human body could survive with all its limbs ripped off.

A bead of water trailed from Wojciech's jaw down his neck, slipping beneath his shirt collar. "You dare much, little flower. Who are you? Did Leszek send you? The Lord of the Forest should know better than to start a war with me. Why are you here?"

A faint moan rang through the air in answer. Across the room, Kazik was beginning to stir.

Wojciech's head turned. A series of emotions played out across his face. Anger chief among them, but it melted into shock. "That's—"

"We're Gisela's friends," Aleksey said quickly, drawing the water goblin's attention back to himself. "We came to talk to her. There was a misunderstanding. She disappeared into the river, so Kazik dove in after her, and I followed to make sure he reached her safely."

He hadn't been about to let Kazik go into the water alone,

knowing what could be down there. He would be the one to take Kazik's last breath, not some other spirit. As it was, if Aleksey hadn't dragged the exorcist that last little way through the wards surrounding Wojciech's realm, Kazik probably would've drowned.

A frown creased the water goblin's impossibly youthful face. The look he shot Aleksey was sharp with suspicion. "What is your name? Or, I should say, what is the name of the boy you are *wearing*?"

A muscle ticked in Aleksey's jaw. "My name is Aleksey." His own name, his true name, was unpronounceable by human tongues.

"Aleksey," the water goblin repeated, shutting his eyes like he was in pain. He opened them again and continued wearily, "Of course it is. You're the boy who gave Gisela that flower. She doesn't know what you are, does she? And I doubt the exorcist does either." He frowned, obviously trying to fit the pieces together. "Explain."

Aleksey cast another wary glance at Kazik, but he was still sprawled in a heap on the floor. Keeping his voice low, he said, "Last spring, I was sent to observe Kazik and his grandmother. The leszy had heard the old witch's God-gifted magic was fading. He thought this could be our chance to take back control of the sacred springs from the humans. But I was discovered. Kazik and I fought, and I retreated into the forest, where I stumbled upon a boy dozing beneath a tree. It's always easiest to enter a body that can't fight back . . ."

"So you took command of that body and its identity," Wojciech finished for him.

"I needed a place to lie low. I was . . . weakened." It hurt his pride to admit it out loud. He hadn't wanted the other biesy to know he'd been beaten so badly either. Strength was prized among the forest spirits. "I was barely conscious for the first few months. It's taken time to recover my full strength, and I realized this boy I had possessed knew a lot about Kazik. I could get close to Kazik like this. Maybe even close enough to take over *his* body."

"And yet you're still in *that* body." The water goblin raised an eyebrow. "A whole year, and you didn't find a single opportunity to possess him? How hard have you really been trying?"

Aleksey bristled. "He's careful. His grandmother left him with protections."

"And Gisela? What does she mean to you? If I'm correct"—Wojciech's voice dipped lethally low; the watery ribbons coiled tighter and tighter around Aleksey's limbs—"*you're* the one who wounded Kasia, and the same night—"

"I never laid a hand on Gisela," Aleksey cut in quickly. "And the witch attacked me first. I was only defending myself. Gisela was simply in the wrong place at the wrong time. She saw me seize control of this body. I don't think she even understood what was happening." And he'd been in so much pain, writhing around on the ground after his fight with Kazik, that he'd been in no condition to try and explain things, nor to stop Roza from chasing her down.

"She ran away in fear and fell from the old pier. Her death was an unfortunate accident."

He did feel bad about it. It was the first time he'd ever felt anything close to guilt. But how could he have known then that

that girl was Gisela? How could he have known then that she was someone he'd come to care for? It wasn't his fault. If anyone was to blame, it was the exorcists. *They* were the ones who demonized biesy. They were the ones who taught girls like Gisela to fear spirits.

"I like Gisela. I admire her." Her influence over Kazik, that slow corruption of his beliefs, was more damaging than anything Aleksey had managed to effect on the exorcist. "I couldn't figure out at first why she was hanging around Kazik. I'm guessing you sent her to seduce him? Did you also help her turn herself human for that purpose?"

Wojciech's expression darkened. "I did not. I would never use the water nymphs that way. Gisela drank a potion containing half a drop of Living Water. She wishes to regain her humanity. But to do so, she must receive a kiss from a mortal. She even managed to charm the exorcist into playing matchmaker for her. Unfortunately, the mortal boy she's set her sights on seems to be not so mortal after all." He pinned Aleksey with a look.

Oh.

Oh.

A lot of things suddenly made sense. So that was why Gisela had been sticking to Kazik's side, and that was why Kazik had wanted *him* to kiss her. Aleksey couldn't help it. He laughed. Truly, Gisela was something else. A girl unlike any he'd met before. Every time he thought he had her figured out, she went and surprised him.

Though at the same time, he felt a small pang of disappointment. Did she find being a spirit so abhorrent?

"Is that even possible?" he said, half to himself. "Can a water nymph truly regain her humanity?" He'd seen Gisela's current transformation with his own eyes. He'd felt the warmth of her skin. But whether it was a *true* transformation was debatable. Death had left fingerprints on Gisela when it refashioned her into a spirit. She'd been changed in ways that couldn't be undone, in ways that might not yet be clear.

No matter what happened next, no spirit would ever see Gisela as an ordinary mortal. Like Kazik, she would always be something more than human.

"If she manages to bring herself back to life, she'll be something entirely new."

"*If* she manages it," Wojciech echoed. "If the potion wears off without her receiving a kiss, she'll fade to nothing."

Aleksey's eyes widened with alarm. He'd noticed the change in Gisela over a day ago. "How long does she have? How long do the effects—"

A soft groan cut him off.

Twisting his neck to look, he saw Kazik pushing himself onto his hands and knees with slow, heavy movements.

"He's going to get quite the shock when he learns what you are," Wojciech mused quietly.

"I don't think it's necessary to reveal that right now, do you?"

"Oh?" A slow smile spread across Wojciech's face, revealing a perfect set of shark-sharp teeth. "Is that your roundabout way of asking me to keep your secret? I *was* going to kill you myself, but I think it will be far more entertaining to watch him do it."

Aleksey kept his face calm, collected, but his heart hammered in his chest. "Are you sure that's what you want? If you tell him what I am, it will undo all of my and Gisela's efforts. Kazik's been coming around to the idea that not all of us are monsters. He's been helping spirits. He's even fallen in love with one."

Wojciech's eyebrows lifted.

"He came after Gisela, didn't he? Dove straight into your river without even hesitating, regardless of the risks." Kazik's grandmother would be rolling in her grave if she knew—and maybe that was revenge enough in itself. "If a kiss from a mortal is what Gisela needs . . ." Aleksey trailed off meaningfully, shoving down a tiny flare of envy at knowing Kazik would have to be the one to kiss her. Aleksey was *in* a mortal body—couldn't that still count? It was probably better not to take the chance.

"If you reveal what I am, it could jeopardize the relationship between the three of us. It could turn Kazik against spirits again. Against Gisela."

Water dripped from Wojciech's hair into his eyes; he didn't so much as blink, his gaze remaining steady on Aleksey. A beat passed, then another.

If Wojciech chose to expose him, there was almost nothing Aleksey could do to save himself. His pulse kicked up a notch, but then, abruptly, the watery ribbons binding him dissolved with a splash.

40

THE WATER GOBLIN

KAZIK

GROGGY CONFUSION BLANKETED KAZIK'S mind. For a moment, he didn't know where he was. His head pounded painfully, competing with the sharp ache in his chest and lungs. His hands found the floor, and he shoved himself up onto his knees—moving just a little too fast. The world blurred.

He blinked hard, and a cavernous chamber came into focus. Rose briars and puddles of water covered a floor patterned with gold crescents and waves, the shapes reflecting the moonlight streaming through the domed crystal ceiling.

Crystal.

Adrenaline surged through Kazik as his memories returned in a rush: Diving into the river after Gisela. The drowner. Being dragged down into the depths. His final hazy vision of the water goblin's Crystal Palace.

A splash, followed by a startled yelp and a loud thud, drew his attention across the room. His jaw dropped. Aleksey was here, too, sprawled on the floor, one hand clutching at his opposite arm, and standing over him . . .

Another drowner?

Kazik forced himself to his feet. He was at Aleksey's side in the span of a breath, his hands on Aleksey's shoulders, scanning him for injury. When had he jumped into the river? "You're hurt."

"Just my shoulder." Aleksey gave him a reassuring grin, but it didn't quite reach his eyes. His gaze fell. "You may want to take a moment to pay your respects, Kazik. You're in the presence of the famous water goblin."

Kazik looked back, his eyes growing wider and wider, drinking the ancient spirit in. He'd been so desperate to reach Gisela, he hadn't considered what, or rather who, else might be lurking in these depths.

Was this really the being Gisela referred to as *that old toad*? The wily and wicked spirit his grandmother had clashed with? Wojciech didn't look much older than Kazik. Even so, there was an air of quiet menace about him that could not be denied.

Kazik's mouth opened and shut. Opened again. *God preserve me*. The words slipped out before he could rethink them. "My apologies, I didn't recognize you. I thought you'd look older."

Wojciech's expression soured.

Aleksey let out a choked sound that could've been a laugh, but it turned into a pained hiss.

Kazik twisted toward him. "What did he do to you?"

"A lot less than he deserved." The water goblin's wine-red eyes seemed to glow in the gloom of this chilly and ghostly place. "So, you've managed to find your way down here, just like your grandmother did. But how were you planning to escape?"

"I wasn't planning to." Kazik's voice came out hoarse. He

cleared his throat. Even the air in here was damp; when he breathed, he half expected bubbles to come out of his mouth. "I didn't come here to fight with you, please forgive our intrusion. I was just trying to reach Gisela. I need to speak with her."

Wojciech gave him a long hard look. "One doesn't grow to be as old as I am trusting the words of humans."

"Please," Kazik said, shivering. Water dripped from his clothes. "I know you have absolutely no reason to trust me. But I swear I mean no harm to her nor to anyone else here. I just need to see her. I—I need to apologize to her."

"I'll vouch for him," someone with a high-pitched voice called out.

Kazik heard Aleksey's inhale of surprise as a small boy poked his head out from behind the great pillar in the center of the room. He was dressed all in black and wore a cloak of ink-dark feathers—no, not a cloak. Those were *wings*. As the boy drew closer, Kazik saw there were even more black feathers mixed in with his dark hair. Understanding dawned.

Latawiec.

"I don't recall asking for your opinion," Wojciech said sharply.

The boy shot Kazik a toothy grin. His eyes were raven blue. "They helped me when I was mobbed by a flock of crows," he told Wojciech. "I'm only returning the favor. You taught me that's good manners."

"I also taught you that it's impolite to eavesdrop."

"Only on you. You said it was fine to listen in on humans."

Kazik marveled at the exchange. He didn't often see spirits of different affinities interacting. His grandmother had said it was fortunate that they fought with one another almost as often as they did with mortals instead of combining their strength.

"Please," Aleksey interrupted. "Let Kazik see Gisela."

Wojciech's jaw tightened. For a second, it looked like he might refuse solely for the sake of being difficult. He considered Kazik for another long moment, searching his face, his gaze dipping to the silver medallion that Kazik wore, that had once been his grandmother's. Wojciech's eyes grew distant, perhaps fixed on some memory in the past. Then he sighed.

"Very well. I will allow it. This once. You may see her. Let's hope you're not too late."

41

FADING

GISELA

"HERE," MIRAY SAID PROUDLY, handing Gisela an all-too-familiar teacup stamped with gold leaf in a delicate pattern of water lilies.

It will make an excellent prison for a soul, Wojciech had told Gisela only hours ago. She almost wanted to laugh at the irony.

The upturned teacup clattered angrily upon its saucer. It had been Miray's idea to seal the bies inside it. *What, you think after almost a century with the water goblin, I haven't learned a few of his tricks?* she'd asked them, as she'd worked the magic.

A faint mystical glow still emanated from the porcelain. It was a fitting punishment, Gisela couldn't help thinking, being trapped inside a teacup and buried at the bottom of a river for all eternity. After all, that demon had wanted to trap her inside her own body. It would've pushed her down into the very depths of herself and kept her there, locked away in the dark.

"Where should we—" Gisela started to cough. Her throat was a tender choker of bruises. Her voice was hoarse.

Miray took the teacup back. "I was thinking to hide it among Wojciech's collection. Unless you wanted to keep it with you?"

Gisela shook her head vehemently.

"Then I'll find a place for it on the shelves in the atrium. It was lucky Wojciech had an empty cup like this lying around." Miray slipped out of the room.

Gisela perched on the edge of Yulia's four-poster bed. Eyes red-rimmed. Waist-length hair a tangled mess. Her knees were bloodied, and her arms were a crisscross of red scratches where the branches had left marks as she'd fled through the forest. The beautiful mint-green dress Kazik had gifted her was hopelessly muddied. She nibbled on a thumbnail, listening to the commotion outside the room: the rushed patter of footsteps, the half- stifled whispers and excited murmurings of the other water nymphs.

Their voices cut off as the bedroom door clicked shut behind Yulia. For a second, she stood looking at Gisela, and then she said, "You took the potion, didn't you?"

"How could you tell?" Gisela mumbled. Even if she hadn't been able to see her hazy bedraggled appearance in the mirror-smooth surface of Yulia's reflective pool, she could feel it. She felt light, and not in the fun breathless way the drinks at the festival had made her feel, but insubstantial, as if the smallest breeze might blow her apart. She'd known taking the potion was a risk, but she hadn't thought . . .

She wrapped her arms around her middle, desperately trying to hold herself together.

"I saw that forest demon swipe its claws straight through you," Yulia said, taking her question literally. "Most of us did."

Gisela winced. "None of the others said anything."

"They don't want to upset you. That, and they're too busy coming up with ways to help."

Gisela sat up straight.

"Zamira's trying to convince everyone to go search for the fern flower in the forest. She thinks its magic could save you. While Miray suggested we break past Villa Violetta's wards and throw you in the spring's healing waters. And Clara and Nina-Marie both want to drag that boy you like down here and make him kiss you by force. They're out there sharpening their knives right now."

Gisela's mouth opened and shut. Her heart felt raw as a wound. She'd tried so hard not to think of this place as home, not to think of these girls as her sisters. But she was so glad to be here, at the end, with them. Surrounded by people who had come to her aid when she needed them even without her asking, who she knew without a doubt cared for her, even if some of them did have a rather murderous way of showing it.

She didn't feel worthy of their love. She'd done nothing to deserve it. She slumped back on the bed and curled in on herself, pressing her forehead to her knees, letting out a panicked shriek when she sank straight through the mattress and the bed frame.

"Gisela!"

Gisela crawled out from underneath the bed. She didn't think she'd ever seen Yulia look so afraid—even when they were fighting the bies. The older water nymph was at her side in an instant, reaching to help her up.

Gisela's hand passed straight through hers. It was only on the second try that she was solid enough to take it. She gave Yulia a watery smile. "Aren't you going to say 'I told you so'?"

"I'll say it when you're not turning into a goddamn ghost. Mother of God. Don't cry. Please. You'll make *me* cry." Yulia scraped a frantic hand through her short brown hair. "We'll fix this. There has to be a way. Wojciech—Wojciech is as old as this godforsaken river. He *has* to know a way around the magic. There'll be a loophole. Something." She was kneeling on the floor now, on the rug beside Gisela, by a heap of discarded clothes, men's shirts and trousers that she'd no doubt been deciding between before she picked her outfit for tonight.

Gisela shook her head. She didn't want to worry Wojciech.

"Maybe we can trap *your* soul in one of his teacups or—" Yulia smashed a fist into her palm. "Back in my village they used to say that if the water goblin claimed a girl as his bride, she'd become a special kind of rusałka. We could hold a wedding!"

"You have got to be kidding me." The flat look Gisela gave Yulia was enough to make the other girl wince.

Yulia pulled her knees up to her chest and rested her chin on them. "It was just an idea," she said defensively. And then more quietly, she added, "I'm sorry. About everything. For how I've been acting. When you said you wanted to go home, I took it personally. I'm not— I wasn't jealous. I like you, but I don't like you in that way. And I know I say shitty things about your liking boys sometimes. Miray's always giving me an earful. I know it's just my own insecurities. But when you were so hell-bent on leaving, it felt like a rejection. You know I walked into this river willingly, don't you? I chose this. And I resented you for wanting to give it all up and return to the normal world. Because it felt like we weren't good enough for you." Her words came out in a rush, like she was trying to get everything out in one breath while she still had the chance, like they didn't have much time left.

Gisela supposed they didn't. Shame surged through her. She'd never meant to make anyone, especially not Yulia, think they weren't good enough. It was just like with Tamara. She'd been so wrapped up in her own pain, so focused on achieving her goal, that she hadn't noticed whom she was hurting.

Why did she always realize these things when it was too late?

"It just felt like you didn't care about any of our feelings," Yulia said. "Your old family might miss you if you don't return, but we, your new family here, will also miss you if you leave."

"Saints," Gisela choked out, on the verge of tears. "Now I *really* feel like I'm dying."

"You're not—"

"I wish I could do both," she confessed. "Stay here and return home." If these were her final moments, she might as well be honest with Yulia, and herself. "The truth is I love it here. I think I've been happier here than I ever was at home. But I felt guilty because I couldn't share any of this with Hugo. I felt bad for enjoying it knowing he couldn't."

If she could've brought Hugo here so he could experience the delights this new life had granted her too . . . But ordinary mortals couldn't survive in the spirit world beneath the waters; in time they would become spirits too. And even as she thought it, Gisela knew deep down that part of the reason why she enjoyed her time here was because she got to live a life that didn't always revolve around her brother.

Swallowing hard, she started to remove the flower wreath from her head, pulling free the pins that had secured it in place. She tried to focus on the good things. To make peace with what was about to happen. She was supposed to have died a whole year ago. Instead, she'd been gifted extra time. She'd gotten to experience more in her short life than people who lived for years and years. She'd met Yulia and Miray and Zamira and Nina-Marie and Clara. Tamara. Wojciech. She'd met so many spirits—some wicked, some good. She'd met Aleksey and Kazik. She'd gotten to do so many things she'd never had a chance to do back home. She'd gotten to experience more than she'd ever dreamed.

She set the wreath on the rug. The blossoms were already wilting.

"My wreath would always drown," Yulia said softly, "when I tried to float it on the river. Every Saint John's Eve. Without fail. Every wreath I made sank like a stone. They say that means you're ill-fated in love. I used to wish a beautiful rusałka would swim up, steal my wreath, and spirit me away."

Gisela huffed out a laugh. "Maybe you'll have to do that."

"What?"

"Steal a human girl's wreath and spirit her away."

"Be the monster girlfriend I want to see in the world, you mean?"

"Why not?" Gisela said. "There have to be other girls out there waiting for a water nymph to steal their wreath."

"But you're forgetting I hate humans."

"You didn't look like you hated the girl you were carrying around earlier tonight." Gisela waggled her eyebrows suggestively. "I saw the way she was looking at you."

Yulia cracked a smile. "Jealous? She was pretty handsome, wasn't she? Almost as handsome as me."

Gisela rolled her eyes, and for a brief second, everything felt so normal: the two of them sprawled on the rug in Yulia's bedroom, exchanging gossip and secrets. She'd missed this. She'd missed talking to Yulia like this. She'd missed her friend.

Yulia had gone teary again, possibly thinking the same thing. She skirted closer, letting her head drop onto Gisela's bare shoulder, putting an arm around her. "I don't want you to go. I want you to stay."

Gisela's face crumpled. Fresh tears trickled down her cheeks. She cried noisily and messily, like a child, squeezing her eyes shut and pressing her face into the crook of Yulia's neck. Yulia tried to rub circles into her back, but again the touch slipped through Gisela as though she were nothing more than air.

What was she going to do? How long did she have? She wasn't ready to leave this world. She didn't think she'd ever truly be ready.

"I'm scared," she whispered.

"It's okay," Yulia said fiercely. "You're not going anywhere. I won't let you—"

Someone knocked loudly on the door.

Gisela pulled back, scrubbing frantically at her eyes. The

door flung open. Miray, Nina-Marie, and Clara tumbled into the room. On their heels followed a skinny auburn-haired figure.

Gisela barred her teeth at Akiva. "What are *you* doing here?"

"Trust me," he said. "I'd rather be anywhere else."

"We have news!" Miray cut in urgently. "Something strange is going on."

"Strange?" Yulia rose to her feet.

Miray nudged Akiva. "Tell them, quickly."

The drowner cleared his throat importantly, taking his time. "So, there I am, peacefully drinking in the moonlight, floating face down in the river, pretending to be a dead body to scare the humans at the festival, and I sense you lot causing a commotion in the water. Of course, I go to check it out."

"Of course," Gisela muttered. He'd probably been hoping to get them all into trouble with Wojciech.

"Anyway the fight, or whatever, is over before I get there. *But*, while I'm looking around, suddenly this boy runs up and dives into the river. Moments after you all went below. And you know who it was?" Akiva paused for dramatic effect. "The damn exorcist."

"*What?*" Gisela and Yulia chorused.

"So I thought," Akiva went on, "I should drown him. He's in our territory. Perfect chance and everything. I begin to drag him down, but then he starts to glow and slams me right here." He pulled his shirt open, displaying a patch of charred flesh. "With holy fire or something. Seriously. Underwater! I thought I was going to die. And then, *another* human boy jumps into the river out of nowhere. There was something about him . . ." Akiva paused, shuddering. "Anyway, you should've seen the look he sent me. It gave me chills. That's when I hightailed it out of there."

Gisela stared at him. She couldn't make head nor tail of the story. None of it made sense. Kazik diving into the river. Summoning holy fire. Had his magic returned? And the other boy . . . Aleksey?

Memories flashed before her eyes, even more vividly this time: The leaf-strewn clearing. The rain of red petals. The crunching of twigs beneath her shoes. The earthy sweet scent of the forest. Her breath catching as she spied the figure hunched over in the grass. A boy struggling to stand, and rising behind him . . . the monstrous antlered shadow of the bies.

The sound of Yulia shifting beside Gisela jerked her back into the present. She was half convinced her mind was playing tricks. Maybe she was remembering wrongly? Maybe that boy hadn't been Aleksey. Wouldn't he have shown some sign of recognition when they'd first met? But those eyes . . .

Gisela glanced sideways. Yulia looked just as confused as she felt.

"Gisela, do you know why Kazik would jump into the river?" Nina-Marie asked anxiously. "Do you think he thinks *we* hurt that human girl? The one who was possessed. Maybe we shouldn't have left her—"

The sound of approaching footsteps had them all tensing up. But it turned out to be only Zamira.

She burst into the room at speed, her shiny black ringlets bouncing over her shoulders, nearly tripping over her own small feet. “Gisela! Gisela! It’s the exorcist! He’s *here*. He forced his way into the palace to see you. Wojciech said he can, if you’re okay with it?”

Gisela gaped at the news. They all did. All except for Yulia.

“I’m going to have a word with that old toad,” she said, looking wrathful. She had a foot out the door when Gisela caught her sleeve.

“Wait! Wait, Yulia. I’ll—I’ll deal with him. I’ll talk to Kazik.” She needed to, even if it was the last thing she did.

42

CONFESSION

GISELA

THEY MET IN THE gallery, a long curving hallway full of rippling green-blue shadows where you could stare straight through the crystal-clear walls of the palace to the riverbed outside.

Kazik was already there, standing with his back turned, watching a school of silvery fish swim through a grass of green reeds twisting on the current. His hair and clothes were dripping wet. It seemed he really had dived into the river after her as Akiva had said.

Why though? Gisela didn't understand. Why bother to come after her at all?

He turned suddenly, sensing her presence. His deep brown eyes caught hers before he dropped his gaze to the floor, wincing, as if it physically pained him to look at her. A petty part of Gisela was glad to see him looking so guilty, like a thief caught red-handed.

He *should* feel guilty. His mouth opened and shut, words and excuses dying on his lips.

She wondered what she looked like to him, if she looked

a ruin in her torn and muddy dress, if she looked angry. She *wanted* to be angry, and she was, but after everything she'd been through—after the terror of discovering the potion was wearing off, after fighting for her life by the riverbank—that anger felt almost shallow, especially compared to the fury she'd felt when she faced the bies.

Too many things had happened at once. It was too much, too fast. She just felt hollow. Empty. She hadn't even processed what had *just* happened. It felt like she'd seen Kazik kiss Aleksey a lifetime ago.

Her bare feet made no sound as she moved closer, each step as silent and soft as a ghost's. It had taken her three tries to will her hand solid enough to even push open the door into the gallery.

She came to a stop before him. A heavy silence settled over them, both waiting for the other to shatter it, neither of them quite knowing how, neither wanting to be the first to speak.

After a long pause, Gisela said, "Well played."

At the same time, Kazik said, "I—"

They stared at each other.

"You really fooled me," Gisela said. "I actually believed you were helping me. Did you enjoy watching me make a fool of myself over Aleksey? Was this all just a joke to you?"

Kazik flinched like the words had slapped him. "No, I—" He ran a distressed hand through his hair.

"Saints, I could even *tell* you liked him." Gisela's throat started to burn. She could feel herself choking up, but she refused to cry in front of him. She was such an idiot. "Why didn't you say something when I dragged you into this, when I asked you if you liked him?"

Because that was what hurt the most.

If he'd told her how he felt, she would've asked him to set her up with someone else. She wouldn't have gotten her hopes up. She scrubbed at her traitorous eyes with the heel of her right hand. "Why are you even here, Kazik? What do you want? Do you even know whose palace you're standing in?" It was a miracle Wojciech hadn't already trapped the exorcist's soul in a teacup. "Do you know how much danger you're in?"

"I was afraid I would lose you. I'm *more* afraid of losing you than I am of whatever might befall me here."

Gisela was taken so off guard by the confession that she forgot what she was about to say next.

"I'd go to worse places for you," Kazik said, stepping closer.

Gisela immediately took two steps back. Her shoulder blades collided with the wall behind her.

Or they should have.

Instead, the solidness of the wall gave like water. She stepped straight through the crystal. For a heartrending moment, she seemed to melt into the wall.

"Gisela!" Kazik lunged forward.

Gisela threw up her hands. "Don't! Don't touch me!"

Kazik froze. Gisela's outstretched arms flickered in and out of sight—gone one moment and then there again the next. Trembling, she tilted forward, removing herself from the wall.

"What's happening to you?" Kazik whispered.

"The potion's wearing off. There may be some, um, side effects."

"What *kind* of side effects?"

Gisela swallowed thickly. She tried to keep the tremor out of her voice. "I'm turning into a ghost?" She could see her own fear reflected on Kazik's face. It was the first time she'd ever seen him look truly afraid.

She glanced at her reflection on the glassy wall. Her edges were wicking away, wispy as smoke drifting from a candle flame. She looked ephemeral as mist, as if all it would take was one breath from Kazik to snuff her out of existence. There was nothing weighing her down. Nothing keeping her here. "What," she said weakly, "no smile? Isn't this what you wanted from the beginning? I thought you'd be happy. One less monster in the world, right? Your saints will be pleased. Maybe that's why you finally have your magic back."

"That's not—that can't be why—" Kazik took a deep breath, fighting panic. His hands balled into fists at his sides. "How do we fix this?"

"You can't. It's how the potion works."

Kazik stared at her in horror. "Did you *know* about the side effects before you drank it?"

Gisela didn't answer.

Kazik raised his eyes to Heaven.

"I feel it's very unfair of you to judge me right now, when I might literally have only seconds left before I fade to nothing. I thought I could make Aleksey kiss me before it wore off! Then I'd permanently regain my humanity. I didn't expect him to kiss someone *else*." Gisela's throat constricted.

Kazik looked at the floor. "Will that still work?" he asked quietly.

"What?"

"Will you still regain your humanity if a mortal kisses you?"

She didn't know. Would she? Did it even matter anymore?

Kazik moved closer.

"Don't! You'll only—" Gisela cringed, expecting his fingers to pass straight through her. But when his hands came to rest upon her shoulders, they didn't slide through. She could feel their weight. Their warmth holding her in place. It was as if his hands on her were the only things tethering her to this world. And maybe, in this moment, they were.

Kazik leaned in. Was he really about to—

"You don't have to," Gisela blurted, when there was scarcely a whisper of air between their lips. "What about Aleksey? What if it doesn't work?" Her heart thundered. What if it was already too late? What if she could no longer regain her humanity?

"Then we'll figure it out together." Kazik tightened his grip on her shoulders. "It doesn't matter to me if you're human or a spirit or something else entirely. No matter what you become, what form you take, whatever demon you turn into. I'm not letting go."

"What if it means you lose your magic again?"

The bump in Kazik's throat shifted as he swallowed. "I don't care."

Gisela's vision went glassy. "Liar. You don't have to force yourself."

"I'm not forcing myself," Kazik said firmly. "I think I've wanted to kiss you for a long time now. I wanted to kiss you even when you were being insufferable. I—I want to kiss you *and* Aleksey. I think I'm a little in love with you both. I know you might not like that." His face fell, his features painted with uncertainty. "If you don't want me to kiss you . . . I can understand why you would feel that way. I can fetch Aleksey. We both came after you. He insisted I talk to you first."

"Aleksey's here too?" Gisela's voice came out a whisper. Again, her thoughts whirled with recently recovered memories. She saw the forest clearing and the great antlered shadow rising behind Aleksey as he knelt in the grass. She saw the violent whirlwind of bloodred petals that had protected her from Domek's fire.

Maybe I'll show you my true face one day, Gisela, if you promise not to recoil in horror.

An awful suspicion was slowly taking root at the back of her mind.

But if there was something wrong with Aleksey, if *he* was possessed by a bies, then surely Wojciech would've noticed. He wouldn't allow anyone into the palace who was a threat.

And would a bloodthirsty forest demon really be willing to follow her down into the depths of the river just to have her back?

Gisela's head swam with doubt. She was too exhausted, her mind too consumed with immediate fears, to even attempt putting the pieces together. She'd cross that bridge later.

"I'll get him," Kazik said, pulling away, taking her hesitation for an answer.

Gisela grabbed the front of his shirt. "No! I—I want you to. Kiss me."

The tips of Kazik's ears turned pink. He searched her face, trying to pick out any hint of disgust. "You don't think it's weird?"

"That you want to kiss us both?"

"Do *you* want to kiss us both?"

"Does Aleksey?" Gisela countered.

Kazik nodded. Gisela took a breath to process this. If she were being honest, she'd admit to feeling a little shocked and slightly scandalized, but not exactly in a bad way. Mostly she was just deeply relieved that they both still liked her, that they both wanted her too. She didn't want to lose either of them, and she didn't think she could've chosen between them if it had come to that.

And if she'd learned anything, it was that life could be agonizingly short. So why not fall in love with as many people as you could?

As always, she fell back on humor to cover what she was really feeling. "Well, if the Heavens want me to have two boyfriends, then who am I, really, to question—"

"For the love of God," Kazik said, "stop talking before I change my mind."

"I'm just saying, if this is my fate—"

Kazik leaned forward and covered her mouth with his. It was only a tiny, almost-shy kiss, a featherlight press, a soft heat, but it sent a searing jolt through Gisela. A bolt like lightning.

Kazik's breath tickled her lips. Their noses brushed.

"Is that the best you can do?" Gisela whispered, pulling back just enough to meet his eyes. "I barely even felt that."

Kazik's hand cupped her cheek, his mouth crashing against hers. He pressed a palm to the small of her back, crushing her to him so tightly, she could feel every hard plane of his body.

Closing her eyes, Gisela slid her hands up his chest and around his neck before sinking her fingers into his hair, drawing him closer still, opening her mouth against his.

A delicious sizzling warmth was unfurling inside her, tingling along her arms and legs, racing all the way down to her toes. The euphoric sensation built and built and built until she felt like she was melting, burning, floating, until the only thing anchoring her to this world was this kiss. Her entire being tingled. Her knees started to cave beneath her.

A soft silvery glow swept over her skin, its radiance expanding, spreading, growing outward like a rose in bloom until it whited out her vision. With a flash of blinding light, everything vanished.

43

NO MORE SECRETS

GISELA

A SOFT MURMURING VOICE pulled Gisela toward consciousness. She felt . . . strange. Her body felt oddly heavy. Drowsiness swaddled her like a blanket, but she had no memory of falling asleep. She was in a bed that wasn't her own. She knew it even before she opened her eyes. The mattress wasn't as soft, the sheets weren't cold silk, and they were scented with lavender and something like incense.

"Gisela?"

With great effort, she opened her eyes a sliver. Spinning shapes and colors coalesced. Sunlight rippled over Wojciech's ageless features. His brows were drawn together in worry. He was sitting in a chair beside the bed.

"Here, drink some water. You must be thirsty." He held a glass to her lips. "How do you feel?"

"I—" The world spun when she tried to sit up. "Dizzy," she said dazedly, taking a sip from the proffered glass. "What happened?" She lifted a trembling hand, staring at the faint blue-green tracery of veins on the underside of her wrist, at her pale palm and slender fingers, half expecting to see them wisp away.

They didn't.

Gisela ran her hands up and down her arms, over her legs, over her torso, reassuring herself that she was still there. She felt . . . tangible. Whole. She could see, *feel*, how solid her body was. She was a creature of warm living flesh and blood. Her heart pounded a reassuring rhythm in her chest.

She turned to Wojciech with a question in her eyes, almost too afraid to ask. *Is this real? Am I dreaming?*

The water goblin's expression was bittersweet. "I suppose I should offer my congratulations?"

Gisela burst into sobs. "I can't believe it actually . . ." She choked. Her shoulders shook. For several long moments, she was at a loss for words. Because it had worked. It had *worked*. She sniffed noisily, swiping furiously at her cheeks.

Wojciech pulled a handkerchief from his shirt pocket, only to frown as water dripped from the sodden square of silken fabric.

The sight made Gisela laugh through the tears. She dabbed at her face with the edge of the bedsheet, took a deep shuddery breath, and shut her eyes, taking a moment to savor, to remember what it was like to be so achingly alive. "Where are we?" She glanced around the room, taking in the slanted wooden ceiling and the underwear drying on the radiator—Kazik's bedroom, she realized.

"This is Kasia's cottage," Wojciech said. "My realm is no place for mortals, as you well know. I had a feeling you wouldn't want to risk becoming a spirit again, so I brought you here with Kazik's blessing. You've been asleep for three days."

"Three *days*?"

She'd been asleep for three whole days? Gisela looked down at herself. She was wearing a clean cotton shift, which meant someone had changed her clothes for her. Heat rushed to her cheeks. She hoped it hadn't been Wojciech.

He adjusted her pillows, repositioning them behind her—Gisela couldn't bring herself to protest. There was something comforting in being fussed over. Leaning back in his chair, the water goblin scanned the simply furnished room with palpable disdain. "It's certainly not a dwelling befitting someone of my status. I will never understand why Kasia preferred a hovel like this to my palace."

"Aw, did you ask the witch to be your beautiful river bride too? Suddenly, I don't feel so special."

"I'm surprised you're jealous. Yulia told me you rejected the idea of marrying me even when you were on the verge of dissipating."

Gisela scowled. "Does Yulia tell you literally everything?"

"Oh, she can't keep a secret to save her life. It's one of the things I love about her. She's a chronic oversharer. She also happened to let slip something about your wishing you could remain here?" It was a question, not a statement. "You're no longer bound to the waters in which you drowned. You are free to return home anytime you wish."

Home.

Gisela's breath caught as the realization hit. She could go

home now. She could see her family again. She was free to stop haunting the river and return to her island, to her old life, to *Hugo*.

Excitement shot through her, along with a bolt of uncertainty.

Wojciech must've read the emotion on her face, because he said, "Wanting things for yourself, Gisela, doesn't cancel out your love for your father and brother."

"I know that." Gisela smoothed a crinkle out of the bedsheets. She did know that. Now. She still loved her family fiercely. But she had a new awareness after everything. Looking after Hugo had given her a sense of purpose and made her feel valued and proud and loved, but it had cost her too. She'd missed out on a lot of things that her peers took for granted. She'd missed out on more than she'd realized.

She'd been lonelier than she'd realized.

Even the demon possessing Roza had said it: She'd become something interesting. She'd become something else. She'd been changed. And maybe it was selfish, but she wanted more for herself now. She wanted better for herself. She still wanted to be a good sister to Hugo, but she didn't want to be his nursemaid. She didn't want to be his mother. She wanted the chance to live her own life. She wanted her father to be present in their lives, and when she returned home, she would fight for that.

"Don't look so hopeful," she told Wojciech. "You're making me feel guilty. I—I'm going to return home. I need to. I *want* to. I know my family isn't perfect, but I still love them. I don't think I'll ever stop loving them." Gisela drew in another deep breath. "But that doesn't mean I won't ever come back."

She was free to come and go as she pleased now without the threat of drying out.

"I'll find a way back here, after I've made sure Hugo's all right, and I'm not leaving *just* yet." Gisela sent a silent apology to her little brother, but she still had to figure out exactly how she was going to get home and how she would even explain where she'd been all this time.

And there were people here she cared about too.

People who had helped her. Saved her. She owed them the same in return. Yulia and the other girls had fought a monster to protect her. She couldn't just leave them to deal with the consequences. What if the bies escaped its teacup prison? What if more forest spirits came searching for it? She had a responsibility to her water nymph sisters and to Kazik—the demon had wanted to use her to get to him. Now that she wasn't panicking about disappearing, she could think more clearly about everything.

About her death.

About Aleksey.

Gisela sat up straighter. "I have unfinished business here and a question I want answered."

Wojciech's eyebrows lifted. He propped a foot on his knee and leaned toward her. "What is it you want so badly to know?"

"Hypothetically," Gisela said, "how can you tell if someone is possessed by a demon?"

44

MONSTERS AND MIRACLES

KAZIK

"SO WHAT YOU'RE SAYING," Zuzanna said, dusting her hands on her skirt and dropping into the chair across from Kazik's at the kitchen table, "is that the impossibly handsome, slightly wet-looking young man upstairs is the water goblin? *The* water goblin? The one from the stories? The one Babcia—"

"Yes," Kazik said, "that water goblin."

Zuzanna gaped at him. "This wasn't what I meant when I told you to make more friends!"

"Maybe you should have specified." Closing his eyes, Kazik took a long, slow sip of raspberry kompot from one of Babcia's crystal-cut glasses—which, coincidentally, their grandfather had once said were a wedding gift from Wojciech.

He'd told his cousin everything. About Gisela. About the unholy bargain they'd struck and how he'd feared he'd lost his magic. He'd told her about Aleksey and how he'd tried to play matchmaker, and finally, he'd told her about what had happened on Saint John's Eve.

His gaze drifted to the ceiling. Was Gisela ever going to wake up?

In the daylight, the exploits of the other night felt almost like a dream. He wanted reassurance that everything that had happened between them had been real. He needed to know where they stood. And he needed to know—was she going to leave now, return home this very instant, after everything?

That was, after all, what she had promised him.

He glanced at Zuzanna, who was looking equally horrified and fascinated. Kazik was just thankful she didn't appear to be angry. He'd been afraid she'd be furious at the risks he'd taken, disgusted by the things he'd done. But at the same time, he'd been almost desperate to confess, to reveal everything and have her absolve him.

Zuzanna pressed her face into her hands. "I can't decide if I should just be relieved you've sorted things out yourself or drop everything and come back here to help you."

"You can't abandon your studies, Zuza. I don't need your help."

"Don't you?"

"Look." Kazik held out a hand and reached for that spark inside him. That fire at his core. He closed his eyes.

May those saints who watch over me . . .

Warmth whispered through him. Heat spread under his skin. He focused, mentally pulling on the sensation until a white flame bloomed in his hand.

"See? My magic's back." He still wasn't sure what he'd done to regain the saints' trust. Maybe it was a combination of things. He couldn't honestly say he was the same person he'd been at the beginning of all this.

"They must believe you'll use your power wisely," Zuzanna mused, "and not abuse it."

"I didn't think I *was* abusing it," Kazik grumbled. "They could've sent me a dream to let me know they were unhappy instead of punishing me."

"Maybe they didn't consider it a punishment. The saints work in mysterious ways. They might have seen stripping your powers away as giving you a gift. A chance for you to learn."

Kazik scowled. Saints or spirits, they all went about things so chaotically. He closed his fist and the flame disappeared.

"Anyway." Zuzanna set both hands on the table. "I'm going to drop by more often."

"You already drop by practically every week."

"I don't like thinking of you being all alone in an empty house."

"It's not so empty anymore," Kazik said, his eyes straying to the kitchen windowsill, where Domek was stretched out sunning himself.

Zuzanna smiled at that. "Still here, Grandfather? I thought the plan was for Kazik to reunite you with your family."

Domek licked lazily at a paw. *I'm comfortable here. Although Kazik doesn't dust the cupboards often enough.*

Kazik snorted.

"Well, knowing you're not alone does make me feel better, but—" Zuzanna said.

"If you give up on university," Kazik cut in, "I'm the one who'll feel bad. Only one of us needs to take Babcia's place."

"It's not that. I mean, I do feel guilty for letting you handle everything on your own. But I still have those dreams about you being devoured by the forest. And I don't think you realize what you've done. You know what this all means, don't you? Adopting Domek? Helping Gisela regain her humanity?" Zuzanna leaned back in her chair with a sigh. "As soon as word spreads, they're *all* going to start coming to you with requests. All kinds of devils and spirits!"

Kazik blanched, the glass of kompot frozen halfway to his lips. "Surely, they wouldn't actually think I'd help them."

She's right, Domek confirmed, shamelessly lifting a leg in the air and grooming his stomach. *I caught a cloud nymph testing the wards only yesterday. She told me she needed your help.*

A sudden terrible vision of the future unfolded before Kazik. He should've known things could only get worse.

"Aw, don't make that face," a familiar voice chided behind him. "You like helping people, don't you?"

For a second, Kazik's heart failed to beat. He rose from his seat, the backs of his knees colliding with the edge of his chair, sending it screeching back from the table. He crossed the kitchen in a blink before grabbing Gisela by the wrists and drawing her into the living room for privacy, uncaring that Zuzanna was watching. "Finally! Are you . . ." His voice wavered. He scanned her anxiously up and down. "Are you okay?"

"I'm much more than just *okay*."

Kazik huffed out a sound that was half snort, half laugh. Gisela flung her arms around his neck. Kazik hugged her back, his heart pounding with relief. For several moments they just stayed like that, simply existing in each other's arms.

Finally letting go, Kazik reached back and, on impulse, unclasped the silver chain from around his neck, removing his saint's medallion. Before he could think twice, he laid the Saint Hyacinth's medal against the shallow dip of Gisela's collarbone and reached around her to close the clasp behind her neck, gently sweeping her hair aside. The action was strangely intimate, almost as intimate as their kiss had been. Kazik felt like a groom shyly slipping a ring onto a bride's finger.

The medallion pulsed hot against Gisela's skin.

She tilted her head at him in surprise.

"There's this old folktale my grandfather used to tell," Kazik said, "about a monk who helps a water nymph to become human. He ties his cross around her neck and promises to marry her, and I just thought . . ." A flush crept up his neck. "It just seemed like the right thing to do. Just in case. I'm not actually asking you to marry me or anything like that."

"I think you'd have to ask for Wojciech's approval," Gisela said, turning the medallion between her fingers. Her cheeks were flushed pink now too. "So you really *do* like me."

"You're the most infuriating spirit I've ever met, and I never want you to stop haunting me."

Gisela broke into a blinding smile. "Good thing I'm not done with you yet, then."

Kazik's stomach flipped. "You're not leaving?" Everyone always left him, one way or another.

"Did you really think I'd be that easy to get rid of?"

"But your brother—"

"Will wait. For now. Don't go thinking this is over."

And why did that feel so comforting to hear?

Gisela gave him one of her damnable smirks, but the look in her eyes was serious. They were still a shade too red to be called brown. Kazik wondered if there were other not-so-human qualities she'd retained from her time as a water nymph despite her recent transformation.

"I can't leave just yet," she said. "I have unfinished business here. A score to settle. Besides, you'd miss me too much."

45

EPILOGUE

ALEKSEY

IT WAS SO QUIET down by the old wooden pier that Aleksey could make out the soft hiss of the grass parting to make a path for him. The ground sloping toward the river was uneven and split where tree roots had torn themselves from the soil. Some remained exposed, twisted into great gnarled knots above the earth.

He stared blindly at the sun-dappled water, imagining how the fight had gone. Seconds ticked by, turning into minutes, and still he stood there lost in thought. A dragonfly flitted past. Aleksey held up a hand and it settled on his fingertips, its iridescent wings fanned out in rest.

It seemed everyone needed rest right now. As far as Aleksey knew, Gisela was still fast asleep, and Kazik was still glued to her bedside, and Roza—well, *Human* Roza—was also bedridden at present. He'd just come from visiting her. According to her mother, she'd been involved in some accident on Saint John's Eve. She had no memory of the night, or much of what had happened over the past year. The doctor thought she may have hit her head.

Aleksey could've told them that it was perfectly normal for a human not to remember the time they spent possessed by a bies. The whole experience would feel like a fever dream she'd kept slipping in and out of. But he didn't tell them that, of course. Instead, he'd come here.

His own Roza had yet to return to Leśna Woda—in any form. He'd waited, ready to vent his anger at her, assuming she must have possessed another mortal or hidden herself away after whatever had happened with Gisela three days ago. Though now, her continued absence was beginning to worry him. Even Human Roza's little dog, Poppy, had returned from wherever he'd been hiding and resumed his place at her side.

So where was his Roza?

As much as she irked him at times, he'd been telling the truth when he told Gisela he thought of her as a younger sibling. She'd been following him around for an eternity, hanging off his every word, tagging along whenever he chose to cause mischief in the mortal world—even if she didn't understand what he found so fascinating about humans. He knew it was partly for protection. No other forest spirit would dare to harm her because doing so meant crossing him. But over time he'd grown almost fond of her presence.

He needed her here. Now more than ever, when his control was slipping, when he was being assailed by all these strange new feelings. He needed her to remind him of who he was and why he was here.

To get revenge. To help take back the sacred springs from the humans who wanted to keep that magic solely for themselves.

The leszy had warned him: *Do not get distracted. Do not get attached to any mortals you meet.*

Aleksey adjusted the sling supporting his shoulder. His expression turned serious as he faced the trees. "I need you to tell me," he said, in the tongue of leaves and branches, "exactly what happened here."

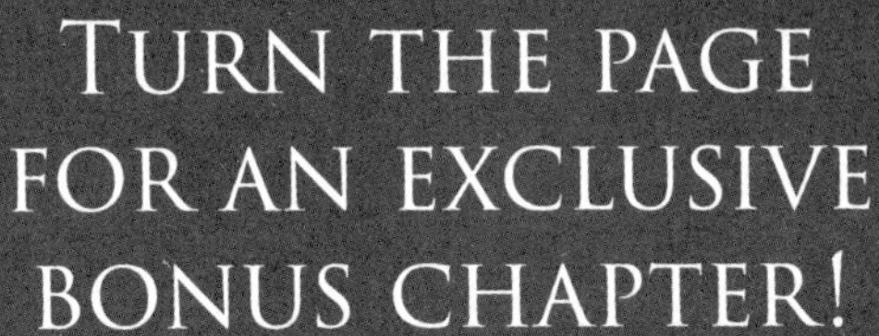
TURN THE PAGE
FOR AN EXCLUSIVE
BONUS CHAPTER!

BONUS

ONE YEAR AGO

THE DEMON

THE DEMON WATCHED THE human men from the shadows of the trees.

There were two of them making their way along the old hunting track. One was tall and slight. The other was short and stocky. Both were getting on in years; silver threaded their wood-brown hair and lines creased their sun-weathered faces. Even from a distance, he could tell from their movements that they were nervous, as well they should be. It was foolish—*dangerous*—to stray from the main trails, especially at this hour, when dusk was falling. But they'd heard what they thought were the cries of a child lost deep in the forest.

"I want the tall one," a voice whispered behind the demon. It sounded like the crackly rustle of windblown leaves. "He looks delicious."

"Really?" a second voice said. It had more of a rumble to it, the undercurrent of a growl. "He's too thin for my taste. I like it when they have a little more meat on their bones."

"Then it's lucky," the demon cut in, "that we're planning to wear them, not eat them."

A beat of silence.

"There's only two of them," the first voice said, as if only just noticing.

The demon lifted his shoulders in a shrug. "I guess one of you will have to stay behind."

Another fraught beat of silence.

Then a thunderous snarling echoed through the forest as the pair behind the demon came to blows over who would have the honor of accompanying him. Ferns and fallen branches crunched and snapped beneath the weight of two massive bodies.

On the track, the humans froze like startled rabbits.

The demon threw an irritated glance over his shoulder at the idiots brawling in the leaf litter. Two others of his kind—biesy. He wouldn't have called them friends, though they'd grown on him over the centuries. If anything, he thought of them as siblings or maybe even minions. Neither of them was particularly good at following orders, but they were loyal in their way and were always down to cause some mischief.

"Enough," the demon hissed, pulling his lips up to bare his fangs. "You'll scare them off."

The figures stilled begrudgingly, then pulled apart.

In their beastly forms, they were equally monstrous. The kind of creatures that had mortals and lesser spirits cowering in terror or fleeing for their lives. The first was a nightmarish cross between a boar and a wild bison. She had enormous gold eyes that glowed like lanterns, wicked tusks, and antlers to rival the leafy pair that crowned the demon's own head.

"I like it when they run," she said.

The second beast nodded in agreement. He was more bearish in appearance. His body bulged with muscle and was covered in matted, mossy fur. His eyes were the deep green of pine needles.

"It whets the appetite."

"Like I said, we're not going to *eat* them." The demon jerked his chin at the gold-eyed beast. "She'll come with me."

"Why does she get to—" the green-eyed beast began.

"Because we both know she'll only try to tag along even if I do leave her behind."

Smugly, the gold-eyed beast moved to stand beside the demon. She loomed over him, impossibly large. He looked comically small in contrast. He preferred a mostly human form—because it lulled those he met into a false sense of security. And, of course, it was easier to mimic the cries of a frightened child with human vocal cords.

He returned his attention to the men. They were scanning the shadowy trees along the sides of the hunting track with obvious fear. One of them crossed himself and murmured a prayer.

"Do you think either of them know the old witch?" the gold-eyed beast asked quietly. "Do you think it's true her god-gifted powers are fading?"

"Why?" The demon raised an eyebrow. "Are you afraid she's going to catch us?"

The gold-eyed beast bristled. "Even the leszy said to be careful."

The leszy had said a lot of things: *Possess a mortal. Infiltrate the town of Leśna Woda. Be careful. Be subtle. Do not get distracted. Do not get caught. Do not get attached to any mortals you meet. This could be our chance to finally regain access to the sacred springs.*

It was amazing how the ancient spirit lord could say all that with a straight face. As if it wasn't *his* fault that they'd all lost access to the magic of the springs in the first place. Humans would never have learned of their existence or location if the leszy hadn't taken pity on a wounded mortal man and led him to the waters to save his life.

The demon wouldn't have made that mistake. He cared for no one but himself. Biesy weren't prone to unnecessary emotions like pity or affection. No feelings grew in the cold, barren soil of their hearts.

"I'm still surprised you even agreed to follow the leszy's orders," the green-eyed beast murmured, attuned as always to the demon's thoughts in a way that was slightly unsettling. "It's not like you to voluntarily do something he wants you to do."

All of the forest-dwelling spirits knew the leszy was determined to mold the demon into a miniature version of himself, and that the demon was equally determined to thwart his efforts. No one else dared, or could, make the leszy tear the flowers out of his beard in sheer frustration. The demon took great pride in his ability to get under the old man's skin—not that it was difficult to make him lose his temper. You only had to whistle or curse loudly while strolling through the woods, chop down the wrong tree or shoot a wolf, and the being that mortals affectionately called "Grandfather Forest" would come storming out of the trees and curse you to wander the forest lost for a hundred years.

Or worse.

The leszy had certainly come close to ending the demon's life more than once—that time when he instructed the demon to guard the legendary, wish-granting fern flower, and the demon grew bored and not-so-accidentally led a human to it instead. And again, when the demon lured a party of hikers astray and they'd trampled all over the leszy's favorite mushrooms.

And then there was the time the demon possessed the body of a shepherd girl who the leszy was fond of . . .

For a moment, the demon could almost hear the old man's bellows echoing in his ears: *I am this close to giving up on you.*

The old man had no sense of fun. He didn't understand. Biesy were the wild and untamed forces of the earth. It was their nature to cause trouble. They couldn't help themselves.

A grin cut across the demon's face like the slash of a knife—sharp, and dangerous. "You really want to know why I said yes to the leszy?"

The gold-eyed beast guessed, "Because you love causing chaos in the mortal world?"

Well, that too.

The demon shook his head. He was careful not to let too much of his eagerness slip out. "The leszy also said that the old witch has a grandson who she's been raising to take her place. A pretty little thing called Kazimierz, or Kazik." The demon rolled the name around his tongue. He liked the taste of it.

"And you're going to put this fresh-faced exorcist in his place?" A hint of admiration bled into the green-eyed beast's voice.

"Somebody has to. We can't have him thinking he'll have an easy time of it." The demon twirled a dandelion between his clawed fingers. It was only fitting that they meet. He wondered if Kazik was as powerful as his grandmother—he hoped so. It wasn't fun unless there was a little danger. He wondered if the boy even wanted to be the witch's heir. If he had a choice in the matter. Did he wish to follow in her footsteps, or did he feel as trapped in his role as the demon sometimes did?

Did he ever feel like he was suffocating, like there were flowers growing in his lungs?

The gold-eyed beast let out a loud malicious giggle.

The sound carried through the forest. It was too much for the already terrified human men. The tall one turned and fled. It was the worst thing he could've done. The gold-eyed beast bolted after him, crashing through the fern-dense undergrowth.

"Really?" the green-eyed beast said sourly. "You'd rather take *her* with you?"

"Try not to sound so jealous. Here, hold this." The demon held out the dandelion he'd been playing with.

"What am I, one of your admirers?" A violent wind sprang up from nowhere as the green-eyed beast dissolved in a blur of sharp-teeth and emerald leaves.

Touchy.

But the demon was in a good mood, so he let the disrespect slide—this time. He turned his attention to the remaining human on the track.

The man stood gaping after his companion. He took a hesitant step, and all around him the dusky forest stirred to life.

Fern tendrils crawled across the soil, threatening to devour the hunting track completely. They coiled like snakes around the man's ankles. While thick tree roots tore out of the earth and wound tightly around his torso. He screamed and struggled desperately until he saw the demon melt out of the shadows. Falling deathly still, he stuttered a single word, "L-leszy?"

The demon's good mood evaporated. His expression darkened as he stalked forward, pausing only to memorize the man's expression—a look of mingled awe and horror—in case he needed to mimic it one day.

He caught the man's stubbled chin and turned his head first one way and then the other, examining his features. The strong nose and warm brown eyes darting in every direction, searching for help that wouldn't come.

If he had more time to pick, the demon would choose to possess someone younger; older minds were rich with useful knowledge, but their bodies came with not-so-fun features like back pain and aching joints. He would've liked somebody closer to his age in human years. The demon had lived for several hundred summers, but he was still considered a seedling.

And he would've liked a face that was a little more . . . handsome for his first meeting with the witch's grandson. The demon wanted to make an impression after all, and he wasn't above seducing his enemies. Making yourself desirable was one of the easiest ways to trick a mortal into lowering their guard.

"Please," the man whimpered. "I'll give you anything—"

"Anything?"

The man nodded frantically, or tried to. The demon stilled the motion, tightening his grip on that stubbled chin. He pretended to think about it.

"Very well. Because I'm exceedingly generous, I'll let you live, but in return you're going to let me borrow your body."

"M-my body? Why?"

"You're from Leśna Woda, aren't you?" the demon leaned in to whisper conspiratorially. "There's someone there who I'm just dying to introduce myself to."

Acknowledgments

THIS FATAL KISS IS probably the longest and hardest book I've written so far, and it wouldn't exist in the form it does today without the help of so many amazing people.

Endless thanks to:

My brilliant editor, Jonah Heller, for helping me shape this story into something I'm truly proud of. Working with you has been an absolute dream!

To Clare Hallifax and Brooklyn O'Connell at Walker Books Australia, thank you for coming on board with Jonah and taking a chance on me.

To my wonderful copy editor: Manu Shadow Velasco.

To my fabulous proofreader: Emily Stone.

And to Andie Lugtu and Lily Steele for creating such a beautiful, dreamy cover for this book.

To the readers of my past works who said they wanted more stories, your words of encouragement have kept me going!

To all my wonderful friends, thank you for cheering me on and not holding it against me when I disappear while on a deadline. (Special shout-out to Aully Qian, who always listens to me rant about publishing.)

To my family, always. Thank you, Mum and Dad, for encouraging my love of books and giving me Polish folktales to read when I was a kid—those stories have lived rent-free in my mind ever since. And thank you to my sister, for never complaining when I ask for last minute help taking photos and updating my website.

And finally, to everyone who picked up this book. I hope you enjoyed this story as much as I enjoyed writing it!

About the Author

ALICIA JASINSKA hails from Sydney, Australia, and is the author of acclaimed YA novels *The Dark Tide* and *The Midnight Girls*. A library technician by day, she spends her nights writing and hanging upside down from the aerial hoop. Visit her on the web at AliciaJasinska.com. Follow her on Instagram @aliciamja.